Adorning the Florida coastline stands Poinciana, the fabulous mansion of the Logan family. Inside its regal walls a volcano of intrigue and violent emotion has begun to erupt, and not one of the Logans is safe.

Especially not Sharon Hollis Logan, the lovely young bride of the patriarchal Ross Logan. For reasons unknown to Sharon, Ross seems to be hated by Gretchen, his daughter from a previous marriage, by her ne'er-do-well husband, Vasily, and by Ross's crazed mother, Allegra—and all their hostility is readily transferred to Sharon. But as she tries to find out why, Sharon uncovers a devastating secret about her own relationship with her husband—a secret that, in the end, will test the limits of her courage as well as her ability to love....

BOOKS BY PHYLLIS A. WHITNEY

WOMAN WITHOUT A PAST
THE SINGING STONES*
RAINBOW IN THE MIST*
FEATHER ON THE MOON*
SILVERSWORD*
FLAMING TREE*
DREAM OF ORCHIDS*
RAINSONG*
EMERALD*
VERMILION*
POINCIANA*
DOMINO*
THE GLASS FLAME*
THE STONE BULL*
THE GOLDEN UNICORN*
SPINDRIFT*
THE TURQUOISE MASK*
SNOWFIRE*
LISTEN FOR THE WHISPERER*
LOST ISLAND*
THE WINTER PEOPLE*
HUNTER'S GREEN*
SILVERHILL*
COLUMBELLA*
SEA JADE*
BLACK AMBER*
SEVEN TEARS FOR APOLLO*
WINDOW ON THE SQUARE*
BLUE FIRE*
THUNDER HEIGHTS*
THE MOONFLOWER*
SKYE CAMERON*
THE TREMBLING HILLS*
THE QUICKSILVER POOL*
THE RED CARNELIAN

Young Adult Novels

STEP TO THE MUSIC*
THE FIRE AND THE GOLD*
MYSTERY OF THE BLACK DIAMONDS
NOBODY LIKES TRINA
SECRETS OF THE STONE FACE
MYSTERY OF THE GOLDEN HORN*
MYSTERY OF THE ISLE OF SKYE*

Adult Non-Fiction

A GUIDE TO FICTION WRITING
WRITING JUVENILE STORIES AND NOVELS

**Published by Fawcett Books*

PHYLLIS A. WHITNEY

Poinciana

FAWCETT CREST • NEW YORK

A Fawcett Crest Book
Published by Ballantine Books

ISBN 0-449-20439-1

This edition published by arrangement with Doubleday & Company, Inc.

Alternate Selection of the Literary Guild Selection of the Doubleday Book Club

Printed in Canada

First Fawcett Crest Edition: November 1981
First Ballantine Books Edition: April 1983
Ninth Printing: December 1991

For PATRICIA MYRER, who has from the beginning held the hands of every one of my heroines through all their tribulations.

With love and gratitude

With special thanks to my sister- and brother-in-law, Mabel and Lloyd Houvenagle, for making my life so much more pleasant, and for driving me around Florida.

My thanks as well to Leone King; to Helen McKinney of the Library, Society of the Four Arts; and to Elyse Strickland of the Doubleday Bookshop, all of whom helped me with my Palm Beach background.

Chapter 1

Outside the long windows of the library, a Florida March was mild, almost balmy. Sunset light touched fine book bindings, turning polished mahogany rosy, but I sat well away from the windows, huddled in a wing chair and hidden by the deepest shadow I could find.

Though the door was closed upon sounds beyond, I heard someone calling, "Sharon? Sharon, where are you?" I shut out the summons. On a table nearby, the tape recorder played, and I listened only to the singing voice.

I had run frantically from the turmoil in the rest of the house—that turmoil when family and friends gather to console one another and dine hungrily on whatever fare is provided for body and emotions. At Poinciana any feast was sure to be sumptuous, and I had needed to give few orders. The household had been beautifully run before Ross Logan had ever brought home a new young wife, and it could run smoothly without me.

The voice on the tape sang poignantly of "purple shadows and blue champagne..." and I steeled myself against the sound. It was that appealing, throaty quality of voice that could only be Ysobel Hollis whispering of heartbreak and loss. Heartbreak—when she had been the happiest woman I had ever known! My mother. The shivering inside me began again as I remembered. Yet it was not Ysobel who had died two days ago.

I had come here as Ross Logan's wife, believing that the very real problems of my life were being solved. I hadn't known then what it meant to be afraid.

Any death in a household such as this one meant an astonishing stir in the presses of the world. What platitudes and banalities had been given out—because the truth was too dangerous to reveal. All the family were on guard now, even against one another. Jarrett Nichols, Ross's powerful right hand, stood behind the story that must be told. None of us were to be interviewed, and the fortress of the house protected everyone in it. Except me.

Within the house, this had not been protection enough. Their eyes accused me. Without words, they were saying, *You are to blame for what happened.*

The taped voice whispered on, and I heard its husky yearning—*I keep a blue rendezvous*... I had endless reasons to find that song disturbing, but I made myself listen, made myself remember every detail.

For the sake of my own sanity, I needed to remember, to retrace, to understand exactly what I was doing here at Poinciana, how I had come to this moment in this room. Death brings its own sense of unreality, and I had three deaths to assimilate. Ysobel and Ian—my mother and father—and now this new and dreadful one.

Everything had begun—such a little while ago!—on

that afternoon in Belfast in Northern Ireland. My mother, her beautiful, funny face alight, had been singing to children brought to the concert hall from an orphanage. My father was in the wings as always, since Ysobel was something of his creation, as well as the focus of his life. Hers was the magic and the talent, but his had been the imagination to recognize, and to present her to her audiences as she needed to be presented. That day I had been sitting near the outside end of the third row, with children all around me. I'd been watching the children's bright faces as they listened, entranced, to the singing of Ysobel Hollis. She wasn't giving them the sad songs of loss and pain that her adult audiences doted on. These children had enough of that in their lives, so she brought them gaiety and hope and life—something she could do equally well. And I was listening, though not as thoroughly entranced as the children.

We were completely different, Ysobel and I. She had been born in New Orleans, I in San Francisco. The outward differences, as I'd always accepted, were not in my favor. She was small and pert, and her black hair fluffed in curls around her face. I was tall and my hair was blond and straight like my father's. I usually drew it back in a coil on the nape of my neck, emphasizing the difference. My father used to tell me I was beautiful, that I had "good bones." I laughed at his words, never believing. I'd have liked a saucy, upturned nose like Ysobel's and dark eyes that could flash with light, instead of blue eyes that Ross had told me were like quiet seas. *I* knew that my seas were never quiet, but I didn't want the world to suspect, and I wore a careful guise that came to suit me like a well-designed gown.

Father adored Ysobel, of course, and he was dramatic enough in his own right. Ian Hollis, Scottish-American, ex-actor. Though sometimes I wasn't so sure it was "ex." He managed Ysobel's fortunes, handled her publicity, built her into the world-famous musical comedy star she became. He was the impresario personified.

I supposed they loved me, when they thought about it, and had time. But it was necessary to leave me in whatever schools were available, from New York to London to Geneva. Never for a long enough time to put down roots and make lasting friends, but enough to give me a background of experience few other children had. Always in a new place there was the whispering behind my back, the eager curiosity because I was the daughter of Ysobel Hollis. Because of this, I was always engaged in a struggle to be *me*. Until recently, a secret struggle that I never let the world suspect.

When I grew up, I could travel everywhere with them, and that was both exciting and smothering. I didn't mind being useful. Mother said I could dress her faster and more skillfully for her performances than anyone else, and she loved to have me do her hair. Little else was required of me—certainly not to attend many parties with them, or be present at press interviews. I could understand that a growing daughter might draw attention from Ysobel Hollis in an undesirable way. As a reward for not being demanding or too conspicuous, I was allowed to go my own way much of the time. Strangely, for a young woman, my fantasy life had to do with museums.

I loved to wander echoing marble halls, until even the guards came to recognize and smile at me. I could imagine myself the elegant doyenne of a mansion housing some fabulous collection about which I was wholly knowledgeable. The Oriental wings drew me especially, and I developed an affinity for Japanese art and culture. China was too big for me to grasp, but Japan was more compact, for all its complexity, and I began to learn about it. Someday I would visit those islands, even though Ysobel had had no desire to travel to the Far East. On my twentieth birthday, when Father asked me what I wanted most, I told him I would love to own a set of Oriental jade, and he took me to Gump's in San Francisco, where I chose a pendant of heavenly clear green, with a gold dragon coiled about it. There were tiny gold and jade earrings to match, and while my father sighed over the cost, he could give generously on occasion. Ysobel never bothered about money, and she didn't mind. She was never the type for jade.

How foolish and how terribly young I'd been. Perhaps "arrested" was the word! But ready for a terrible awakening.

On that afternoon in Belfast, there was no warning of danger. Ysobel was laughing one moment, singing her heart out, and in the next she was gone in a flash of light and shattering sound.

It was as though the seats around me exploded and I was thrown outward against the wall of the theater. When I opened my eyes the stage was aflame, the wings burning, and there were shouts and screams everywhere. Pain stabbed through my arm, and there seemed to be blood streaming down my face. My brain had given up working properly. There was no way I could reach the stage, and I knew only that I must get as many children as possible out the side door of the hall.

I grabbed and pulled, shouted myself hoarse, and somehow managed to bundle a few of them through the door, starting an exodus, so that others followed. Fright and agony were screaming inside me, yet I went on doggedly, bringing a number of us out to the sidewalk.

I don't know what happened after that. I was told later that I'd collapsed. When I opened my eyes again it was to find that I had been in the hospital for two days. The sister at my bedside hushed and soothed me, refused to answer questions.

Then Ross Logan came. What Ross Logan ordered, people provided. A private room for me, the best of doctors, and Ross himself there at all hours. He had been my parents' great friend for many years and I remembered him from my childhood as an always impressive figure. In London he had heard the shocking news, knew that I was alone, and had come at once by plane. As always, he was possessed of an enormous vitality. Phones around him were never still, and he could talk with equal authority to Washington or Tokyo, London or Bonn.

He sat at my bedside, his athlete's body erect and youthful, because at nearly sixty he still kept himself in top condition. He sounded like the American he was, exuberant most of the time, and always handsome and dynamic—his hair barely touched with gray, an intensity brimming in dark eyes and tightening the corners of his mouth. As I was soon to recognize, he exuded power. I, who had never felt so weak, could begin to learn and trust a little.

It was Ross who told me they were both gone. Ysobel and Ian. They had been killed at once and hadn't suffered, he assured me. I, their daughter, had helped to save a great many children from the fire that had followed the bombing, and was something of a heroine. It was a comfort to me when Ross took over all the dreadful funeral arrangements, requiring nothing of me but agreement. However, the most comforting release he brought me was his own grief. He had loved my parents, he told me, and felt it no shame to weep—so we cried together, and my healing began. I didn't understand until later why he cried, or how angry such tears could be. My own, as well as his.

When I had recovered enough physically, my damaged arm in a sling, he carried me off to his town house in London. His housekeeper, a sensible older woman, took me in charge, and again I need take no action, make no decisions. Ross went away to his business meetings, flew to New York and back again. When he was in London he took me everywhere. To the best plays and restaurants, on a flying visit to friends in Scotland in his own plane. I began to see as never before what a figure of power and importance he represented wherever he went. The press was apt to follow him, and they even took an interest in me, as they would in any woman to whom he paid attention. That I was also Ysobel Hollis's daughter, with a tragedy behind me, whetted their appetite for sensation. Ross handled them skillfully, and escaped them when he could. He seemed to inspire an almost awed respect on every hand, and I began to feel a little giddy in such high-powered company. Giddy, but not very real.

As far as my own affairs went, I was still in a state of shock and unable to plan for myself. I couldn't believe I would never see my parents again, and I was glad for any distraction possible.

My future stretched ahead blank, empty, a question mark. Ysobel and Ian Hollis had been bountiful spenders. I had my mother's few jewels and that was about all. There were astonishing debts. Her income from recordings soon went to pay those off. I had been trained for nothing practical, but must now somehow find myself a job. Perhaps as a model? I was told I might do well enough at modeling. What people called my poise would get me by, with no one ever guessing that it was an outer casing I wore that made me seem cool and confident and remote—with no hint of the disturbing emotions that might be surging underneath. I wanted *not* to be theatrical, not to be like Ysobel—whom I could never emulate anyway—and not to be like my father, who sometimes played at charades. So who was I?

There weren't any permanent men in my life, only casual friends. I'd learned when I was thirteen not to bring young males around my mother. She couldn't resist captivating them. I didn't blame her, but perhaps I grew a little cynical about men before I was old enough to have one of my own. Later on, I suppose I put men off. They didn't know how to smash through the protective glass that encased me, and I hadn't met the man who could coax me outside. They thought I was cold, when sometimes I felt as though I were burning up in futile anger.

"So you're Ysobel Hollis's daughter?" they'd ask, and we would talk admiringly about *her,* while *I* went into hiding and seethed.

My relationship with Ross was something new. I

began to relax a little in response to his enormous charm, his skill with a woman, his tenderness. That he was fifty-six to my twenty-five was only reassuring. A younger man might have stirred up my uncertainties, my resentments, while Ross offered strength and dependability, as well as a total concern with me. A concern such as no one else had ever given me.

He had been married twice before. Helen, his first wife, had died. His second, Brett Inness (as she called herself now), he had divorced. An impossible woman, he said. There was one daughter by this second marriage, and he appeared to love her dearly. Yet when he talked about her, I found myself unexpectedly wary. I knew about fathers who loved their daughters, but were too busy to pay them much attention. Without ever having met her, I began to harbor a secret sympathy for Gretchen Logan.

"She's a difficult girl, Sharon," Ross told me. "Unruly. And too sexual too young. At twenty, she's already had an affair or two and seems quite willing to throw herself away on any man who shows an interest in her. Right now, she's running around with a man named Vasily Karl. He's some sort of Balkan fellow—Rumanian, Bulgarian? Maybe a dash of Hungarian or Russian—who is obviously after her money. I'm trying to put a stop to it, but she's not likely to listen."

I could grieve for him about his daughter, even while I instinctively sympathized with her. By way of advice I offered nothing, but I was a good listener, and Ross liked to talk. Especially about his family.

His father, Charles Maynard Logan, had made his own great fortune and had been the founder of Meridian Oil, as well as establishing the Logan banks. He'd known as well how to spend and how to collect. Among other things, he had collected the midwestern beauty who became Ross's mother, and who gained her own fame as Allegra Logan. Allegra had taken to Florida with enthusiasm, perhaps in reaction to Minnesota cold, coming to the island of Palm Beach in the twenties, and setting her mark upon it. It was there she had built her fantasy house, Poinciana, flinging down the challenge to Marjorie Merriweather Post, a lady who had a few fantasies of her own. Ross smiled a bit ruefully as he spoke of his mother.

"She must have driven her architects crazy, stealing from Mizner and anyone else whose houses appealed to her, so that she built a hodgepodge so spectacular that it made its own name and importance, and no one dared to laugh."

I gathered that both his parents were gone now, though he wouldn't talk about their death. Ross had kept Allegra's creation, and Poinciana was clearly his favorite place on earth, though he owned several houses elsewhere. It was to Poinciana that he brought his father's collection of art and antiques, and it was there he chose to make his headquarters for at least part of each year. Let New York and London and Washington come to *him*.

During those days of our getting acquainted in London, while I convalesced, I began to recognize Ross's growing interest in me, and I could hardly believe in what was happening. For the first time in my life I could fall in love without being fearful of Ysobel. Ross was vitally exciting and virile, and he aroused feelings in me that had never been stirred before. The hidden cynicism I had developed as a protective coating for my emotions was melting away. The inner turmoil was dying.

When he brought me a stunning ring of diamonds and sapphires and put it on my finger, I knew all my problems were over. Ross would rescue me, protect me, love me forever. I needn't ever be adrift and lost again, and *I* would have someone to love.

As he talked to me about his growing up in Poinciana, I began to glimpse its magnificence in my mind, and the thought of it revived old fancies. I had visited splendid houses often enough with my parents, and I had as well all those museum hours behind me. Ross told me frankly that one of the things that impressed him about me was my background of sophistication and my surprising knowledge of Oriental art. I could accept the latter, but I wasn't sure about that word "sophistication." Disguise was my specialty. Nor was I sure that I could cope with either the legend or reality of Poinciana—though something in me wanted terribly to try.

The house, Ross told me, contained not only the treasures collected by Charles Maynard Logan and his wife Allegra, but Ross's own celebrated Oriental prints, lacquers, ceramics, and Japanese netsuke. The idea of the Oriental collection excited me. All those exquisite pieces of cloisonné and Satsuma, to say nothing of the prints and the miniature world of netsuke art, about which I knew very little at that time, since such collections were rare. My imagination was fired. All my life I'd viewed, but never been able to touch, to hold, to relish. Now all the old dreams were about to come true.

Before I knew it, Ross was making plans. We would be married quietly outside of London to avoid the press, and then we would honeymoon in Japan. I was nearly speechless with delight. I knew that he had been stationed in Japan under MacArthur long ago, and had fallen in love with the country and its people. Later he had been American Consul in Kyoto for a time. He had always been interested in things Oriental, and his wealth and power had made him useful to his government. He could have been an ambassador, had he wished, but he was no career diplomat. The oil business was still the main focus of his life. He was less interested in the banking aspects, but it was possible to make friends in Japan who would further business interests later. That I should match this passion of his for Japanese art made me one woman in a million in his eyes—or so he assured me.

Now and then I would catch him studying me with a look of appreciative delight, yet no hint of warning touched me. No one had ever appreciated *me* before, so how could I not respond? How could I possibly suspect what lay hidden so terribly in the background?

We could stay in Kyoto as long as we liked, since Ross was thinking of early retirement, and there were many executives in charge of Logan interests. He had already stepped down as chairman of the board of Meridian Oil. And the great Logan trusts and foundations, the philanthropies, were in the hands of others, though under the advisorship of a man named Jarrett Nichols, Ross's principal aide and consultant. He had taken Jarrett on some years ago as a young lawyer and molded him into his most valuable assistant and executive. I would meet him when we returned to Poinciana, where he had his headquarters at present, awaiting Ross's return.

There, Ross said, was where we would live. Perhaps even in the summer, if I could face it. He'd always hated his mother's habit of flitting around from season to season, living in different houses. His daughter Gretchen was there now, and it was the house he had grown up in and most wanted me to love. I would be the one to restore it from shabbiness to new beauty. I would understand Poinciana and what Allegra Logan had built. He already knew that about me. What he wanted most of all for himself when our honeymoon was over was to return to Florida and write the book on Japanese netsuke that he had long been planning, and on which he'd done too little work.

I still felt dazed and unable to resist the avalanche that was sweeping me along. What he expected of me in Florida, I would not think about now. A line had been held out to rescue me, and all I could do was cling to it for my very life. If at times I found Ross a little moody, if some communications from the States caused him to be preoccupied at times, I made nothing of this. The oil business was, to say the least, in a state of unrest, and this must cause him considerable worry.

Nevertheless, Ross decided to put all business matters away from him for now, and this time he would travel with no entourage. He sent the young man who was his personal secretary off on a long holiday, and told Jarrett Nichols by phone to handle all mail and messages at that end, unless something very important came up. I was delighted at the prospect of traveling unencumbered and having my husband all to myself.

Our wedding was quiet, with only a few of Ross's friends present, and the press for once evaded. There was no one whom I especially wanted to invite. Before I quite knew what was happening we were on our way to Kyoto. Long plane flights were a familiar enough experience for me, but to travel on Ross's private jet was something new and exhilarating. Every luxury was at our disposal, and I became increasingly aware of the strange world of the super-wealthy that I had married into.

At the airport outside Tokyo we were besieged by reporters, but welcoming government officials were on hand to take us through. We went by one of Japan's crack trains to Kyoto, and stepped into a quieter and older world. I could understand very quickly why Ross had wanted to bring me here.

The Miyako Hotel was set on a hillside with mountains all around, and I loved it at once, as I loved the temples and gardens, the narrow streets of the older part of the city that had once been a capital, and which had never been destroyed by war. The reality of Japan was even more fascinating than all my reading had led me to expect. Teahouses and Japanese food were both attractive under Ross's tutelage, and not a cloud marred my happiness.

One day in a curio shop, Ross held up a lovely ivory figurine and said it was like me—exquisite. He bought it for me, and told me that we would both grace Poinciana on our return. For just an instant, standing beside my husband in that dark little shop with its unfamiliar, not unpleasant scent—was it camphorwood or sandalwood?—a question flashed through me. What was I doing here? I was no ivory figurine. Nothing so perfect as that. What did Ross really know about *me?* But reality was dangerous. Reality was a theater in flames and screaming children and the terrible pain of loss. I put it away from me quickly.

Only sometimes when Ross made love to me there was a return of uneasiness. In this one aspect I could only feel that I disappointed him. Inexperienced as I was, I knew only a passive, submissive role, expecting him to teach me, feeling very little myself. He sensed my concern and was gentle with me. Wait until we reached Poinciana, he said. Everything would be better there. I didn't understand, and I wondered uncertainly why it should be different in Florida.

Unexpectedly, I didn't always have Ross to myself during our honeymoon. There were certain Japanese businessmen who came quietly—almost secretly—to consult with him at the hotel. On these occasions I was sent off in a car contributed for my pleasure, to sight-see, or wander in temple gardens. The first time this happened, I asked questions, wanting to share all that interested my husband. But Ross had been curt and preoccupied, and I began to realize that there were some interests he didn't want to share with me. I knew without rancor that this would be a fact of marriage that I must accept.

Then something shattering happened in Kyoto, cutting our visit short. A long-distance call came from Jarrett Nichols, and I was with Ross in our suite at the hotel when he picked up the phone. I saw the dark flush of anger rise in his expressive face.

"We'll come home at once," he told Jarrett. "I'll cable arrangements as soon as they're made." When he hung up, he turned to me, more shaken than I'd ever seen him.

"Gretchen has married Vasily Karl," he said. "Totally against my wishes. And they've moved into Poinciana."

I wondered to myself how he could expect anything

else, considering that he was so seldom with his daughter, but I said nothing, watching his anger in alarm. I had never seen him in a rage before, and it was frightening. When he stamped out of the hotel and went walking alone in the streets of the city, I went into the garden beyond the glass walls of the dining room and sat trying to be quiet and calm, watching goldfish dart about in a small pond.

Again I found myself thinking about Gretchen. After all, her father had given her no warning of *his* marriage to me. He was foisting an unknown stepmother upon her with no preparation. A stepmother only a few years older than Gretchen herself. He had never even told me how his daughter felt about Brett, her mother. Now I couldn't help wondering if Gretchen's sudden marriage was a deliberate slap in the face for a father she might both love and resent.

I knew what that feeling could be like. Love for one's parents could very well be mixed with a flavoring of resentment. I had been raised to recognize that Ysobel's career was all-important in our lives. Yet sometimes I'd thought rebelliously that she and Ian might have come for a birthday, wherever they'd left me, or even have brought me to them. Christmas at school, with Ysobel and Ian across a continent, could be utterly lonely, even though they phoned and sent me wonderful gifts. As I sat waiting for Ross's return, I began to hope that I could win Gretchen's liking, let her know that I could understand, that perhaps we weren't too far apart and might be friends. I longed suddenly, unexpectedly, for a friend, and knew with disturbing clarity that true friendship was something I would never find with Ross. A man didn't make friends with an ivory figure on a shelf. Certainly not a forceful, vibrant man like Ross.

We were to have stayed in Japan through cherry blossom time, but when Ross returned to the hotel he was the man of action again. All had been arranged. We were going to Tokyo tomorrow, flying home the day after. First, however, we would make one more visit here in Kyoto.

We took a taxi to a small Japanese house off a side street and enclosed by a high bamboo fence. There were dwarf pines and the usual fishpond in the garden, with a little red lacquered bridge arched across it.

A bowing Japanese woman wearing a kimono led us to stone steps, where we could sit and remove our shoes. Then we followed her into the house, through sliding paper shoji, padding across springy straw tatami, climbing polished stairs to a room that opened upon a narrow wooden gallery overlooking the garden and nearby rooftops of gray tile. An old man with a fringe of white hair rose from his cushion to greet us. He was dressed in the old-fashioned way in a fine silk kimono of charcoal gray, with a small white crest on each sleeve.

He bowed deeply, then gave his hand to Ross Logan in a warm clasp of friendship, and I knew there was respect between these two. I was presented to Gentaro Sato with a formality that emphasized this respect. Cushions were brought for our comfort and I sat cross-legged, unable to fold my knees under me for long, as Japanese women did. A low tray-table was brought in by the woman, set with a flowered teapot that had a curved bamboo handle, and accompanying small, handleless cups. She poured our tea and offered a plate of bean paste cakes shaped like four-petaled flowers of pink, green, and white.

I looked for the alcove I'd read about, with its single treasured vase and flower, the hanging kakemono, and other spare ornaments of art. But in this room something different was evident. On shelves here and there were displayed tiny carved objects, some with cords threaded through them. These were netsuke. I'd seen them occasionally in museums here and there.

"Sato-san is a sculptor who makes fine netsuke," Ross told me. "Not for sale to the public as a rule, but to satisfy his own creative talent and preserve an old art form that is being lost."

Mr. Sato rose, went to a shelf and made a selection, returning to hand me a tiny wood carving. "For you," he said.

I thanked him warmly, and turned the beautiful little thing about in my fingers. It was no more than an inch and a half wide—a carving of a mother frog with a baby frog clinging to her back, one foot set carelessly over its mother's eye. There was humor and great delicacy in the carving, and the detail in so small an object was amazing. The eyes of both frogs were inlaid in shell and black coral.

"Netsuke aren't popular in Japan any more," Ross said. "When men used to wear the kimono, they tucked pouches into the obi band around their waists, with the netsuke on a cord with a sliding bead, hanging outside to anchor the pouch."

As I listened, I had no idea that these little objects were to become so important in my life—and so disturbing. But I realized that the art had fired Ross's imagination, and he was ready to go on talking about them.

Unfortunately, the creation of so utilitarian an art had not been properly valued in the past, and the carvers were often neglected and unappreciated. Even the museums of Japan had been negligent about collecting them, so that it had been the foreigner who had delighted in this miniature art, and taken most of them out of the country into private ownership. Ross himself had a fine collection at Poinciana, which he was eager to show me.

When I commented on the charm of the little frogs Mr. Sato had given me, he motioned gently toward the garden, where there were undoubtedly real frogs in the fishpond.

"My teachers," he said, and I looked about at the carvings with new eyes. Some were pure fantasy, or based on myth or legend, but even those were glimpses of life and nature as one man perceived them.

Apparently Gentaro Sato now sold some of his own modern work to a few respected collectors, but he also kept an eye out for such ancient netsuke as surfaced from time to time around Japan. He harbored a slight bitterness against his country for not having placed sufficient value upon such artists and their work in the past. Ross had promised him that someday his own private collection would be given back to the government of Japan, to form a nucleus of netsuke art.

When his business with Gentaro Sato was concluded, and a neat wooden box had been packed with several carvings Ross had chosen, we returned to the hotel and prepared for our journey home.

All that evening, Ross continued remote and preoccupied. Once I tried to talk to him about Gretchen, but he closed me out with a coldness I hadn't seen in him before. It was as though he said, "Keep your place. Don't touch my real life," and I found myself alone again. Alone and bewildered. It was his very directness that I'd most admired, and now he seemed coolly evasive.

That night I put on a kimono of golden chrysanthemums that Ross had given me, and that he'd been delighted to see me wear. But when I went to him he looked at me as though I were suddenly a stranger, and turned away. Later, I lay on my side of the bed, finding that I was still shut out, and that for the first time since our wedding there were no loving arms to hold me. I told myself that his strangeness was not due to me, or anything I had done. Undoubtedly the news about Gretchen had upset him, and he would come back to me in time.

Nevertheless, I lay awake for a long while that night. Once during those hours when he became aware that I wasn't sleeping, he touched me lightly and repeated those strange words he'd spoken before: "It will be better when we reach Poinciana," and again I asked myself: *Why?*

From Tokyo we flew to New York for a brief business stopover—a trip many hours long, even by private jet. Ross was still preoccupied and distant. This time we couldn't avoid the press and we were besieged with questions that Ross handled skillfully out of long experience. He spoke for me and I said very few words and smiled a lot. We stayed overnight at the Pierre Hotel, rather than open up the New York apartment, and the next day we continued on the short flight to Florida. It was midafternoon when we reached the West Palm Beach airport.

There I had my first glimpse of the elegant Rolls that was only one of the cars that would be at our disposal at Poinciana. Albert, the Logan chauffeur, met us, attended to our baggage, and answered Ross's rather testy questions as to why neither Jarrett Nichols nor Gretchen had come to meet us.

It seemed to me that Albert, after his first smile of greeting, was edgy and uncomfortable.

"Miss Gretchen had an accident this morning, Mr. Logan," he said. "I understand it was nothing serious. She—uh—fell on the stairs coming down from the belvedere. Mr. Nichols thought he should stay at the house until you arrived."

Ross was anything but satisfied. "Gretchen is as surefooted as a goat, so what happened? Where was this new husband of hers?"

Albert busied himself putting our bags in the trunk of the car. "Sir, he seems to have gone out. I'm sure Mr. Nichols will explain."

Albert was past middle age and belonged to an older era, his behavior impeccable and correct. Ross had told me that he had been with the family for a long time, and I suspected that he knew very well what had happened to Gretchen, but he would say nothing at this time. Especially not in front of me.

Ross helped me into the luxurious back seat and

plumped himself down beside me. I had looked forward to having him show me Florida, but Albert's news had disgruntled my husband, and I watched the passing landscape in silence, continuing to feel a little lost.

This was one state I had missed in my travels with Ysobel and Ian, and I found it different from any place I'd known. The country seemed to be made up of palm trees and sand, and a land as flat as the ocean we had flown over, its rises marked only by condominiums.

At least I had done my homework on Palm Beach, and I knew that the Intracoastal Waterway flowed into Lake Worth, which bordered most of Palm Beach on the west. The island was only thirteen miles long, and a mere three quarters of a mile at its widest. Beyond, to the east, lay the ocean.

We crossed at a bridge near the Bird Sanctuary and drove along South Ocean Boulevard. On our right, as the road dipped near it, ran a continuous stretch of beach, and I had glimpses of whitecaps out on the water. Large houses, most of them dating back to the twenties or earlier, came up on our left, and I saw the trademark of red-tiled roofs that belonged to the Spanish revival that architect Addison Mizner had created here. Most of the houses were of stucco or stone, since wood rotted easily in the salt air, and they were painted pink or cream, or a dazzling white. Between the houses and the ocean a natural sand dune rose in protection, and sea grape grew rampant everywhere, its big tough leaves a dirty rust color at this time of the year. Inland they were greener.

The houses faced the ocean behind walls and hedges, though only Poinciana and one or two others occupied property that ran through from ocean to lake. Behind most of these ocean houses were streets and other houses that fronted on Lake Worth. Those that faced the ocean had marvelous views of the Atlantic from their upper windows, but their residents had to cross the boulevard to reach their private beaches.

Everywhere, palm trees grew tall—the stately royal

palms as well as slender coconut palms that leaned away from the prevailing wind.

"Here we are," Ross said, and my heart jumped. I hadn't lost my sense of uneasiness about coming to Poinciana.

A high wall of coquina rock, with bright hibiscus growing against it, ran along on our left until it reached wide gates with pillars of the same coral rock on either side. Once these gates must have been fashioned of wrought iron, but now they were modern steel, and were electrified. At a beep from Albert's horn, they swung open away from us, and a man came out of the gatehouse and touched his cap to Ross Logan. We drove in, following a curved way that led between well-trimmed ficus trees, and I had my first unimpeded view of the house.

Allegra Logan's fantasy had indeed been just that. Poinciana was built of rosy stone brought from the Spanish Pyrenees, and decorated with roofs of red tile. This was not Spanish architecture, however, nor, in fact, any sort of identifiable architecture. It jutted here, and indented itself there, in a rapturously experimental way, inviting amazement, inciting in me an eagerness to explore. Commanding the entire rambling structure was a high, curiously domed cupola, with windows and a tiny balcony all around. This must be the belvedere, on whose stairs Gretchen had fallen. What a view there must be up there, I thought, and planned to climb it as soon as I could. Off to the right, beyond the house, I could glimpse smaller cottages, with their own red-tiled roofs. The grounds, Ross had told me, occupied some thirty acres, and the house was rooted sturdily into an ancient reef of coral, hurricane-proof.

As we neared the porte cochere, he slipped an arm about my shoulders, and I turned to him eagerly. Ever since we'd left the airport I had felt alone and increasingly anxious.

"Welcome to Poinciana, darling," he said. "I want

you to be happy here. I had always hoped that Ysobel would visit this house someday, but there never seemed to be time in her busy life. So I'm glad her daughter has come to us."

It was a strange welcome, and I could have wished that the emphasis had been less on my mother. Nevertheless, I turned to him eagerly, relieved by this thawing of a remoteness that had seemed to shut him away from me.

Albert drew the Rolls up before an arched entrance, the huge, carved front door set well back for weather protection—an impressive door of heavy Florida cypress, with brass ornamentation. It opened as we mounted the few steps, and I knew that my life at Poinciana was about to begin.

Chapter 2

A woman stood framed in the open doorway. She was tall and rather heavily built, and wore a trim gray skirt topped by a white blouse. Her hair was even blonder than my own and had been coiffed into a complex of coils pinned neatly and securely on top of her head.

This, of course, was Mrs. Broderick. Helga Broderick, who had come here from Norway as a young girl in Allegra's day, later marrying an American, Tom Broderick. Tom had once been in charge of everything outside the house, but he had died a few years ago, and Mrs. Broderick was a widow. All this I knew from Ross's previous briefing. He had also warned me that she was never to be considered a servant, even if I'd been likely to use that term. She was an administrator, and one spoke of the "staff" in referring to employees. Allegra Logan had been nothing if not democratic, for all that she lived like an aristocrat.

Ross shook hands with Mrs. Broderick warmly and introduced me.

"Welcome to Poinciana, Mrs. Logan," Mrs. Broderick said, but her handclasp offered no warmth and her pale blue eyes dismissed me quickly. Obviously I wasn't up to exclusive Palm Beach standards, and for a moment I felt subtly diminished. I could never live up to Allegra's measurements, I was sure, but something in me stiffened. I mustn't think like that. Perhaps Mrs. Broderick would need to live up to mine.

"Mr. Nichols will be right down," she said to Ross, stepping back from the doorway. "He is with Miss Gretchen. There has been an unfortunate accident—though nothing serious."

"Albert told me," Ross said. "I'll go up at once. I want to know what happened."

Mrs. Broderick bowed her head in compliance. "Miss Gretchen—that is, Mrs. Karl—and her husband have moved into the south wing," she added.

Ross nodded, his mouth tightening, and motioned me in ahead of him. Albert had already vanished around to the rear with an armload of bags. I stepped into the entry hall and forgot everything else as its stunning impact struck me.

It was an utterly beautiful and formal room done entirely in red and white, and not as large as might have been expected in such a house.

The walls were covered with tapestried silk the color of Chinese lacquer, the square of floor was white marble, lightly veined, and a suspended white stairway rose on the left, carried upward by wrought-iron balusters and rail. The lacy iron curved across the back of the hall at half-level, without visible support, and then turned toward the front, the treads vanishing as they reached the upper floor. The underside of the stairs gleamed white as they performed their act of magical balance.

Straight ahead at the half-level, white columns framed the red of a wall that held portraits, except for one conspicuously blank in the center. Beneath the floating stairs, more columns framed a door at the back, guarded on each side by marble busts on tall pedestals. Where the stairs began, a pot of Sèvres porcelain held a glowing rhododendron.

I must have been standing open-mouthed, for Ross put an arm about me, laughing. "Allegra used to watch for just that reaction the first time any guest stepped into her house. That stairway is still famous in architectural circles."

"It's *so* beautiful," I said. "It takes my breath away. Yet for all its formality the room seems almost modern. Perhaps a classic modern."

Ross approved my words. "My mother could do things like that. She had the imagination to fly ahead into new worlds at times. She didn't want marble staircases and the ballroom-sized entry hall that Flagler chose for his home, so she created this out of clouds and made someone build it for her."

"I already admire her tremendously," I said.

In some strange way, he seemed to withdraw a little from the warmth in my words, and went on more coolly. "The empty space up there above the stairs used to hold a portrait that Sargent painted of Allegra. It's at the Metropolitan in New York now. Perhaps we'll replace it with one of you."

"Oh, no!" I said too hastily, and he laughed again. I hadn't earned the right to be up there, and I wondered uncomfortably if other wives had hung there too, and been in turn removed. But that wasn't fair. I tried to cover my haste. "I'm going to love everything about this house."

"Don't be too sure yet," he said in the same cool tone. "It's a difficult house to know. But come along. I want you to meet Gretchen before we settle into our rooms."

I wasn't sure this was wise, under the circumstances, but I knew better by now than to object to anything that Ross proposed. We mounted the beautiful white stairs and I touched wrought iron lightly. The handsome foyer hardly prepared me for the drab and rather shabby hallway that stretched across the wide front of the house. Once its carpet had been rich with glowing color, but now it was faded and threadbare. Here and there a Louis Quinze chair or console interrupted the emptiness, and the flowered wallpaper was peeling in one corner.

"So much neglect, as you can see," Ross said. "Some of the house has been kept up, but Allegra would hate what has happened to the rest. Poinciana needs you, Sharon."

That pleased me more than anything. I wanted to be needed, and I meant to live up to what was expected of me. Somehow.

The curious architecture of the house became evident as we followed the hall. Other corridors turned off at odd angles, and unexpected flights of steps led up or down. At the end of the hall, double doors of mahogany had been closed across the far apartment. Near the doors a tall, red-haired man in jeans and a blue pullover stood beside a table talking on a telephone. He gave Ross a salute of finger to temple, glanced at me with appraising gray eyes, and went on speaking in a low, assured voice.

Ross didn't knock, but opened the far doors that gave upon a formal parlor, and crossed it to a door that stood ajar upon a darkened bedroom. Here he tapped a warning of our presence.

"Gretchen?" he said. "Gretchen, I'm home. I missed you at the airport. What's all this about a fall downstairs?"

"Go away!" said Ross's daughter.

The words made no impression on her father. He pushed the door wide and drew me with him into the bedroom. It was high-ceilinged, with two tall windows across the front. Draperies of some light, neutral material had been drawn across to shut out sunlight and leave the room in shadow. I could barely make out the double bed with its rumpled covering, and a dark head just visible on the pillow. Bits of clothing had been strewn around the room and I stepped over a scuffed sneaker.

Ross advanced upon the bed, leaving me to stand hesitantly near the door. "None of that now! Sit up and let me have a look at you. I want you to meet Sharon."

The girl under the covers groaned deeply and flung a sheet over her head.

"Open the draperies, please," Ross said to me. I wanted to escape, but there seemed nothing to do but obey, permitting bright Florida sunlight to flood the room.

Gretchen bounced indignantly and tried to burrow further under the covers. To my astonishment her father reached out and grasped the bedclothes, pulling them down, and when Gretchen would have turned over to hide her face in a pillow, he pinned her shoulders with both hands so that she had to look up at him.

Gretchen Karl was developing a very colorful black eye.

"So!" he said, as she went limp under his hands. "That creep hit you, didn't he? No fall downstairs did that."

"Oh, Daddy!" Gretchen wailed, and held out her arms. Ross sat on the side of the bed and enveloped her in an angry hug.

I slipped quietly back to the hall, postponing any introduction, and found the man at the telephone just hanging up.

"Hello," he said, and held out his hand. "I'm Jarrett Nichols, Mrs. Logan. It's too bad this had to happen right when Ross was coming home."

When I'd shaken his hand and murmured some agreement, I could find nothing more to say, and I stood in uncomfortable silence, waiting for someone to tell me what to do next. What had happened to that poise I was so noted for?

"Anyway," he went on, "it's a good thing you're here, both of you. I don't believe in feuds."

"I didn't know there was one," I said hesitantly.

He seemed to concentrate on me for the first time since that initial cool look in my direction, and I stood my ground and studied him back, starting at the top of his tousled red head. Somehow, I had expected that the man in whom Ross put so much trust would be older—and different. More polished in appearance perhaps, and not so informally dressed. The gray eyes I'd already noted were emphasized by scraggly red brows, his nose had a slight bend in it that was not unattractive, and his chin had a fighter's look. Above it, the mouth was unexpectedly tender in a face so strong—though I had a feeling that this man smiled very little. I felt wary with him at once. Like Mrs. Broderick, he was ready to weigh me and find me wanting.

"Mm," he said, finishing his own appraisal. "You don't look much like Ysobel Hollis."

"Did you know my mother?" I asked directly.

"Not really. I met her a few times. And of course I saw her on stage. What happened in Belfast has hit everyone who admired her. I'm sorry about all that horror you've had to go through."

He sounded sorry enough, but my distrust remained, and I was glad of that glass case I could close around me, concealing what I felt. I had always backed away from talk about my mother, however admiring. And now I did so more than ever. Ysobel was in the past and it was safer for me if she stayed that way.

"You've come as a surprise to this house," he went on bluntly. "You might as well be aware of that."

"Marrying Ross was a surprise to me, too," I admitted.

His look continued to measure, but told me nothing of his conclusions. "Never mind. It's done and you're here. I suppose we'll all get used to one another."

Again, a strange welcome. I wished Ross would come and rescue me from this outspoken man.

"What do you think of the house?" he asked when the silence grew between us.

"I haven't seen much of it yet. The foyer downstairs took my breath away. I'm eager to learn more about Allegra Logan. Did you know her?"

"A remarkable lady," he said, but there seemed an odd inflection in his voice, as though he held back when it came to any discussion of Ross's mother.

Again there was silence, and Jarrett Nichols went a bit impatiently to the door of Gretchen's suite and looked in. Ross beckoned to him from the bedroom, and he left me with apparent relief. It was obvious that he did not approve of Ross's marriage and that all he could offer me was cool courtesy. Never mind—I could play that game, too!

Just talking to him, I had begun to feel geared for resistance. How often in the past I had lived in a state of quiet combat. Even inside a glass case, one could be quietly stubborn. This wasn't what I wanted now, but I had to find my own way to acceptance and respect, and I'd had more practice at this sort of resistance than Ross dreamed. I mustn't bristle, but I wouldn't be put down either.

At that moment Mrs. Broderick reappeared around a far corner and came toward me. "Would you like me to show you to your room, Mrs. Logan?"

I glanced toward the open door of Gretchen's suite and saw that Ross and Jarrett were already deep in discussion. It occurred to me wryly that I hadn't been formally dismissed by Ross as yet, but it was time to make a choice.

"Thank you," I told the housekeeper, and followed her down the hall.

She led the way along a secondary corridor past a flight of circular steps that ran upward.

"That's the way to the rooms in the belvedere," she told me. "Mr. Logan's mother had a sitting room up there at the top, and her nap room, as she called it, was just below. We've prepared a room for you next to Mr. Logan's, down this corridor, though of course you may want to make changes if you are going to live here."

I knew very well the customs of the rich. In Ross's case there was a house in East Hampton and in Virginia, and the apartments in New York and London, but he had spoken as though he might not make the usual seasonal exodus. He never minded hot weather, he'd told me, and had thrived on it as a boy, just as his mother did.

The wing we were now in seemed to extend at a right angle from the back of the house toward the lake. At the end of the corridor were two open doors, and Mrs. Broderick gestured toward the one on the left.

"This is the Ivory Room. Mr. Logan's room is on the right, with a connecting door between." She stepped back to let me enter ahead of her.

The room was indeed ivory. Pale and beautifully elegant—a silken room with hardly a touch of color except for light yellow draperies and a golden pillow on the chaise longue. A perfect room for a woman who lived in a glass case, I thought, and wondered why I felt depressed.

"Your bath is over there," Mrs. Broderick said, her feet whispering across the champagne carpet. "The dressing room adjoins it and I see that Albert has brought up your bags. I'll send one of the maids to unpack for you, Mrs. Logan."

I told her that I preferred to unpack for myself, and she indicated the bell, in case I wanted to summon assistance.

"Or you can always reach me on the house connection," she added. "Just dial three."

I looked into the bathroom and found it enormous, with mirrors and gilded fixtures, and a great deal of old marble, including the huge sunken tub. The gold rug would be furry and soft, shielding one's feet from the marble floor.

In this suite there was no shabbiness and I wondered if Brett, Ross's second wife, had done it over for herself.

"How large is the staff at Poinciana?" I asked, moving back to the bedroom.

"We're somewhat shorthanded these days. There are only eight of the indoor help at present. Not including kitchen and laundry, of course. I want to consult with Mr. Logan about hiring more when he has time. Though help is difficult to find these days, and in any case Mr. Logan doesn't like a house cluttered with people. The maids are supposed to keep out of his sight as much as possible. So you'll need to ring if you want anyone. Of course, old Mrs. Logan had at least seventeen servants in the house when she was in residence here." Apparently Mrs. Broderick didn't mind the word "servant" if it wasn't applied to her.

The fact that she hadn't considered consulting with me about the hiring didn't disturb me. I had no feeling that I was in any way mistress of Poinciana as yet, but merely a stranger, visiting.

Looking about at all this ivory perfection, however, I felt an urge to muss up the pillows, rumple the well-dressed bed, set the furniture askew.

"This wasn't Allegra Logan's bedroom, was it?" I asked.

Mrs. Broderick permitted herself a faint smile, and the intricate coils of her blond hair dipped slightly in my direction. "No, this wasn't one of Mrs. Logan's rooms. She preferred richer colors. That is, in the old days. Her rooms have been shut off for a long time. We don't use them any more. There's no need, with so many other rooms available and empty. Mr. Logan has done very little entertaining here for many years." She hesitated. "Though of course that may change now."

If there was a question in her voice, I didn't know the answer, and I remained silent.

"Old Mrs. Logan designed and furnished the entire house originally," Mrs. Broderick went on, a hint of pride coming into her voice. "Though I worked for her only in her later years, I know what wonderful taste she had. She knew all about the antiques and fine paintings her husband had collected, and often she brought in experts to advise her. Until—" She broke off and I had the same sense of something suppressed that I'd had with Jarrett Nichols.

"What happened to her?" I asked, trying to sound casual. I was beginning to feel increasingly interested in the woman who had built this house. In some ways she seemed more alive to me than those I had met within its walls.

Mrs. Broderick's expression reproved me for my question. "Perhaps Mr. Logan will be better able to tell you about that. If there is nothing else you wish, Mrs. Logan, will you excuse me? Word that you were coming was rather sudden, and there has been much to do to get ready. Dinner will be served at eight, but Mr. Logan usually likes cocktails downstairs around seven-thirty."

When she'd gone, I stood for a moment lost in thoughts of Allegra. There always seemed to be a sense of hesitation when her name came up, as though something of importance was being held back. I had been ready to admire her as the creator of Poinciana. In her role as mother, I wasn't so sure. Talented and dramatic mothers could often leave something lacking where their children were concerned, but this had not seemed to be the case with Ross's mother. After all, she had done a spectacularly good job with him. Hadn't she? Anyway, I had other things to think about now.

I stopped pretending to be sure and in command of all I surveyed.

Across the room were arched doors that opened to the outside. I stepped through them eagerly and found myself on a wide upper loggia floored in terra cotta tiles. Moorish arches framed the view of the lake and ran along past a series of rooms, mine being one of them. Tiled steps led down to a pebbled courtyard, where tropical trees grew against the walls of the house, and bougainvillea clambered to the roof. Beyond, a wide lawn sloped toward the lake, its lush green dotted with coconut and royal palms. Strange to think that in the beginning there had been no palm trees in

Palm Beach. They had all been imported when the island was built up from its sandbar state.

In the distance, from the other side of the house, I could hear the ocean murmuring, rushing up on a beach, but on this side the lake lay calm and blue-gold in warming sunlight. Out on its waters a sailboat moved under power toward one of the bridges, and on the far side rose the buildings of that busy commercial city that was West Palm Beach.

As I knew, Palm Beach itself had been the invention of Henry Flagler, Rockefeller's partner in Standard Oil. He had seen the possibilities for an exclusive resort, and had run a railroad down to make the island accessible. It had been reclaimed from its wilderness of sand and shell and scrub growth into very much what it was now. Then he had built West Palm Beach across Lake Worth, to house, as he said, those who would serve the wealthy on the island of Palm Beach. West Palm Beach had thrived and spread and continued to marvel at the fantasies of the rich islanders whom it often served.

I turned against the rail of the balcony and looked about at what I could see of the house. It rambled away in all directions without apparent plan—which made it all the more interesting, though, as Ross had said, Allegra must have driven her architects mad in its building. Dominating all else, rose the tower that I'd heard referred to as the belvedere. There were windows and a balcony up there beneath the curiously domed roof that would command a splendid view in all directions. I liked to think of that room as belonging to Allegra, and I was already calling it Allegra's Tower in my mind.

At the far end of this pleasant arched loggia, with its long chairs intended for sunning, a small door of carved cypress had been set into a rounded bulge of wall—obviously not the door to a bedroom. I went to it and turned the brass knob. Circular walls closed around me as I stepped inside, and I felt along the edge of the door for a light switch. When I touched it a ship's lantern that hung from the ceiling came on, lighting a narrow flight of stairs curving away at my feet.

I smiled, remembering a secret staircase in a castle I had visited with Ysobel and Ian in Portugal. Clearly Allegra had loved her little surprises. Holding to the rail, I descended the flight and tried the knob of another closed door. Nothing seemed to be locked, and it opened easily. Once again I caught my breath in astonishment, as I'd done when I first entered Poinciana.

The room was enormous, its shadowy length cut into by long beams of sunlight from the tall windows at one end, turning it into a golden room, bathed in yellow light. Truly a golden room, I thought, for unless I was mistaken, the coffered ceiling was done in gold leaf, and so were panels along the end wall. No furniture occupied the center of the great room with its gleaming parquet floor, but there was a recessed dais for an orchestra, and little French chairs of tarnished gilt and frayed satin stood in place all the way around the walls, like guests waiting for the music to begin.

I wished I could have seen Allegra dancing here! What beautiful gowns she must have worn. Perhaps some of them were still hanging in the closets of her unused rooms. She must have been a great beauty in her time, and in that vanished era such parties must have been given regularly here as were never seen today.

Feeling like Cinderella wandering in a deserted palace, I walked across the room, peopling it in my mind with waltzing couples. No—not the waltz! Those were the Scott Fitzgerald days, so they'd have been dancing the fox-trot, and perhaps those who were young and daring would have Charlestoned madly across the parquet floor. More than ever, I wanted to see a picture of Allegra, wanted to know more about what she had been like.

A sound surprised me into turning and I saw that a door nearby had opened and a man stood staring at me. I recognized the uniform and cap of a guard, and after an instant of startled exchange, he touched a finger to his cap.

"Sorry, Mrs. Logan," he said, and the door closed quietly as he disappeared.

Ross hadn't mentioned guards, but I supposed they would be necessary at Poinciana, where several valuable collections were housed. For the first time, I had a sense of walls, not only holding out the world, but imprisoning those who lived here as well.

I shook off the fancy impatiently. Certainly I could come and go as I pleased and the walls had nothing to do with me. But now I had better find my way back to the other part of the house. Across the ballroom were wide double doors, arched and gilded, but I would explore where they went another time. I ran up the stairs and through the cypress door to stand at the loggia rail again. Someone shouted below me, and as I watched, a boy of about ten came running into sight, with a small nondescript brown dog at his heels. He slid to a halt on the grass as he saw me, while the dog leaped around him.

"Hello," I called down. "My name is Sharon Logan. What's yours?"

He didn't answer me directly, though his curly red hair hinted at his identity. He simply stared at me for a long, unblinking moment before he spoke.

"So you're the new one?" he said.

He was like his father, blunt. "And you must be Jarrett Nichols's son? Do you have a name?"

"Sure. It's Keith," he informed me. "Keith Nichols. Gretchen said you were coming."

And she hadn't said it flatteringly, I suspected. "Do you live here?" I asked.

"Of course. All the time. My father stays here when he's not in New York or Washington or someplace. We live over there in Palmetto Cottage. That's the one closest to the lake." He waved an arm, but from my balcony the cottage was out of sight around the next wing of the house.

"What a wonderful place to grow up in," I said.

He nodded, and as his look moved to the right and left of me, I sensed in this boy a certain proprietorship about the house.

"Anything you want to know about Poinciana, you can just ask me," he said. "I know things *they* don't know. Things *she* told me."

"You mean Mrs. Logan?"

"Of course." Gray eyes that were like his father's seemed suddenly bright with mystery. "Come on, Brewster!" he shouted, and boy and dog went racing toward the lake.

Brewster? Whose whimsy was that? He had spoken of his father and himself living at the cottage, with no word about a mother. And what was all that about some mysterious knowledge concerning the house? Well, the Nichols family was not my affair. There was too much else to occupy me now.

I turned back to my ivory room and began to unpack, while water ran in the marble tub. I hadn't recovered from jet lag, and a hot soaking would be pleasant. But first I went to the door of the adjoining bedroom and tapped on the panel. There was no answer and I opened it, feeling almost surreptitious.

The room matched my own for size, but there was nothing of feminine elegance here. The big bed was covered by a woven hemp-colored spread, and the window draperies were of the same natural weave—suitable for warm weather. An easy chair of red leather sat near the inevitable fireplace—that could also be needed in Florida—and above the mantel hung a colorful hunting scene, with red coats on horses that were dashing for a fence. An open cabinet revealed a record player and stereo set, making me wonder what Ross's tastes were in music. There was still so much to learn about my husband, but now, with an oddly guilty sense of spying, I closed the door and went to take my bath.

Later, dressed in a silk tunic and trousers of pale coral, I sat at the rosewood dressing table and brushed my hair, wound its coil at the back of my neck, and tucked in a tortoiseshell comb. Then I opened the fawn leather jewel case that had belonged to Ysobel and took out the jade my father had given me. In the padded ring tray were emerald earrings that were Ross's gift, but for tonight I chose the jade. The golden chain that suspended the dragon pendant held jade beads at intervals along its strand, and when I put it over my head the green glowed with life against the pale coral of my tunic. When I'd fastened the matching earrings in ears that Ysobel had long ago caused me to have pierced, I was ready.

There was an instant, looking in the mirror, when I had the feeling that all this luxury was playacting. Make-believe. Out there somewhere was a real world where women worked for a living, and no one had eight indoor servants, let alone seventeen, or a house with a hundred rooms.

Ah well, I would playact for a while longer. Never in my life had there been enough money to do anything I wished. Ysobel might spend as she pleased, but I had never been permitted more than a small allowance. Everything was bought *for* me that I might want. So now I might as well enjoy and try to become accustomed. Nevertheless, it still seemed unreal, and sooner or later I would have to come down to earth and find something useful and interesting to do. Goodness only knew what, since apparently I was not expected to run the house or get a job.

Earrings secured, I searched the jewel case for the tissue-wrapped netsuke of frogs that Gentara Sato had given me in Kyoto. Once more I admired the intricate delicacy of the carving, and especially its subtle humor. If a frog mother could wear an expression that spoke for all maternal tolerance, this little frog wore it. Obviously, she was fatuously satisfied to have her heedless child put his foot in her eye.

There were holes for the cord, so perhaps I could have it made into a pendant. I really liked it much better than the ivory figurine Ross had given me, and which was still locked away in a trunk.

A light tap sounded at the door. I set down the frog carving and turned about on the dressing table bench to call, "Come in."

A curly head of dark hair popped around the edge of the door, and a pair of bright green eyes regarded me speculatively. Then a dimple appeared in one cheek, and a small, rather pert woman pranced in. She was probably thirty-eight or forty, but her manner seemed more youthful.

"Pranced" was the word. She moved rather like a pony, and she skittered around the room without the slightest by-your-leave, looking all around before she came opposite my bench, where she stopped to smile at my astonishment.

"Hello," she said. "I'm Myra Ritter." The accent was slightly Germanic. "And of course you are the new Mrs. Logan. Ysobel Hollis's daughter. Mm."

That considering "Mm" was already familiar to me. "I know I don't look like her," I said dryly.

Myra's smile broadened. "I wasn't going to say that. I thought you might be feeling a bit oppressed and that a friendly face would help. Do I look friendly?"

I recognized that she wasn't being impertinent, or rudely familiar. She was clearly an original and it was evident that neither Poinciana nor its occupants impressed her to a point of subservient respect.

I had to smile. "Thank you. You've given me a name for yourself, but I still don't have an identity to go with it."

"Sorry! The room rather stunned me. Though I should be used to the house by now. I'm Mr. Nichols's assistant. That sounds better than secretary, doesn't it? I was just leaving and thought I would look in on you first. There's been quite a stir about your coming, as you can probably guess. I've only worked here a few months myself, so I know what it's like to spend your first days at Poinciana. At least I can get away at night. I don't think I'd stay if the pay wasn't so good!"

By any of the "proper" social standards that I had been quietly resisting most of my life, what she was doing was entirely outrageous. But she was being human, and I immediately liked her for it. Also, Myra Ritter, as I would come to know, had the ability to fly to the heart of a problem, discarding the extraneous. There was a shrewdness in her, seasoned by an enormous curiosity that she hadn't the slightest interest in stifling.

"Thank you for coming," I said. "Everything is strange and quite wonderful, but I don't really believe in any of it yet. Won't you sit down?"

She dropped into a chair and crossed a pretty pair of legs. She was young enough in years, yet older in intuitive wisdom, and she possessed a rather intense vitality.

"Money is always real," she observed. "A very practical matter when one doesn't have much of it. Though I find I can adapt to all this quite easily. But then, as I say, I can go home to my little apartment every night."

"Tell me about yourself," I said.

She pursed her lips thoughtfully. "I was born in Vienna, but my parents brought me here when I was very young. I've been to school in Switzerland. I've worked at all sorts of jobs, here and there. Both in America and abroad. There was a marriage that broke up. Not a lot to tell, really."

We chatted for a moment about schools in Switzerland, though mine were different from hers. I wondered if she might inform me about other members of the household. There was so much I needed to know.

"What is Mr. Nichols like to work for?" I asked.

"Considerate. Most of the time. He works very hard and he suppresses his suffering. Sometimes I think Americans can be as inhibited as the English. And the men of course are worse."

I had no idea what she meant by the word "suffering."

She went on without my asking, quite ready to gossip. I suppose I should have stopped her, but I didn't. "Perhaps you don't know? His wife died in an auto accident two or three years ago. There was some question about what really happened—whether it was suicide on her part. He's a very good father to his son but the loss has been hard on both of them."

I felt both shocked and sorry. "How dreadful," I said, and wondered why Ross had never mentioned the tragedy. "I'm still ignorant about a great deal," I went on. "I know some of the things that Mr. Nichols does for my husband, but just what do they encompass?"

She cocked her dark head on one side, grinning impishly. "I might quote one of the Mellons and say that Jarrett Nichols hires *presidents* of companies. Perhaps that's not it exactly, but he does keep on eye on all those Logan Foundations, among other things."

The picture of enormous power was coming clearer, but I turned from it with a conscious effort. "This house is what fascinates me. All the care Allegra Logan must have given to building and furnishing it!"

Myra nodded. "Yes—a fabulous lady. I've been reading about her in books from Poinciana's library. She must have been very dramatic and willful when she was young, and always given to getting her own way with all her husbands. There were three of them, as you probably know. The first two she couldn't stand and threw out. But I gather she was faithful to Charlie Logan all his life. There are several books in the library downstairs with whole chapters on Allegra Logan. Everything she did was news. And she's the one who started a lot of the philanthropies Mr. Logan keeps up, and which Mr. Nichols helps to administrate. It's his job to check new causes they might invest in. Tons of requests come in every year. Of course it's all wonderful for tax saving, and of course makes Meridian Oil look soundly virtuous."

Clearly, respect for the Logan empires was not uppermost in Myra Ritter's mind, and I didn't especially care.

"This is the first time I've met Mr. Logan," she went on, "though of course I've talked to him by long-distance on any number of occasions, taking messages for my boss."

Apparently, she had sat still long enough, and now she jumped up. I was to learn that Myra never made smooth, easy movements. She jumped and darted nervously, and now she skittered toward the door.

"Just wanted to say hello. I'll run along now. Don't let Gretchen put you down." Again there was that intuitive leap to an understanding not altogether welcome, so that I felt unmasked.

She waved her fingers and disappeared through the door, closing it briskly behind her. For a moment I sat staring at its panel, not entirely comfortable at having been seen through so easily. It was as though with Myra Ritter my protective glass casing didn't exist. She had seen straight into the uneasy truths that hid at my very core. Uncertainty and self-doubt had seemed visible at a glance to this odd little woman.

I turned back to my mirror and used my lipstick brush. So Gretchen was sure to be a problem. I wished I had asked Myra about Vasily Karl, the "Balkan" husband. It would be more useful to know about him than to study Allegra Logan's life in the library downstairs—much as the idea appealed to me. Had he really given his wife a black eye? And if he had, what would Ross do—throw him out?

These were questions that would eventually answer themselves. Now that I was dressed, there was still time before cocktails, so I might as well move about the house, learn to find my way through its maze. I stepped into the corridor and met Ross coming from the stairs. He hurried to put his arms around me, then held me away.

"Beautiful, Sharon! That coral silk becomes you. You

do have an elegance your mother never had. You make me very proud, you know."

What my mother had had was love. Love pouring out to her from every audience she faced, love cradling her from her friends, and most of all, Ian's enveloping love. Mine too. At least I had been eager to give it whenever she had time to accept the giving. But such a thought came close to something I'd never had the courage to face fully, and I moved away from it now, pleased that Ross had compared me with Ysobel and found her wanting. Ross was one man whom Ysobel would never have been able to manage.

He had returned to me fully, and when he kissed me I felt again the marvelous warmth of his protection. All my uncertainties could go into hiding, and I need only drift with Ross's arms around me and be forever safe. I thrust back the small inner voice that asked if this was all I wanted of life—just to be safe?

"Where are you off to?" he asked.

"I thought I might wander about the house for a little while. Get acquainted with it. I've already found the ballroom. Do you mind?"

"Of course not. It's your home now. I'll give you a proper guided tour tomorrow, but you can explore in the meantime. I'll shower and change, and then join you downstairs. Have fun."

His second light kiss sent me on my way, and I knew this wasn't the time to ask about Gretchen.

Much of the upstairs floor, as I discovered in my roaming, was shut off and unused. Allegra had obviously done a great deal of entertaining in her day, and there must have been times when every room was full. But now bedroom after bedroom closed its door upon whatever life remained in the house. All were beautifully, tastefully furnished, though a little frayed and worn. Often they had their own sitting rooms, and fine paintings hung on their walls. Allegra must have liked the French moderns, and it was surprising to find a Cézanne sketch or a Renoir watercolor tucked away casually in a sitting room where no one came any more. The art collection downstairs was undoubtedly fabulous.

Once Mrs. Broderick heard me opening and closing doors, and came out of her own room to ask if she could help me. I thanked her and went on in the face of what I sensed as disapproval. To her I was still an intruder, but she would have to get used to me.

Looking out a window, I discovered for myself the servants' wing, set on a lower level from the main floor, and apart from the house by a roofed passageway.

Of course the tower drew me. I wanted to see it when I was alone, and not with anyone who would instruct and inform. Information could come later. Right now I wanted to sense Allegra as she must once have been. If old houses were haunted by ghosts, then Allegra's must surely walk these halls, and perhaps had already begun to haunt me, filling my imagination, leading me in a direction in which I felt compelled to go.

I found my way to the iron treads that circled up to a third-floor level in the tower, and climbed, clinging to the rail. The steps opened from a landing into a room where all the shutters were closed and little light penetrated. There was a musty odor, a slight dampness, and what furniture remained had been shrouded in white covers.

The stairs led me upward, and I climbed to the top level, where window shutters stood open, and a breeze blew in from the sea. At one side a door opened onto a tiny, circling balcony, and I went through it to stand high above the red-tiled roofs of the house. It was like being at the top of a lighthouse, and I loved the mild wind on my face, the view of ocean breakers rolling in upon a narrow strip of beach. I could see the swimming pool down there, and the tennis court. But the room itself interested me even more, and I returned to examine it.

Here no shrouding had been done. Comfortable rattan furniture covered with bright chintzes invited one.

Across one corner was set a small desk and chair. Allegra had perhaps come to this tower room to free her mind when it was troubled, to feel close to the shaggy tops of the palm trees outside, and to view sky, sea, and lake, as they were visible from every window.

This, however, was not an unused room. An open portfolio of photographs lay on the desk, and tacked on the brief space of wall between windows were double photos in black and white. Both were pictures of Ross, and I went to stand before them, my interest caught.

Each was an action shot in which Ross had been moving toward the camera. In one he was striding free, his arms swinging, athletic and handsome, as I had so often seen him, his head up and eyes alight with characteristic vitality. He seemed to move with force and purpose and that eagerness for life that I loved in him, since it was the force that had brought me back to life.

The other photograph was in startling contrast, and it disturbed me deeply. Again Ross moved toward the camera, but now his arms were bent at the elbow, fists clenched, as if he were running. Late sun threw shadows slanting across his face, giving it a look of dark fury. I had never noticed that faintly diabolic slant of his brows before, or the way deep lines could etch his mouth, giving it a sinister look. Yet in this picture too he was driven by some vital force, so that he charged at the camera angrily, as though he meant to destroy it.

The contrast between the two shots was startling and unsettling. In the one picture, he moved into sunlight with confidence and courage, and you knew he was a man who could do anything he chose. In the other, he charged like a bull and the force that drove him was destructive—an ancient, dangerous force that grew out of some terrible frustration and despair. Only a despairing man could be as angry as that.

"What do you think?" said a light voice behind me. "Which one do *you* think he is like?"

I whirled about and knew that the small, sturdy

young woman in tight jeans and plaid shirt must be Gretchen Karl. If no other clue was given me, the spreading purples of the bruise about one eye would have been enough.

Chapter 3

"Hello," I said. "I'm Sharon. I hope I'm not intruding up here. The tower drew me, and your father said I might explore."

Her expression reminded me of the dark look worn by the man in the second photograph, with no smile, no brightening of the dark eyes that stared at me. She was examining me carefully, rudely, detail by detail from head to toe, and I stood quite still, meeting her searching look.

Then she said coldly, "You'll be just fine for his collection." Her meaning was clearly insulting.

I tried to ignore her manner, studying the picture again, searching for something to say.

"You haven't replied to my question," she went on. "What do you think of those photos?"

"I only know the man on the right," I told her quietly.

"I've never seen the other one." Or had I, briefly, that last night in Kyoto?

"He tried to smash my camera on the day that was taken." Her lips twisted wryly. "I grabbed it and ran—so I saved the picture."

"What was it that made him so angry?"

Her eyes flashed with the indignation of memory, and she moved her head so that black hair, cut in the thick, swirling bob that Sassoon had stamped upon the country, flew out, and then fell back, with every strand in place.

"He was angry with my mother—and so with me for defending her. It's a wonder he didn't kill her one of those times before they were divorced. You have something to look forward to if you haven't seen him angry yet. My father can be a very destructive man."

She was throwing out one challenge after another. Antagonism toward me seethed in her voice, in her contemptuous look. Yet I wanted to make some tentative gesture toward her that might lessen this hostility. I glanced down at the open portfolio of photographs on the desk.

"You're very good," I said. "Do you do this professionally?"

"I don't do anything professionally." But her tone softened just a little and she seemed to relent. "The library asked me about exhibiting some of my work, and I've been wondering whether to let them."

"It's a wonderful idea. Have you picked out the pictures you might use?"

"I couldn't make up my mind."

"May I look at them?"

For an instant, I thought she might refuse, but she shrugged instead and flung herself into a rattan chair, legs outstretched, toes upturned in dirty sneakers. I was uncomfortably aware of my silk tunic and trousers and Saint Laurent perfume. I had a feeling that she disapproved thoroughly of everything about me.

Trying to move as quietly as though I were in the

company of a wild animal cub, I went behind the desk and sat down. One by one, I turned over the large glossy prints, now and then setting one aside, aware of her watchfulness that was still guarded and suspicious.

The photographs were good. Very good. "You've a special gift for seeing," I said. "The lighting is exactly right and your subjects come to life. But a photographer has to see quickly and choose the perfect instant—which you've done. These pictures are never static."

"I hate studio portraits," she admitted.

"They'd be easier to do than this. It takes tremendous skill to catch someone in motion at the one precise moment." I was speaking the truth, but if I'd thought to win her with it, I'd failed.

"What the hell do you know about it?" she challenged.

"Very little. I know more about painting. Mostly from visiting museums when my parents parked me somewhere while they traveled."

I could sense her thinking about that, but I said nothing more, turning the pictures again. One photograph stopped me. It was of a young woman standing against a strange, many-trunked tree, looking up at a boy of five or six stretched upon a massive branch above her head. I had met an older version of the boy—Keith Nichols.

Gretchen came out of her chair to see which picture had caught my attention. "That's Pamela Nichols, Jarrett's wife. Was. She's dead."

I looked more closely at the slim figure in Bermudas, her dark hair thick about her shoulders, her small, rather humorous face tilted to look up at her son.

"She doesn't look unstable," I said. "Myra Ritter told me there was some concern about possible suicide."

With a quick, violent movement that startled me, Gretchen reached for the print and ripped it in two, tossing the pieces on the floor. Then she closed the portfolio with a slap.

"That's enough! I'll pick the ones I might show myself. If I show any."

For an instant I considered trying to talk to her about the really good prints I had pulled out, but I knew this wasn't the time. I rose and came around the desk, moving slowly toward the stairs.

"This is a charming room," I said. "Was it your grandmother's?"

Her voice changed. It was a voice that could show lively color and resonance, or could be as light and wispy as air. Now she sounded wistful.

"Yes, it was Gran's. I haven't changed a stick of it since the days when she used to come here." She went around the desk and dropped into the chair I had left, suddenly forlorn. "I miss my grandmother. She was the only one around here who knew how to be kind. She would tell me what to do—if only she could!"

To my dismay, tears spilled over as I watched, and rolled down her cheeks. She wept openly, like a child, and I wanted to comfort her, but dared not make a move, certain of rejection if I did. Instead, I turned my back and went to look out one of the windows, my eyes following the driveway that wound between ficus trees toward the front gate. What did Ross really know about his daughter? I wondered. Had he any idea that she was as lonely as this, that she still longed for her dead grandmother? How little parents really knew about their children.

I spoke softly. "Your father was disappointed when you didn't meet him at the airport today."

She raised her head and stared at me with tear-blinded eyes. "I hate airports!"

I agreed. "Airports are for saying goodbye. I hate them too."

For just an instant there was a hint of understanding between us. Then her rejection of me surged back.

"Why did you have to come here? You'll be sorry! He makes everyone sorry!"

I edged toward the stairs. There was nothing more

I could say to her now. Just as I reached the top step, however, a man came rushing up, brushed past me and threw himself across the room, to kneel and envelop Gretchen impetuously in his arms.

"My darling! How I've hurt you! Will you ever forgive me?" It was all theatrical and more than a little startling, but Gretchen's face lighted and she leaned into his arms for comfort.

"It was my fault, Vasily," she told him, her wet cheek against his. "What could you do with a wildcat coming at you? You're the one who must forgive me."

Embarrassed by this outpouring, I turned away. I had found that retreat was the only solution when raw emotion reached out to engulf me. That was what throbbed in this room—raw, ungovernable emotion. Fury, despair, anguish, love, were all a part of it, and it was more than I wanted to face. I'd started down the stairs when Vasily Karl left his young wife and came to grasp my hand and draw me back to the room, speaking with his precise, foreign-born English.

"No—don't go, please. You are Sharon, yes? This is all very unfortunate, but we are glad to have you here. I was a devotee of your mother's. I saw her many times in London, Paris, Rome. My heart goes out to you in your loss."

I kept my head down, shrinking from being pulled into this vortex. "Thank you. I must go downstairs now and find Ross."

He continued to hold my hand, restraining me, so that I really had to look at him for the first time—and I received a shock. Somewhere, perhaps a long time ago, I had seen this man, and recognition seemed to carry with it a sense of unpleasantness, even of fear.

He was not someone to be easily forgotten. Probably in his mid-thirties, he was rather thin, with blond, waving hair and a face that just missed being too good-looking. It was his eyes, most of all, that gave me a sense of remembering. They were very dark in contrast to his light hair, and with a slightly Oriental tilt. A short white scar lifted the edge of his right eyebrow, giving him a permanent expression of cynical surprise.

"You are very lovely," he said. "Mr. Logan is to be congratulated."

I ignored this. "I've seen you somewhere before, haven't I? Surely we've met somewhere?"

The hand that held mine gently, yet with such strength, was long, with slender, sensitive fingers, and it tightened slightly on mine. He bent his head to kiss my hand in a gesture that was natural to him, and then looked at me with an amused, almost sleepy expression.

"Had I ever met you, Mrs. Logan, I would remember," he said.

I withdrew my hand firmly, further embarrassed, and this time he let me go. Without looking back as I went down the circling stairs, I knew that he watched my flight, and that perhaps he was not altogether amused. I *had* seen him somewhere before, and not under happy circumstances. That much I knew, though memory eluded me. The answer would probably return when I wasn't searching for it. Now all I wanted was to put the tower room behind me.

Outbursts of theatrical emotion were not unfamilar in my life. Both my father and mother had lived at a top vibrancy of feeling, and in self-defense I had learned to insulate myself. I was glad that most of the time Ross was the cool businessman, who would never let himself go in an emotional tantrum. I had seen him angry, but even then it was a sternly controlled anger that got him whatever he wanted. Certainly I had never seen the dark, destructive side that Gretchen had caught in her photo. At least I didn't want to think I had.

Now I searched for the floating stairway that had brought me up from the foyer, and when I found it I followed its descent past red walls and white pillars, until I reached the marble floor below. The double doors beneath the stairs were open, and I could see a fire burning across a vast room. Ross stood beside a scrolled black marble mantelpiece, glass in hand, waiting for me, and I was struck again by his distinguished good looks.

In relief at the sight of his calm presence, and aware of soft and soothing colors, I crossed the gray-green carpet to a chair of rose brocade drawn beside the fire. Candles had been lighted in delicate girandoles that reflected their gleam from the walls, and here and there a lamp shed further subdued light on the elaborate and exquisite room. Pale draperies of rose damask were pulled across windows closed against the chill of evening. From one large wall a large classic mirror framed in thin gilt gave back the scene, increasing the room's depth and width still more, and adding a further glow of rose and gold.

With a sense of luxury, I sank into the chair, accepting the glass Ross brought me, and let all thoughts of what had happened in the tower room flow away from me.

"I wish we could have the house to ourselves," Ross said. "Perhaps that time will come. At least we can have our own rooms. Tomorrow you must look through the house and see if you find something that suits you better. I've been using my present bedroom for years whenever I came here for visits. But now I'm going to stay and work on my book, so we might as well settle in."

"The book on netsuke?"

"Of course. I've been working on it off and on for some time, and Gretchen's been doing the color photographs for it. Tomorrow I'll show you my collection, and perhaps you can help me with it."

There was unexpected fervor in his words, as though this was something he cared about with a passion that I'd not seen in him before. I had an odd sense of revelation—but of what? It was as though some basic emotion had surfaced in Ross that was new to me, and I wondered why it made me slightly uneasy. But he was waiting for my response, and I gave it hurriedly.

"I'd love to help, if I can. And of course I'm eager to see your collection."

He was pleased with me, and that very fact warmed and reassured me. I sipped my drink, sitting quietly before the fire, and for the first time in a long while I began to feel entirely at peace. As though, at last, I had come home. Ysobel would have been astonished, and perhaps Ian too. They had always seen me as an adjunct to themselves. Someone not quite grown up as yet. Someone for whom marriage lay in the distant future—if ever. Ysobel had sometimes been openly doubtful about my appeal for men. Too cool and chaste, she'd said, teasing me, and had never suspected the small, angry flame that had leapt inside me at her words.

Now I was mistress of this stunningly beautiful home, and I could have anything I wished, do anything I wanted. Though it might take a little time to convince myself of that. Most of all, I had a husband who loved and needed me, and I would never again doubt my own appeal for a man.

"You're looking pensive," Ross said. "What are you thinking about?"

I had no words to tell him. I had never learned how to express what I was feeling, and I was afraid of being laughed at for the turbulent emotions that could boil up inside me. So now I withdrew into being matter-of-fact.

"There's so much to consider. So much that is new. So much to learn." It was time now to tell him. "I've met Gretchen and Vasily," I said.

The sense of peace was shattered in an instant. Ross came to my chair with a quick movement that set his drink tilting to the rim of the glass.

"He's had the gall to come back? I hope Gretchen has told him where to get off. If she hasn't I'll see him myself and do it for her!"

"When I left them they were in each other's arms

and she was telling him that it was all her fault. It sounded as though she may have instigated their quarrel."

"Nonsense—a little thing like that! There's something vicious about that fellow. He actually struck her! Of course he only married her for her money, and the sooner she wakes up, the better."

I wondered if I should tell him of my sense of recognition when I'd met Vasily Karl, but with nothing definite to recall, it was too nebulous to talk about. Besides, my sympathy was really with Gretchen and I had to make some mild protest against his words.

"Perhaps Gretchen needs someone of her own in her life." After all, *I* knew what that yearning could be like.

"There are plenty of men in America. She could have her pick."

"Perhaps he *is* her pick. She looked very happy in his arms."

"I won't have it! I won't have my daughter exploited. He'll wind up breaking her heart."

Though I knew I shouldn't, I went on. "Why don't you wait and see? Isn't her happiness worth it?"

His expression was colder than I'd ever seen, and I wondered with a faint twinge of disloyalty if he was capable of considering Gretchen's happiness. This was a man who possessed a power that I was only beginning to understand. Presidents listened, financial empires trembled at Ross Logan's edicts. What he commanded must be done. I had begun to recognize this in small ways as we traveled together, and I saw it in the attentions and services that were paid him, and paid me because I was with him. But could a man who had found his way to such a position learn to accept defeat in anything? Was that what made him strong—refusing ever to be defeated? If so, there might be a painful time ahead for Gretchen and Vasily, and I wondered if his daughter could be equally strong in order to fight him. Her rage was very great. I had already seen that. But had she the iron in her to best him?

Ross sipped his drink and looked at me again, his gaze softening. "I'm sorry, darling. I don't want anything to spoil our first night together at Poinciana."

I was a little like Gretchen, I thought with unexpected clarity. When Ross looked at me the way Vasily looked at her, I melted. I wanted so terribly to be loved, cared for, protected, and I didn't want to live with my guard up all the time.

Shortly before dinner was announced, Jarrett Nichols came into the room, greeted me with distant courtesy, and accepted a scotch and soda from Ross. Again I was conscious of his striking red hair, and of the strength this man too seemed to exude. Though it was a different strength from Ross's. Not so much a power that commanded outward events, but something inner that could be relied upon by others. This was undoubtedly why Ross depended on him, trusted him implicitly. And because of this I wished he might look at me with less antagonism.

Jarrett, as became clear quickly enough, was here at Ross's invitation. I gathered that he usually dined with his son in their cottage when he was at Poinciana, but tonight there were more business affairs to discuss.

A butler, whom I hadn't seen before, came to announce dinner, and we went down an inner hallway to a pair of open doors. On the threshold I stopped to view a room that was a perfect picture in itself.

"Allegra again?" I said.

Ross smiled. "My mother believed that any room worth doing must be seen like a painting on first sight."

A painting it was, done in glowing pink and silver gray. The walls were of pale gray satin, the Directoire chairs, about an oval table, upholstered in deep pink moiré. Mantelpiece and ceiling were a cloudy gray, and a shining Waterford chandelier hung above the table, glass tapers alight. A centerpiece of luscious pink rhododendron graced a cloth of heirloom lace.

Ross's hand guided me to my chair opposite his at

the long end of the oval. Places were set for only three and Jarrett sat between us.

"This is the family dining room," Ross told me. "There's a larger, more formal room for grander affairs. In Allegra's day it was used frequently, but this was one of her favorite rooms. Brett had these chairs done over, but the rest is just as it was in my mother's time, and the colors have never been changed."

I sipped white wine and thought again of Allegra Logan. She must sometimes have been a little bizarre and ostentatious, yet capable of creating this room of delicate beauty. A lady of contrasts and great imagination. Once more I saluted her and hoped humbly that her spirit would bear with me.

"How old would Allegra be now if she had lived?" I asked.

Ross glanced at Jarrett before he answered—a look I didn't understand. "Ninety-two," he said. "She was thirty-six when I was born. There were two other children ahead of me who died. A girl and a boy."

I was aware of Jarrett, staring at his plate in a fixed way, and remembered his previous withdrawal at the mention of Allegra's name. There was something here that I didn't understand.

I began to spoon my cream of parsley soup, and it was Jarrett who finally turned the conversation to me by asking how I had liked Japan.

I told him of our visit to Mr. Sato in Kyoto, and about the gift the old man had made me of the mother-and-child frog netsuke.

"Perhaps I can have it made into a pendant," I said. "It's so beautiful and I would love to wear it."

Ross looked shocked. "Of course you will do nothing of the kind. That is a valuable collector's item. Tomorrow you can bring it to the netsuke room and we'll find a proper spot for it."

For just an instant I wanted to protest that the carving had been given to me, that he had no right to order what I should do with it. But I wanted no quarrel, and he was probably right, so I said nothing, though I was aware of Jarrett's frank look upon me. A look that might be derisive. My intense awareness of this blunt red-haired man made me uncomfortable. What did it matter if he didn't like me? I turned away quickly.

For the rest of the meal, Ross talked mostly with Jarrett, and though my attention wandered now and then, I became aware of a certain tension growing between the two men.

"I'm out of all that," Ross was saying. "I haven't been on the board of Meridian for more than a year."

"You're still the major stockholder and you vote. Your influence isn't likely to be overlooked. You know very well that new explorations for oil are vital. Ours should be moving ahead a lot faster. You need to urge this on personally."

"You worry too much," Ross told him, and gave his attention to the steak that had been perfectly broiled with mushrooms.

Yet even while Ross ate his dinner with obvious relish, I grew aware of a certain choler that had arisen in him. A flush had mottled his face at Jarrett's words, and I wondered at its cause. Jarrett himself seemed coolly controlled, betraying nothing, and he let that particular topic go and turned to less irksome matters. I wished I might ask questions, learn more about my husband's empire, but I knew that I lacked the knowledge to ask with intelligence, and that probably both these intimidating power figures would regard any words of mine as frivolous and ignorant. If I wanted to learn, I would have to go about it in more indirect ways.

We finished the meal with a sherbet, and I became increasingly aware that I would not be needed in this house for the planning of meals. Not that living in hotels and schools had prepared me for a kitchen. But sometimes I had the whimsical wish that I might be turned loose with a cookbook and assorted pots and pans, just to see what adventures might await me in that unfamiliar world. At Poinciana it was likely to stay unfamiliar. Of those who worked here, no one but Mrs. Broderick had paid me the slightest attention, and I was quite aware that her acceptance of me had been laced with polite disapproval. I had yet to earn my wings.

After dinner, Jarrett returned to his cottage, and Ross went up to my room to fetch me a shawl. We walked outside, and the sound of traffic seemed far away beyond the coquina rock walls that guarded Poinciana. Nearby sounds were only the rattle of the wind in palm fronds and the rushing of waves onto a beach. What a perfect jewel of a world! An antique if not archaic jewel, really, to be thus removed from everything that was ugly and painful and threatening. All those things that had hurt me so deeply could never touch Poinciana.

I walked with my arm through Ross's, safe in my imaginary sphere, able to believe for a little while that clocks could be turned back, and that a life like this was still possible.

Lights burned in the windows of several cottages and I waved a hand in their direction. "Who lives down there?"

"Some are empty. They were guest cottages in Allegra's day. Jarrett and Keith and their housekeeper occupy the largest. A few of the staff who've been with us a long while live down there if they have families. Let's go this way. I want to show you something."

We walked around the front of the house and toward the boulevard, where Palm Beach traffic went by. Ross led me to a locked gate, which he opened, and we went down several steps to a stone passageway that led under the road. Allegra had seen to everything, including a private way to the beach.

The echoing stone tunnel was damp, but it was free of debris and had obviously been swept. I could feel the rush of the wind through the arched openings as we approached the ocean. Another short flight of steps, another gate, and we were out on the sand. Off to our right were the tennis court and swimming pool. I smiled to myself, remembering what someone had told me about Palm Beach: "Nobody who is anybody swims in the ocean." But *I* would.

The beach ran the length of the island—not very wide, and bordered by sea grape on the land side. We went to the water's edge, where the sand was packed damp and firm, and walked together, my hand in Ross's. Though the beaches along here were private, no one could be barred from walking the sand, but no one was out tonight. Beyond the sea walls and the road, the great houses, their windows alight, seemed remote and of another world. The world of the rich and the favored that I didn't really belong to.

Appropriately, a huge Florida moon hung over the water, and I smiled to myself, thinking of Ysobel's *Moon Songs* in a long-ago album, remembering that I'd thought them sentimental, when she herself was not. Tonight I could dare to be sentimental myself. The scene about us was so beautifully, unbelievably romantic, and I knew when Ross slipped an arm about me as we followed the strip of sand that he was feeling it too. Under his breath he began to hum an old song that Ysobel had helped to popularize—"Blue Champagne." I might have wished that he had chosen some other tune, but I would not let thoughts of Ysobel trouble me now.

Perhaps anticipation is one of the essential parts of lovemaking. To be close and to know what lies ahead, so that excitement begins to build in a warm awareness of what is to come. How lucky I was to have been chosen by a man like Ross. A man who knew every tender, arousing touch of love, who knew what a woman wanted. Especially a woman who had known so little about love until now.

When he bent his head to kiss me, my mouth responded and I felt the tiny pulse awaken in my lips.

"Let's go up to the house," he said, and we turned

together and walked quickly across the sand, eager now, hurrying back through the tunnel.

High in Allegra's Tower, a light burned, but I turned my eyes away from it. I didn't want to wonder who was up there. I didn't want to think of Gretchen and Vasily, but only of Ross and me. Tonight there would be no repetition of that strange rejection I'd experienced on our last night in Japan. Tonight we were ready for each other. Perhaps more than we'd ever been before. I remembered that he had told me everything would be better at Poinciana, and I was beginning to understand what he meant.

Up the lovely front staircase we floated, and at the door of my room he let me go. "Come when you're ready," he said, and went through the next door.

Even though eager haste befuddled my fingers, I undressed tidily. Living in schools taught one not to drop clothes heedlessly about. When I'd put on a gown of sheerest chiffon, I sat at the dressing table to remove my jade earrings. For just an instant, my eyes rested on the frog netsuke, and a feeling I didn't want to entertain ran through me. He had no right... But I wouldn't think of that now. For this whole entrancing night I would think only of Ross and of how much I loved him, how much he loved me.

As I moved barefoot toward the closed door to his room, I heard the sound of instrumental music starting—the same tune he had hummed earlier down on the beach. How lovely, how perfect! How well Ross understood that a woman needed the romantic. I adored that beautiful sentimental tune, and I no longer minded his choice. I knew it would make just the right background for our expression of feeling for each other.

I had reached the door, my hand on the knob, when the singing voice began—and I froze. That was Ysobel in her old recording, and for a moment I couldn't move. The idea of music was beautiful, but not my mother's voice singing to us at a time like this. *I keep a blue rendezvous*... It was all wrong, jarring. Wrong for some instinctive feeling in me that perhaps went back to my childhood. Perhaps a confusion about sex and love—and what one's mother mustn't know. A confusion about my own feelings toward Ysobel.

Quickly I opened the door and went into the room. I meant to go straight to the stereo and turn it off, but I never reached the machine. Ross was there, waiting for me.

"Come here," he said. "Come here, my darling," and there was something in his voice that I had never heard before. In one terrible, rending realization, I understood. And there was nothing I could do. Short of utter rejection, there was nothing at all I could do.

I heard the note of undisguised sexual feeling that could throb in Ysobel's tones, and knew that it held and stirred my husband as I had never been able to. Stirred him because *she* was in his mind.

I went to him slowly, unable to help myself, and he held me in his arms as he had always done, yet with a difference. That I had stiffened in something like horror seemed to matter not at all. For him, I wasn't there as myself. He held another woman, from another time, and made love to her with a passion I had never felt in him before. A passion tinged with a strange hint of anger, though he had never been rough with me, as he was now. And all the while Ysobel's velvety voice cradled us in its warmth. A warmth that was totally false. Though this was a bitter thought that I had never accepted fully until this moment, when it helped to make what I had believed was Ross's love for me equally false. I lay beside him while tears wet my cheeks. He never knew. He had fallen into a deep, satisfying sleep, after pouring out his love for Ysobel through Ysobel's daughter.

Chapter 4

Ross had always awakened early, and I was adjusting to the same pattern. I heard him rise and go into his bath, and I got out of bed hastily and fled to my room. There must be no repetition of last night, and I was glad that he had spent himself, as a younger man might not have done.

Under my shower I tried to wash myself clean of memory. An impossible wish. What had happened had completely shattered me. For most of the night I had lain awake with my thoughts churning. The escape from the past, from Ysobel herself, that Ross had offered me, had been no escape at all. If I believed in what had just happened, then all my newfound confidence as a woman must be denied. As always, I was nothing—Ysobel everything.

But morning light could bring a remembered courage, a lessening of night terrors. A slow, deep anger began to grow in me—against them both. Against Ross and Ysobel. If this was what Ross wanted in me as a wife, he must be shown how wrong he was, no matter how furious that might make him. I recalled the photographs Gretchen had taken of her father. I had seen in it a man who could charge furiously, like a bull, and I shivered.

Moving automatically now, I dressed in cream-colored slacks and a silky shirt of pale amber, braided my hair into a thick strand down my back, and was nearly ready when Ross tapped on my door and opened it. I sat stiff and frozen on the dressing table bench, watching him indirectly in the mirror, steeling myself against whatever might come. He seemed no different than on any other morning in our brief married life, except that he was at home now and ready to return to his own busy and ordered existence. For the first time since last night, a faint uncertainty stirred in me, and I grasped at the fragile straw. Was it possible that I hadn't really understood? Oh, if only that could be true!

He kissed me with affection, and if I held back a little, he appeared not to notice as he linked my arm through his when we went down to breakfast. I found that I could still play my old game of concealment. If others were false and not to be trusted, I could be like that too. It was a game that sickened me, because it had never been what I'd wanted in life. In marrying Ross, I had believed myself free of Ysobel, free of all pretense. This morning, however, pride was everything, and all that mattered was for me to hide the remnants of my shattered fantasy. What had happened must never happen again, but in the meantime I must play the role required of me as the new mistress of Poinciana.

The breakfast room was still another, smaller room done with green bamboo wallpaper, and accented in tones of lemon. Ross seated me at a small table set with woven place mats, and rang for the same man who had served us last night. I found I wasn't especially hungry, and I settled for papaya, toast, and coffee.

Glass doors opened on a pebbled courtyard and looked out toward the lake. The water seemed as calm as it had been yesterday, with only a tiny breeze to rustle the palms. It was good to engage myself with the physical details of my surroundings and put last night far, far away. Putting something out of my mind, pretending it hadn't happened, was an ability I'd developed over the years when I'd felt hurt and lonely. It was nearly always possible to enjoy the small pleasures of the present and not allow what stood outside the circle of the immediate hour to threaten me. Postpone the hour of reckoning, and the evil thereof!

Listening to Ross and watching him, I could almost convince myself that my interpretation of last night was wrong. I was Sharon to him again, and he condescended to me just a little, as he often did, and I didn't especially mind. How could he not, with the difference in our ages, so that sometimes he must look on me as very young indeed, and in need of educating and directing. Besides, I admired him in so many ways—for the ease of his bearing, his brilliance and knowledge, for his natural authority.

"I want to show you the netsuke collection first of all this morning," he told me. "You must have something to occupy your time, and I think I may be able to involve you in this work—if you're willing."

I brightened a little. I was more than willing to make any sort of plan that would keep me busy. One of the things I'd been dreading was too much idle time. I wanted to develop a purpose, a direction—something to engage my full and enthusiastic attention. When I'd been with Ysobel and Ian, there had always been so much to do that life progressed at a breathless pace. Perhaps I hadn't been using *me* fully then, but now that they were gone, I seemed to be drifting and becalmed.

On the other hand, I knew all about the wives of

wealthy men, who engaged fervently in work for charity, for one cause or another. All laudable enough as far as it went, but not for me. I wanted something that would use whatever talents and abilities I might have.

After breakfast, Ross needed to confer with Jarrett Nichols for a half hour or so, and I said I'd go for a walk.

"Just stay away from the cottages," he directed. "We like to give them privacy, as we enjoy ours."

I was glad enough to get off by myself for a little while. Ross's company still left me uneasy this morning, though more and more I was trying to be reasonable about last night. The sick conclusion I'd jumped to must be wrong. It had to be. If it were true, the consequences to me would be more devastating than I knew how to face.

Outdoors, I gulped deep breaths of salty, invigorating air as I walked along. I stayed away from the beach this morning, since it would remind me of last night. Besides, there were other parts of the grounds that I wanted to explore.

Most of the plantings seemed old and well established, so Allegra must have had a hand in them, as she had in all else about Poinciana. Best of all I liked the great spreading tree that Ross had pointed out to me as a poinciana. Flowers came before the foliage, and I could see pink buds starting along graceful gray branches. Before long it would glow with red blossoms, its other name being the flame tree.

Paths of ground shell wound along and I followed them at random. Rounding a bed of tall Spanish flag, I found that my circling path had taken me after all in the direction of the cottages. I stopped to look toward them for a moment before turning back. Most were painted a clean white, with red-tiled roofs for contrast, and they were not set too close together. One, in particular, was remote from the others, and unlike the rest, its color was pale pink. Shutters had been the style in the day when these structures were built, and all the shutters on the pink cottage were closed, so perhaps it was unoccupied.

I wondered who had lived in this rather special little house that was set apart from the others. Palmetto, where Jarrett and his son lived, was closest to the house, while this was the farthest one of all. In the distance I could hear the sound of a riding mower being driven by one of the yardmen, but around the cottages no one moved. Probably the occupants were all busy with their duties by this time. Then, as I watched, the door of the pink cottage opened and a woman came out, to start along the shell path toward me.

Sheltered as I was by the flower bed, I hadn't been seen, and I stood my ground, watching her. She was an arresting figure, moving with an authority and assurance that would make her notable anywhere. Though she was well into middle age, her hair was carefully brown, and she had pulled it into a knob on top of her head in a style that was fashionable, but not especially flattering. Though I suspected that wouldn't matter to this particular woman. Her very wearing of the style gave it a certain elegance. Her well-cut jacket, vest, and trousers were of a deep lime color. She was anything but the jeans type.

As she came closer, she glanced in my direction, saw me, but did not slow her steps. Once, she must have been a strikingly beautiful woman, and she was still handsome, with eyes of an odd, dark violet, strongly carved features, and a skin that had suffered from too much sun.

"Good morning," I said as she came closer. "I'm Sharon—"

"I know who you are," she said with a touch of hauteur. "Good morning." And she walked straight past me without troubling to introduce herself.

I watched in surprise as she strode off with a long, free swing that took her rapidly away from the direction of the house. In a few moments she disappeared around a grove of live oak, and didn't come into view again. What lay over in that area, I had no idea, but there was no time to explore. I suspected that this woman was not one of Ross's employees. Her air of authority was too evident; even her manner of dressing wouldn't have been suitable for someone coming to work around a house or office. My curiosity was thoroughly aroused and I would have to find out who she was. But not right now. A glance at my watch told me I'd better get back to meet Ross.

On the way, Keith Nichols crossed my path, schoolbooks under one arm, red hair slicked neatly down.

"Hello," I said. "Where do you go to school, and how do you get there?"

He grinned at me in friendly fashion, his red hair shining in the sun. "Albert takes me when he's not busy. There's always somebody around to drive me. I go to Palm Beach Day School."

Perhaps Keith Nichols might give me an answer to what had been puzzling me.

"Can you tell me who lives in the pink cottage that is farthest from the others?" I asked as he fell into step beside me.

"That's Coral Cottage," he said, but his eyes evaded mine. "*She* stays there. But I'm not supposed to talk about her. Not ever. Mr. Logan says so." He broke away from me and ran off toward the huge garage that housed the cars of Poinciana.

I walked on thoughtfully, and let myself in a side door. Another mystery! Poinciana seemed full of them. Now, more than ever, I wanted to learn the identity of that remarkable-looking woman. Yet at the same time I smiled and said to myself, "Mrs. Bluebeard, be careful." For some reason—perhaps because of Keith's words—I knew I wasn't going to ask Ross who she was.

The room in which Ross kept his netsuke collection had been his mother's morning room. It was a more intimate room than some, but still large enough so that shelves and cabinets didn't seem to crowd it. Again, it was on the lake side, with long French doors that opened upon a little patio surrounded by potted plants. The desk at which Allegra had once worked on her plans for each day was now Ross's, and manuscript papers were stacked upon it, presided over by a portable typewriter.

But what caught my attention, what drew me most were the rows of shelves with their marvelous display of Japanese Satsuma and cloisonné, ivory and lacquer. I stood open-mouthed until Ross came to me, pleased at my reaction.

"Yes, there are some remarkable pieces here. And I found every one of them myself. The rest of the house belongs to my parents, but these things are mine."

I'd not heard such pride in his voice before, and I understood something new about Ross that gave me an unexpected feeling of tenderness. Both Allegra and Charles Maynard Logan must have been overpowering figures, and Ross had grown up in their shadow. So of course he would prize especially something he had created, brought together out of his own knowledge and taste. Some of my resistance toward him began to fade.

He had brought a stack of mail from his office to sort through, and he set the pile down on the desk. There were several invitations, and the office phones had already been ringing with calls from old friends, and with requests for interviews with both of us. But Ross was postponing all that for the moment, and letting Jarrett, with Myra's assistance, handle anything that seemed urgent. Ross's own secretary wasn't due back from his holiday for several weeks, and Ross seemed to enjoy the freedom of being without him. Now his collection could have his full attention, and he wanted me to learn all about it.

"First," he told me, "I'd like you to familiarize yourself with the netsuke pieces. There are over three hundred items on those shelves at the far end of the room, and they've never been properly catalogued. Perhaps that's one job you can do for me, if you'd like. Of course, I have records of purchase of everything in the collection, but they should be numbered and identified in one journal. My manuscript is a narrative account and will cover some of them. I'll want you to read what I've written and look carefully at Gretchen's photographs."

All of which I was happy and eager to do. At Ross's direction I started at the far end of the room, where shelves covered the wall from waist height up, with cabinet doors below. Ross sat at the desk and began to work on his papers.

Fatefully—because I didn't know then the role she would play in all our lives—the first netsuke I picked up was carved of pale pink coral, and represented a tiny mermaid, sleeping sweetly with her hands clasped under one cheek, and her tail curled up to shield her body. Again, there was the light touch of humor, of whimsy, lending reality to the fantasy. The mermaid was so exquisitely rendered in every tiniest detail that it seemed as though she might open her eyes at any moment and look up at me.

"How beautiful!" I said. "She's absolutely exquisite!"

"They're all exquisite," Ross agreed, sounding faintly impatient at my interruption. However, he did look at the tiny object on my palm and his tone changed. "Oh—the Sleeping Mermaid. That was my mother's favorite of the entire collection. Sometimes she used to carry it up to the tower with her. For a 'visit,' she used to say—so the mermaid could see her home in the ocean. Of course, I never approved of any of the collection's being taken out of this room. We can't have them scattered about the house. They're always here to be admired and enjoyed, but let's keep them here."

I hadn't proposed keeping them anywhere else, except for my frogs, but I was glad that Allegra had been capable of her own little conceit about the mermaid.

As I went on along the shelves, pausing to pick up a piece now and then, I came upon one that caught my interest especially. It was hardly more than two inches long—the crouching figure of a man in a pointed straw hat and grass cape, with every blade of straw visible in the carving. His head was turned so that he looked backward watchfully, his large eyes rolled, his mouth sly. Again I was enchanted.

Ross saw my face and relented to come and stand beside me.

"Oh, all right. I'd better introduce you—or at least make a start. They won't mean much to you otherwise. That little fellow is probably a ronin disguised as a farmer. You can just glimpse the sword hidden beneath his body. Do you know about the ronin?"

I remembered them from my reading and nodded. A ronin was a masterless samurai turned robber, and this one was undoubtedly waiting to ambush some helpless passerby.

"He was carved from a whale tooth," Ross pointed out. "Unsigned, as so many of the netsuke are, unfortunately, because, as you know, so humble an art was thought not worth signing."

He pointed out others among his favorites. A Lion Dancer in a gold lacquer kimono, no more than an inch and a half in height—a No dancer wearing the mask for the lion dance. This one was signed with characters that Ross translated as the Koma Bunsai. Next Ross pointed out a snail carved of wood, with the shell and soft part of the body clearly distinguished by the texture of the carving. The body actually looked damp and shiny, in contrast to the shell.

I was particularly taken by the Fox Priest—a taller figure than most, being nearly four inches. The pointed fox head and feet contrasted with human hands and the body of a man dressed in a flowing kimono. Often the figures illustrated some legend, and these, Ross said, I must learn from books he would give me to read.

He had just picked up a tiny temple dog when Jarrett Nichols looked in the door.

"Good morning. Ross, there's a Japanese friend of yours on the phone from New York, if you'd like to talk to him. A Mr. Yakata."

"I'll take the call in my office," Ross said, and went out of the room.

Jarrett looked around. "So he's breaking you in?"

Again I seemed to hear a hint of derision in his words, and I bristled inwardly. "There's so much to see that I hardly know where to begin. Ross wants me to learn about the collection so that I can help catalogue it."

"That should keep you busy."

I didn't like his tone, and I changed the subject. "I want to learn about Allegra too. She *was* Poinciana and her mark is on everything in the house. Are there any pictures of her when she was young?"

Jarrett opened a cabinet door beneath a netsuke shelf. "Those are Allegra Logan's scrapbooks. She kept them faithfully over the years." He pulled out a fat, leather-bound volume and laid it on the desk, turning its pages. "There you are. That's a color photo of the famous Sargent portrait that hangs in the Metropolitan."

The period was early in the century and she wore an evening dress of summery blue, cut with a round neck that showed her beautiful throat. No jewels were needed to add to such shining beauty. Though perhaps not beauty in a conventional sense. Not prettiness. One became aware of an overpowering strength of personality that attracted and held. She wore her dark hair puffed over her forehead and there was an eagerness for life in the eyes that looked out at the world. Her chin still wore the soft curves of a very young woman, and there was a certain willfulness about the mouth that hinted of a lady accustomed to having her own way. The only ornament in the painting was the rose she held in her hand.

"Did you know her?" I asked.

"Not until she was in her late seventies. She was the one who picked me out of law school and told Ross he could use me. A marvelous lady—always."

"She interests me even more than the netsuke," I

confessed. "Everything she was is stamped somewhere in this house, and I want to learn about her, about what she was like and what she wanted. Ross feels that some restoring should be done, but I hope he'll keep the house the way she planned it."

Jarrett's look softened a little. "Good for you. I was afraid you'd want to bring everything up to date."

"Of course not! I wish I could have known her—Allegra Logan."

"You'd better get acquainted with the netsuke first," Jarrett said curtly.

"Oh, I shall. It's an exciting art. And of course it must be recorded, preserved. But I've already studied Japanese art a bit and I'm used to it. It's not alive—not any more."

"And you think Poinciana is?"

I warmed to the subject. "Of course! After all, it's the creation of a woman who is still close to us in time. Lives have been lived here. People have died and been born and suffered and laughed—as it is with any old house."

"It belongs to the past, nevertheless," Jarrett said. "A museum piece, and I hope it will be cared for as such."

"I'm not so sure of that. From the little I've seen, the present is shaking its walls right now. But I expect they've withstood storms before this."

He knew what I meant. "Yes—Gretchen and Vasily. Sometimes Gretchen reminds me of her grandmother. The way she digs in and won't be budged, once she has an idea between her teeth. Of course, that's Ross too. You'll need to understand that."

The faint resentment toward this man that I had felt before rose in me again. He had no right to tell *me* about my husband. As though I were a stranger whom he needed to instruct. He presumed far too much.

Again I changed topics with an abruptness that I hoped would show him my displeasure. "This morning when I went for a walk, I saw a woman coming from the direction of the pink cottage that is farthest away. Quite a striking woman. Perhaps in her fifties. With her hair in a knot on top of her head, and very well dressed. I tried to introduce myself, but she barely acknowledged me and hurried off right away. Rather rudely, I thought. Do you know who she could have been?"

Jarrett sighed. "I'm afraid I do. That must have been Brett Inness, Gretchen's mother. I haven't told Ross yet, since he has enough problems on his hands with Vasily. Brett has been around regularly, and Gretchen has given her a key to the north gate so she can come and go as she pleases. The guards have been told not to interfere with her. If Ross stops this, there will be an explosion from Gretchen. But he must be told. He won't want her around."

I felt decidedly upset. I hadn't expected a former wife of Ross's to have such easy access to Poinciana—especially when this was a woman he seemed to detest.

"I've talked to your son a couple of times, and I liked him very much. This morning he told me that the woman I saw lives in the pink cottage. He called it Coral Cottage."

Jarrett's answer was firm. "You must have misunderstood him. Of course she doesn't *live* there. She must have been visiting, that's all."

I let the matter go, and sat down on the floor before the shelf of scrapbooks, with the one he'd opened for me on my lap.

Jarrett said, "I'll see you later," and went out of the room.

Relieved to be alone, I began to turn the pages. There were numerous news clippings of elaborate affairs held at Poinciana, and I found I could pick Allegra out of any group in which she had been photographed. Even as styles changed, she had kept that puff of hair above her forehead—her own distinctive hairdo—and she was always the most imposing woman around, for all that she hadn't been very tall. Seen alone, she looked tall because of the proud way she held her head, her shoulders, and I could well imagine that she had made a formidable impression.

One page showed the Logan yacht, in which she had been sailing the Mediterranean, visiting the Isle of Rhodes. There was a delightful picture of her in the ruins of Lindos, where I had been long ago with Ysobel and Ian on one of those rare times when they had taken me with them on a holiday. Allegra looked almost Grecian herself in her flowing scarves. Of course the yacht, bought for her by Charlie Logan, had been called *Allegra.*

So engrossed was I in these accounts of Ross's mother that I didn't hear his return.

"I thought you'd be going through the netsuke," he said. "Not mooning over dead history."

He bent to take the scrapbook from my knees and returned it to its place on the shelf. Once more, a hint of resentment sparked in me, but I managed to suppress it.

"I asked Jarrett Nichols if there was a picture of your mother I could see," I explained as Ross pulled me up. "That's why he showed me these scrapbooks. I want to read them all eventually. If I'm to know her house, I must know her. Will you show me the house now?"

For some reason he was not entirely pleased with my interest in Allegra's scrapbooks, and I wished I could ask him why openly. But I had already learned to tread with caution around Ross's sensibilities, and I recognized that the subject of his mother was one he wanted to drop. Showing me Poinciana was different, however. He put an arm around me as we started on our tour.

The downstairs rooms were extensive. Hundreds of people could have been lost in them. There were drawing rooms and small parlors, a wing of offices, a huge library with thousands of books on the shelves—a place I would return to again and again, I knew. Shabbiness was evident in those rooms that went unused today, but I could glimpse what they had once been. On every hand were antiques of a value that could hardly be estimated, and I felt a small thrill over fulfilling my dream of my own private museum to learn about and study.

The formal dining room was enormous, with high-backed chairs down each side of a long, shining table, bare now of place settings. No concession to Florida climate had been made here, and there were no flowered fabrics, no warm-weather lightness. From elaborate plaster rosettes hung two chandeliers, their shining pear drops of rock crystal. As Ross touched a switch their reflection gleamed from the long table. Against light green damask walls hung family portraits.

The place of honor above the mantel was held by a handsome portrait of Charles Maynard Logan, and I went to stand before it. He had chosen to be pictured sitting at his desk, with a globe on a stand nearby—symbol of far-flung Logan interests. I could make out the lands of the Middle East, from which Meridian Oil had made its billions. He wore the sober clothes of a businessman, with the wider collar and foulard tie of another day. His hair had been gray when the portrait was painted and it was not a young man who looked down at me, but a man of great assurance and strength.

I wondered what he would have thought of his son's new marriage. Would he have disapproved of Ross's taking so young a wife? I thought I saw a glint of humor in the eyes of Allegra's husband, as though it amused him to find himself sitting for his portrait.

Making a sudden comparison that disturbed me, I realized that humor was a trait Ross seemed to lack.

"I think your father must have enjoyed a good joke," I said.

"He did. Too often and sometimes inappropriately," Ross told me. "My mother was forever trying to hush him when he got out of hand."

"Couldn't she laugh too?"

"Oh, she laughed all right—but mostly at her own jokes."

I ventured on delicate ground. "I've never heard you tell a joke, Ross. In fact, I don't think you laugh a great deal."

"Perhaps I find very little to laugh about. But aren't we getting too serious about humor?"

His arm around me tightened, and I felt again a twinge of apprehension. As the day wore on, the hours would move relentlessly toward night. It was easy to assure myself that I would never allow last night to be repeated. But how could I stop it when the time came? I hadn't stopped it last night. If what I'd believed then was true, what was I to do? There seemed a sudden void at the very pit of my being. Perhaps I wasn't facing the truth because I didn't dare to.

I moved from his touch to walk beneath other portraits on a side wall, and Ross introduced me to them, one by one—aunts and uncles, the young brother and sister who had died. But oddly, no grandfathers or grandmothers. The heritage of wealth that led to portraits must have begun wholly with Ross's father. There was, however, a fine painting of Ross himself.

He had chosen to stand with his back to a window, through which Poinciana's belvedere could be glimpsed. On the other side of the window in the painting stood a handsome vitrine, its glass cabinet on high spindly legs. It was probably of walnut, with fruitwood marquetry, all meticulously painted in by the artist. The inlaid motifs had obviously been inspired by Japanese art, and the glass shelves held tiny netsuke. I stood before the picture, fascinated by its detail.

"This is hardly a standard portrait," I said. "Much more interesting, though some of the focus is taken away from the central figure."

"Not really. Like that globe in my father's portrait, the details here show *my* interests." He seemed pleased that I liked the painting. "You can't tell much about a man's life from most of these portraits."

I went on, looking for the one picture I didn't see. "Isn't there one of Allegra?"

"She never liked to be painted. The Sargent was the only one she would ever sit still for, and that was when she was young. She knew the value of being painted by an artist like Sargent, but she was too active and vigorous a woman to give up time to a lot of foolish sittings. So she preferred to have photographs taken. How many times I've seen her bustling about this room, giving orders for some enormous dinner party. And then presiding in style—her own inimitable style—for a great occasion."

"You must have given a few dinner parties in this room yourself?"

His mouth seemed to tighten. "Too many. That's over now, thank God. I hated it. Come along and I'll start you on the art collections. There's something in the gallery I want to show you. A surprise I've been saving."

As I went with him, I was still puzzling over his remark about too many dinner parties. Had the life Ross inherited been far more of a burden than I had guessed? Again I felt a touch of sympathy for the imposing, complex man I had married.

As we followed another branching corridor, I tried to speak of pleasanter things, and told him of my admiration for Gretchen's photographs that I'd seen in the tower room. Again he seemed pleased.

"I saw the double shots she did of you," I told him.

"Ah yes—my dual nature. Which one do you think I am?"

Perhaps this wasn't a pleasant topic, after all. The question was casually asked, never doubting my answer, and I should have replied quickly. But the right words wouldn't come, and my hesitation lasted a moment too long.

His eyebrows went up a little. "So you're not sure?" he said, yet, strangely, he sounded almost pleased.

I looked into a face that seemed more saturnine than

I'd realized, and saw that his silver-flecked eyebrows really did have an upward twist.

"She caught your eyebrows very well," I said.

His laughter rang out along the corridor. "There! You see, I can laugh. As a matter of fact, I felt rather flattered by that picture. I would say that fellow was a very forceful man."

Like his father? There had been unquestioned strength in Charles Maynard Logan's face. One couldn't doubt that he had been a powerful force in his day. I had taken it for granted that Ross possessed much of the same quality, yet now I sensed his need for reinforcement—as though he himself might doubt that very fact. Somehow a disquieting thought.

"There was one thing that happened when I was in the tower that I don't understand," I went on. "I was looking through a portfolio of Gretchen's pictures when I came across one she took of Jarrett Nichols's wife and son. I was interested in it, but Gretchen snatched it out of my hand and tore it up. Why?"

"Come along," Ross said, his hand firm on my elbow. "We'll never be through with the house at this rate. And I want to get back to work."

For once I didn't let him overrule me, but pulled back. "No! Please, Ross. I'm tired of mysteries. I've been running into blockades that you've set up against me ever since we arrived at Poinciana. Topics that seem to be forbidden. I've even thought of Bluebeard's wife!" I managed a smile. "Don't you think that when I ask a question it should be answered?"

The saturnine look was back—that dark look of Gretchen's picture. For a moment I thought he might stride angrily away from me. Instead, he made an effort and returned my smile.

"Sometimes you provoke me a little, Sharon. There's a time and a place for your questions. I don't much like it when they come popping out of nowhere. We'll talk about Pamela Nichols some other day."

I couldn't accept either his tone or his words, but I

had to be satisfied for now, and we went on toward the gallery wing. Allegra, he told me, had built it especially to hold Charles Logan's collection of paintings, and she had added many finds of her own. Wealth was to spend, and there were no limitations in Allegra's day.

Again there were generous double doors, and when Ross opened them we stepped through into a long, narrow room that stretched toward the lake at the southwest end of the house. I remembered noting it earlier when I'd explored the grounds. The Italian influence was in evidence here, with marble floor and arches, and a high, ornate ceiling. But the lighting of the pictures was excellent, and nothing was lost in distorting shadow.

As we came in, a guard left his chair near the doors, saluting Ross with finger to cap before he disappeared behind us, clearly obeying the edict that those who served around the house were to remain invisible.

I saw at once that it would take months of returning to this room before I could appreciate all of its treasures. The first look was bewildering. I was more accustomed to the carefully spaced displays of museums. Here, every inch of wall space had been covered with framed pictures. There were Cézannes and Renoirs that I had never seen in reproductions. Several Gauguins occupied a corner, and there were two Van Goghs.

"My mother bought all of those," Ross said. "Dad leaned more toward Turners and Constables, as you can see."

As he spoke, I caught a faint movement from the corner of my eye. A door at the far end of the room seemed to be open just a crack—as though someone might be standing there listening. Ross didn't notice, and as we moved on I decided to ignore whatever I had seen.

"Did your parents collect any of the American artists?" I asked.

"Of course. You'll find Mary Cassatt, Bellows, Eakins, even a lesser Whistler. And with his interest in landscape my father was attracted to the Hudson River school, with all those mountains and rather rigid outdoor scenes."

As we moved on, I paused in delight before a Breughel—a charming winter scene of white snow and black tree trunks, with little figures of dogs and men, and a distant pond dotted with skaters.

"How on earth do you protect all this?" I asked.

"There's an excellent alarm system, and a special inner room for the most valuable paintings. Here is the door. I've turned off the alarm for the moment."

The same door that had been left ajar was closed, but when we went through there was no one there. No other exit from the room seemed evident, so I must have been mistaken.

This extension of miniature gallery was less ornate and lighted entirely by ceiling fixtures along the top of each wall. I gasped at what I saw. Rubens, Vermeer, Tintoretto! A Study of a Spanish town done in brooding tones of green and black. El Greco! Just to walk among such paintings outside of a museum sent shivers up my spine. Yet somehow, so private and protected a collection seemed a sad fate for work that deserved to be seen by hundreds of thousands.

"Shouldn't these be in a museum?" I asked.

"Some have been given away, when the tax savings were right. But my father liked the idea of owning them, and so did Mother."

"Do you feel that way too? About owning?"

"Of course. I can spend hours here whenever I please. I enjoy what I possess. I suppose I'll eventually will them to one of the museums that are always begging for them."

The way he spoke of possessing made me uneasy again. I was beginning to find certain aspects of Poinciana more unsettling than I'd expected, and I remembered too what Gretchen had said about my fitting into her father's collections. Rebellion was stirring in me, but I mustn't let it out. Not yet.

"My mother was a great accumulator," Ross went on. "She had her own wealth to spend as she pleased, but she had a good business sense too. She knew that what she bought would increase in value. There are antiques in some of those rooms we walked through that are priceless."

I turned from the magnificent paintings, feeling invisible walls moving in around me. Suddenly I wanted to escape from this private, self-absorbed world.

"Mrs. Broderick told me that your mother's rooms have been kept as they used to be," I said. "May I see them?"

"If you wish. But first there's that surprise I have for you. Come over here."

A small half-circle of alcove had been built into one end of the room. I had thought it empty at first glance, but now I saw that curtains of azure blue velvet hung across the space. Ross stepped to one side and drew on the cords of a pulley. The curtains parted to show the portrait hidden behind them. I gasped as Ysobel Hollis smiled down at me from a background of more blue curtains. My mother was younger in the painting than I remembered her, but it was so lifelike, so real, that if I reached out I would surely touch flesh and blood. My own flesh and blood. She was wearing a favorite primrose yellow dress, her short curly hair black in contrast, her face pert and smiling.

Ross's arm came about me and for a moment I leaned against him weakly, then drew away. "Do you remember when that portrait was painted?" he asked.

I did indeed. It had been done a number of years ago, and its painting had become something of a joke in our family. Some "secret" admirer of my mother's had commissioned it. It was to be his if my mother would pose and accept a fabulous sum as a gift for the children's hospital she was sponsoring. We were in London at the time and a notable English portrait painter had been engaged to paint her. When the portrait was done, Ysobel had liked it so much that she had been reluctant to part with it. The artist had caught not only her verve and vitality, but a lovely generosity that looked out of the canvas, saying the same things she always told her audiences with her eyes and voice: "I love you. Come to me."

I stared dry-eyed at the portrait, remembering something strange my father had said in a soft undertone that first time he had viewed the finished portrait: "Things are not always what they seem."

Only now was I beginning to understand a little what he had meant. Now, if I looked long enough at Ysobel's face, I might discover truths that I had long kept hidden from myself. Truths that I was perhaps not yet ready to face. In any case, what did they matter now? Only Ross mattered to me at this instant, and the terrible inference of the portrait. He too had seemed to be what he was not.

Tears came at last, not only because the portrait had opened wounds, but also because it was Ross Logan who had commissioned the painting. Now I must confront what I had been trying all morning to deny: *Last night had been real.*

He was clearly dismayed by my tears. "Darling, you mustn't cry over this. I thought you would be pleased."

He tilted my head to kiss my lips and I kept my eyes closed because I didn't want to know whether he looked at the portrait while he kissed me.

When he gave me a handkerchief, I dried my eyes, trying hard once more to save my pride. "I'm sorry. It was just—just the shock of seeing that portrait again. Everything came back so sharply."

"Of course. I understand," he said, and I knew that he didn't understand at all.

When I turned to escape this small space that had begun to stifle me, he put a hand on my arm.

"Wait, Sharon. I want to show you another whimsy of Allegra's. Look here."

He pulled back a portion of the curtain behind Ysobel's portrait to reveal a door. It opened away from us into a passage that moved into darkness.

"Where does it go?" I asked.

"It opens into an annex at one end of the ballroom. Allegra always liked to have her escape routes handy."

"Escape from what?"

"Bores. People she disliked or didn't want to see at that moment. When she chose, she could disappear with the expertise of a magician."

Now I understood that something I had noted earlier would have been possible. "Ross, when we were in the big gallery, I noticed that the door to this room was ajar. Or thought I did. But when I looked again it had closed. Do you suppose someone could have been here, and gone away down the passage? Isn't it dangerous to leave this entrance to the gallery unprotected?"

"Oh, it's not unprotected," he said. "The door at the far end of the passage is kept bolted from this side. And the alarm system works there too."

"Is it bolted now?"

He touched a switch that lighted the passageway, and went to the door at the far end. The bolt was open. He closed it impatiently and came back to me. "Of course, others in the house have access to these rooms. But this door is supposed to be kept locked at all times. I'll speak to the guard about it. Then if you want to see Allegra's rooms, I'll take you to them."

When he'd spoken in imperious anger to the man he addressed as "Steve," he led the way out of the long gallery, and up one of those unexpected flights of stairs that Allegra had caused to be placed around turning corridors.

At the top I was startled by the sudden appearance of Keith Nichols. The boy had been nowhere in sight, and then without warning he was there, staring at us, equally startled. I wondered if he had been the watcher who had opened and closed the doors downstairs. Since this was Saturday, he had no school.

Ross regarded him sternly. "I thought all this was going to stop. Were you down in the gallery just now?"

"Yes, sir, I was." Keith tilted his head of red hair, looking up at Ross, undaunted. "I lost Brewster, and I think he's hiding in the house. Mrs. Broderick said he wasn't to come inside, so I'm trying to find him."

"That had better be the truth," Ross said.

"Yes, sir!" Keith grinned at us impishly and seemed to disappear through the wall.

"Where on earth did he go?" I asked in astonishment.

"Never mind. That wall is a *trompe l'oeil* touch that hides a real door. Keith grew up at Poinciana and he knows every trick that Allegra built into it. She used to show him her secrets herself."

"What an imagination she had," I said. "I'm glad Keith can enjoy it while he's young." I listened to my own words and felt far removed from them. Only that portrait of Ysobel was real, and must eventually be confronted.

"I don't want him to have the run of the house unsupervised," Ross went on. "But most of all I don't want you to become obsessed with Allegra. Don't build her into some romantic conception in your mind. This house and most of what is in it was her vocation. She was very good at what she really cared about. But the extravagances she indulged are done and gone. Her reign is over. This is another day. *Your* day. Remember that."

My day—or Ysobel's?

Again we followed a shabby upper corridor into a wing that jutted out at the opposite end from Gretchen's suite. Ross opened the double doors with a key.

"This was my mother's favorite room in her later years," Ross said. "It's a bit different from what you've seen downstairs."

It was indeed. I found myself on the threshold of an airy, uncrowded space, with wide windows that looked out toward the ocean. The muted reds of a Turkish rug contrasted with pale walls, and a long couch of plump cushions was oyster gray. Over a chaste, uncarved mantel of white marble hung a painting of angular design in shades of blue.

"Picasso!" I cried. "A marvelous one too."

An open door opposite the sea window led us into a wide room with more windows on the far side. Allegra's bedroom casements offered a view of the lake, while at the end glass doors opened on a balcony overlooking walks and flower beds that led in the direction of the cottages.

The room itself surprised me, even more than her quiet sitting room. That Allegra Logan's bedroom should have been as austere as a cell was unexpected. The walls and ceiling were a soft, cool white, and there was a rug of palest pewter. The only color to be found blossomed in tiny yellow buds on the borders of two bedspreads. The beds were of brass and quite narrow. This was a time when Allegra would have slept alone. On a bed table were a few books, as she might have left them, but no pictures hung upon the plain white walls. It was a room in which you could close your eyes and rest.

"It's astonishing," I said. "With everything so elaborate downstairs, that she would want her own rooms—"

"She was nearly eighty when she moved in here. She'd begun to reject her old life. She began to retreat. There are two beds only because she would sometimes invite Gretchen to stay with her for the night. Something Gretchen always loved."

I could easily understand why. A lonely little girl with a fabulous grandmother might very well come visiting here whenever she was permitted.

"Did she die in this room?" I asked. "I hope she did, and not in a hospital."

Ross made a queer, choking sound, and then cleared his throat. "Come here," he said, and there was a rough note in his voice, as though I had somehow angered him.

He took my arm and walked me firmly to the French

doors, opened them and stepped through to the balcony, drawing me with him.

"I haven't wanted to tell you," he said. "I wanted you to get used to the house first, and learn to be happy here before we brought in tragedy. But now, with this infatuation for Allegra developing, I think you'll have to be told. Look out there. That farthest cottage—do you see it?"

I followed his pointing finger and saw that the cottage he indicated was the pink one that young Keith had called "Coral." It was the cottage from which Brett Inness had emerged this morning.

"Yes," I said. "I see it." Dread had started somewhere inside me. I wanted to keep my fantasy of Allegra Logan secure, and I sensed that it was about to be destroyed forever.

"I never told you that she was dead," Ross said. "You leaped to that conclusion yourself. Unfortunately, my mother is still alive. She lives in that cottage with her nurse, Miss Cox. She is ninety-two and has to be taken care of and watched constantly."

"Is she ill?" I asked sadly.

"She's mad," Ross told me. "Mad as any hatter. Before long I'm going to send her away to a good place where she will be cared for properly. I've avoided this because of the publicity it'll bring. But I'm afraid the time has come. We lack the facilities to care for her here. I'm only sorry this wasn't done before you came. But now you have it—the skeleton in my closet."

I felt a shock of loss, as though someone I'd known and loved had met with disaster. Yet at the same time I experienced a disturbing chill. In Ross's words there had been no real mourning for his mother, for the woman she had once been. No pity for what she had become. His concern seemed to be with the avoidance of unfavorable publicity, and with the expediency of removing her from Poinciana. *Her* Poinciana. If she had lucid moments, what did she feel about that?

"I would still like to see her," I said. "Will you take me to her cottage sometime?"

"No! Absolutely not. Leave her alone. She won't understand who you are, and it would only upset you. Now, my dear, let's get back to the netsuke and go to work."

I stood for a moment longer looking out toward Coral Cottage, stirred by pity. No matter what Allegra had become, she had been all that I imagined in her youth, and even into old age. There was a new longing in me to reach out to her. A longing I must conceal from Ross. What he didn't know about me, what I had hardly admitted to myself, was that my life with Ysobel and Ian had taught me to dissemble and move quietly toward goals that were my own. I had one now.

Something drew me irresistibly to Coral Cottage.

Chapter 5

After a quiet lunch, at which I found I wasn't hungry, we returned to the netsuke room, and I began the task of identifying various items in Ross's collection. It was difficult to postpone an examination of all the other treasures of lacquer and cloisonné and ivory, to say nothing of the files of Japanese prints. But I must please Ross and work on the netsuke first as he wished. They were certainly fascinating in themselves.

He gave me a thick folder of vouchers to use as reference, many of them written in awkward Japanese-English. These indicated what Ross had paid for each, and gave dates and other descriptions that would guide me. He also handed me an envelope of glossy prints—the photographs Gretchen had taken as illustrations for his book.

Those netsuke that were brightly colored had been placed against backgrounds of mossy green, or a soft, hollyhock red, while the black-and-white pictures were done against textureless neutral backgrounds. All had been skillfully lighted and photographed. These would be useful in helping me to identify the pieces, and were also small works of art in themselves.

"How very good she is," I said, turning them over one by one.

Ross shrugged. "Some of them will need to be done over."

I felt impatient with his lack of appreciation, but I said nothing. Giving my attention to the vouchers, I began to sort them into piles that represented signed and unsigned netsuke. Then I began the long task of matching each item to its corresponding voucher. Once I had found an item and identified it, I placed it on a shelf I had cleared, and entered it in the journal Ross had given me. After each entry I left a space for Ross to set down those details that I couldn't know. At his suggestion I used a simple numbering system.

I was glad to have something painstaking to do with my mind and my hands. Glad to be able to hold off my growing confusion, my fears. I wasn't always successful. Once I simply stopped what I was doing for a little while and sat with my eyes closed, trying to find a calm place to go to inside me. Instead, there was only a churning of questions. I must find a way to talk to Ross—talk about *us*. Talk about a marriage in which Ysobel Hollis could play no role. But the thought of such a confrontation frightened me. It was the sort of thing I had fled from all my life. It was so much easier to step inside my glass case and close the door upon anything that might shatter me.

Around three that afternoon, Ross told me he had an appointment in town and would be away for a couple of hours. I needn't feel that I must be tied to this room if there was anything I wished to do. I was progressing well with the netsuke and they could wait.

I was in the middle of a search for an ebony carp done by Kiyoshi, and I said I would find it before I stopped. Perhaps then I would do something else. So much awaited me throughout the house. So much to distract me, and keep me from thinking.

Shortly after Ross left, Myra Ritter came into the room carrying a tray with cups, a steaming pot, and some English tea biscuits. I hadn't seen her since last evening, and she grinned at me cheerfully, her wide green eyes alive with interest, her dark, curly hair fluffed about her face.

"I've instituted the custom of having tea since I've come to work at Poinciana," she said. "I understand that Mrs. Logan always used to serve tea in the afternoon. I thought you might join me. Here—I'll find a place."

She set the tray down on a corner of Ross's desk, opened a small folding table, and waved me toward a chair. Her ability to enjoy life was evident again, and so was the faintly sly look that took amusement from everything around her. Today she wore a blue jump suit that suited her small, unbulging person. It also suggested that Jarrett Nichols's informality of dress spilled over to those who worked for him.

While she poured tea, I went on with my search for the elusive carp, sounding my frustration aloud.

"I've been over every single netsuke three times, and I can't find anything that answers to the description," I said. "Do you know if Mr. Logan keeps any of his collection somewhere else?"

She shook her head. "I wouldn't know. It's not my territory."

"This is the second netsuke I haven't been able to find," I said. "The other is a coiled dragon done in cherry wood. I didn't want to bother Mr. Logan about this, but now I might as well give up until he gets back."

Myra's brew had a jasmine fragrance, and I hadn't tasted such frosted biscuits since my last stay in London. It was pleasant to sit with this sprightly little woman and chat about the unimportant. I needed distraction from my own thoughts.

"My boss is off having a conference somewhere," she told me. "I've finished my work until he gets back, so we can take our time. You've been on a Poinciana tour, I understand."

I was to learn that almost anything one did in this house was immediately reported on the grapevine.

"Yes. I've been through the downstairs rooms, and to see the gallery of paintings." I left that subject quickly, lest I find myself talking about Ysobel's portrait. "The rooms that interested me especially were Allegra Logan's. They're such a contrast with what she did in decorating the rest of the house. Almost without color. Comfortable, but utterly plain. Have you seen them?"

"I've hardly been invited on a tour," Myra said wryly. "About your missing netsuke—one thing occurs to me. Do you suppose the old lady could have taken them?"

So she knew about Coral Cottage and Allegra Logan's present state? But then, everyone at Poinciana must know.

"What do you mean?" I asked.

Small shoulders moved in an expressive shrug. "I've heard that this collection has a special fascination for her."

"I thought her fondness was for just one piece," I said, and went to the shelves I had not yet listed. The Sleeping Mermaid was in the same place it had occupied this morning. "Besides, how could she come to the house? I understand she has a nurse."

"Who can't stay awake all the time, watching her. Mrs. Logan doesn't always swallow her sleeping pills, and she likes to run away every chance she gets. I understand that Mr. Logan is considering taking her to some more suitable place."

I was growing curious about the grapevine. "How do you know all this?"

"Mr. Nichols was talking with Mr. Logan about it just a little while ago." She sipped her tea complacently. "Why not go down to Coral Cottage and find out for yourself? Not that you'll get any answers easily. It's hard to talk to her. I've tried."

I was surprised. "You have?"

"Oh, I probably wasn't supposed to, but I feel sorry for the poor old thing. Sometimes when I bake at home, I take her coffee cake or raisin bread. I expect the nurse eats them, but Mrs. Logan nibbles, and sometimes she's glad to see me."

My own resolve began to rise. Why shouldn't I do as Myra suggested, and do it now? Ross wouldn't like it, and I might be seeding his wrath, but the spirit of rebellion was growing in me. No matter what she had become—perhaps all the more because of it—I admired Allegra and I wanted to see her and tell her so.

"Perhaps I will go down there," I said to Myra. "Though I'm sure the two pieces will turn up in some place I don't know about."

We finished our tea, and when I'd thanked her, Myra picked up the tray in her usual quick way, and went to the door, where she paused.

"Are you all right, Mrs. Logan?"

I stared at her in surprise. "Of course I'm all right. Why shouldn't I be?" But even as I spoke I heard the edge in my voice.

She lowered long lashes demurely and went away, leaving me even more uneasy than I'd been before. Did what I was feeling show that much?

I put my cataloguing aside, but before I left the room I ran quickly through Gretchen's photographs. When I came upon those of the carp and dragon I knew they were nowhere on the shelves. These I hadn't seen before.

Without further delay, I found my way out of the house, and as I followed a shell path in the direction of the cottages, I had a sense of windows watching me. The invisible "staff" had lives and curiosities of their own, undoubtedly—like Myra Ritter. And they would be curious about me. Perhaps they would even report my movements to Ross. Well, let them! The time had come to be myself, if I was not to be forever smothered. There were matters to be resolved between Ross and me, and one of them had to be my freedom of movement.

The afternoon was pleasantly warm, and buds on the poinciana were beginning to open, so that spreading gray branches were dotted with color. Along a wall that hid a service center for the house, a row of ficus trees had been planted—one of the variations of fig. Allowed to grow untrimmed, a species of these could turn into the exotic banyan trees that dripped aerial tendrils to root in the ground and form myriad trunks. Trimmed and shaped as these were, they became beautifully formal.

Ahead of me, Coral Cottage drowsed in the sun, its shutters open now to receive the light that would be less welcome later in the year. No one moved around the cottage, as I approached from the rear, but I heard voices drifting out through an open window. Probably nurse and patient talking. But then I heard another voice—a man's tones—and hesitated. I would rather visit the cottage when Allegra and Miss Cox were alone. However, since I had come this far, I would at least walk around it.

As I turned a corner of the small pink stucco house, I stopped in surprise. A bench had been placed on the side nearest the lake, and Vasily Karl lounged there, staring out at the water, a cigarette in his fingers. He got up with alacrity at my appearance, stamping out the cigarette in the grass. I was aware again of his good looks. His fair hair shone in the sun, and his teeth flashed as he smiled. I was aware too of the small scar that lifted one eyebrow and gave me a sense of familiarity.

"Good afternoon," he greeted me. "If you've come to call on old Mrs. Logan, this might not be the best time. There is, it seems, a certain controversy."

His glance indicated the window behind him, and I could hear voices again. Gretchen's, for one. And the man sounded like Jarrett Nichols. I hesitated between flight and curiosity, staring openly at Vasily.

"I'm sure I've met you somewhere," I repeated.

"I would remember you," he said, as he had before. "But if you have really come to call on Mrs. Logan, perhaps I can help you."

He put an assured hand on my elbow and turned me in the direction of the cottage's front door. Somehow, I was certain that he knew very well where we had met, and perhaps eventually I too would remember. I went with him, no longer caring whether I intruded or not. Who could tell but what Allegra might need someone on her side. That I was already there, I knew.

Vasily pulled open the screen door and waved me ahead. "You have a visitor," he told the three in the room.

Jarrett and the nurse stared at me, and Gretchen's already stormy look turned upon me, the bruise about one eye slightly subdued by makeup. Allegra Logan herself was not present.

"Go away," Gretchen said rudely. "You aren't wanted here."

When I would have retreated, Vasily stopped me, and I saw the look in his dark eyes that so contrasted with his fair hair. He was enjoying this, I thought uneasily. It was quite possible that Vasily Karl was a man who liked to stir up fireworks.

"Now, now, darling," he said to his wife. "Didn't they teach you more politeness in all those schools you went to? I would say that Mrs. Logan has every right to be here, if she pleases."

I broke in before Gretchen could respond. "I just wanted to meet Allegra. Ross took me around the house this morning, and I—I wanted to tell her—" I hated myself for dissembling.

Jarrett, who had been silent, seemed to make up his mind. "Come in and sit down, Mrs. Logan. Perhaps it's just as well if you're in on this conference."

"So she can tattle to my father?" Gretchen snapped. "So she can fight me on his side?"

"I suspect," Jarrett said shrewdly, "that Mrs. Logan isn't one to take sides."

The quiet words stung. Why should he think that about me? I had exchanged only a few words with him since my arrival, yet whenever we were in the same room a spark of antagonism seemed to flame between us.

"Oh, all right!" Gretchen said crossly.

"That's my good girl," Vasily approved.

I sat stiffly in the chair Jarrett indicated, and looked around. It was clear that Allegra Logan had done no decorating here. The room had been made comfortable enough with white wicker furniture and grass green rugs. The pictures on the walls were undistinguished, and it was as impersonal as a hotel room. Two doors led off from it, and both were closed.

The nurse—"Coxie," as Gretchen called her—was introduced to me by Jarrett Nichols. She was probably in her mid-fifties, with determinedly curled brown hair, and a short white uniform that showed too much of a sturdy pair of legs. If it were necessary, she would be capable of restraining her patient physically. At the moment a worried frown creased her forehead and she kept pressing her lips together, as though the talk had upset her. When I sat down she gave me a look of sharp appraisal, and then didn't glance at me again.

"Perhaps I'd better explain what this is all about," Jarrett said. "First, though, may I ask if Ross knows that you're here?"

I felt myself flushing. "I came on my own. I asked if I could meet Allegra Logan. I didn't know she was still alive until this morning. But he told me to stay away from her cottage. So I came."

Jarrett looked faintly surprised, which pleased me in a contrary way. Gretchen merely grunted. Vasily was smiling again, enjoying himself.

"If Ross doesn't wish it, perhaps it wasn't very wise of you to come," Jarrett said.

I didn't want to discuss my small rebellion with any of them. In fact, I hadn't really analyzed my own motives, though I'd given myself excuses for coming.

"I'm here," I said curtly, and he accepted that with a nod of his red head.

"To explain," he went on, "Ross feels that his mother can no longer be cared for suitably here. He has several people looking into good nursing homes that take only a few privileged patients, and where she would be treated well."

"If they send her away, she'll die," Gretchen said flatly.

"She will do that before long in any case," Vasily reminded her.

"The point is," Jarrett said, "that Mrs. Logan puts herself into unnecessarily dangerous positions. She has become cunning about escaping from Miss Cox, who certainly can't stay awake all night to watch her. Ross is reluctant to bring in another special nurse. After all, Coxie has been with the family for years and isn't given to talking outside."

The nurse ducked her head in quick agreement.

Jarrett continued, speaking directly to Gretchen now. "Last week your grandmother nearly slipped into the lake on one of her midnight ramblings. If I hadn't been sleepless and out there myself, she might have fallen in and drowned."

"She can be watched better right here," Gretchen protested. "Dad's got to be made to understand that."

I surprised myself by speaking. "Are *you* in favor of putting her away?" I asked Jarrett.

"I don't like your phrasing," he said. "I'm neither in favor of, nor against it. I'm trying to find a reasonable solution."

"He's in favor of," Gretchen said. "And I'm against. I won't have this done to Gran. She hasn't earned such treatment from us. And I know my mother will help on this." She threw me a quick, defiant look.

"I don't think there is anything Brett can do," Jarrett said.

"But there's plenty *you* could do. My father listens to you."

I thought of the missing netsuke that Allegra might have taken, but said nothing. I wanted to add no further coals to this kindling fire.

"Does Mrs. Logan herself know about this?" I asked. "Why isn't she present at this conference?"

The white cap on Coxie's head moved from side to side in denial. "She's altogether out of it most of the time, poor lady."

"Then why," Vasily asked, "does it matter where she is? Perhaps it would be more interesting for her with people around, things she might do?"

Gretchen's small, sturdy person seemed to take on a look of disapproval. "Gran *is* Poinciana. Take it away from her and she'll know, all right. She'll just stop breathing. Jarrett, you've got to make my father see!"

Jarrett walked to a window to stare out at slanting coco palms, and Gretchen turned to me.

"What do *you* think? Even though you've only been here so short a time, you must have an opinion. Where do you stand?"

I couldn't decide how to answer her. "I'm not sure. How can I be, when I've never even seen Allegra Logan?"

"Then why not see her?" Jarrett turned from the window and went to open the nearest door. "Come here," he said to me.

I was beginning to wish I'd never come. I'd been seeking a fantasy. I had wanted to find, somehow, a hint of the Allegra who had created Poinciana. I didn't want to see the wreckage age had made of her. But there was no escape now. He beckoned me, and I walked to the door of the adjoining bedroom and looked in.

A small, frail woman in a dark green robe sat in a

rocker beside a window. She didn't look around as Jarrett spoke to her, and I could see only a coil of white hair piled on her head—much as she'd worn it in younger photographs. From the back, she looked shrunken and fragile as a doll. I closed my eyes.

"Please don't disturb her," I said, and knew that I sounded angry. I was angry. Angry at life for destroying a legend, for ending like this. Ysobel would always be young and beautiful, but perhaps Allegra Logan had lived too long.

The woman heard my voice and turned her head. "Oh, you've brought me a visitor?"

Jarrett drew me into the room. "Mrs. Logan, this is Sharon, Ross's new wife. You remember—he told you that he had married again. She admires Poinciana and wants to meet you."

There was a certain elegance of bearing about her as she sat waiting for my approach. An air of authority in the way she held her head, and in the entirely calm look she turned upon me. I had been wrong—she was still beautiful. Neither the lines of age nor the falling away of flesh could destroy good bone structure and the fine carving of temple and cheek and chin. The hand she held out to me bore the stigmata of age, but there was grace in her gesture, and the welcome of a woman who had spent a great many years in the role of accomplished hostess.

I went to her and took her hand, holding it in mine like a small bird. Then it tightened in a grasp that still carried strength behind it, as though she sensed support in me and clung to it.

"Mr. Nichols is right about how I feel toward Poinciana," I said. "Ross has been showing me through the house, and it's so beautiful. So much that was creative and imaginative has gone into it. I've wanted very much to meet you."

Thin lips moved in a faint smile. "I'm glad you approve, since you're going to live there. Ross might have brought you himself to meet me. I hope you will be as happy in our house as I have been. What did Jarrett say your name is?"

"Sharon," I told her. "I was Sharon Hollis before I married Ross."

"Sharon Hollis. How very strange. I thought your name was Brett." She shook her head in gentle confusion and sighed. "You must come to see me again. I want to know all about you."

"I will come," I promised. Then I spoke softly to Jarrett. "Is there a way out? I don't want to go back through the other room."

He led me to a door that opened upon an entryway at the back of the cottage, and came with me when I left. By the time we were in warm sunshine again, my anger was ready for release.

"Why can't she live in her own house, her own rooms? Why can't she be among all the things that belong to her? She doesn't deserve to be banished like this!"

He must have known that I was close to angry tears, but he walked beside me without comment. When we were well away from the cottage, he paused beside a huge banyan tree that I recognized from one of Gretchen's photographs, studying me thoughtfully. I was intensely aware of his long, solemn face beneath red hair that blew untidily in the breeze, of gray eyes that were cool, and a mouth that could be unexpectedly tender. A man of power. One to be feared if he set himself against me.

"You had better ask Ross your questions," he said.

I didn't try to hide my indignation. "Everyone puts me off! Ross said his mother was completely mad, that she had to be restrained. But it's only old age she suffers from. She's gentle and helpless."

"Not gentle. She was never that. And probably not as helpless as you might think."

"She only seems confused. So why must she stay in that horrid little place? Why can't she be brought back to the house? Perhaps something can be arranged."

"You'd better ask Ross," he said, and turned away from me.

I caught his arm, surprising both of us. "No! Oh, I will ask him—believe me, I will! But I want you to tell me too. I want everyone at Poinciana who knows her to tell me why she has to live like a prisoner. What harm can it do if she wants to wander about a house that she built and will always belong to?"

He was watching me, and his eyes were no longer cool. "You *are* a surprise! Ross isn't going to like this, you know. He doesn't care for anyone to disobey his orders, and he doesn't like explosive women."

I faltered, caught up in my own astonishment at the way I'd behaved. "I'm sorry. I didn't mean to get angry. I don't usually. I—" I floundered to a stop and found tissues in a pocket to wipe my sudden tears. This was the second time I'd wept today. Once for Ysobel, once for Allegra Logan. And perhaps both times for myself. What was happening to me? Where were my disguises? Had I already shattered my crystal case?

"Let's walk down to the water," Jarrett said. "I'd better tell you a few things."

I walked beside him toward the lake. On the way my toe kicked something that I thought was a croquet ball, but when I stopped to look down, I found it was a half-grown coconut. Perhaps because it gave me time to delay, I picked it up. The shell had no shaggy coat, but was smooth in texture and slightly tapering at one end. I carried it with me and moved on, never guessing that someone besides Jarrett was watching me even then.

"A souvenir," I said. "I'll take it back to my room."

"If you want to. But it will rot, you know, and the ants will come."

At least I carried it with me to the bench beside the lake, where I sat down. Jarrett stood beside me, with one foot on the low stone wall that held the water from the land.

"How long has Mrs. Logan lived in that cottage?" I asked.

"Several years. I've lost track. She's accustomed to

it now. And some of the time she doesn't really know where she is, so it can't matter to her all that much."

"I think it does," I said, beginning to heat up again. "I agree with Gretchen. Somewhere in her mind she knows."

Jarrett sat down beside me. "Don't go overboard, Sharon." It was the first time he hadn't called me "Mrs. Logan," and I felt reproved, as though I'd been a child. "It may be that Ross is right and she would be happier among others close to her own age. And in a place that offered more to interest her, take her attention. She's being bored to death now."

"She wouldn't be bored at the house among her own things. Tell me why she was put there?"

He was watching a sailboat skim along the lake, its course smooth as a flying bird's. For a moment I thought he would once more sidestep my question. Then he spoke quietly, evenly, without emotion.

"She tried to kill Ross one night, and she very nearly succeeded."

I could only stare at him. "That little, frail woman? A man in Ross's superb condition?"

"A gun can be effective, no matter what hand holds it. He still carries the scar of the wound on his upper arm."

I had seen the scar and asked about it, but Ross had brushed aside my question.

"But why?" I pleaded. "Why would she do a thing like that?"

"Perhaps because she isn't always in her right mind. Isn't that a good enough answer? Isn't that a good enough reason for her being moved to the cottage? Of course, no weapons are ever left unlocked any more, though Ross keeps a gun in his desk and one in his bedroom upstairs."

"Why guns?"

He repeated his usual refrain. "Ask Ross. Anyway, there have been other times when Allegra escaped Coxie and came to the house. Though I don't think she has ever again wanted to kill him. Allegra always cared a great deal about her son."

We sat in silence for a little while, and Jarrett stared across Lake Worth at the skyline of West Palm Beach. His profile had a cold, carved look. He often seemed a stone man, I thought. Yet not always. I knew so little about him, about what he did for Ross Logan, and why he served him with such deep loyalty. If that was what it was. It was difficult to be sure of anything with a man like Jarrett Nichols.

He stood up abruptly. "I must get back to the house."

"Thank you for telling me," I said.

He nodded remotely and strode off among the coco palms. From another part of the grounds a small figure came running. Jarrett stopped and waited until his son reached him and they walked on together. There seemed a difference in the man as he turned his interest upon the boy—certainly a loosening of tension around his shoulders, a bending of that stiff neck. How would he behave toward a woman he liked? I wondered. That he disliked and distrusted me had been clear from the first, so I would probably never know.

Soon Ross would be coming home, and I must tell him what I had done, what I now knew about his mother. And I must tell him as well about the two missing netsuke. Later on, there was still the night to be faced. None of these thoughts raised my spirits, and I too was staring fixedly at the shimmering pane of water that reached to the city on the opposite shore, when I heard someone beside me and looked up at Gretchen Karl.

She dropped onto the far end of the bench and I glanced around to see Vasily walking toward the house alone.

"Well?" Gretchen challenged. "Now that you've seen my grandmother, do you think she should be sent off to some horrible institution?"

"I don't think your father will pick a horrible place, do you?"

"You were talking to Jarrett. Did he tell you what happened? What Gran tried to do?"

"Yes, he told me. But not the reason."

"I was the reason. And my mother. The hideous things he has tried to do to my mother! I hope someone pays him back sometime. I really do!"

In a gesture that I wasn't aware of until after I'd made it, I crossed my arms and hugged myself—as if in protection from all the ugly things that were being hurled at me in too brief a space of time.

Gretchen snorted in wry amusement. "After a while you'll start rocking yourself the way my grandmother sometimes does. The way they do in madhouses. I'm tempted to often enough myself. Or was until I met Vasily. Poinciana is a place to drive anyone mad. Because of my father. Only because of my father!"

She jumped up and started off toward the house, then stopped and turned around. I was still watching her in dismay.

"Will you come with me to town tomorrow? Just tell Dad you have to shop on the Avenue and we'll go in for lunch. Can you do that?"

Her about-face was surprising, but I would accept anything that might bring me closer to Ross's daughter. "Of course," I said. That Gretchen left me bewildered didn't matter. She was one of the more important problems to be faced at Poinciana. Much as I wanted to help Allegra, her life was mainly behind her, while Gretchen's lay ahead—equally threatened by Ross. He had already shown how much he detested Vasily, and I suspected that it was only a matter of time before he used his power to interfere with his daughter's marriage.

I was not ready to look closely yet at my own relationship to Ross. I was still holding that time away, but if I could make friends with his daughter, I wanted to try.

The afternoon was nearly gone, and after a time I started reluctantly back to the house. The bald coconut I'd picked up stayed behind me on the bench.

Mrs. Broderick must have seen me from a window, for she came to meet me. "Mr. Logan has telephoned," she said. "He will not be home for dinner, Mrs. Logan. He has been detained."

I thought with distaste of sitting alone in the dining room. "May I have a tray brought to my room, Mrs. Broderick? Not a full dinner. And perhaps earlier than the usual dinner hour?"

"Of course, Mrs. Logan." She gave me a regal bow of convoluted blond coils and went away.

I walked around one end of the house to enter the beautiful red and white foyer, and my footsteps echoed on marble. Somehow a lonely sound. More than ever I began to feel the emptiness of Poinciana. It was as though no one lived within its walls. Now and then I glimpsed a maid or a workman, but they were like shadows, fleeing from my approach.

I went slowly up the beautiful floating staircase and down branching corridors to my room. There I closed the long shutters and lay on the bed. As long as I was awake, I would be aware of time ticking along toward the hour I dreaded. It was better to lose myself in sleep than try to solve all the problems I had stumbled into that were churning through my mind. I shut my eyes and tried not to see Allegra Logan's face. Or Gretchen's. Tried not to remember the portrait of Ysobel. I wanted to see only darkness and emptiness. I had not yet begun what was to become a struggle for my very life.

Chapter 6

A tap on my door brought me awake, and I sat up on the bed. A young maid in a gray and white uniform came in, carrying a tray.

"Mrs. Broderick said you would like something to eat early, madam."

"Thank you. You can put the tray on that table near the window, and I'll open the shutters."

But she was well trained and wouldn't allow that. Quickly and efficiently, she managed tray, table, and shutters. Then drew up a chair for me.

"Will there be anything else, madam?"

"Yes," I said. "Tell me your name."

She was a pretty young thing, brown-haired, with dark, intelligent eyes. "Susan," she told me.

I wasn't content with that. A whole person had a last name. "What is the rest of it?"

She hesitated, eyes downcast. "It is Broderick."

"Mrs. Broderick's daughter?" Somehow I was surprised.

She agreed and was silent, waiting for dismissal.

"Do you like working here?" I asked.

"Of course, madam. It's a beautiful house."

"But what else are you going to do with your life?"

She relaxed a little, and suddenly her brown eyes were faintly impish and the polite smile turned into a grin. "I'm only here part-time—to help out with extras for college. I'm interested in archaeology."

"You play the role of maid very well." I smiled at her. "Can't you sit down and talk to me?"

"My mother would kill me. But thanks, just the same, Mrs. Logan. Madam." She ducked me a slightly exaggerated curtsy and slipped out of the room.

Surprise, surprise, I thought, and wondered how Mrs. Broderick felt about her Susan going into archaeology. I hadn't imagined Mrs. Broderick in the role of mother.

My supper was delectable. A mushroom omelette, delicately brown, corn muffins with sweet butter, a tossed salad and a choice of dressings, with a slice of papaya for dessert. The coffee steamed hot in a silver container, the china wore a scattering of pink buds, and the heavy silverware was cool to my touch. Across the linen napkin lay a red hibiscus blossom. I tucked the flower into my hair and proceeded to enjoy every mouthful of food. From outdoors, the distant sound of waves rushing upon a beach was endless and soothing. I was beginning to feel a great deal better. And more hopeful. A foolish optimism.

When I was through, I rang for the tray to be taken away, but this time a more stolid young woman appeared and I didn't try to talk to her. Determinedly, I thrust all problems away and sat at an elegant drop-leaf desk to write a letter to an acquaintance in London. Stationery and pens had been provided and I saw that the paper wore the tiny emblem of a flowering poinciana tree. I gave myself to a rapturous description of the house and my new life that was just beginning here. It wasn't hard to whip up enthusiasm when I thought only of pleasant things.

By the time the letter was finished—written as much to me as to my casual friend—the moon had risen. It would be pleasant to walk outdoors again. Alone.

I drew a light stole around my shoulders and left by the loggia stairs that took me directly outside. The moon was still low and huge, its reflection glimmering in the lake as I turned away from the ocean to walk among leaning palm trees. No one was about. There were lights in Gretchen's apartment, but no sounds, so perhaps she and her husband had gone out. Some of the cottages were lighted, but I could see no glow at the windows of Coral Cottage, so perhaps Allegra and Coxie retired early. Palmetto Cottage was a magnet, drawing me toward its bright windows, but I turned away. There was nothing for me there. Jarrett's abrasive qualities would only destroy the healing peace that I was seeking.

Once I thought I saw something move a little distance away, but when I stopped to watch, all the shadows cast by house and trees were still. The staff of Poinciana continued to guard its invisibility by night, though I could hear muted voices from the servants' quarters.

In the mild evening, my thoughts were quiet as I wandered about the grounds. I had found my way back to my own quiet inner enclosure, and I didn't want to come out again. I had no sense that these would be my last peaceful moments for a long while.

When I had walked long enough, I returned to the house and used a door I hadn't come upon before. It opened into the ballroom, where only moonlight filtered through arched windows, illumining the vast expanse. I crossed the floor lightly, as though I danced to some ghostly whisper of music, and found my way to the same curving stairs I had explored yesterday, and which led to the loggia outside my room.

The narrow tiled steps were dark and I couldn't find the switch at the bottom. It didn't matter. There was a faint patch of light where they turned upward at the top, which meant that the door must be open around the curve. I knew my way and started up, my hand on the rail.

There was no time for me to be startled, no time to draw back against the wall. The rush down the stairs came so rapidly, the hands that reached out were upon me so unexpectedly, that I had no chance to tighten my grasp on the rail. Ugly whispered words carried the same vicious intent as the push against my chest. My hand was torn from the rail and I went pitching backward into space. I turned as I fell and struck my shoulder and the side of my head, stunning myself.

When I opened my eyes, my head was throbbing, and the tiles were cold under my body. As I lay there, the frightening whispered words that had come with the attack seemed to buzz in my ears. "Go! Go away or you'll be sorry!" Had I heard them or dreamed them in my daze?

No guard seemed to be about to help me, and I had a feeling that no scream would be heard in other parts of this enormous house. Gradually I pushed myself to a sitting position, and then stood up. At once dizziness assailed me, but my head cleared a little as I leaned against the wall, trying to collect myself.

These stairs were still the quickest way up to my room, and my assailant had rushed past me, running the other way. I pulled my body up one careful step at a time, until I could breathe fresh air on the loggia outside my room. I had left a lamp burning, and the French doors were open. Quickly I went inside and closed them, sliding the bolt.

Someone had to be told what had happened, but first I went into the bathroom and splashed cold water on my face. A gingerly exploration of my head showed a rising lump, but no bleeding. I went out into the hall.

Standing there, still feeling dizzy, was like looking

down a hotel corridor, except that in a hotel I would know there were people behind the closed doors. Here there was no one. At least I knew the way to Mrs. Broderick's room, but when I went to tap on her door, there was no answer. Since I was ignorant of the workings of the house, I had no idea where to find her.

As long as I was able to act, I could hold off the fright that waited to engulf me. So now I would try Gretchen. Perhaps she and her husband had come home by this time. Again I followed what seemed an endless corridor to Gretchen's suite. Before I reached it, however, the doors opened and Myra Ritter came through.

She saw at once that something was wrong. "You look faint. What has happened?" she asked.

"I—I had a fall."

For all her skittishness, Myra could take charge capably when she had to. "Come down to the office, where I can telephone. When you've collected yourself, you can tell me what happened, and if you need a doctor. Mrs. Karl has gone out. I've just checked. Why didn't you ring for help?"

"I never thought of it," I confessed wryly.

"I know. All these conveniences take some getting used to."

I was feeling shakier by the moment, and willing enough to give myself into comforting hands. We went downstairs to the section of offices, which I hadn't seen before. Myra's desk occupied a pleasant space with an outside window. The two main offices opened on either hand, and she led me into Ross's elegant room, with its Chinese rug of sapphire blue, its great mahogany desk and black leather chairs. There was a leather sofa as well, and she helped me to it.

"Now then, tell me what happened."

I told her of the thrusting hands that had come so suddenly out of the dark, and of my fall backwards. I said nothing about that whisper I thought I'd heard.

"Luckily, it was only a few steps, but I banged my head on the tiles, and it's still throbbing."

She felt the scalp under my hair. "There's a good-sized lump rising. Would you like to see a doctor?"

"No. I'll be all right. But the guards should be alerted, shouldn't they? Someone should be searching. Though I'm afraid it's already too late."

"I'll call Mr. Nichols." She went to the phone on Ross's desk and spoke to Jarrett, then hung up and rang the gatehouse.

It was all out of my hands now, and I stretched out on the leather couch and closed my eyes.

"It's lucky I was here," Myra said as she came back to me. "Mr. Nichols had some urgent letters, so they sent in some dinner and I worked right through. He was coming back this evening, anyway. I took a letter for Mrs. Karl too, but when I went to her room with it just now, her husband said she was out."

I closed my eyes again and waited for Jarrett to come. He brought one of the guards with him, and I answered questions as best I could. No, I hadn't seen anyone clearly. Just a dark shape rushing down the stairs to push me. Yes, I thought the push had been deliberate. But I didn't say why. I wasn't ready to face that yet.

A call was put through to Ross in town, and I could hear the crackle of his anger over the line as Jarrett held the receiver. He would come home at once, Jarrett told us.

The phone was busy after that, with reports from various parts of the house and grounds. Apparently nothing unusual had been noted by guards or staff. They were still talking on the phones when Ross arrived in a black fury. He considered the attack upon me to be an attack upon him, and he spoke to those around him with a barely controlled anger. Myra skittered back to her outer desk to escape the storm, while Jarrett heard him out implacably. No answers were to be found tonight, but the grounds would be thoroughly searched again by daylight for any clue to an intruder.

I wished that Ross would stop giving orders and just come to sit beside me and hold me. I wanted to be protected, comforted, told that I couldn't possibly have been so viciously threatened.

During the discussion, Vasily was summoned from his rooms and came to lounge in the doorway of Ross's office, watching us all with his usual air of sardonic amusement. It was a look that further infuriated Ross. But being angry with Vasily was like fighting with fog. He never stayed quite where one expected him to, always moving away from any direct confrontation. He was, I was beginning to realize, on everyone's side—and on no one's. He'd been reading a spy novel, he said, and hadn't stirred out of his room all evening. So he had heard and seen nothing. Gretchen was off visiting friends, and he hadn't cared to go. But she would know nothing either.

"All right—go back to your damn book," Ross told him.

Vasily said gently, "Perhaps someone should pay attention to the young lady and her hurts."

Jarrett threw me a startled look that carried a certain guilt, but it wasn't for him to apologize.

"I will take care of my wife," Ross told Vasily.

When he had gone, Ross came and sat beside me solicitously. "I'm sorry that this should have happened. Tomorrow we will get you to a doctor if you wish, but now I'll take you to your room, darling."

I thanked Myra, and went with him a little stiffly, feeling sorry for myself. Vasily was right. Everyone had been so concerned with capturing the enemy within the walls that very little attention had been paid to me, the victim. My injury and fright seemed of little importance to anyone but me. "Sniff-sniff," I thought, and halted this course of self-pity.

In my room, I told Ross that I could get to bed by myself, and to my relief he made no effort to help me.

"I'll come back when you're in bed," he told me. "I've a couple more phone calls I want to make."

Through the closed door I could hear him on the telephone, his voice still grim. I undressed quickly, and when he returned in response to my call, he sat on the side of the bed and held my hands.

"What if it wasn't an outsider?" I asked. "What if it was someone inside this house?"

"That's nonsense. We've had break-ins once or twice before, in spite of security. We can't live in a fortress. You just happened to be in the wrong place at the wrong time."

I bristled a little. "There's something you ought to know. I'm sure that what happened was deliberate and intended for me, because whoever pushed me whispered something like 'Go away, or you'll be sorry.' "

"Why haven't you told me this before?"

I wasn't entirely sure why I had held back. Perhaps because I'd feared his disbelief. "It all happened so quickly. I'm not certain—"

"Of course you aren't, darling. All sorts of frightening thoughts must have gone through your head. But don't you think you're imagining this whisper?"

There had been some uncertainty in me, but now I began to feel stubbornly sure. I *had* heard those words, and they'd been intended for me. But I knew that no matter what I said, I wouldn't be able to convince Ross.

"Go to sleep now, darling," he told me. "We'll talk again in the morning."

He kissed me lightly on the cheek and went away, and I watched him disappear into his room, feeling a strange mixture of relief and resentment. I wanted to be believed. But for one more night at least, all the problems that tormented me could be postponed. I needn't tell him about my visit to Coral Cottage. And I needn't listen in dread for the sound of Ysobel's voice in that recording of "Blue Champagne." At the moment I was too tired and sore—and frightened—to be anything but a coward.

It wasn't very late and with the lamp off I could see the moonlit sky over the lake. Ross had checked the loggia doors that I'd locked, and opened only the windows at the side of my room. I could hear the sound of the ocean—a pleasant lullaby. With Ross in the next room, I was not afraid. My picture of him as strong and invincible persisted, and I could at least trust him with my physical safety. If, otherwise, it proved that I had fallen in love with a man who lived only in my imagination, I wasn't sure what I would do about that.

I left a lamp burning when I went to sleep.

It was two-thirty in the morning by my watch when I came suddenly wide awake. Sleep was gone for good, and turning in bed meant once more giving in to the terrors of my own thoughts. I should have brought something to read from the library, but the idea of venturing through a dark house in search of a book was more than I could face.

Restlessly, I sat up in bed. As my attention drifted idly about the room, I saw something unfamiliar on my dressing table—a lumpish something. I got out of bed and crossed the room to see what it was.

Resting upon my hand mirror lay the smooth brownish sphere of a coconut, such as the one I'd picked up on the lawn. For an instant I felt pleased. Someone must have noticed my interest in the coconuts and brought me one—my souvenir.

Then I saw the nastiness. I saw with disgust the oozing mass at one end, aswarm with ants that fed upon it. Ants that crawled across my mirror, over my comb and brush, carrying morsels of decay among my intimate possessions. Sickened, I understood. This was no gift. Nor was it some child's prank. This was something far more unnerving, more disquieting—faintly obscene. This was to remind me that the whispered warning on the stairway had been real—and intended for me.

How long this had lain here I didn't know. I had undressed in the bathroom and I hadn't sat down at the dressing table before I went to bed. But at some time this infested object had been placed here—clearly to make me uncomfortable, to put further pressure upon me to leave Poinciana. I could almost hear that whisper again: *Go away!* Well—I wouldn't go.

Sudden, absolute fury shook me. I picked up the coconut, catching an odor of decay as I did so. Scattering ants, I carried it to the loggia door, unbolted it, and strode into the wind in my nightgown. With all my strength I hurled the thing from me into the yard, and then slapped crawling ants from my arms. I was so angry I was trembling.

I had had enough. Enough! Poinciana had given me nothing but pain and fright and humiliation since I'd stepped beneath its roof, but I would take no more.

This was the moment when I began to fight for my own sanity. I had no idea what I must oppose, or whom. Perhaps all of them. Good enough! I would not be intimidated by malicious tricks. Not even in the matter of getting myself something to read. If I wanted a book, I would go downstairs and get one. Now.

I pulled on my robe defiantly, thrust my feet into slippers, taking no care to be quiet. Ross always slept heavily and I could hear his breathing in the next room. At least my head was no longer throbbing as I let myself boldly into the corridor, where wall lights had been left burning.

I was still too angry to be cautious, but the very hour gave me protection. Who would expect a victim like me to be up and about in these empty corridors? I was through being a victim. From now on, let the enemy beware!

By the time I reached the lower floor, I was ready for anything, armored by my own outrage. But nothing threatened me. Only when I turned a corner in the lower hall and saw a streak of light that fell through an open door, did I make some effort to get myself in hand.

That was the door to the Japanese collection room, and clearly someone was up ahead of me. Perhaps the very person who had removed the missing netsuke. Perhaps the same person who had met me on the stairs, and put the coconut in my room. Fine! An open confrontation might do both of us good.

Nevertheless, I moved more quietly as I edged along the wall. I would look cautiously into the room and see who was there, before I burst in with accusations. Without making a sound, I reached the door and peered around the jamb.

At the desk that had once been hers, nibbling thoughtfully on a pencil, sat Allegra Logan. She had changed into slacks and a brown pullover, and she was talking to herself in a light whisper.

"The John Pillsburys, of course. And Mrs. William Randolph Hearst. The Vanderbilts and the Huttons. Mrs. Post, if she's home at Mar-a-Lago."

The white head, with its still regal neck, bent over a sheet of paper on which she was setting down names, a tiny smile of satisfaction curving her lips. This was not my enemy, and some of my anger began to fade. I stepped into the room and she looked up, imperious and questioning.

"Who are you?"

"I'm Sharon Logan," I said gently. "Do you remember meeting me this afternoon at the cottage?"

"I've never seen you before. I don't know anyone named Sharon. Where is Brett? Where is Gretchen?"

I tried to reassure her. "I'll go and tell Ross you are here. I know he'll want to see you."

"No! I don't care to see him. He's behaved very badly lately. He's trying to get rid of me...." Her look changed, sharpened into recognition, as though she'd remembered who I was. "Don't trust him," she went on. "There's something you ought to know. Something I must show you. Only I've lost it. I came here tonight to look for it, but I can't remember where I've put it." The mists seemed to close in again, and her lined face crumpled with the effort of thought. "I'm sorry. I can't always remember clearly these days. But he's trying to do something I don't like, and if you stay here he'll hurt you. The way he did *her*."

I wondered how I could call the cottage. Perhaps I could phone Mrs. Broderick's room and she would let the nurse know, so she could come and get her patient. But when I went to the desk to pick up the phone, Allegra tapped my hand sharply with her pencil.

"Leave that alone. I know what you're going to do. But I have work to finish here. After all, the party is only two weeks away, and I haven't sent out all the invitations yet. It's so difficult these days trying to do everything without a social secretary. I can't think why Ross sent Madge away."

I drew a chair close to the desk and sat down. "Ross showed me around Poinciana this morning, Mrs. Logan, and I've never seen a more beautiful, more fascinating house. It must have taken you years to finish it."

She relaxed perceptibly and put down her pencil. "It was never finished. After Charlie died I lost interest. Oh, there was plenty of work for me to do, but I could never care about it as much as I did before. He was so proud of everything I built here. He was proud of me. The only one of my husbands who wasn't afraid of me! I wish Ross were more like him."

"I saw your husband's portrait in the dining room yesterday. He must have been a very strong and forceful man."

"He was. The only man I ever knew who was stronger than I was. At least in those days. It's different now. I don't know how to fight Ross. He was never all that strong, really. Only obsessed. But he knew how to put strong people around him. Only now—now... oh, never mind. Gretchen won't let it happen. She has promised me."

Allegra broke off and stared at me with bright, sharp eyes. "I'm sorry. I have so much trouble with my memory these days. I can remember perfectly things that happened long ago, but I can be confused about today. Old age is a dreadful nuisance, my dear. You'll have to tell me who you are again."

"I'm Sharon Logan, Ross's new wife. You remember that he was divorced from Brett?"

"Yes, of course. Though Brett still comes to see me. And I can remember Helen very well. The first one. Poor little Helen. So beautiful and so inadequate. She was the most determinedly unhappy young woman I've ever known."

"Helen was Ross's first wife? The one who died?"

She nodded. "Sick all the time. Hypochondria. Frightened to death of him. It never pays to be afraid of Ross. Brett never was—which is one of the reasons he divorced her. But now Brett comes to see me oftener than Ross does. Sharon? A pretty name, though not one that was popular in my day. Are you in love with him, Sharon?"

"That's why I married him," I said. "Has he told you anything about me?"

She thought for a moment and then drew the right answer from the tumbled files in her brain. "Of course! You're the daughter of that singer, aren't you?"

"Yes. Ysobel Hollis."

"The only woman Ross ever lost. Of course, he never forgave her for that. I remember how angry he was when she turned him down for that enterprising fellow she married."

I spoke quickly. "I don't think that's quite right. Ross was always my parents' friend. I remember his visits from the time when I was small."

"Oh, I'm sure he would visit. Ingratiate himself. Because he never gave up on anything he wanted. Though there was a difference between him and his father. My Charlie worked hard for everything he had. He was a brilliant man and he could handle being important and wealthy. He could even handle me! But everything was *given* to Ross. Too much power too early. He's been clever enough to hire men around him as executives and advisers. What he wants, he takes, and he never forgives anyone who thwarts him. Like Jarrett Nichols, who is a treasure. I found him, you know. But to thwart Ross is to make him a lesser man than his father. Such people he destroys. Remember that. Oh, I could tell you about the lives he has destroyed!"

I stood up, not daring to hear any more, dreading corroboration of what I had begun to believe last night. This was the one thing for which I couldn't fight—Ross's love.

"You really must return to the cottage now, Mrs. Logan. I'll call Ross and he will take you back to your bed. It's nearly three in the morning, you know."

She fluttered a glance at a wrist that was free of any watch, and shook her head despairingly. "I'm sorry. I do get so confused about time. It goes by so quickly." The names she had jotted on paper caught her attention, and astonishment came into her eyes. "Did I write these? Just now? But they belong to years and years ago! These people are dead. I'm the only one who is still here—outliving my time, outliving my life."

There was anguish in the look she turned upon me, and she did not resist as I raised her gently from her chair. I wasn't sure how to manage this, since she opposed my phoning for help. The easiest solution would be to walk her across the grounds myself. Perhaps a guard could be found to escort us.

Before we reached the door, however, I heard running feet, and Gretchen burst into the room, her expensively cut dark hair as tidy as though it had just been brushed, while everything else about her was thrown together—slacks, a cardigan, under which a pajama top showed, sneakers on her bare feet. The bruise about her eye had grown in discoloration without makeup, and somehow increased her look of dishevelment. She rushed to her grandmother, pushing me aside.

"Oh, darling! You promised me you wouldn't run away again. Coxie just phoned, and she was frantic. I thought you might be here, writing notes for the day. You must come back to the cottage with me now, Gran.

If Dad finds you here, he'll be angrier than ever—and that will only hurt you." She whirled suddenly on me. "Don't you tell him—you hear? It's hard enough to stop what he's trying to do, and this will only make it worse. They feed her drugs that confuse her, and can even make her hallucinate. Then he takes advantage."

"Stop chattering!" The command came with complete authority, and for an instant I glimpsed the woman Allegra Logan had once been. "*I* don't matter now," she went on. "I've lived my life and it's been a good one. But you matter, Gretchen, and so does this new young wife Ross has brought home. He's angry about your marriage, Gretchen, and he'll break it up if he can. And *this* young woman he'll use in unspeakable ways." She looked at me sadly as her vision clouded and the moment of sharp intelligence dimmed.

Like a chastened child, she stood up with her granddaughter's arm about her. "I know I shouldn't be here. I just came to get this. At least I *think* that's why I came."

She reached one birdlike hand to the desk and picked up a small object that I hadn't noticed until now. It was the little pink coral netsuke—the Sleeping Mermaid.

"No, darling," Gretchen took it from her and handed it to me. "Put it back, Sharon—wherever it goes."

"But Ross gave it to me!" Allegra wailed. "He said it was always to be mine."

"He never keeps his word," Gretchen said harshly. "Put it back, Sharon. He'll have a fit if he finds it missing."

I spoke for the first time since Gretchen had rushed into the room. "Mrs. Logan, do you suppose you could have picked up any of the other netsuke the last time you came to this room?"

She looked about vaguely, confused again, and I knew she would not remember. But I had caught Gretchen's attention.

"What do you mean? Are there others missing?"

"I'm not sure if they're really missing. There are two

I haven't been able to find. I expect they'll turn up somewhere. Do you suppose you could look among your grandmother's things at the cottage?"

"Gran wouldn't take them. It's only the mermaid she wants. Come along, darling. I'm going to get you back to bed."

"Perhaps I could call a guard—?" I began.

"No, of course not. Why should I bother with a guard?"

"Didn't Vasily tell you what happened to me earlier?"

Gretchen and Allegra had reached the door, and Gretchen turned for a backward glance. "Oh, that! But no one will be after me. You're the one who's getting all the backs up, you know. You're the only one who would get pushed downstairs. Unless it was my father."

I wanted to ask what she meant, and why I should be anyone's target, but she was moving briskly down the hall, with Allegra trotting along beside her, content to be in her granddaughter's charge.

Feeling too limp to move, I sat in the chair Allegra had left, staring at the pitiful list of names she had jotted down. I must destroy this paper, so there would be no evidence that she had been here in these early-morning hours.

Absently I tore the slip into bits as I sat on, considering Gretchen's words. There were only two possible reasons behind that push on the stairs. One would be Gretchen's—that I was deliberately the target. The other was that I had been about to discover someone who shouldn't be there, and who had to silence me and escape. Which of these choices might be the right one, I couldn't tell. Surely there was no reason why *I* should be a target, yet there was the matter of that coconut, placed so maliciously where I would find it strewing decay. And the whisper that had been directed at me.

Was the reason behind this torment simply the fact that I had married Ross Logan?

I put the ugly thought away from me and considered again the missing netsuke.

In spite of what Gretchen had said, perhaps Allegra in her confused state might have picked them up on one of these nocturnal visits, when she escaped from Miss Cox. Suddenly I considered something else. If she could get away to roam about the house, could she have been on the stairs earlier in the evening, coming in from outdoors and mistaking me for some imagined enemy? She wasn't feeble, by any means, for all her frailty, and it wouldn't take much of a shove to throw someone off balance on those narrow, turning stairs.

I would have liked to believe this because it was a fairly innocent explanation. But I didn't. It was possible, but not probable. As I sat there in the stillness of early morning, with the house hushed around me, and my first anger gone, fear began to rise, coursing through me, so that my heart thudded, and I felt chilled to my fingertips. I dropped the torn bits of paper in a wastebasket and walked out of the room.

This time it took courage to follow the dim halls, find my way upstairs, and let myself into my room, the books I'd gone down for forgotten. I went first to my dressing table, but the ants that had crawled there had dispersed, cheated of their source of food. Before I got into bed I listened at Ross's door and heard his breathing. Luckily he hadn't wakened. I slipped between cold sheets and lay on my back, all my concerns rushing through my mind in a confusion as great as Allegra's.

"Mad as a hatter," Ross had said about his mother. But Gretchen had spoken of the drugs she was given. There were certainly times when she was perfectly lucid and aware of the present—not in the least mad. I wondered if he had tried to have her certified and had failed. Clearly she had become an embarrassment to him in her present state, and if he had once held any love for his mother, it must be gone.

Anger began to stir in me again, but this time it was a quieter, stronger, more reasoned emotion. Tomorrow, somehow, the struggle must begin. It must begin with *me*.

Chapter

7

After a breakfast that Ross sent up to my room, I felt somewhat better. My head was reasonably clear, though I had discovered new bruises, and my shoulder was sore. The quieter anger, with which I'd fallen asleep, had not abated, but this morning I knew I must move with care. I mustn't flail out blindly against whatever threatened me.

Ross came into my room as I finished dressing, and we sat outside, where morning shadows darkened the arches of the loggia. He kissed me with tender affection, and I felt again the aura of protection he could place around me. I had only to relax and do exactly as he wished and nothing dreadful could happen to me. For a moment I didn't want to remember his mother's words. I didn't want to remember that portrait of Ysobel, or her voice singing as he made love to her daughter. I wanted to forget hands in the dark, that whisper, and the obscenity of a coconut on my dressing table.

I remembered everything.

While I was asleep, Gretchen had slipped a note under my door, reminding me that she still hoped to take me into town for a late lunch and some shopping on Worth Avenue. The note was typed on her personal stationery with her name and "Poinciana" engraved at the top of heavy cream paper. She hadn't signed it, but had drawn at the bottom of the sheet a smiling face with upcurved mouth, round eyes, and three hairs, coming out of the top of the head.

I showed it to Ross and he chuckled. "Typical. Gretchen's handwriting is illegible, so she always types. And when it's family or friends, her signature is one of those faces. Smiling, or sad, or with a zigzag for anger. I'm really pleased. This means she's making friends with you. You can be a good influence on her, I know."

Which probably meant that I was to influence her in a direction he might want her to go. Anyway, I wasn't convinced that the invitation was a friendly gesture. Gretchen's motives were likely to be devious, from what little I'd seen of her.

Ross assured me that a further search had been made of the grounds this morning, but no trace of last night's intruder had been found.

I asked the same question that I'd asked before. "What if it was someone inside the house?"

Again there was quick dismissal of the notion. "Nonsense! There's no one in the house who would want to hurt you. In any case, the security men are on the alert now. I've put one hell of a scare into them. It won't happen again."

I considered bringing up the matter of the coconut, but that was minor compared with everything else that Ross must be told this morning, and it could wait. I plunged into an account of my visit to Coral Cottage, and he sat listening, his expression forbiddingly dark, and once, when he would have interrupted, I hurried on, my inner anger sustaining me.

"Ross, I can't live here as a semi-prisoner. I hate this atmosphere of secrets around me, and of motives I don't understand. Can't we bring everything into the open? I'd like to know more about your mother."

I could see that my plea was useless. Even as I spoke, his mouth had tightened in displeasure. "I do not choose to discuss the problem of my mother. It's not something you can deal with intelligently when you have so little to go on."

"Jarrett told me about the attack she made on you a few years ago. But isn't it possible that she's better now, so she could be brought back to her own rooms? You can have her constantly watched."

He was already dismissing the suggestion. "I prefer not to be murdered in my own bed."

I wanted to ask the question I had been silent about when I talked to Jarrett. I wanted to ask why Ross's mother had made such an attack, but I held back words that might further anger him and asked another question.

"Why do you need to keep guns about?"

"Don't be naïve," he told me with biting scorn. "Anyone in my position faces constant danger from the crazies out there."

I supposed I must accept that. But I couldn't leave the subject of Allegra without another try.

"I'd like to visit your mother now and then," I went on. "I'm sure there are times when she could talk to me about the days when she lived in Poinciana and I would enjoy listening."

Ross left his chair and walked across the tiles to stand for a moment at the rail. When he turned about he was smiling. He had made his decision not to be angry. This time.

"Life with you isn't going to be dull, Sharon. You are full of surprises."

"I'm not that figurine you said I was in Kyoto," I reminded him.

"I'm beginning to see that. And I rather like it—providing you don't carry these notions too far."

I hurried to a subject less personal, though I suspected that it might upset him a lot more.

"After you left yesterday, I went on with my work in the netsuke collection. It's coming along well, but there are two items that I haven't been able to locate. The vouchers for them are there, and so are Gretchen's photographs. One is the carving of a carp done in ebony, and the other a dragon carved in cherry wood. I've gone over every netsuke several times, and I can't find either of them."

Ross was on his feet before I finished. "Come downstairs with me, and we'll have a look together. Perhaps you just haven't recognized them."

I doubted that was the case, and when Ross himself had gone over the shelves piece by piece, he could only come to the same conclusion. Two netsuke were missing. After that, phones began to ring around the house. Jarret was summoned and Myra Ritter came with him, steno book in hand. Gretchen and Vasily were found and brought in. Mrs. Broderick was instructed about questioning the staff.

"If necessary," Ross told us as we assembled in the room, "I'll call in the police. But I hope it won't come to that. If the missing netsuke are returned to this room at once, I will ask no more questions. These are not toys. Such pieces are irreplaceable. I've collected them over the years at great trouble and expense. We'll wait a few days and institute a search. That's all for now."

Vasily put a proprietary arm about Gretchen, with a sardonic look for Ross. Myra ducked out of the room in Jarrett's wake, and Mrs. Broderick bustled off to confront the household staff.

Gretchen nodded to me. "If you're ready, we can go into town now." For once she was wearing a dress instead of jeans, and I wondered at her insistence upon this trip.

"Would you like me to stay home?" I asked Ross.

"Of course not. Run along, you two."

Gretchen came with me when I went upstairs to change, as though she was afraid I might have second thoughts about this luncheon date.

"Do you really think anyone in the house would dare to touch your father's netsuke collection?" I asked her when we reached my room.

"Who knows? The staff has been with us for years. And there aren't many of the rest of us to choose from, are there? Besides, what would any of *us* want with the netsuke?"

That seemed true enough. Gretchen was wealthy in her own name, and the money a few such objects would bring could hardly be an incentive. Not even if it ran to thousands of dollars.

She went out on the loggia to wait for me, and I put on a white dress flowered in pale blue, and changed to open-toed shoes. When I sat before the dressing table mirror, I discovered a lone ant wandering over my comb, and I brushed it away in disgust, considering whether I should tell Gretchen about what I'd found here last night. Better not. Better to play everything by ear for the moment until I knew my true direction. Anger could wait, and perhaps be strengthened by the very delay. The intent against me—which others were discounting—was too serious and alarming for me to dismiss. Nor could I be sure that Gretchen wasn't behind what had happened.

When I rejoined her, we went down to the front door, where a car was waiting for us. She got in behind the wheel and I sat beside her, still puzzled by her manner, which seemed to alternate between antagonism and an effort to be friendly that I didn't really trust. Right now some secret purpose seemed to be pushing her, and the very fact made me watchful and alert.

In her red Jag we drove along South Ocean Boulevard past impressive houses. She pointed out the Addison Mizner touch of red-tiled Spanish roofs visible amidst tropical growth. We cut across the island on Royal Palm Way, where handsome, big-boled palms marched down a wide strip of grass that divided the street. No Palm Beach street that ran east and west could be very long, because of the water boundary each way. Our destination, Gretchen said, was Worth Avenue, and we turned off to reach it.

Among the magical shopping streets of the world, Worth stood near the top, though it was only a few blocks long. Rimming its sidewalks were the most famous of shops, where elegance and wealth were almost commonplace. Here were offered jewels and perfume, clothes by the great designers, to say nothing of fabulous art works. On this island where the Gulf Stream flowed nearest the shore, thus moderating temperatures the year round, there existed what some had called the American Riviera. The rich and famous played and rested in Palm Beach, and celebrities abounded. Worth had been called the "Mink Mile."

At the end of the First World War, Addison Mizner had appeared to put the mark of his own architectural whimsy upon the island that Flagler had developed, giving Palm Beach its Spanish-Moorish-Mediterranean character. He had lived in Spain and South America and California. He had borrowed, and he had also created out of his own imagination. It was he who designed Worth Avenue, with its Spanish façades, and charming arcades. As an architect, he had sometimes been more imaginative than practical, and odd "mistakes" sometimes turned up in his houses.

His own apartment, Gretchen pointed out, had been up there under the red-tiled tower that dominated the street.

We drove past Bentleys and Rolls-Royces, Cadillacs and Mercedes-Benz cars that were a common sight at the curbs of this famous street, and found a place to park. Palm trees grew along the way, and there were plants everywhere, in tubs, or thriving lushly in courtyards. Bougainvillea climbed the walls and spilled over balconies, and the scarlet of hibiscus could be glimpsed everywhere.

In some ways the street reminded me of the French Quarter of New Orleans, and as we walked along I was treated to glimpses of fountains, tiled walks, archways, and arcades.

Gretchen drew me past an inner fountain to stop before a Gucci window. She seemed to move in a leisurely way, yet I had the feeling that she was merely marking time as we approached some event that lay ahead. It wasn't likely that she had invited me out for the pleasure of my company. Something was going to happen—eventually—and when it did, I suspected that I would not like it.

Out again on the street, she stopped for purchases in a shop with shining mirrors and a gleaming marble floor, where the saleswoman knew her and greeted her by name.

I bought nothing. How could I need for anything with all that Ross had given me from the stores of London and Tokyo and Kyoto? Yet all the while as I followed Gretchen, I felt as though I floated in a sea of unreality. This was a world of such expensive artifice that it had little to do with the realities of living.

It wasn't that I couldn't respond to luxury with my senses, or that I couldn't enjoy this sort of artificial beauty. I had lived very close to this world for a good part of my life. I had seen such shopwindows in New York, London, Paris, Rome, but I had never really belonged to this fantasy world, and I couldn't belong to it now.

As we left the last shop, Gretchen said, "You look a bit dazed. What are you thinking about?"

"I'm not quite sure. I love to look in the windows, to go into the shops, watch the people. But I feel as though I were attending a not very real play."

"I know what you mean!" There was a sudden passion in Gretchen's words that startled me. "I grew up with all this, and sometimes I hate it. Sometimes I hate everything about the Logan money, and all my father's power. Sometimes I hate everything about Poinciana except Gran. And Gran is being sent away because he is afraid of her. She was always the *real* one. Even though she could make unreal things happen, she kept in touch with life. My father has never had that touch. That's why he employs men like Jarrett Nichols, who are real. That's why I married Vasily Karl—because he's real."

That surprised me still more. We were walking back to her car, and I could think of no response to make.

When we got in and she drove away from the curb, Gretchen gave me a smiling look that challenged whatever I was thinking. "A fortune hunter can be very real, you know. Oh, don't feel embarrassed. I know exactly why he married me, and I know why I married him. We understand each other, and we have something very good going between us. But I've made you uncomfortable, haven't I? Because you aren't used to talking about things as they really are. Are you, Mrs. Ross Logan?"

"I don't think you know very much about me," I said. "Are you judging me?"

"Of course. Why shouldn't I? Don't we all judge everyone else? It just surprised me a little that you would even recognize that all of this is make-believe. Of course, we compromise and satisfy our egos. Jarrett Nichols too—though he's closer to the real world than the rest of us."

"I wish I could be as sure as you are," I said. "I don't know where the boundaries are any more. Perhaps you've escaped to some extent through your camera."

She said nothing to that, and we drove a block or two in silence before Gretchen parked the car again and glanced at her watch. "I've made a reservation at the Brazilian Court, so come along."

We walked through a large open court where tables

were shaded by bright umbrellas, and went up a few steps to an enclosed pavilion. Here again Gretchen was recognized and we were seated by a window. I noted a third place setting, and Gretchen cocked an eyebrow at me.

"I've invited someone to join us. Someone you really ought to know. But we needn't wait. We can decide about lunch right away."

So this was the event we had been moving toward. I studied the menu, while my uneasiness grew. When I looked up and saw Brett Inness coming toward us across the room, I knew my fears were justified.

"She doesn't know you're to be here either," Gretchen whispered, grinning.

I was furious with her for her presumption, but there was nothing to do but face it out now.

Her mother wore a sleeveless blue linen frock, elegantly simple, with a strand of white coral beads at her throat. Gretchen commented first on her dress.

"I do like that. It's your own design, isn't it?" And then to me, "My mother is a marvelous dress designer. She has her own shop here in town. Sharon, I'd like you to meet Brett Inness. And Brett, this is Ross's new wife, Sharon. I thought you two ought to know each other."

Long experience in dealing with the unexpected around Ysobel came to my aid, and I managed to be polite and a little remote. Brett was clearly as annoyed with her daughter as I, but she acknowledged the introduction and sat down opposite me.

"Outrageous," she said to Gretchen, and then looked at me. "I suppose we'll have to make the best of it."

"I'm sorry that I didn't know who you were when I saw you on the grounds the other day," I said.

"I thought it just as well if you didn't. I'm trying not to annoy Ross, since I want to be able to visit Allegra on occasion."

"He can't forbid you the grounds," Gretchen said.

"If he tries, there will be a bang-up fight between us. So he'll pretend not to know."

My attention was on Brett at that moment, and my first impression of a woman of will and authority was growing. She still wore her hair in the brown knob on top of her head, and perhaps it was right for her angular style. Florida sun had not spared her skin, and I noted the lines, the weathering. Now I could see her odd, violet eyes more closely, and I was aware of their chill regard. She showed no warmth, even toward her daughter, and in spite of Gretchen's outrageous behavior, my sympathy for her grew. I knew about mothers.

When we'd ordered, Gretchen looked from one to the other of us, serious now, and no longer impish.

"I didn't do this just to upset you both. There isn't any reason why you should be friends. Or even acquaintances."

Her mother broke in. "Oh, I don't know—we may have a lot in common. Though perhaps Mrs.—ah—Logan hasn't worn that name long enough yet to be aware of this."

Anger would not serve me now, or resentment. I retreated into my glass case, where no words could reach me, and smiled politely, distantly, saying nothing. Neither of them could possibly touch me. That was the thought I must hold on to.

Gretchen continued. "I brought you both here to talk about Allegra. To help me plan a battle—a war, if necessary. You're already on her side, Brett, though I think it's only because you like to oppose Ross. And I can tell that the Allegra legend has gotten through to Sharon, so perhaps she'll help us too. Then we can work on this together."

My self-imposed retreat wasn't working too well, I discovered. In spite of myself, I was becoming involved, and wondering about Gretchen. Ostensibly, she was fighting a battle for her grandmother, but I suspected that whether she knew it or not, this was only part of a larger war with her father. And there my sympathies were engaged, even more than for Allegra. Gretchen's life still lay ahead of her.

"How can you stop your father if he's made up his mind?" I asked.

"That's what we have to figure out. My father isn't an easy man to stop. But the way each of you feels should help. You're a softy, Sharon. You'd like to help Gran because you're tenderhearted. Oh, don't look at me like that. You hide behind that front you wear, but the softness still shows. That's the reason Dad married you. One of the reasons. He likes people close to him that he can hurt. Don't I know!"

"Stop it, Gretchen," her mother said, her voice low. "You used to have a few manners."

Oddly enough, Gretchen subsided. "Well, what can we use for a lever with my father?" she asked, faintly sullen. "It's not only Gran, you know. He's after Vasily, too."

Someone was also after me, but this wasn't the time to point that out.

The waitress brought our orders and we said little until she went away. I had nothing practical to offer, and I felt increasingly uncomfortable in the presence of these two. Brett watched me obliquely, and Gretchen was obviously hoping to make me squirm. I wasn't sure how fond she was of her mother, but I was still the interloper on territory that Gretchen had no wish to share. If Ross liked to hurt people, perhaps his daughter shared something of that trait as well.

When the waitress had gone, she put her question again. "Any suggestions to offer?"

I looked out the open windows at bright umbrellas in the courtyard and at people dining cheerfully at small tables. I tasted my shrimp-stuffed avocado, but I had no appetite.

Brett said, "There is always *l'affaire* Pamela Nichols. A touch of blackmail can be useful at times. Ross has gotten away with too much for too many years."

I found it hard to swallow my food. "What about Pamela Nichols?"

"Shut up," Gretchen told her mother, as if for the first time she regretted her plan. "You don't have a thing to go on."

"But Allegra does," Brett said sweetly. She was enjoying her pompano almandine with an appetite neither Gretchen nor I had. "She knows *something*. She's hinted as much to me. Don't underestimate your grandmother when she's lucid, Gretchen. Why else do you think Ross wants to put her away, except that she has something on him when it comes to Pam?"

My attention was caught. I remembered Gretchen's burst of temper that day in the belvedere when she'd snatched the picture of Jarrett's wife and son from me and torn it up. And I remembered Ross's evasion when I'd mentioned the incident to him.

Gretchen glowered at her mother for a moment, and I knew this was a topic she was unwilling to face.

"Pay no attention," she told me. "I can tell you the real reason why my father wants to send Gran away. And it's not this nonsense Brett is trying to foist on you."

I was silent, waiting. Brett waited too, but with a gleam in those violet eyes.

"Of course, Dad is the main stockholder in Meridian Oil, but Gran holds the next-largest block of stock. Not that she does anything about it these days. Jarrett makes a big thing of consulting with her, and she votes her proxies as he and Dad think best. But if my father could have her declared incompetent, then everything of hers would pass into his hands, and he'd feel a lot surer of total control."

"That's only part of it," Brett said.

"If this is true, why hasn't he taken the step of sending her away before?" I asked. "She seems to have lapses of memory at times that would give him cause."

"I'll tell you why," Brett said. "He's afraid of her—that's why. When she is thinking clearly, she can be dangerous to him. So he's afraid to bring in anyone else she can talk to openly. He probably feels that it's also risky to send her away. But at least in the company of other loonies, no one is likely to pay much attention to what she says. Now that you're here, Sharon, he hasn't been able to keep you apart. She might talk to you at any time and let a few tigers out of the bag."

"What tigers are *in* the bag?" I asked.

Gretchen answered me curtly. "I only want to see my father persuaded. I don't want to damage him."

"Our goals aren't exactly the same, are they?" Brett said. "But since you've called this little meeting and asked for suggestions, I've made one. Poor, foolish Pam might still be useful."

There was more than a hint of venom in Brett's cultivated tones, and I retreated again, saying nothing more, not wanting to hear, willing myself not to participate. I didn't know what they were talking about, and I didn't want to know. To know might, on top of everything else, be more than I could bear. Nevertheless, I listened carefully to every word.

Gretchen had cut her mother off sharply. "Pam has nothing to do with us now. We've got to decide what action to take in the present." She buttered a roll, scowling.

"You've always been clumsy, darling," her mother said sweetly. "Impetuous. You thought that bringing Sharon and me together would be entertaining. But somehow it's you who usually winds up in deep water. Nothing ever turns out right for you, does it?"

"I don't want anything to eat," I said. "I'd rather not stay and listen to this."

"You'll stay." Gretchen's hand was on my arm, and I couldn't rise without a struggle.

"You'd better not oppose her," Brett said to me. "My daughter has a dreadful temper. Like her father. Being so unsure of themselves basically, they keep trying to prove something. And they fly into rages when they're opposed." Her angular face with its strong features seemed bright with a malice that equaled Gretchen's.

I made no further attempt to rise. Once more, it seemed to me that Gretchen needed help, even more than Allegra did. My sympathy for her had its roots in the past, in my own girlhood, and it continued even in the face of her behavior toward me.

She released her hold on my arm and gave it a little pat, ignoring her mother's words. "That's better, Sharon. Everyone's been giving in to me ever since I was three—just because I could make such awful scenes. People who are well brought up have a terrible handicap. They've been taught that the greatest sin of all is to be bad-mannered. So they're at the mercy of people like me—who just don't care. But to get back to our problem. I won't stand by and see Gran railroaded. She's not all that crazy, and maybe she's the only person I've ever loved. Or who's ever loved me."

"You aren't always lovable, darling," Brett said. "What about Jarrett Nichols. Won't he help you?"

"I've already talked to him. He's not sufficiently *against* her being sent away. He even thinks it might help her. But I know what would happen. She'd be put away in some posh place where the horrors of rich families are kept hidden from the world. Gran doesn't belong with the horrors, but she could become one of them if she's put in that sort of big happy family!"

I told them about speaking to Ross. "I asked him to bring Allegra back to her own rooms in the house. I still think that could be done."

"What did he say?" Gretchen seemed surprised.

"He doesn't want her in the house. Because of what happened. I've been told about her attack on your father. He feels she's not responsible."

"She only did what a lot of people might like to do," Brett said with quiet venom. "I still think we should consider Jarrett. Ross is a little afraid of him. You know that, Gretchen. So what happened to Pamela might still be useful now. After all, she was Jarrett's wife."

"What are you proposing to do?" Gretchen demanded.

"Oh, *you* would have to do it. Just drop a hint or two, raise some doubts in Ross's mind. Hint at something you might want to talk to Jarrett about if your father doesn't see things your way about Allegra. Nothing too heavy."

"You really can be poisonous," Gretchen said. "How could I possibly do that? He would wind up hating me."

"Of course, that's your biggest problem," Brett said. "You brag about not caring, but you do. You've always wanted to be loved, and you never knew how to be lovable."

I hated what Brett was doing. Hated her mockery and her willingness to hurt her daughter. I could forgive Gretchen's attempts to be outrageous better than I could her mother's deliberate cruelty. I had to say something—anything.

"Don't put yourself down," I told Brett, and was pleased to see her startled look. "You've raised a very talented and clever daughter. I can't blame her for the way she feels about me—an outsider coming in without warning. I hope I can live that down in time. If there's anything I can do to help your grandmother, Gretchen, I'd like to. But I don't have any other ideas."

Gretchen was watching me as though I puzzled her, for all that she'd been so quick to judge my character.

"Perhaps you'll be the one to find the way," she admitted grudgingly. "This isn't only the matter of keeping Gran at Poinciana, you know. It's your freedom too that's involved, and mine. Our happiness. If there is such a thing as happiness. Gran can help us as well as herself. Power against power."

Before I could pursue this, she looked toward the glass doors, and her face brightened. When I glanced around, I saw Vasily Karl coming up the steps of the pavilion.

"Here comes more support," Gretchen said. "I asked him to join us."

He moved with a graceful, jaunty air, and I realized for the first time that he was a rather small man. His slenderness, the high sweep of blond hair, and his erect carriage gave an illusion of height that I recognized now as only an illusion.

He greeted Gretchen with a kiss on the cheek, bent over Brett's hand, and gave me his most charming smile. "How fortunate to be meeting three such lovely ladies," he said.

"No games," Gretchen told him. "We're into a serious discussion about my grandmother, Vasily. Will you sit down and have lunch?"

Someone pulled out the fourth chair for him, but he waved the menu aside. "When you're ready for dessert I'll join you. The library exhibit is going well, dear. I've been consulting about the hanging of your photos."

I hadn't realized that Gretchen's proposed exhibit was this far along.

"Vasily used to have his own art gallery in London," she explained. "That's where I met him."

I had wondered what Vasily Kari had done in the past, and I suspected that he'd held a few other jobs as well. Once more I found myself staring at the little scar that raised one eyebrow. It hypnotized me with that sense of having seen it before. Perhaps in London?

Despite his smiles and compliments, and the looks he cast upon each of us in turn, I sensed that all was not entirely well with Gretchen's husband. He was not lazily at ease, as I'd seen him before.

"What's wrong, Vasily?" Gretchen asked. "Something has upset you."

He shrugged eloquently. "It's nothing, darling. One of your father's whims. He's having me investigated. A full-scale detective job. It was to be expected, of course."

Gretchen flushed angrily, her face mottling, the bruise about her eye becoming more vivid. "Brussels?"

"No, no, of course not. All that was cleared up long

ago. There is nothing he can do. It just upsets me to know that I am so little trusted."

I had a feeling that Vasily Karl was quite accustomed to being little trusted, but Gretchen said, "Don't worry—I'll talk to him."

"That will help a lot," Brett said.

"Never mind." Vasily patted his wife's arm. "Let's not discuss unpleasant matters now. What will Sharon think of her new family?"

At times he watched me and I saw that he had a curious way of stroking the scarred eyebrow as though to erase the mark. My feeling of recognition became stronger. Yet I be couldn't be sure. It was too dim a memory—if it was even that. Something to do with my mother?

"Of course it's typical of Ross to take such action," Brett said. "He will get rid of you if he can, Vasily, and he'll stop at nothing. So I hope you have a spotless past."

Gretchen spoke grimly. "My father has to be stopped. Sharon, you're the only one who has his ear right now. Maybe he'll listen to you. You've got to persuade him not to send Gran away, and to cut out this nonsense over Vasily."

Brett was shaking her head. "Don't put any heavier load on Sharon than she's able to carry. She has her own problems. You're the one, Gretchen. You or Jarrett. You're the only ones he's ever been afraid of."

What did she know of my problems? I wondered. What could she know—and how?

Gretchen's expressive mouth had twisted in anguish. "I don't want any of this! I don't want to struggle and fight and throw tantrums. I only want to be left in peace!"

"Then why did you move back into Poinciana?" Brett asked. "Never mind—don't try to think up an answer. Peace would bore you as quickly as it bores Ross. You started out a fighter back in your playpen, and you're still one. Thank God I'm on the outside now, and I prefer to stay there. I've told you what you can do to help, but I expect you'll play everything by ear as you always do, Gretchen. Now let's order dessert and end this impossible luncheon."

Menus were brought and the other three ordered. I wanted nothing but coffee, and a chance to escape as quickly as possible.

Nevertheless, having all three of them here together was more of a temptation than I could resist. I wanted to watch their reactions, and I told them quietly about finding a rotting coconut on my dressing table last night.

There was a moment's silence while they all stared at me.

Vasily spoke first. "How very shocking! And how extremely vindictive!"

"Disgusting," Brett said, wrinkling her sharp nose. "Sharon, have you been getting up on the wrong side of the servants?"

"I've hardly spoken to any of them," I told her.

I was watching Gretchen, who had picked up her napkin and was creasing it thoughtfully.

"Have you any ideas?" I asked her.

My question broke through her concentration and she shook her head vigorously, setting her short hair aswirl. "No, of course not. What a silly trick!"

I let the matter go, and Vasily, with his usual skill, turned the talk to safer subjects. The hanging of Gretchen's best photographs interested him, and she listened to his words, his suggestions, in almost pitiful agreement. What a strange, prickly girl she was—wanting so much the very things she seemed to have little talent for winning. Puzzling too. I had a feeling that she knew something about that coconut. She was even capable of playing such a trick herself. It would be futile, however, to press her, and I found myself thinking of Brett's odd references to Jarrett's late wife, Pamela Nichols.

Direct questions, I was sure, would never provide

the answers I wanted, but this was something I must pursue when I had the chance. Perhaps with Gretchen—who had torn up Pam's picture so angrily.

When Gretchen and I returned to Poinciana, Vasily came with us, filled with good spirits that I suspected were artificial. His presence kept me from asking any more questions then, and I left them at the door.

When I reached my room, I went out on the loggia, where I could refresh myself with a view of the lake, and try to recover from what had been a disturbing experience. On a blanket, down near the edge of the water, Susan Broderick, my part-time maid, was seated cross-legged, her books around her. I ran down the outside steps and across the lawn.

"May I join you?" I asked as she looked up.

She shook her head despairingly. "If you sit down, I'll have to stand up. In fact, I suppose I should stand up anyway. Mother is a great one for the proper behavior of her housemaids. We're not supposed to fraternize."

"You're off duty," I said, and dropped down on a corner of the blanket, my hand out to keep her from rising. "I'll talk to her. I just want to relax for a few minutes. I've been doing Worth Avenue with Gretchen and having lunch with her husband and her mother, and I'm feeling a bit limp."

Susan bent her head so that a wing of dark hair fell across her face, hiding her expression.

"I grew up with Gretchen," she said after a moment. "There weren't any restrictions on us as kids. Old Mrs. Logan was very proper on the surface, but she was human, and she was always interested in the problems of those who worked for her. She even set up a trust to put me through college, you know."

I picked up one of the books from beside her. "Is archaeology the subject that really interests you most?"

"Yes, it does. Last summer I went on a dig out in Arizona. It's what I'd really like to do. When I'm through with school, maybe I can get a job with an expedition. I'd like to go to any of the Middle East countries, where so much history is buried. Though there's also a lot of it buried right here at home that's never been dug up."

"What does your mother think?"

Susan wrinkled her nose. "She hates me to get dirty. Dirt is the enemy. And that I should want to go out and dig in it offends her. What about you? What do you want to do?"

It was a strange question, but from this young woman perhaps a natural one. Unlike the others, she didn't take it for granted that being Mrs. Ross Logan was the whole of my existence.

"Right now I'm trying to learn about my husband's netsuke collection," I told her. "It's never been properly catalogued, and I'm trying to correct that."

"I heard about the ones that are missing. We've all been questioned. Though I can't imagine any of the staff touching anything at Poinciana. They've all been here a long time and they're quite loyal. This has upset everyone a lot. Mother's in a real tizzy. But it's even more important that you were pushed down those stairs last night. I hope you weren't badly hurt."

"Just a few bruises. Susan, is there any talk about who might have done that to me?"

She looked away, out across the lake. "There's always talk. Gossip. But it's only speculation."

"Would you be willing to tell me?"

"If I believed in it, I would. As it happens, I don't."

"Gretchen?"

There was no answer, and I couldn't expect one. She had been Gretchen's friend when they were small. I asked another question.

"Susan, did you know Pamela Nichols?"

"Of course." She relaxed a little, as though this was a safer topic. "I wasn't working here then, though I lived at Poinciana with my mother. In a way, we were friends. I can still cry when I think of her terrible death."

"What happened exactly?"

"They say her brakes must have failed. She always drove too fast. There was a truck—and she couldn't stop in time. She must have died at once."

I could feel the sickness and hurt along the nerves of my own body. I hadn't known Pam, but I knew Jarrett, who had lost his wife so terribly.

"What was she like?" I asked.

Susan began to stack her books. "My mother would say that it isn't proper for me to talk about her." Blue eyes looked up at me ingenuously. "But I will, anyhow. Pam was always happy and laughing. Except that she was a little afraid of her husband. It's strange, really. She was the one with a good family and inherited money, while Mr. Nichols was someone Allegra Logan had pulled out of the slums. But he was the one who grew and became really important, while she could never keep up with him. I think he loved her, but she didn't have much confidence in herself, and he was too busy to build her up in the way she needed." Susan broke off, suddenly aghast. "I'm talking too much! I should never be telling you these things."

I had listened in some astonishment. "You're a psychologist too!"

The long fall of hair swept across her face again. "Just because I like to dig up shards and bones, doesn't mean I'm not interested in live people. Growing up at Poinciana was always like living in the first row of a play. Old Mrs. Logan liked to talk to me sometimes. She wanted me to stretch my mind, and she'd make me tell her about the people I saw and listened to. Tell her what I thought of them. She was a great one for figuring out human nature. So some of what I've just said about Pamela came from her. Mr. Nichols wanted all those things his wife had stood for naturally. I suppose she was the unreachable that he finally reached for."

I was glad that this girl had been one of Allegra's protégées. But the remarks Brett Inness had made at our lunch table still puzzled me. How could anything about Pamela be used against Ross?

Susan Broderick gathered up her books and rose to her feet. "I have to go in now. It's time to get back to work."

I helped her fold the blanket and watched her run across the lawn toward the house, dodging palm trees. For a while I sat on the wall beside the lake and stared at rippling water. Everything that had been said at lunch today came indirectly back to Ross—to his influence upon all our lives. A fierce anger began to rise in me against him. I was beginning to see what his mother had meant—about the lives he'd destroyed. I couldn't know about the past, but I could see what was happening right now. All around him human beings were being used and manipulated. Allegra and Gretchen. Brett, who was still filled with bitterness. Me. Perhaps even Jarrett Nichols, though I wasn't sure about him. Almost without my being aware of it, I had begun to trust in Jarrett's strength and good judgment.

"Mrs. Logan! Mrs. Logan!" The voice had an excited ring. I turned to see the nurse, Coxie, coming from the direction of Coral Cottage, and I left the wall to hurry toward her.

"Please," she said as we came together, "will you come inside the cottage with me? I want to show you something. I've phoned the house, but I couldn't reach Mr. Logan."

"Is anything wrong?" I asked.

"No, no! That is, not exactly. I just want to show you."

At the door of the cottage she put a finger to her lips. "Mrs. Logan is asleep, and sometimes she sleeps very lightly, so we'll try not to wake her."

She led the way through the small living room and into the bedroom, where Allegra lay on her side, looking tiny and withered beneath the afghan tossed over her. Her eyes were closed and lashes that were still long, but very white, lay upon her cheeks. She looked rather like a child, lying there.

Coxie went to the dressing table and opened a drawer. "Look!" she whispered. "Just look in there."

I looked and saw the two netsuke nestled together beside a box of face powder. The small ebony carp and the cherry-wood dragon! I picked up the carp and examined the intricacy of a carving in which every fish scale was represented in meticulous detail. I was playing for time, dismayed that these should be found in Allegra's possession. When Ross knew, it would make everything that much worse for her, and I didn't suppose he could be kept from knowing.

"How do you suppose they got here?" I asked.

"Why—she brought them, of course. She's done that before, you know, with that mermaid she says belongs to her. But she's never touched anything else until now."

I found that my anger hadn't died away. What if she hadn't touched these either? With everyone alerted, warned, wouldn't it be clever of the real thief to place them here, where Allegra would be blamed?

"Have you been out of the cottage today?" I asked.

"Yes, of course. I always take her for a walk in the early morning. She likes to go down to the lake and watch the boats go by."

Like a child, I thought, and winced. "So anyone could have come into the cottage while you were out?"

"I suppose so, Mrs. Logan. The doors can't be seen from the water. There's never been any point in locking up down here in the cottage. But I don't see—"

"It's all right," I assured her. "It's not your fault. No one could watch her every minute."

She bristled a little, a frown on her broad face. "I do the best I can. Mr. Logan doesn't want anyone but me to take care of her."

Because he paid her well not to talk, no matter what Allegra said to her?

"I understand." I pulled some tissue from a box on

the dressing table and wrapped each netsuke carefully. "I'll take these back to the house and explain. I know everyone will be relieved to find them."

"Thank you, Mrs. Logan."

She looked relieved herself over not having to face Ross's possible ire.

As I started back, I wondered what I could do under these circumstances to protect Allegra. And myself, if I hid the truth. Perhaps Jarrett Nichols could help us both. Perhaps this was the time when I could talk to him, whether he approved of me or not.

Chapter 8

I found Jarrett in his office seated behind a desk equally as large as Ross's, and a great deal more untidy. When I spoke to Myra, she motioned me into Jarrett's office, glancing curiously at the small parcels in my hand.

He rose as I appeared and I went to sit in a green leather chair beside his desk. Today his red hair had been combed into some semblance of order, and he wore tan slacks and a pullover. Gray eyes that always made me uneasy—as though he could see past any dissembling—watched as I unwrapped the carp and the dragon and placed them before him.

"These are the netsuke that were missing?" he asked.

"Yes. Miss Cox found them in Mrs. Logan's dressing table drawer."

"That's unfortunate. It's terrible that she's had to

deteriorate in this way. I wish something could be done to help her, Sharon."

I hesitated before I went on. "I suppose we have to tell Ross where they were found?"

His manner seemed slightly less brusque with me than before. "I can understand how you feel. You've become fond of Allegra, haven't you?"

"It's not only Allegra. It's Gretchen too. We're all involved. What if Allegra didn't take these in the first place?"

He looked mildly startled. "What do you mean?"

"After they were discovered missing, perhaps the real thief became nervous and put them in the cottage so everyone would think Mrs. Logan had taken them?"

"An interesting theory, but unlikely. According to your idea, who would you pick for the thief?"

"No one. I haven't anything to go on except a feeling that Allegra never touched anything but the mermaid she believed was hers. Even Miss Cox said she was only interested in the mermaid."

"I suppose you can suggest this to Ross." He sounded doubtful.

I must have sighed, because once more he was studying me disconcertingly. "How are *you?* Have you recovered from your fall?"

I sat up straight in my chair. "Don't you see? Something is happening in this house! And I don't think Allegra has anything to do with it. Sometimes... sometimes I feel I'm being watched. And I know there was real vindictiveness behind that push on the stairs when I fell. And do you remember when I picked up a coconut from the lawn and you said it would rot if I tried to keep it? Well, someone carried one into my room that was in worse condition, crawling with ants, and left it on my dressing table."

If I'd shocked him in the least, he showed nothing. He was the perfect lawyer, playing it cool, and my anger began to include him.

"Have you told Ross?" he asked.

"No! I don't want to. He'd just call another meeting and dress everyone down." I lost my last trace of patience. "Don't be so smug and blind! There's some sort of dreadful purpose behind what's happening! Only I haven't a clue as to what it can be. Or even what the source is. That's the awful part. And we're all going to suffer if it isn't stopped."

He didn't take offense at my anger, but shook his head at me. "You mustn't get so excited. You mustn't let foolish tricks upset you like this. Or frighten you."

"I'm not frightened! Not any more. I'm just mad clear through. I feel outraged and—and furious!"

His guard had slipped a little and he was at least betraying astonishment. "And to think I believed that you were the unruffled type."

"I used to be. I liked being that way. Poinciana has done something strange to me, and I'm not enjoying it. I've never lived in a place so thick with secrets."

"Secrets?"

It was useless to try to explain. Jarrett Nichols was a realist. How could I explain feelings which were still nebulous? I could hardly reveal anything so personal as the eerie playing of "Blue Champagne" on my first night in this house, or tell him of the way I felt when I saw my mother's portrait in the gallery, admired in secret by my own husband. And there were those other secrets Gretchen and Brett and Allegra were all harboring—some of them concerning Jarrett's own wife.

"That push on the stairs was real," I said sharply. "Yet no one seems to know what lies behind it. If I can't walk around the house safely in broad daylight—" I broke off, remembering what Susan had said about the brakes of Pam Nichols's car. Others had not been safe either. For the first time I questioned that "accident."

Myra came scurrying through the adjoining door, halting her rush at Jarrett's desk. "Mr. Logan in coming up the driveway in his car. If he starts upstairs, shall I ask him to come in here first?"

"Yes, do that," Jarrett said.

She bounced off with her light walk, as though she moved on rubber. I imagined she couldn't help hearing every word we'd spoken, and I wondered what scraps of information she might have about Poinciana that might be useful to me if I found the right questions to ask her. At least her interruption had helped me to relax a little.

"How was your morning on Worth Avenue?" he asked.

"It didn't make me comfortable," I told him. "It's hard to believe in all that money. Somehow such a lavish display of wealth seems almost—obscene."

His smile was wry. "What's this—reverse snobbery? As Mrs. Ross Logan, you'd better be aware that money is very real. Though I don't suppose you have even a beginning notion of the tremendous good Ross does with his money. All the philanthropies, the trusts and foundations—have you any idea of what they do for thousands upon thousands of people?"

"Of course I do," I protested. "Oh, I don't know all the details. But what has that to do with high fashion and priceless gems, exotic perfume, and custom-made cars?"

"Well, well, well! What have we here—a proletarian at Poinciana? You mean you don't care for any of those things?"

I was growing indignant. "My mother and father had them to some extent. But they came as a reward for years of hard work and sometimes doing without. Perhaps it's just as well that Allegra Logan can't run Poinciana the way she used to. It's too—too—"

"Decadent?" He was laughing at me.

"Where do *you* fit in?" I challenged.

He sobered at once. "Perhaps the channeling I do is useful. Isn't that possible?"

I suspected that he did a great deal more than "channeling." I remembered the few facts I'd been told about Jarrett Nichols—the way Allegra had picked him out and put him in Ross's charge. Of his marrying a woman who had by inheritance all the things he'd never had. Yet I felt that the basic man had never changed. Money had not used him, as it had used Ross. In some instinctive way I believed this, and I quieted a little.

"You undoubtedly do a great deal of good yourself in Ross's world," I said, and knew how lame the words sounded. Even when I stopped being angry with him, there seemed no way to get through to Jarrett, much as I might want his help.

I was relieved to hear Ross's voice in the outer office at that moment, so that I could end this disquieting discussion. Yet I dreaded what was to come and wished I could sweep the two netsuke into a drawer. I did not move, and when Ross reached us the first things he saw were the small carp and dragon lying on Jarrett's desk. He bent to kiss me on the cheek and I looked up at him as he stood beside my chair, with one hand resting lightly, possessively, on my shoulder. For just a moment I was intensely aware of the two men. Ross, vital and dynamic, as he always seemed, quick of temper and explosive, as he could be. Jarrett, all quiet control over whatever fires raged within. Often sardonic, always strong. He would be able to stand quite still at the center of a storm and he would probably master it, I thought. In the same instant I wondered if a real hurricane would blow Ross away, and winced at my own disloyalty.

Ross was already speaking. "Where did you find them?" he asked us, picking up the netsuke.

"Mrs. Logan found them," Jarrett said, and Ross looked down at me.

"They were in a dressing table drawer in Coral Cottage," I told him. "Miss Cox discovered them and called me because she couldn't reach you. I brought them here."

"Did you talk to my mother about them? Not that it would have done any good."

"She was sleeping. I didn't want to disturb her."

"She'd never remember taking them anyway. I'm glad to have them back, but this means I'll need to make a decision all the more quickly. I was in town this morning talking to an old friend who has an aunt in a fine home in upstate New York. When we've had a look at the place, I'll take Mother there."

"New York?" I cried. "Upstate—in the winter? When she's used to Florida?"

"There are heated houses," he said mildly. "She won't be abandoned in a snowdrift. And, after all, she grew up in Minnesota."

I gave up trying to contain myself. "I think it's a terrible thing to do! I think it's disgraceful, when you have all these empty rooms, where she could be happy and live out her life in a familiar and loved place—with nurses to care for her constantly."

His expression darkened as I spoke, and I saw the anger in his eyes. He moved away from me and placed a sheet of paper on Jarrett's desk.

"I'd like you to talk to the woman in charge of this place, Jarrett. Draw up a list of practical questions to ask. And then make an appointment for me to go there."

As they discussed Ross's plan, I became aware of Myra in the doorway, wiggling her fingers at me and making faces. But before I could understand her signaling, Gretchen was in the room. Myra hurried back to her desk and Gretchen faced her father.

"What's this about a home? Dad, you can't send Gran away! I won't let you!"

Ross held the netsuke out to her. "These were found in your grandmother's dressing table drawer. She's become totally irresponsible, Gretchen, and she can't be controlled any longer at Poinciana."

"You're not going to do it!" Gretchen's look was as dark as her father's and they glowered at each other.

"*You* are going to stop me?" Ross demanded.

"If I can." Gretchen whirled and walked out of the room, her rage with her father almost sizzling.

"I'll take care of this," Jarrett said quietly, picking up the sheet of paper.

I gave him a look filled with scorn. Of course! He would always do whatever Ross Logan required. That was why he was behind that desk. My brief vision of strength and solidity had vanished. I couldn't stand either of them any longer, and I couldn't stand this house. I jumped up and ran through the outer office, where Myra stared in wry amusement, and went out the front door to the driveway.

Immediately a man in uniform appeared from the gatehouse and came toward me. "You'd like a car, Mrs. Logan?"

"Yes, please. And someone to drive me."

Albert, the chauffeur who had met us on arrival, was still putting the Rolls away, and at the gateman's signal he turned it around and drove back to the porte cochere.

When he held the car door open for me and asked where I wished to go, I told him to take me to some peaceful spot where I could get out and just walk around.

He knew exactly the place, Albert assured me, and we went north along South Ocean Boulevard in the direction of town. We drove through Palm Beach streets until Albert drew up to the curb before a great Gothic church near the lake.

"Bethesda-by-the-Sea," he told me. "The gardens are very beautiful, Mrs. Logan."

It was the open-air solace of the gardens I sought, rather than the shadowy nave of the church itself. I walked through a long stone arcade to find a courtyard where palm trees slanted up through paving stones that had been set around each bole, and where bougainvillea climbed the walls. My steps echoing on stone flags told me I was alone. Through an archway I saw the graceful gray branches of a poinciana tree, where blossoms were turning to flame. Another archway and stone steps with fanciful stone abutments led me to a higher garden of patterned flower beds in contrasts of red and green. A bench invited me, and I sat down and raised my face to the constant Florida sun, letting its healing warmth pour over me from a limitless blue sky.

All I wanted was to quiet my thoughts, my emotions. When Ross Logan had come into my life at its lowest ebb, taking away my load of problems, helping to assuage my grief, I had wanted the peace he'd seemed to offer more than anything else. With his arms around me, I had felt safe and able to breathe again. Some of the soreness of memory began to abate, and I could love a man for the first time. I had been grateful for his love and his rescue of me in my need. Yet in the short time I had been at Poinciana, all the good feelings of safety and peace had been shattered, and my world turned upside down in more frightful turmoil than ever. A turmoil that was part of a fearful present. I could no longer be an observer on the sidelines. I had been plunged into the tumultuous heart of whatever was happening. Perhaps I was really coming to life for the first time. The movement of blood through frozen limbs is always painful.

From the corner of my eye I was aware of movement in another part of this formal garden. Without turning my head, I was aware that a man walked alone beyond the flower beds. I didn't look at him, and he kept to himself. We would respect each other's solitude.

But the small distraction had disturbed the peace I was seeking. Everything crowded in upon me, centered upon fears that I knew were justified, even though others discounted them. Gretchen, Allegra, and I were all tied together now, but because of my presence, some unseen enemy had moved—where perhaps there had been no need to move at all before. And an enemy who is faceless is the most terrifying of all.

True, it was Ross who wanted to send his mother away, but I'd begun to sense some other ominous movement behind the scenes, and it frightened me not to know the hand that moved us as if we were chess pieces.

Which one played the powerful role of Queen, and was the disguise worn by male or female? I'd been unable to tell about the sex of whoever had pushed me down the stairs.

I sat with my head bowed in my hands, only to become suddenly aware that the man who shared this solitude had come close to my bench and was watching me. With a sense of shock, I looked up into the face of Vasily Karl.

Chapter 9

Again the sharp sense of recognition assailed me, and with it came memory. The last time I had seen that face it had worn a beard, thick and blond and slightly curly.

"I knew you'd remember," Vasily said. "I knew we had better talk when I could find you alone. So when I saw you rush out of the house a little while ago and drive off in the Rolls, I followed you. I'm sorry to disturb your contemplation in this beautiful spot, but it is necessary, don't you think? You were only thirteen, I believe, but you remember now, don't you?"

Yes, I remembered. It had been in Amsterdam. How I'd loved that museum filled with Vandykes. Ysobel wouldn't look at them in spite of my pleading. She was upset because a handsome emerald necklace that had been given her by a Spanish nobleman had been stolen. I couldn't remember the necklace as well as I did the

Vandykes because it had been sold later for a tidy sum when Ysobel and Ian had found themselves in debt.

"Emeralds," I said. "The necklace, I mean. And a few diamonds sprinkled in. I never understood what happened, but I was in the room when the police brought you to see Ysobel. I remember that I was fascinated by your beard and your eyes, and that scar over one eyebrow."

I didn't tell him that I'd also been terribly frightened that day. There had been something about the young man who was brought to see my mother that I didn't like. Perhaps a child could sense more deeply beneath the surface than an adult did. I hadn't liked him, and I was afraid that he meant to hurt my mother.

Vasily sat beside me, studying me with those slightly tilted eyes that I remembered. "A distant Mongol ancestor must have furnished the eyes," he said. "The scar was made by a knife. Together, they make disguises difficult. What else do you remember?"

"I'm not sure of the details. Was it you who took the necklace?"

He laughed softly and his amusement seemed genuine. "No—my career has usually operated well inside the law. But I was living at the time with an uncle who was, I believe, an excellent fence. I happened to have seen the necklace in his shop. So when I read about it in the papers, I decided to go to the police. After all, I had been charmed by your mother in a recent performance and I couldn't bear to see her unhappy. My uncle was a rascal anyway, and we were never very good friends after that. But your mother was generous in the reward she gave me and best of all in her kindness."

He made it all sound so innocent, so light and amusing. Yet I had been afraid.

"Yes," I said, "I do remember. I was there in the room when you put the necklace into her hands."

"And I remember you. A small girl with very big eyes and already with a beauty far greater in promise than your mother's would ever be. I wished at the time that I could have brought you chocolates or a nosegay. But I gave you neither, and now I am in your hands."

"Why do you think that? I don't know anything about you, except that you brought back something which my mother valued."

"Mr. Logan is bent on investigating my life. And not all of it bears investigation. He will not be pleased if he goes back to Amsterdam. In those days I had another name."

"Then you must have been in trouble with the law?"

"But never caught. There is a difference, I think."

"Does Gretchen know about any of this?"

"She knows all there is to know. Or almost all. I must throw myself on your mercy. If you will give me your silence about ever having seen me in Amsterdam—give it for just a little while—perhaps you will be doing Gretchen a favor. She needs our help, wouldn't you say?"

He had a winning charm of his own, and besides, I had no wish to see Ross destroy whatever happiness Gretchen had found. I mustn't rely too much on the instinctive fear of that child in Amsterdam.

"There's no reason for me to say anything about my mother's necklace, or about meeting you in Amsterdam," I told him.

"Thank you." He took my hand. "I'll leave you to your solitude now. My car is on another street, since I thought it wiser not to have Albert see me come into the gardens."

He bent his blond head and kissed my hand, but when he stood up to leave, I stopped him.

"There's one other thing. Do you know that the two netsuke—the ones that were missing—have been found among Mrs. Logan's things at her cottage?"

"I had not heard that," he said gravely. There was a slight lift to that already raised eyebrow and I wondered if he spoke the truth. Certainly I had the feeling that I had given him something slightly disturbing to think about as he bowed again and turned away. Intrigue was his medium, however, and I suspected that he would come through his troubles, whatever they were.

Watching him cross the grass, go down the few steps, and walk off toward the arcade, I continued to wonder about him. Wondered about Amsterdam, and about what had led Gretchen to marry him. Again I remembered my father's words—"Things are not always what they seem." She must have met a great many charming, fortune-hungry men. So why Vasily? Never mind—this wasn't the main problem that faced me. That, as always, was my husband, Ross Logan. How would I ever find the truth behind his façade? To this puzzle, my father had given me no key.

When I returned to the car, Albert was leaning against the hood, smoking a cigarette. He put it out when he saw me and sprang to open the door.

"Thank you," I said. "This was a perfect place to bring me. I'll want to come back another time and go inside the church. But now I'll go back to Poinciana."

"You look a little better, Mrs. Logan," he told me, and got behind the wheel. He was a kind man, and very loyal to Allegra's son and the old regime.

"Of course, you were here in Allegra Logan's time?" I said as he started the car.

"Yes indeed, Mrs. Logan. I've driven her all around this area many times."

"How can I help her, Albert?" I wanted to add, *How can I help myself and help Gretchen?* But I wouldn't shock him like that. I could tell by the stiffening of his shoulders that I'd startled him as it was.

He turned the car around before he spoke. "Mrs. Charles Logan has always been devoted to Poinciana, Mrs. Logan. If there is something she could help with around the house—?"

"Yes. That's what I think too. But what?"

He thought for a moment as we drove through pleasant tropical streets. "There are those paintings she used to collect, Mrs. Logan. Is there anything you could consult her about that concerns them?"

"Perhaps there is. A very good idea. Thank you, Albert."

We were silent for the rest of the short drive home. When I left the car at the front door, I walked down a long corridor to the gallery wing and opened its door cautiously, half fearing to hear the alarms go off. But the security guard was inside, snoozing in his chair, and he sprang to attention as I entered.

"I don't know the rules," I told him. "When is the alarm usually set?"

"It's on for the door behind the curtain right now," he told me. "But during the day there is always a man on duty at this end of the gallery."

"I'd like to walk through again," I said, "but I won't open the far door."

He touched his cap, and I started along the marble aisle of marvelous paintings. Albert's suggestion might be a good one. Perhaps Allegra could be consulted about the rather haphazard hanging. But to answer that was not my purpose now, and I went on down the long gallery to the second, smaller room, where the real treasures were kept. I knew what drew me like a magnet.

I hadn't wanted to return to this spot. I'd run from it before—because of Ross. But now I wanted to see Ysobel's portrait for myself. There was a need in me to face the truth about my mother. The truth, not only about her, but about *me*.

The curtained recess reminded me of a shrine, and again I hated it fiercely that Ross should have hung her picture like this—in a secret place that only he would come to. If her portrait had been hung where everyone could see it, that would have seemed more normal, and it would have pleased Ysobel. I was sure she would have hated being hidden away like this.

An audience for this rendezvous was the last thing I wanted, and I was glad to be out of sight of the guard when I reached the curtain pulleys.

I put my hand on cords that would open the curtain, hesitating, wondering if I could ever forgive her. Ever forgive myself for hating her as much as I loved her. Now, before I looked into her face again, I must accept that truth, accept the opposing feelings that warred in me and accept them without guilt. None of that lovely generosity Ysobel had directed toward the world had ever been for me. I need not feel guilty. *I* had been the lonely one, watching their happiness together from a distance.

Once, at a time when I was too young to handle bitter reality, she had explained it all to me. She'd done it jokingly, but I had known what she said for the terrible truth it was—that she had never wanted a child. Though if she'd had to have one, a son would have been more acceptable. A son could have been properly adoring, and would never have made her seem old. A daughter could grow up to be a rival. Not that she ever intended that to happen. By the time I was grown, I'd been reduced to a position of useful attendant. She often forgot to introduce me to new friends, and kept me away from the press.

I'd withdrawn into my protective case and tried to feel nothing. It was the only way to live, and I was not actively unhappy or sorry for myself. Resources of my own began to develop. Besides, when I had really wanted something, I had learned how to fight her quietly until she gave in. But now, here at Poinciana, it had all begun to spill out. I could stand before her portrait and for the first time accept the ugly truths. Only then could I send them away from me. Somehow I must forgive her in order to forgive myself. She had never been able to be anything but what she was—a tinsel woman who *had* to be loved, but who had never learned how to love back. I was better off than she, because I had found out that I could love. I had even loved Ysobel in a hungry sort of way. And I had hated her—always concealing both emotions from myself because it hurt too much to indulge them.

Reasoning was no use now, however. I couldn't rid myself of old angers so easily. With a sudden, compulsive movement, I pulled the cords. The blue velvet curtains parted, and the shock of surprise stunned me. I was keyed to face Ysobel, but the space on the wall where the portrait had hung was empty. For several moments I stared blankly at blue curtains. Then I ran back through the small room and down the long gallery to where the guard waited for me.

"My mother's picture is gone," I said. "Do you know what has happened to it?"

He stood up hurriedly. "No, Mrs. Logan. I didn't know it had been removed."

He came with me through the rooms to the recess and looked in some dismay at the empty wall. "Mr. Logan must have given some order that I don't know about. I should have been told. I'm responsible for the security of these galleries."

Steps echoed loudly down the long marble room, and I turned to see Gretchen hurrying toward us. She had changed to her usual shabby jeans, and wore a blouse with a button missing. She moved with an accustomed, purposeful vigor, though sometimes I wondered if she really knew what that purpose was.

When she stopped beside me, her words were almost accusing.

"So here you are! I've been looking for you, Sharon. Susan Broderick told me she'd seen you coming this way."

"My mother's portrait is gone," I said. "It was here only yesterday, when Ross showed it to me."

Gretchen nodded to the guard. "It's all right, Steve. My father took the picture down himself. I saw him this morning when he was carrying it upstairs."

"But why?" I asked, my sense of surprise increasing. "Why did he move it?"

Gretchen looked at me soberly, and for once without mockery. "Maybe we'd better talk. We'll go out the rear way, Steve. You can put the alarm back on when we're out."

She opened a small panel behind blue curtains. Inside was a gray metal box. Gretchen turned the alarm key and led the way through Allegra's "secret" door that Ross had showed me.

"I know the very place for a quiet, intimate conversation," she said, the mockery creeping back. "Come along."

By the time we had made a turn or two, I was lost again, but this was the home that Gretchen had grown up in, and when she opened a pair of double doors I saw that we were in one of the vast drawing rooms that I'd visited on my tour with Ross.

The outer shutters were closed and the great room was dim. Gretchen touched a switch and two priceless chandeliers of rock crystal flashed into light. This was what Allegra had called the French Drawing Room. She had furnished it with gilded Louis XVI chairs upholstered in the pictorial designs of Gobelin tapestry. The wall vitrines on either side of a gold and white marble mantelpiece were filled with Sèvres porcelain that picked up the color motifs of chairs and Savonnerie rug. Upon a cabinet inlaid with mother-of-pearl stood a gilded ormolu clock, its hands stilled at some forgotten hour. Pink Fabergé Easter eggs rested on their own stands on either side of the clock.

"When she was young, Gran turned her rooms into museums," Gretchen said. "You'd never know the same lady furnished the austere suite she took for herself after Grandfather Charlie died."

She went to a window and pulled heavy cords to open the draperies that hung from ceiling to floor. Then she opened the glass and set shutters ajar to let in air and filtered light. When she'd turned off the chandeliers, she led the way to a place by the open windows.

"Gran always arranged little islands for conversation in these big rooms, so this is as good a spot as any. No one will disturb us here."

We sat in tapestried chairs beside a table inlaid with more mother-of-pearl. A collection of millefiore glass paperweights graced its surface. I still felt a reverence for everything around me, but I had no time for appreciation now.

"Why do you think your father moved the picture?" I asked.

"You haven't found out the truth about him yet, have you? You're still infatuated with his position and money and power. All that tremendous effect he makes wherever he goes!"

I was shaking my head before she finished. "No! Those things have never impressed me in the way you mean. Except, perhaps, to make me feel safe."

"Then why did you marry him?"

Somehow it was easy to say the words in this dim and shadowy room that belonged to the past. "He was kind to me. He rescued me and loved me, and I loved him."

"A very pretty picture. But that you believe it only means you haven't discovered that my father is a very sick man. He's powerful and can't be touched, but he's a whole lot sicker, I sometimes feel, than Gran ever was. That's why he's taken the picture upstairs. Because he has an obsession with Ysobel Hollis. He's had it for years. It's one of the things that drove my mother away. It will be a whole lot worse for you because you're *her* daughter."

I could feel the rush of blood to my face, feel the trembling start inside me. She was telling me a truth I had already known, but I'd wanted neither to believe nor to accept it.

When I started to rise, she put out her hand to stop me. "Wait. Vasily told me about finding you in the Bethesda-by-the-Sea gardens this afternoon. He told me what you said about not giving him away to my father. At least I can thank you for that. I know I've resented you. I've wished you'd hate it here and go away. Maybe I still do. But I think you really do want to help with Gran, and it could be you're the only one who can get through to my father. So don't take it too hard about the picture. He can't help himself. Be careful you don't destroy what you care about most."

I already felt that what I'd cared about in Ross Logan was disintegrating because it was based on something that existed only in my mind. I was growing very tired of people who couldn't help themselves—myself included. Somewhere along the way we all had to be responsible for our own actions. But I could say none of this to Ross's daughter, no matter how she might criticize her father herself.

She seemed not to notice my silence. "You must have missed the big battle between Dad and Jarrett today," she went on. "Or have you heard about that?"

I couldn't care a great deal right now, though this would have startled me at another time. "What do you mean?"

"Jarrett seldom loses his temper. Sometimes he has too much control, so that he explodes when he lets go. I was too far away to hear anything but the shouting. I'll have to pump Myra when I get a chance. Jarrett rushed off in a rage just as I reached the office, but I don't think Dad would ever fire him. He couldn't operate without him. Dad was all right—just sputtering mad. It was something about Meridian Oil, I think. About some Japanese businessmen who want to come to see him. He wouldn't talk to me except about Vasily, so I left too and came looking for you."

My mind was still upon what Ross had done with my mother's portrait—my *fear* of what he had done with it—and I listened without much comprehension. I wanted no more of Gretchen's company at the moment, and I left my chair slowly, carefully, as though something were wrong with my balance. It was just that trembling feeling again. I thanked her politely, though I wasn't sure what for, and I didn't hurry until I was out of the room.

In the corridor, I wandered blindly for a few moments

before I got my bearings and found a back way that took me upstairs. Once I knew where I was, I fled down the hall and into my room. There I started through an automatic routine, not allowing my eyes to stray toward Ross's closed door. Postponing. Because I was afraid of what I would find when I opened that door. I'd thought that nothing could become much worse between Ross and me, but I already knew better.

When I'd taken off the coral earrings I was wearing, I pulled my jewel box toward me to put them away. Ysobel's jewel box. It seemed only partially closed, and when I lifted the lid I saw why. A packet of envelopes had been stuffed into the top tray just under the lid. They were nothing I had placed there and I picked them up with a sense of fatality.

At first glance I saw that the top envelope was addressed to Ysobel in San Francisco, where she had taken her last show. By this time I knew the handwriting very well—the letter was from Ross. Quickly I ran through a dozen or so envelopes—all addressed to Ysobel in various parts of the country and the world, all in the same handwriting.

I had no intention of reading them, but I had to be sure. I opened the top envelope and took out the letter on stiff Poinciana stationery, turning quickly to the last page, where Ross's name had been signed, "lovingly." My eyes scanned the page, and the words of love leaped out at me. Someone with vindictive intent had placed this collection of love letters that Ross had written to my mother here in Ysobel's jewel box for me to find. One more thing I had to know. Quickly I ran through the postmarks. Most of them were old letters, a few bore dates of more recent years, but there was nothing in the immediate past.

How they had come back to this house, I had no idea, unless Ysobel herself had returned them to him. Which was likely, of course. In that case, someone in this house had taken them from wherever he'd put them, and left them here for me to see—intending to hurt me as deeply as possible.

With fingers that fumbled in their haste, I started to fold the letter I'd opened, in order to replace it in its envelope, when a name on the page caught my eye—"Brett." I read the paragraph. Ross had written rather chattily about the weapon he could hold over Brett's head if she ever became a threat to him. Apparently Gretchen's mother had gone deeply into debt in order to open the exclusive shop where her designs were sold. Unknown to Brett, it was Ross who held the note for the loan she had taken, and if he chose he could call it in at any time. If he did this before she was ready, he could very well ruin her. A sense of malevolence, of a cruelty he might enjoy, marked his choice of words, and I felt further sickened.

If someone else had found these letters—Gretchen?—then it was possible that Brett knew very well the dangerous position she might be in, if she had not yet paid up the loan. I wondered what threat she might hold over Ross that had resulted in an impasse.

I stuffed the letter quickly back in its envelope and sat for a moment with the packet in my hand. When I glanced at my own reflection in the mirror, I saw how wide and staring my eyes were, and how pale I looked. There could be no more postponement. I thrust the pack of letters into a lower drawer of my dressing table and placed a box of tissues over them. Later I would decide what to do with them, but now there was the matter I had come here to face.

I got up and went to the closed door of Ross's room. When I tapped there was no answer, so I opened the door and looked in. A hunting scene that had hung over the fireplace was gone, and the portrait of Ysobel Hollis had been put in its place. I crossed the room and stood before the picture, looking up into eyes that had always laughed, as if at a joyous secret, and at lips that smiled for her audience. Any audience. This must be my own private moment of truth.

The secret had been that Ysobel had looked forever in a mirror, and that anything or anyone who came between herself and her flattering self-image was likely to be treated with subtle, smiling cruelty. My father had known well enough, but he had loved her and he had learned how to play the game that would hold her to him. He only took my side when we were alone. At times I'd felt a great impatience with him, yet I could understand his predicament more clearly now. Now I was out of my protective case, and at least I could thank Ysobel and Ross for that. I would never go back.

It was going to hurt a lot out here in the open, I thought fiercely—but here I would stay. Ross's hanging of her portrait in his room erased the last of my doubts. This time I would not wince away from the confrontation that lay ahead. Nor was I in any mood to forgive Ysobel now.

Filled with a new, quiet determination, I returned to the pale champagne colors of my room and lay across the bed. I had no need to will myself into the escape of nothingness now. My mind was clear and I was deeply weary. Sleep carried me restfully into late afternoon, when I awoke to the touch of Ross's hand on my arm, and opened my eyes to see him standing beside my bed.

Chapter 10

Ross was wearing the blue tie-silk dressing gown I'd bought as a gift for him in London, and he smelled pleasantly of soap and shaving lotion. He sat beside me on the bed, leaning over to nuzzle his face into my neck.

"You've had a good sleep," he said. "You're warm and soft and relaxed—the way you should be. Darling, I want to show something."

He scooped me up easily in his arms and carried me through the open door into his room. When he laid me on the bed, I could look up at Ysobel's picture over the mantel and I stared at it fixedly.

"Aren't you pleased?" he said. "I thought you wouldn't want her hidden away in a museum. Besides, she must see how happy we are, my darling. Don't move now. Close your eyes and wait a moment."

I knew what was going to happen as he reached for the switch on the stereo set. The recording began near the end of a phrase, and I heard the huskiness of her voice—"...memories of blue champagne..."

"No!" I cried and sat up on the bed. "Don't play that! Don't ever play it again!"

"Of course I'll play it." His voice was low, gentle, but it brushed aside my objections. "It's the one perfect tune for *our* lovemaking. Her voice, her song. And let her watch—*let* her!"

I pushed against him, rolling to the far side of the bed. "No! I won't let you do this! I won't let you make love to her through me."

He pulled me back to him and all gentleness was gone. "Is that what you think? That I'd make love to her through you? Don't you know how much I hated her, detested her? But I want her here now—here in this room so she can see that I've beaten her. That I've married her daughter."

The singing voice went on beside us, disembodied and terribly wrong, when there was nothing of flesh and blood behind it. What he was telling me was even worse than the sickness I'd suspected. Ysobel was the only woman who had ever refused him, denied him, sent him away, so now he must try to punish her through me, by making love to me.

"Let's get you out of all these clothes," he whispered against my cheek.

Only humiliation could result in a physical struggle against him. There was a better way.

"What a fool you are!" I said softly. "What fools we've both been. Can't you see that Ysobel has won? We are her discards—both of us!"

He let me go and sat up beside me with a curious blankness in his eyes. I slid off the bed and stood up.

"Get out of my room!" he said, his tone ominously low. "Get out of my sight!" The threat in his voice was terrifying.

I rushed into the hall, and it didn't matter where I ran. I only needed, as he said, to get out of his sight.

I had made him a *nothing*, and that was the one thing Ross Logan could never endure to be.

It was all over—everything I'd trusted in so mistakenly, everything I'd hoped for so stupidly and innocently in this marriage. There were tears on my cheeks and sobs were catching my breath as I ran down the nearest stairs, stumbling, clinging to the rail to keep from falling, hoping that I would meet no one until I could find a place to hide. Because I was afraid of myself—of falling apart in some disastrous breakdown of the sort I'd been close to after that fire in Belfast. I no longer had any inner place of concealment to run to—and no confidence in my ability to face what lay outside.

Because I was hurtling blindly, I ran directly into Jarrett Nichols as he came out of the offices into my path. By this time I was weeping wildly in reaction, and he shook me hard, shook me back into my senses, so that I gulped for air and went limp in his hands.

"Come in here," he said, and drew me into his office, thrust me into a chair. Myra had gone for the day, and he closed the door to the outer office and came back to sit on a corner of the desk beside me. "Would you like a drink? Do you want to talk?"

I shook my head and wept into my hands. How could I ever tell anyone, when what had happened was so painful, so shameful? Only Gretchen would have understood, yet in her way she loved her father, and I could never talk to her, never talk to anyone.

I'd been wrong about the office being empty, however. In my distress, I hadn't seen the quiet figure in a corner of the room. When I heard movement, I took my hands from my face in surprise. Allegra Logan left her chair and came to touch me gently on the shoulder. She was wearing slacks and a sweater again—her costume when she went roving from the cottage.

"What has my son done this time?" she asked. Her eyes were bright in her lined face, and they were perfectly sane and aware.

I only shook my head.

"Jarrett, get her a glass of something. It will help her to relax. She's obviously had a shock. My son has always been a vulnerable man, and that makes him dangerous."

Jarrett brought me a small glass of brandy and put it in my hand. Then he pulled a chair for Allegra close to mine, and seated her in it.

"This house still needs me," Allegra said. "He's going to spoil Gretchen's life, and he's trying to destroy this poor young thing. I'm needed here, but I haven't the strength any more to do what ought to be done. Besides, he means to send me away—and how am I to fight that?"

If in the past Jarrett had wavered in what he thought might be best for Allegra Logan, he now made up his mind. "No one is going to send you away. I'll do my best to prevent that."

I managed to sip brandy, letting its warmth flow through me, relaxing a little, watching them both.

Allegra looked up at Jarrett. "I had one weapon, if only I could have used it. He doesn't know it exists, or that I lost it somehow when they moved me out of the house. Perhaps I put it away somewhere carefully. Only I can't remember where. Of course, it's all in my head, as well, and that's what he's afraid of. But having it in my head isn't strong enough to use against him now."

She had caught Jarrett's attention. "What are you talking about, Mrs. Logan?"

"Nothing I have any intention of telling you," she said calmly. "You don't need this, as I do. You already have the power. You're the one person he won't dare to go against if you make up your mind to oppose him. Though I'm not sure you'll really go that far. You've protected him for too long."

"I stopped protecting him today," Jarrett said bitterly. "We had the worst row this afternoon that I've ever had with him. And I was the one who walked out. We've trained him for too long to believe in his own fantasies."

"Of being a great man? Yes. I don't know how you've stayed with him for so long. Or perhaps I do. You've put the money in the right places. Without you as his conscience, he'd never have cared."

"This afternoon he lost the last of his conscience," Jarrett said.

"But he's no longer on the board, is he? He's been letting the reins go, turning to other things?"

"Ostensibly. Outwardly—to give himself protection. But the board chairman is still in his pocket. Ross never lets go of what he wants." He glanced at me in sudden embarrassment and apology.

"It's all right," I said. "I must try to understand."

Allegra closed her eyes wearily. Then she opened them and looked at me.

"What about you, child? If you love him, that's important too. God knows, I've loved the wrong men at times. But you're not another Brett. We all know what she wanted of marriage. But whatever Ross has done, he will get over it if you give him time."

"*I* won't get over it," I told her. "Not after what has happened." My voice broke again, and suddenly the words came pouring out—words I'd thought I couldn't speak. "He hung Ysobel's portrait in his room. That painting of my mother that he commissioned years ago. And he played a song of hers—with *her* voice singing! He's still in love with her!"

But I couldn't tell them the rest, and I broke off as Jarrett started pacing around the room. Allegra leaned forward to touch my hand with thin, dry fingers.

"You must be very careful now. He can never bear to be thwarted—my son. He came to see me earlier today. Because of the two netsuke he says I took from his collection and hid in my room. Of course I didn't, but this is why I gave Coxie the slip and came here to talk to Jarrett. I tried to persuade Ross that I would never have taken them. I never much liked that collection, except for my little mermaid. It's become too much of an obsession with him—as though this book he wants to write will give him the distinction he's never really been able to grasp in other ways. But he wouldn't believe me. He doesn't want to believe me."

Jarrett paused before her chair to take her hands in his. "If I'm to help you, I have to be sure of what I'm doing. I'm going to say something now that it may be hard for you to hear. Do you remember the time when you fired a shot at Ross? That time when he moved you out of the house? Can you remember why?"

"Certainly I remember! It was just after your wife's death. I shot at him because I knew he would never be convicted of anything he did, and he would just go on destroying people. Good people. He had to be stopped. I gave him his life, so perhaps it was my duty to take it away. Unfortunately, I wasn't a very good shot. Perhaps at the last moment I didn't really mean to be. Charlie would have been ashamed of such terrible aim. But it was more than that. There was a *special* reason why I shot him...only...only..." Her voice faltered to a halt as her strength faded.

Jarrett was at her side at once. "That's enough now. Never mind the reason. Let me take you back to your room at the cottage."

She rallied a little, however, and reached a hand toward me. "I meant what I said. If you want to leave him, then you must do it quickly, before he can guess what you intend. You must be very careful of his anger."

I already knew this and I nodded mutely. I had seen that look in Ross's eyes, and I'd fled from it instinctively. But while she could still talk, I needed to know whatever she could tell me.

"You said a little while ago that Ross was vulnerable. What did you mean?"

"If Charlie had lost every bit of money he made, it wouldn't have mattered. He'd have been perfectly sure that he had the brains and gumption and character to do it all over again. But Ross is a second-generation *heir*. He didn't earn it himself out of a business that he'd built and loved. I suppose some heirs do fine, but Ross knows he'll never be much on his own without money to back him. So all he can think about is getting more and more, without really having any good reason for needing it."

"Right now," Jarrett said, "he's trying to prove what he can do on his own, and he's stepping into deep and dangerous waters. The trouble is that a great many more innocent lives hang in the balance than his."

Allegra bowed her head in agreement. "He's frightened to death of losing anything that belongs to him. He couldn't stand it when he almost won Ysobel Hollis, and then she turned him down for your father, Sharon. That's what he can never take—ridicule, defeat. Our defeats make most of us tough. Not Ross. Now he is trying to undo all this by strking out in some new direction. He has never understood that he's vulnerable. That's what makes him so dangerous."

She had talked for too long, and she sank wearily back in her chair. I saw that her hands were trembling.

"We'll go to the cottage now," Jarrett said. "Do you think you can ride with me in the golf cart?"

"Of course. If you'll boost me into it. I just came to find out where you stand, Jarrett. At least I know that you'll try to help me—even if you fail."

"I will try," he said. "I'll talk to Ross. Will you come with us, Sharon? You're still looking rocky. I don't want to leave you here alone."

The phone rang on Jarrett's desk and he picked it up.

"That will be Coxie," Allegra said, and it was. Jarrett reassured the nurse, and we went into the outer office. Myra Ritter, busy at her desk, looked up at us innocently.

"I thought you'd gone home," Jarrett said.

"I did leave, but then I remembered something I hadn't finished, so I came back. I didn't want to disturb you."

"We're taking Mrs. Logan down to the cottage," Jarrett told her. "If anyone asks, you haven't seen her."

"Of course I haven't, Mr. Nichols." I suspected that she was on our side and would say nothing to Ross if the matter came up.

Outside, the golf cart that was often used for quick transport around the grounds waited for us at a side door. But before she got in, Allegra looked sadly up at the house. "It's too quiet and empty these days. Palm Beach used to be so full of parties. Everyone gave parties and there was always some charity ball coming up. We did some good while we had all that expensive fun."

"It's still going on," Jarrett said. "You can go to three parties a day on the island when the season is on. If you wanted to. This little stretch of land holds more ball gowns and jewels and magnums of champagne than most of the population of America ever sees in a lifetime."

If she heard the sting in his words, she paid no attention, and her face, for all its myriad lines, looked dreamy with an illusion of youth.

"But they were never like the parties *I* gave. Rajahs and maharanis came to Poinciana in those days. Kings and princes and all kinds of presidents. Of countries and of businesses. If we got bored with what was happening on land, I took them all off on the *Allegra* and we would sail to the Bahamas, or the Greek isles—or anywhere our fancy chose."

She stood transfixed beside the car, her thoughts in the past..

"Let me help you." Jarrett spoke gently.

"Wait." She turned to me. "You must bring it all back. You must make it come to life again—my beautiful house. With all my chandeliers lighted, and all the crystal and silver shining. Guests will come, you know, the minute you whistle—because you're a Logan and this is Poinciana."

Already she had forgotten that I might be leaving Ross.

"I'm not sure I want all that," I told her.

For a moment her eyes looked directly into mine. "No, I suppose you won't want it. You've much better sense. In the end, of course, I didn't want it either. When Charlie died and Brett gave the parties, I never went. I moved into those lovely, peaceful gray rooms. I had time to read books then, and listen to music. Not music played just for dancing. All right, Jarrett, take me back to the cottage. It's antiseptic and ugly. But I'm used to it now. I don't even see what's around me most of the time, and I can still look out the windows and walk outside."

He lifted her into the front seat, and I climbed into the back, facing the other way. Which is why I had a full view of the house as we drove off across the lawn. Ross had come through his mother's rooms and was standing on her small balcony looking out this way, watching us go, his face expressionless. In bright sunshine I felt chilled and more than a little frightened.

"He's watching us," I warned. "Just standing there on a balcony watching us."

"Let him," Jarrett said.

But I couldn't shrug off that chilling emptiness on Ross's face. I must get away quickly, while there was still time.

When we reached the cottage, Jarrett took Allegra inside, and I saw that she faltered now as she moved, and that her mind had lost its moments of clarity and taken her far back into the past.

Jarrett returned to the cart, where I waited. "Are you all right now?"

"I'm not sure. I'm not sure of anything, except that I must leave."

"You'd better *be* sure, because Ross will be very sure of everything. But you need to be sure because you've thought it all through, not because you're running away scared."

I wanted to trust him, to listen, to lean on a strength that I felt was real and to be counted on. But I'd been learning the hard way not to trust, and I must lean on no one but myself.

"I'm angry now, but I'm frightened too," I told him. "I have to go away. Perhaps I can move into town for a while. Just to have time to think. Alone."

"Don't act in too much of a hurry. It's better not to antagonize him, if you can help it. Besides, have you considered that you may be needed here more than you believe? Allegra knew she was needed at Poinciana, but she's too old to cope now, and she realizes that. So perhaps it's your turn. You've made a start with Gretchen. She and Allegra both need you here."

"Need me! Allegra had forgotten me by the time we reached the cottage. And Gretchen doesn't like me."

"If you think those things, you're blinder than I believed. Isn't it possible that you could be good for Ross as well, if you stay and see this through? Have you ever considered that he might be running scared too?"

My indignation surged. "Allegra, who knows him best of all, thought I should go. She believes he's dangerous. Besides, just a little while ago in your office you were critical of Ross. You didn't sound sympathetic toward him then."

"That doesn't mean I'm going to walk out. I can be critical of him, and sorry for him at the same time. Allegra spoke the truth. He *is* vulnerable. More so than you know."

I hardly listened. "Allegra knows something," I mused. "Something in particular that might be used against Ross."

"That's probably all in her imagination. And no matter if it were true, I wouldn't want to see it used. A great many issues are involved here—complex issues."

"But I have to save myself. I can't stay here and be destroyed."

"I think you're stronger than you've let yourself discover. And if you leave, he'll come after you. You have to realize that. You have to recognize the fact that you're surrounded by the enormous power of one of the most omnipotent men in the world. In a sense, I'm in the same position you are. But I'll stay because greater issues *are* involved. I'll stay and compromise, in spite of my mixed feelings about Ross Logan."

"I don't know if I can compromise. Or if I should."

"You're a woman. Win him. Win him over Ysobel!"

I stared angrily at Jarrett—at the blowing red hair, into eyes that watched me coolly, at a mouth that seldom smiled. I resented him utterly. Resented most of all what he had just said to me. Words that were an affront and that I couldn't accept.

We'd reached the house and the cart came to a stop.

"I can't think of larger issues," I told him. "I can only think about getting away."

"Gretchen is frightened too. And so is Allegra. So think about yourself, but think about them too."

I didn't want to listen to any more. I jumped down from the cart without waiting for Jarrett's help, and ran toward the nearest door.

Susan Broderick stood in the doorway, waiting for me. She was in uniform again, and playing the proper maid.

"Mrs. Logan, Mr. Logan would like you to come to the library as soon as possible, please."

Alarm ran through me, but I managed to thank her and went into the shadowy coolness of the house. By this time I knew my way to the library, and I moved reluctantly down the hall, feeling totally unprepared for an immediate interview with my husband.

At the doorway I hesitated, looking into the big, slightly gloomy room. Ross sat at a long refectory table at the far end. The only light came from a Tiffany lamp on the table. Behind him a Coromandel screen of lacquered black and gold formed a luminous backdrop. When he saw me he left his chair to come toward me quickly, and it was clear that all the earlier rage had gone out of him. But my own emotions couldn't shift so quickly, and though my immediate alarm lessened, I moved toward him stiffly.

"Sharon darling, we must talk," he said. "We haven't understood each other at all, have we?"

"I understood that you wanted me out of your sight. I was just going upstairs to pack and move into town. Perhaps I can stay at the Breakers for a while."

He put an arm around me and walked me to the leather couch, where he sat beside me. "I'm sorry I lost my temper. You'll have to get used to that at times. When I'm angry, everything pours out and I may say things I'm sorry for later. Listen to me, darling. The portrait of your mother will be taken down. And I'll put away that recording. Ysobel Hollis has nothing to do with us."

"I think she has everything to do with us. I realize now that I'm only here because I'm her daughter."

He put a hand against my face in the tender way I'd loved, and drew me close to him. "You're wrong to think that. Perhaps I did have my own foolish fantasy of revenge, but it's been played out now. It's over with—done. You are my young love, who has brought me more happiness than I've ever known. And I think you've loved me too."

All the old charm and tenderness were working and I felt his appeal. Yet a part of my mind stood away, distrusting and unaffected. I didn't believe anything he was saying, and I moved so that I could sit apart, so that his hands couldn't weave their caressing spell.

"I don't know," I said.

"You don't know what?"

I faltered in my uncertainty. "I mean I'm not sure of anything right now. Cruelty frightens me."

"Cruelty? Oh, come now, Sharon. I'm hardly a cruel man. Am I being cruel now?"

"I don't know," I repeated. "I really don't know. Not only because of what has happened between us, but also because of what you're doing to your mother and to Gretchen."

He stood up against the rich golds of the Coromandel screen, impatient with me again. "Don't you think that I must be allowed to judge what is best for my mother?"

"I can't help feeling the way I do," I said. "I believe your judgment is wrong on this. I had a chance to talk with Allegra today. She can be perfectly normal and sensible. Quite wise, really. What happened that one time shouldn't be held against her. If she came back to live in her own rooms, she might improve."

I sensed a sudden wariness in him. "She might also improve if she were placed in the care of a resident expert in mental illness."

"She would only be put on drugs and she could become really senile then. Why not give her a chance here first? You could always send her away later. Is this too much to ask?"

I knew we were playing a game. If Ross had reason to fear the knowledge Allegra possessed, the issue was not where he sent her, but how he stopped her from talking. As with Brett, in that mention in the letters. I wondered if Brett knew the same thing Allegra claimed to know.

"I'll think about it," he said. "But now let's talk about Gretchen and Vasily. There is a great deal about her husband that she doesn't know. For instance, that he was married for a couple of years to an actress named Elberta Sheldon. In London. Oh, they were divorced, all right. The records show that, but it's a little matter he hasn't told Gretchen about. I know, because I asked her this afternoon. He's an adventurer of the worst sort. He was still married to this woman when he met Gretchen, but he got out of his marriage pretty quickly when better prospects came into view."

"I think Gretchen looks at him realistically, whatever he's done," I said, feeling that nothing I learned about Vasily would surprise me.

"She's a baby! He got out of Brussels just ahead of the law and changed his name. If he's sent back there he'll be arrested and tried, and probably put in prison.

So I have him where I want him. I talked to him an hour ago and gave him a choice. He will either leave Gretchen at once, or I will have him sent back to Belgium. Gretchen will have to accept this and let him go."

For a moment I could only stare at Ross in dismay. "She'll hate you forever if you do this. Can't you see the effect on Gretchen? She knows about Brussels. Vasily has told her everything."

"He's an expert liar. I won't have you defending him."

"I'm only trying to keep you from injuring your daughter. And yourself, too, because I think you do love her. Ross, if Vasily is really no good, then let her find it out for herself. If you give her time, perhaps she'll be ready to leave him on her own. But if you do what you're planning, you'll lose her for good."

"I must be the judge of that."

There was nothing more to be said. "I'll go and pack," I told him. "I don't want to spend another night in this house."

At once he dropped to the couch beside me. "Now you're the one who is acting hastily. Most of the time you are a very mature young woman, and you try to think things through sensibly. So don't rush off in haste and regret it later."

He didn't understand anything about me, I thought. He had no idea of the way I'd been shattered, damaged as a woman, from the moment I had realized that it was Ysobel he was making love to, not me. He really believed that a few denials and apologies would now make everything all right. If I hadn't been so thoroughly spent by my own emotions, I might have stood my ground and opposed him further. But I couldn't fight him any longer right now.

"I'll stay for tonight," I said. "Perhaps I can think more clearly in the morning."

"Good." He was pleased over what he must regard

as the winning of a disagreement. He seemed to have no idea of how deep this went with me.

I stood up and he rose to hold me for a moment and kiss me warmly. "That's my girl. Let me take you out for dinner tonight. Let's get away from Poinciana and recapture what we had in Kyoto. It's still there, you know. Let it surface again."

I was already shaking my head before he had finished. "No, Ross, please. I want to spend some time alone. Let me have that before we talk again."

He let me go reluctantly and I went upstairs to my room. Susan Broderick was there, turning down my bed for the night. I told her I had a slight headache and would have supper here—something light. She was at once concerned and kind.

"I'll bring a tray up for you myself," she promised.

I undressed and drew on a long robe. Then I went out on the loggia to look at a sky that was taking on hints of sunset vermilion. As I stood there a flock of flamingos sailed past and as I watched the flight of exotic birds some of the tension went out of me.

Ross had been right, and so had Jarrett, even though I'd resented his words. I couldn't dismiss everything lightly, but I would wait and think about it, allow what had happened to fall into some sort of perspective.

When I heard sounds in my room, I returned, to find that not Susan, but her mother, had brought up my tray.

"Mr. Logan asked me to look in on you and see if there is anything you wish," Mrs. Broderick told me. "He's concerned that you aren't feeling well, Mrs. Logan."

I sensed a disapproval behind her words that she couldn't entirely hide.

"I'll be fine," I said. "Thank you for bringing me a tray."

She sat it upon a table she pulled near the loggia doors, where I could sit and watch the sunset.

When I'd finished my light meal I went outside by

the loggia steps and crossed the lawn to sit on the wall beside the lake. My thoughts had quieted to some extent, but I was only holding away the time of decision, of taking a stand. Nothing could ever be the same again between Ross and me. The simple element of trust was gone, and no matter what he claimed, I would doubt him from now on.

What Jarrett had said about my usefulness here seemed unreal. Even if there was anything I could do for Gretchen or Allegra, I would be of little use to anyone until I could mend myself.

As I sat there on the wall, Brewster, Keith's dog, came trotting over to examine my presence. Jarrett's son followed him and sat beside me, his legs dangling toward the water. They were undemanding company. The boy told me that Brewster had been named for a gardener at Poinciana, whom Keith had liked.

"I want to be an air pilot when I grow up," he went on. "I want to go everywhere. Like you. Dad told me you've lived in all sorts of countries. What was it like?"

So simple a question, and one so difficult to answer. What would seem strange and different to this young boy had been everyday to me. Alps on the horizon were commonplace, and so was the sight of Big Ben across the Thames. I knew the Paris Métro well, and I had once stayed in a castle on the Rhine.

I tried to tell him a little about all this, tried to make it amusing. As I related a funny story about a concierge in Paris, I heard myself laugh, and realized that it was not only Ross who had lacked a sense of humor lately.

Boy and dog were good for me. Before the afterglow was gone from the sky, they walked me back to the steps and then ran off toward their cottage. I felt more relaxed than I had all day.

Inside, I bolted the loggia doors, locked my hall door, and got ready for bed. All the while, those letters to Ysobel seemed to burn in my consciousness—their physical presence in this room a further threat to me.

Not because Ross had written them, but because secret malice had brought them to me.

There was no key to Ross's room and nothing I could do about that. I was enormously tired, physically and emotionally. In the morning perhaps I could face what had to be faced.

Fortunately, sleep came easily that night, in spite of the early hour, and at first I slept soundly. There were dreams and in the hours after midnight they grew disturbing. But they were gone in a flash when I awoke to a dreadful sound of disaster.

An alarm bell was ringing wildly, clamoring all through the house. I sat up against my pillow, stiff with fright, and listened to that horrible, shattering sound that seemed never to end. A glance at my watch told me that it was two-fifteen in the morning. I rolled out of bed and pulled on my robe, ran through the door into Ross's room. It was empty and his bed had not been slept in.

Chapter 11

I ran into the empty corridor and rushed toward the nearest stairs. In this vast house a dozen people must be moving about, summoned by the clamor, yet corridors and rooms seemed ominously empty. As though only I could hear that terrible, shrilling alarm.

It was coming, I realized, from the direction of the art gallery at the other end of the house. When I reached the lower hall, I saw light from the offices cutting through an open door, and I ran past Myra's desk into Ross's office. He was there, and so was Jarrett Nichols, but if either of them heard that terrible ringing, they gave no sign.

Ross, fully dressed, lay slumped across his desk, while Jarrett, in a terry robe, stood beside him, a sheet of notepaper in his hand. He stared at me as I came into the room, and I had never seen him look so desperately grim.

"I just found him." As he spoke, Jarrett thrust the sheet of paper beneath an engagement book on Ross's desk. "Sharon, I'm afraid he's gone. I'm going to try mouth-to-mouth. Help me get him out of that chair."

Together we managed to lower Ross to the floor. I was too numb and unbelieving to do anything but what I was told. Jarrett scribbled a number on a pad and handed it to me.

"Call this doctor," he ordered, and knelt beside Ross's prostrate body.

I hardly knew what I was doing as I dialed the number. And all the while the hideous clamor of the alarm bell seemed to go on and on. Then, just as a sleepy voice answered on the line, the sound stopped with an abruptness that left the silence ringing.

Since I was using Ross Logan's name, there was no question but that the doctor would come as soon as he could get here. I set the phone down just as Jarrett looked up at me.

"It's no use," he said. "He's gone." He rose and went to Ross's desk, where papers lay scattered.

Still numb with shock, I knelt beside my husband and touched his shoulder, half expecting him to respond to me. His expression was contorted, as though he had died in a moment of great distress. Only a short while ago I had loved this man, depended upon him, and trusted him. Yet during the last days, even the last hours, all that had gone out of me, and kneeling here beside him, I could feel nothing. It was only numbness, of course. Feeling would come later—a sense of loss and sorrow.

Jarrett had begun to gather and stack the papers across which Ross had fallen. "Before the police come," he said.

I echoed the word dully. "Police?"

"He died unattended. The doctor will report this."

"Then should you touch his desk? Won't the police want everything left as it was?"

He paid no attention, but took an empty folder from a drawer, thrust the stack of papers into it.

"Remember," he said, "you know nothing about these."

I came to life a little. "I don't understand. Why are you putting Ross's papers away?"

"It's only for the time being. I can't explain everything now, Sharon. It's too complicated. I'll tell you later."

"Tell me now. Tell me what happened to Ross."

Without answering, Jarrett went to the phone, and a moment later he was talking to the police. Next he telephoned the gatehouse and spoke to the guard who was posted there. When he'd questioned him about the alarm, he explained that Mr. Logan had had an accident.

"Why did the alarm go off?" I asked when he hung up.

"They don't seem to know. Sit down, Sharon—you're looking shaky."

He was clearly shaken himself, for all his control, and when I didn't move he picked up the folder of papers and carried it into his own office.

Almost without thought, I went to the desk and drew out the sheet I'd seen Jarrett slip beneath Ross's engagement book. Something was wrong here, and I had to know what it was. I could tell as I folded it into the pocket of my robe that the note was on Poinciana notepaper. There was no time to examine it, however, before Jarrett was back.

"Gretchen must be told," he said. "This shouldn't be done by phone, but I can't send you, Sharon."

"I'll go," I said. "I can manage."

There was no need. Even as I spoke, Gretchen burst into the office, still in pajamas, a gown clutched about her.

"What's happening?" she demanded. "The alarm woke me and I went down to the gallery. But no one was there, so I turned it off and came along here."

"It's your father, Gretchen," Jarrett said.

She looked at him, and then at me, saw the direction of my eyes, and came around the desk. Her cry was one of true anguish as she dropped to the floor and tried to rouse him, calling to him, pleading for him to answer.

Jarrett raised her gently and took her to a chair. "You have to face this, Gretchen. We've called Dr. Lorrimer, and the police as well. And I've notified the gatehouse. They don't know who set off the alarm. Guards are searching the grounds now. Shall I phone your rooms for Vasily to come?"

Gretchen stared at him blankly, emotion draining out of her. "Vasily's not there. He must not have come to bed at all last night." She broke off, trying to get herself in hand. "Tell me what happened."

I still wanted to know that myself, and I sat down beside Gretchen.

"Your father called me on the phone just a short time ago and asked me to come here at once," Jarrett said. "He told me it couldn't wait until morning. So I came as fast as I could—and found him slumped across his desk. I'd barely stepped into the office when the alarm started. Sharon heard the ringing and came. She called the doctor, while I tried to revive him. I don't know what happened, Gretchen. He may have felt a heart attack coming on when he phoned me. He was upset about something."

Gretchen started to speak, and he stopped her.

"Before anyone comes—is there anything you know about this?"

A strange question to ask, I thought, as I saw her bristle.

"What should I know? You're the one who upset him badly with that row you had. You and—and *her*. He's had nothing but pain and disappointment from Sharon!"

That hadn't been the way she had talked to me about her father in the library. But now she was growing excited.

"He's had too much from both of you! And I'm going to tell the doctor that. Believe me, I am!"

Jarrett answered her quietly. "You'll need to get yourself in hand, Gretchen, before anyone comes. You know as well as I do how explosive anything that's said here now can be. It won't help if you fly off with wild charges. What we need to know is the truth. If there is something you know about this, you'd better tell us now. About what shocked him and brought on this attack."

She shrank into her chair, her anger evaporating. "I don't know anything about it. How should I?"

I wondered uneasily about Jarrett's insistent probing. Was she trying to protect Vasily in some way by accusing us? Her husband—who had every reason to quarrel with Ross—would be in the clear if we were to blame. Now, at least, the detectives would be called off from their investigation of Vasily, and he would no longer be held to a grim bargain by Ross Logan.

Jarrett went to the coffee maker in a corner of the office and brought us each a cup of hot coffee. I warmed my hands around the china cup, wondering if the chill would ever go out of me. Nothing would ever be the same again. Not for me, not for Gretchen, or even for Jarrett. Allegra would be saved from the fate that had awaited her. Strange that Ross's death should bring hope to so many people. But I couldn't deal with that now. I couldn't even assimilate the fact that he was dead. At any moment he would surely open his eyes and take up his life as the strong, dynamic man we had all known. It was he who should be giving orders in this crisis, not any of us.

The sheet of notepaper seemed to burn in my pocket, but I dared not take it out and examine it, though I had a strong feeling that it would tell me something—something that ought to be known, and which Jarrett had instinctively tried to hide.

As though the intensity of my thoughts touched him, he set down his cup and went casually to Ross's desk, where he moved the engagement book an inch or two. I saw him freeze for an instant. Then he looked directly at me. I stared back, willing myself not to let my eyes falter, while unspoken accusations leapt between us.

Gretchen suddenly began to cry. She wept like a child—wildly and with abandon, and I wished that I could cry in the same way. During the last few days I had seemed to weep easily and often. Yet now, when there was terrible cause, no tears came.

Jarrett let her cry. He left the desk to stand before me. "Give it to me," he said softly. "It doesn't concern you."

Once more, I managed to meet his eyes. "I will not," I told him.

The gray, shaken look was still upon him. "Be careful of the damage you may do," he told me. "It will be better for everyone if you burn that note without reading it."

Were these Ross's last words that burned in my pocket? What damning things might he have written? But I didn't know yet what I would do with the note—except that I couldn't do as Jarrett asked. It was time for the terrible secrets that had haunted this house to come into the open. That one thing I knew.

"I wonder why Mrs. Broderick isn't here?" I asked. "She should have heard the alarm, like the rest of us."

Gretchen looked up woefully. "She left last evening with Susan to visit a sister in Boca Raton. She told me they would come home today."

For the first time I missed the presence of Ross's efficient housekeeper. But at least others of the staff were about, including the reliable Albert, who had chauffeured me only yesterday afternoon. He came in, bringing with him the doctor—a slightly stooped, elderly man, with an air of authority. Ross would have had his personal physician for a long time, and he would be the best.

Dr. Lorrimer began his examination at once, and a few moments later the local police arrived. In charge was Lieutenant Hillis, a quiet, youngish man, with sandy hair that had begun to thin. He was clearly respectful of these august surroundings, yet hardly awed by them. I sensed a strength in him that would probably get results without any barking of orders.

He explained that it would be necessary to ask a few questions of those present. Dr. Lorrimer informed him with an air of complete assurance that the cause of death was heart failure, making his findings very clear. Undoubtedly he was aware that no questions must be left hanging for police or press to pick up. His patient had had heart difficulties for years, he pointed out. He had been warned repeatedly that he must avoid disturbing emotions, avoid any overtaxing of his strength. Apparently he had driven himself hard last night, working past midnight without rest. The expected penalty had at last been exacted. All this was news to me. Not once had Ross mentioned any trouble with his heart.

Gretchen had stopped crying and sat curled up in her chair, her legs under her, and I knew she listened intently to every word. As we all did. Because of so many guilty secrets? I wondered. I was sure that Jarrett and Gretchen did not believe that Ross's death had come about so simply as Dr. Lorrimer claimed, though not one of us was going to dispute his words. In spite of her threat that she would blame Jarrett and me for upsetting her father, Gretchen said nothing now.

Lieutenant Hillis informed us of what would happen. An autopsy would be performed, after which the body would be released to the family.

Jarrett nodded. "It's better that no questions about Mr. Logan's death be left unanswered. May Mrs. Karl and Mrs. Logan go back to bed? I'll stay as long as you need me."

The lieutenant agreed readily. There would be time later in the day for more questions, if they seemed necessary.

Dr. Lorrimer had been watching Gretchen, and he

spoke to her gently. "I'll see you up to your room now and give you something to help you sleep. You mustn't stay alone at this time. Where is your husband?"

Before she could answer, the telephone rang shrilly and Jarrett picked it up. His reply was curt. "Don't let anyone past the gates. Tell them I'll come out and make a statement shortly."

The press, of course, I thought. The media! This would be no quiet, private death. The news line of the world would hum furiously for days, weeks, and we would be given no peace unless Jarrett set up the barricades.

Before the doctor could repeat his question about Gretchen's husband, Vasily himself appeared in the doorway, pausing a moment to take us all in before he went to his wife. He looked properly grave and regretful, and had apparently heard what had happened. However, I was beginning to know him a little by this time, and I suspected that he could barely conceal the mood of elation surging up inside him. It was there in the very spring of his step, in the brightness of his eyes. Vasily would always think first of himself.

"Darling," he said. "This is all too terrible. I came as soon as I heard."

She sprang from her chair and let herself be folded into his arms. I noticed that she didn't demand to know where he had been.

"Good," Dr. Lorrimer said. "I'll go with you to your bedroom and give her something to help her sleep. You must stay with her now, Mr. Karl." Then he turned to me. "Are you all right, Mrs. Logan? Would you like—?"

I reassured him quickly. "I have a prescription I can take if I need it." After all, I had been through two deaths recently. I was well prepared, wasn't I?

He gave me a slightly doubtful look, as though he feared some delayed reaction in me, and I spoke again quietly.

"I really am all right." It was strange how calm I

could manage to be, and a little frightening. Had I lost all ability to feel?

Gretchen glanced at me with eyes that were faintly accusing before she allowed Vasily and the doctor to help her from the room. More than anything else, I was aware of Jarrett's stillness as he watched them go—a stillness that covered whatever he was thinking.

No one asked aloud the question that must have been in Gretchen's mind, as well as in Jarrett's and mine. Where had Vasily been, and how had he heard what had happened? Apparently, since everything seemed clear cut and settled about Ross's death, this was not a question that Lieutenant Hillis had any need to ask.

But even as it stirred in the silence of our minds, Vasily came back to us through Myra's empty office.

"I should have explained," he said quickly. "I have been in Allegra Logan's company all evening. When I went to see her earlier, I found her very much upset. So I stayed until the nurse got her to sleep. It must have been nearly two in the morning, and afterwards I dozed in her living room for a while, lest she waken and be upset again. I heard the alarm go off, of course, and I was awake when one of the guards came to tell us what had happened. I instructed Miss Cox to say nothing to Allegra until a member of the family could tell her. Then I came straight to the house."

He looked from Jarrett to me as though his words carried some barely hidden triumph, and then hurried after his wife and the doctor. No one said anything.

The medical examiner and further police entourage were arriving, and Jarrett came over to me.

"You needn't stay for any of this. Let me take you up to your room."

The last thing I wanted was to be alone with Jarrett Nichols. Not until I knew the contents of that note. He looked quite capable of taking it from me by force if he chose.

I jumped to my feet with a suddenness that caused

Lieutenant Hillis to stare at me. "I just want to be by myself!" I cried. "I know the way to my room!"

I ran into the hall, and heard Jarrett coming after me. One of the guards had posted himself near the door to the offices, and I rushed up to him.

"Please take me upstairs. Mr. Nichols has to stay with the police, and—and I feel a little dizzy."

He was the man called Steve, who was usually posted in the gallery. He showed quick concern. "Of course, Mrs. Logan. I'll get her upstairs all right, Mr. Nichols. And I'll call one of the maids to come and stay with her. Everyone's up by now."

Jarrett nodded grimly and went back to Ross's office. I clung gratefully to Steve's arm, discovering that I really did feel uncertain about where I put my feet. On the way I thought of one question to ask.

"Were you in the gallery when the alarm went off?"

"Yes, Mrs. Logan. This was my night to be on duty. When it rang, I ran through the gallery and out the far door. I didn't even stop to turn off the alarm, because searching at once was more important. But I couldn't find anyone."

When we reached my room, I refused to let him call a maid, thanked him, and sent him away.

Safely inside, I went through the now familiar ritual of checking and locking my doors. After a moment of hesitation, I went through Ross's room and locked his door to the corridor as well. Ysobel watched me, smiling warmly from her place on the wall. Before I returned to my room, I stood for a moment looking up at her.

"I don't know who has won, or who has lost," I told her.

Back in my room, with the connecting door closed, I dropped onto the chaise longue and stretched out. The lamp beside me gave light for reading, and there was just one thing I must do at this moment.

I unfolded the notepaper I had thrust into my pocket and saw that it had been typed, and then signed with one of Gretchen's curious little signature faces. This one displayed zigzagged teeth—the sign, Ross had told me, that indicated displeasure or bad news. There were only a few lines.

> Dad:
> If you send Vasily away, I will tell Jarrett what I know about you and Pam.

That was all, but it had clearly been enough. Ross must have read the note and reacted with a heart attack that had killed him. Yet he had first summoned Jarrett, and perhaps we would never know why. He had been working alone over papers that Jarrett had not wanted the police to see. Had he actually meant to show Jarrett the note from Gretchen and perhaps discount it? Or had he felt the attack coming on, called for help, and then been overcome before Jarrett could get there? He must have fallen across his desk with the note from Gretchen close at hand, and Jarrett had found it.

No wonder he had looked so shaken when I'd walked in. No wonder he had thrust the note out of sight, meaning to retrieve it later, and had been so deeply disturbed to discover that I had taken it from its hiding place. Now I remembered with more understanding that moment in the belvedere when Gretchen had torn up a picture of Pam. If she knew something about her father and Jarrett's wife, then Pam must have been a sore subject with her, and when I praised the picture, she had reacted by tearing it up.

This note, certainly, was something that must be kept private at all costs, so Jarrett needn't worry about what I would do with it. Somehow, the typed words gave me no sense of shock concerning Ross. There had been previous hints now and then about Pam, though I'd never paid much attention to them. I had no doubt that Ross would have gone after any woman who appealed to him, regardless of whether she was the wife of a man he needed and trusted above all others.

A man he dared not lose?

That was the point, wasn't it? That Jarrett must not know? Yet how could he not have known? He was anything but obtuse, anything but trusting and simple, and he had grown up the hard way, subjected to the harshness of life at an early age. Even more important now were Gretchen's actions. Surely she must guess that her note had brought on her father's heart attack—which would account for Jarrett's earnest questioning of her, and also for her defensive accusations against Jarrett and me. She might have been stirring up a smoke screen.

A sudden knocking brought me up from the chaise longue in dismay. The knock sounded again, and I had to respond.

"Who is it?"

"It's Jarrett," he said. "I must talk to you, Sharon."

I couldn't face him now. Not with this knowledge about his wife so newly in my hands. "No," I said. "Not any more tonight. I'll talk with you in the morning. You needn't worry—I won't do anything. You can have the note back then."

"I'm sorry," he insisted, "but it's necessary for us to talk. Not only about Gretchen's note. In the morning everything will explode around here. I've made a statement, shut off the phones, but tomorrow the world will move in on us. We have to talk together *now*. You are Mrs. Ross Logan. You have responsibilities."

I pulled my robe more closely about me, feeling not only the chill of this Florida night, but the coldness inside me, the coldness of fears that were all too ready to possess me. I took several deep breaths to steady myself and went to unlock the door.

Jarrett came into the room, looking even more weary and grim. But not beaten. At least he would be here for all of us to depend upon. And as Ross had trusted him, so must I. Until I had good reason not to. I gestured him toward a chair and went back to the chaise longue, drawing a crocheted throw over me. I felt utterly, achingly tired, yet far from ready to sleep.

He ignored the easy chair I'd motioned him toward, and pulled a straight desk chair around, to sit astride of it, his arms resting on its back as he faced me.

"I've read Gretchen's note," I said. "I can't blame her for trying to save Vasily by accusing us. But she must know now that her note is what shocked her father into a heart attack. That will be a heavy load for her to carry."

"I didn't come here to talk about that. Except to ask you to burn the note."

I shook my head listlessly. "Not yet. Perhaps I'll give it back to Gretchen."

"To punish her?"

I wasn't sure about that. I wasn't sure about anything.

He looked at me long and steadily, and I was reminded somehow of a boxer who was still in the ring. Perhaps it was his slightly crooked nose, that might once have been broken when he was young, that made me think of a pugilist—and that stubborn chin.

"What I want to talk about," he went on, "concerns the papers Ross was working on, and which I put into a folder and locked in a drawer in my own office. You were concerned that I seemed to be concealing something. I am. And I want your promise to say nothing about this."

"How can I give you a promise when I don't understand what I'm promising?"

"That's why I'm here now. To explain a little. It's very complex, both in the ramifications and in the reasons that lie behind what Ross was trying to do. He wanted to keep me from finding out, because he knew I'd oppose him. But he couldn't get away with that. It was Yakata, the man who came here from Tokyo to see him, and whom Ross went to meet in Palm Beach yesterday, who gave things away. I began to suspect, so

I searched for the evidence. Because what he intended has to be stopped without any publicity."

"What do you mean?"

"It was nothing illegal, but certainly something that would let down the best interests of the United States. Japan needs oil. So do we. Ross would have seen to it that millions of barrels needed here would go into the hands of an element in Japan that would profit from it mightily. So would Meridian Oil. Not the government of Japan, but a few sleazy businessmen there who are interested only in profit."

"But there'd have been an enormous scandal when it came out. And it would have to come out, wouldn't it?"

"I don't know. Not for a while. I'd have kept it quiet if I could."

I had enough strength left for indignation. "To protect Ross?"

"No. I told you it was a complex matter. If the stock of Meridian Oil plunged, it would mean not only catastrophe for the charitable foundations—not all of which are self-sustaining—and a collapse of all the good they do, but disaster for millions of stockholders as well."

"Stockholders!" I put scorn into the words.

"Don't be stupid, Sharon. Stockholders aren't only corporations, some of which might go under with disastrous results. They are also people—*individuals*—who have invested their money, trusted in the integrity of Meridian Oil. There are times when the truth can cause more havoc than it mends."

As might have happened if Jarrett had faced the truth about his wife and Ross Logan? I wondered.

"Perhaps there are times when the truth ought to come first," I said grimly.

"I wish I knew how to make that simple choice, Sharon." There seemed no sarcasm in his words, but only weariness and a deep sorrow.

"Ross must have known that he had a great deal to lose if this came out," I said.

"He was ready to gamble. He fooled himself into thinking he could handle anything that happened and ride it through. That he was powerful enough to do as he pleased."

"And wasn't he?"

"That was his delusion. Allegra could tell you. She understood. Oh, not about this deal, but about what he was trying to prove. It was always the same thing. He wanted to show that he was as powerful and clever a man in his own right as Charles Maynard Logan had ever been."

"But—but that's childish," I protested. "Ross *was* a great man."

"Deep-seated motives often go back to the child in us. Any psychiatrist can tell you that. A great many of the world's problems come straight from the childish self-delusions of men in power. You've only to look at history. You've only to listen to the screaming of today's headlines. The madness, the ferocity, the crying out for vengeance. By men. This is the way that wars are started. The child in such men can be enormously dangerous."

"What will happen now?"

"None of this will come out, if we choose to keep it quiet. It hasn't gone far enough yet. Yakata and his pals must be told that the deal is off. They have no legitimate hold on Meridian, and I can take care of this myself. It's not something that's been brought up before the board. Ross was acting in a completely clandestine way. By the time anyone could have tried to stop him, the whole thing would have been too far along to be halted without an even bigger scandal. That's why he was trying to keep it from me. That's why he was working late hours to accomplish what he needed to do before I could take any action to oppose him."

"He was trying to prove something to you, too." I didn't put it as a question. I was beginning to understand just a little the love-hate relationship that must have existed on both sides between Ross Logan and Jarrett Nichols. Ross would have needed him desperately in all sorts of ways, yet how bitterly he must have resented such a needing. Jarrett was no ordinary aide-de-camp. All too often he must have been the brain behind whatever was accomplished, and that was the weight Ross had been trying so recklessly to escape. His growing compulsion to prove himself—evident in his life with me too—had begun to verge on the unbalanced.

"Perhaps he was stopped just in time," I said, and felt chilled by the sound of my own words. As though Ross had been *deliberately* stopped. I went on quickly, veering away from implications I didn't want to make. "I mean for his own sake, as well as everyone else's. What might have happened if he'd lived could have been worse than anything he dreamed of. Or are we being callous? About Ross's death, and about something called truth?"

Jarrett shook his head. "Only realistic. It's tragic to have to recognize how many people will be saved by what has happened to Ross."

Myself among them, I thought, and winced at the silent admission. There was a great deal I was going to have to examine inside myself in the coming weeks.

"You can count on me," I said at last, and my voice was empty of emotion.

Jarrett didn't leave at once. Instead, he sat staring at me with so searching a look that I closed my eyes. I didn't want him to see all those things that I wasn't yet ready to face in myself.

"You'll be all right," he said with strange conviction, and started for the door.

The ringing of the telephone stopped him. I got up to answer it, and found that my legs were no longer shaky.

It was the nurse, Miss Cox, on the line. "I've been trying to reach Mr. Nichols. But no one seems to know where he is, so I'm calling you. Mrs. Logan is awake and she's listening to the radio, as she sometimes does at night when she can't sleep. News programs. I'm afraid..."

I broke in. "Mr. Nichols is here now. We'll come right down and talk to her. I don't think we should disturb Mrs. Karl. Try to distract her until we get there."

"Allegra?" Jarrett asked as I hung up.

"Yes. She's awake, and Coxie is afraid of what she may hear on the radio."

"I'll take care of it," Jarrett said. "You needn't come."

I was already getting a coat from the closet, flinging it on over my robe and gown, thrusting my feet into shoes. "I can't sleep anyway, and perhaps I can help."

Some of the tension seemed to leave him and he smiled wryly as he held out a hand. "Thank God Ross married *you,*" he said.

I wasn't sure whether I could agree to this sentiment, but I took his hand, accepting his strength, and let him pull me along as we hurried through the house. Outside, the golf cart stood beside the door, and I climbed into the seat beside Jarrett. The sound of its starting seemed to shatter the night, and a guard came running toward us. Jarrett waved to the man, and we went off toward Coral Cottage, shortcutting across the lawn. The cart had been equipped with head lamps, and there was no difficulty about finding our way in the dark.

Coxie came to the cottage door, a vast relief on her face. "You're just in time! I couldn't keep her away from the radio any longer."

We went into the bedroom together, to find that Allegra was sitting up, dwarfed by the huge pillows around her, her face looking almost young and eager in the softened light. She greeted us with lucidity, and I sighed in relief. It would be too hard to get through to her if she were living in the past again.

She reached out with a thin, still graceful hand and switched off the radio. "You've taken your time about getting here," she said. "Ross is dead, and I've been waiting for someone to come and tell me what happened."

I could hear the catch in Jarrett's breath. "We didn't want you to hear it that way. We hoped you'd sleep straight through the night. The moment we knew you were awake, we came."

"Thank you. Though I thought it might be Gretchen. But I expect she's having a bad time right now. His dying will make everything easier for her, but she loved him a great deal. I suppose I loved him too. Once. At least, I loved the little boy and young man he used to be. I haven't loved the man he became for a long while."

For just an instant I felt an unfamiliar sympathy for Ross. Then I remembered what he'd been doing to Allegra, and I pulled a chair close to her bed.

Surprisingly, she reached out to pat my hand and then looked up at Jarrett.

"I wish you had been my son. You'd have been worthy of Charlie. Tell me whatever you can."

Jarrett explained that Ross had had a heart attack, and that there were police formalities, which would soon be over. Then the funeral could be arranged for.

"Keep it private," Allegra said.

Jarrett agreed. "Of course. As far as we can. That will suit you, won't it, Sharon?"

I could only nod, remembering that it had been Ross who had taken the details of that other terrible funeral out of my hands. Now others would help me again, but I would be expected to make decisions. Or would I? Gretchen must be consulted tomorrow. Today. It was really her wishes and Allegra's that must be considered. I didn't even know if I had any wishes.

We stayed with her for a little while until she grew weary and let us go. Then we returned to the cart.

"She's a marvel," Jarrett said. "That was a lot easier than I ever expected. I might have known that she can still come to grips with reality when she has to. And when she's not being drugged."

We rode back toward the house, where lights still

burned aplenty. As we passed the spreading shadow of the great banyan tree, a slimmer shadow detached itself and came toward us. Jarrett braked the car, and in its lights Brett Inness emerged. She wore slacks and a jacket, and for once her hair was not wound in a knot on top of her head, but hung to her shoulders, caught back by a clasp.

Jarrett switched off the motor. "Hello, Brett. You've heard what has happened?"

"Yes." In the bright shock of intense light all color seemed to have been washed from her face. "There was a news broadcast that I heard because I couldn't sleep."

How few of us seemed to have slept through this night.

"How did you get in?" Jarrett asked.

She seemed to draw herself up with a touch of that hauteur she could assume so well, and she ignored me completely. "Why shouldn't I come? He was my husband once, and Gretchen's father. It's possible that she may need me now."

"I merely asked *how* you got in," Jarrett said. "Guards have been placed at every entrance—even the beach tunnel."

"Of course. But I do have a key, and the guards were given orders by Gretchen long ago to let me in whenever I pleased to come. You know I've visited Allegra often."

Jarrett nodded, but I sensed his suspicion toward this woman and her motives. "Why tonight? Gretchen will have been sedated by now. What can you do?"

She seemed suddenly forlorn and lonely, standing there, and I remembered that all this had belonged to her, as Ross's wife. And she was still, as she'd said, Gretchen's mother.

I spoke for the first time. "You may want to be with Gretchen in the morning. You're welcome to spend the rest of the night at Poinciana. Can we take you up to the house?"

"Thank you," she said with dignity. "I'll walk. I can certainly find my way."

Jarrett gave me a long look, but he had nothing more to say, and we went on toward the house. I was aware of a lightening of the sky out over the Atlantic. Dawn was not far away. When we stopped, Jarrett came around to help me down from the cart, and he still looked quizzical and a little surprised.

"What will happen to me now?" I asked, the momentary authority I'd assumed with Brett already dissolving. "Where will I go? I don't know where I belong any more."

"That will be up to you, won't it?" Jarrett said. "You took charge quite capably just now. So of course that's what you'll continue to do."

I shook my head wearily as we went in through a side door. "I'm not in charge of anything."

"Of course you are. You're mistress of Poinciana now. Ross left it all to you. I've seen his will."

Once more, my knees betrayed me, and Jarrett steadied me with his arm. His words had shocked me, and I couldn't absorb their full meaning at once. This was something I'd never thought about at all. Ross *was* Poinciana.

Jarrett helped me up the stairs to my room and came in for a moment to make sure I'd be all right. The sometimes hard, life-weathered look was gone from his face, and his eyes were kind.

"When you came here," he said, "I took it for granted that you'd married what Ross Logan stood for, and all that he could give you. I know I was hard on you in my judgment. Now I can understand better that you were frightened and needed to be looked after."

I let Jarrett help me off with my coat. "I know what you thought. You never troubled to hide it."

"I'm sorry. But I think you'll manage now, though it won't be easy. Get to bed, Sharon. You're tired enough to sleep. I'm almost that tired myself. Don't think about anything. It can all wait until much later today."

He let himself out the door, and I felt grateful to him, as I'd never felt before. Grateful for his talking to me so honestly. Grateful because he had let me glimpse his own torment and moments of not being sure. He would help me if he could. And I would need all the help I could get. There were those in this house who had hated me—and now that might be even worse.

Soon the sun would be up, but I must sleep now and do as Jarrett had said—think about nothing.

At once as my head touched the pillow, I thought of Ross, and felt a pang of loss for something I'd never really had. And something of sorrow for him, too, because all that he'd been, the good and the bad, had come so suddenly to an end.

I thought curiously as well of Brett Inness. How long had she been on Poinciana grounds? Had she come here, perhaps, before Ross had died? And I thought of Gretchen's note. For the first time, I questioned it. Had she really written it? Was it even possible that someone else had copied her simple method of note writing? Perhaps someone who wanted to hide behind Gretchen might have done that very thing. But such suppositions were beyond me now.

When sleep caught me, I went out completely, and I heard nothing at all for a good many hours into the new day.

Chapter 12

It was all over. The ceremonies, the eulogy, the funeral, the visiting relatives—a few of them still in the house. Ross's "close" friends had been there—though I think he had been close to very few. For a "private" affair, it had seemed distastefully large to me. The press members who had been allowed to attend had been issued only the most carefully worded statements.

This hardly stopped the media from clamoring for more details concerning Ross's death, and as often happens in such cases, unpleasant rumors and speculation began to circulate, appearing in the sleazier journals. Everything was brought to me, on Jarrett's orders, though I read little of what was printed.

Allegra had appeared for some of the ritual, a proud and fragile lady, who could not be wholly grief-stricken over the death of her son, yet put up a very good front. Coxie hovered in attendance, watching her charge, but

Allegra, free of "pills," performed admirably and with great self-possession. Whenever she was present, Jarrett kept watchfully close.

There had been a lavish buffet luncheon afterwards, which had been a strain for me to endure. It all seemed a sham to me, a ritual to be observed, though the signs of true grief, of deep regret for Ross's passing were few. I resented this more for Gretchen's sake than for my own. Of those who thronged the house, her mourning was the most genuine, even though in her, too, it must have been laced with relief.

Vasily stayed by her side every moment, making an effort to be properly solemn for the occasion, but now and then allowing elation to break through to the surface and gleam in his eyes.

Jarrett kept his distance where I was concerned. Those early-morning hours of revelation between us had slipped into a hazy past, and we'd spoken impersonally whenever we met. I had no idea what he was thinking and I wasn't sure now of what his function was, or mine, or exactly what our relationship should be. There was an unspoken understanding that he would go on as before for the time being, and that at the appropriate moment we would talk and sort a few things out.

By the time I could escape from the social part of the day, it was nearly evening, and I had come here to the gloom of the library, where sunset light touched the windows. I had come here to try to put some sense into the confusion and disorder of my thoughts.

Beside me, the tape recorder played "Blue Champagne," and Ysobel's voice filled the empty cavern of the room. I played this song of hers deliberately, allowing my emotions free rein. I had gone back every step of the way, trying to understand, trying to find answers. My life had lost its simplicity even before Ross's death, and with the making of his will he had plunged me into complications that I had no idea how to handle.

If only he had left Poinciana to Gretchen, instead of

to me. Perhaps he would have done so, if she hadn't married Vasily. This was her punishment—Ross still reaching out to hurt her from his grave. He had left Gretchen even more wealthy than she was, Jarrett told me—something she cared little about—but he had not given her what she wanted most: Poinciana. Nor had he left her his shares in Meridian Oil. Those, as well as a sizable fortune, came into my hands. Everything, of course, wisely invested, giving me an income that was big enough to support the estate, and do anything I wished besides—even after the enormous inheritance taxes. It all seemed completely unreal and beyond my comprehension.

There was only one stipulation. Poinciana was to be mine for as long as I chose to live here and care for it. Otherwise, it would go to Gretchen. Or it would go to her if she outlived me. My first impulse was to walk away from the burden, and I told Jarrett so. He had said, "Wait. Don't do anything hasty. If it goes to Gretchen now, it also goes to Vasily Karl. *Her* will leaves everything to him—in defiance of her father, of course. I see no reason why she might change this, now that Ross is gone. Vasily will see to that."

Other reasons were developing to keep me from walking away. There was still the question of the note, purportedly from Gretchen, but which anyone could have forged—and which had surely been the cause of Ross's heart attack. I had not yet confronted Gretchen with the existence of that note, but I must do so soon. It would be difficult to talk to her, because she was blaming me quite vocally for Ross's death. Though not to the police. I was the one who had so wickedly shocked and upset her father, she kept pointing out. By this time, she was brushing past the earlier quarrel with Jarrett that she'd included in her first accusations. *I* was the one, and she was ready to tell this to all who would listen. I'd felt a little sorry for bewildered friends and distant relatives, who were not yet sure of my position in the house, and reluctant to offend Gretchen by befriending me.

The sound of Ysobel's voice on the tape broke into my thoughts insistently, and I knew that one unhappy problem, at least, had been ended. I would never again be made love to because I was Ysobel Hollis's daughter. The need to leave Ross was gone. He had escaped from us all, and from his own torments that he had tried to conceal.

Already Brett Inness came and went about the house as she pleased, and I could only regret my earlier generosity. Gretchen had told her about the will, and she too resented the leaving of Poinciana to Ross's present wife. She and Gretchen had clearly allied themselves against me.

The gossip columns were not ignoring us. The hint had appeared of some serious quarrel between Ross and me shortly before his death, and I could guess that Brett was its possible source. Such columns would be only too ready to pounce upon anything connected with Ross Logan. Fortunately, there were those in powerful places who had stepped in to play down rumors that might affect the stability of Meridian Oil, though no one cared very much what I might be feeling.

Except for Jarrett. He saw what was happening. "You can put Gretchen and Vasily out of the house, if you like," he told me curtly. "It's up to you. There's nothing that says Gretchen and her husband are entitled to live here. And you don't have to take Brett's presence at all."

Put Gretchen out of her own home? Forbid her the comfort of seeing her mother in her own surroundings? I wasn't tough enough for that, but I must certainly have a talk with Gretchen as soon as she could be persuaded to listen to me. I wanted to know whether she had really written the note Jarrett had found in Ross's possession at the time of his death. If she had, it might account for her desperate effort at self-delusion by placing the blame elsewhere.

The song on the tape came to an end, and the recorder turned itself off. The big room, with its Coromandel screen darkened now in the gloom, seemed more forbidding than ever. Once this library had been the courtroom to which Ross brought those who displeased him, and from which he issued his judgments and punishments. I had stood for arraignment here. Now it was only an empty shell of a room, yet I had chosen it to flee to in order to judge myself.

Behind me, someone opened the door and tiptoed in. "Mrs. Logan? Are you here?" The voice was Myra Ritter's.

"I'm here," I said, and she came to stand before me.

For once she was formally dressed in a dark frock, suitable for the occasion, though I'd seen plenty of floral prints at both church and cemetery. Myra had heard the radio early the morning of Ross's death, and she had wasted no time in coming to Poinciana and making herself useful. If I sometimes had the faint impression that she was part of the audience at a dramatic and entertaining play for which she had a box seat, I could forgive her that. So what if she was interested and involved with all that happened at Poinciana, when she had no great life of her own? This was a vicarious thrill for her, and I suspected that her one regret was that she hadn't been present when it had happened.

She had run errands, given advice, whether asked for or not, answered hundreds of telephone calls with skill and diplomacy, and served us all tea when our spirits faltered. Even Mrs. Broderick, shocked almost to the point of tears—but not quite—had found her useful.

Now Myra dropped into a chair opposite mine and kicked off her high-heeled shoes, sighing with relief. "Back to flats tomorrow," she said. "How are you feeling? Is there anything I can get you?"

"Nothing," I said. "Thank you for all you've done, Myra. I just wanted to escape from everyone for a little while. Are the guests thinning out by this time?"

"Mostly. They've been asking for you to pay their courtesies before leaving, but you're supposed to collapse in private grief now, so that lets you off the hook. Though I'm not sure how many in this house have done any grieving. I mean besides you and Mrs. Karl, of course."

She lay back in her chair and wiggled her toes, sighing again with pleasure.

There was no need to answer her, and pretty soon she would go away. Or else she would come around to the real purpose behind this visit.

"I found out something pretty shocking today," she said at last.

I thought I was past all surprises, and I said nothing. Gossip was not something I wanted to encourage in Jarrett's secretary. Though it was hard to discourage in the face of her open enjoyment in other people's affairs.

"Did you know that Brett Inness isn't Mrs. Karl's real mother?" she asked.

That brought me up in my chair. "I don't know what you're talking about."

"Mrs. Karl was having a row with her mother this afternoon after the funeral. Mr. Karl and I were there and we stepped out of the room because it was getting embarrassing. He was upset, and that's when he told me."

"He told you *what?*"

She shrugged. "He can get pretty emotional and Russian at times, and he blurted out that Mrs. Karl isn't Miss Inness's natural daughter. I wasn't to tell anyone—and of course I won't. The newspapers would love this."

"So why are you telling me?"

Again the shrug. My question didn't seem to disturb her. "You're family. Maybe I'd like to keep my job here. Maybe I can be useful at times, and it's not Mrs. Karl now who can get me fired."

At least she was direct and down-to-earth. I suspected that she was quite ready to tell me more of whatever she had picked up, but I didn't want it to come from her. What she had revealed might furnish a strong clue to Gretchen's behavior, and I would need to think about it.

"Mr. Karl was right," I said. "There are things that shouldn't be talked about. It's more important now than ever, since almost anything can be blown out of proportion."

Reluctantly, she wiggled her toes for a last time and put on her pumps. "You can count on me. If the time comes when you need a social secretary, you might consider me," she said, and slipped out of the room as quietly as she had entered.

After a moment I roused myself to follow. I didn't know what to do with the information that had been given me, except to bleed a little for Gretchen. An adoptive mother could be as loved and loving as a natural one, if she behaved like a mother. But I wondered if Brett ever had.

Upstairs, I stood before the long mirror that hung on my bathroom door. "What am I to do?" I asked the woman in the glass. She had no more idea of the answer than I did, and she looked as helpless and ineffectual as I felt.

With an effort, I straightened my shoulders. I could remember that strengthening moment only a few days ago when I had made a stand against the things that beset me. But now I knew less than ever what to struggle against, or what I really wanted—except to get away from Poinciana. Everything here threatened me, and if there had been animosity toward me before, it must be a hundredfold greater now. With Gretchen as the source?

Aimlessly, I went outside to stand at one of the arches of the loggia. In the fading light, Jarrett Nichols walked among leaning palm trees. As he approached the house, he raised his head to see me standing there above him. At once he came to the foot of the steps.

"May I come up?"

"I don't mind," I said. The words sounded ungracious, but I seemed to have no desires left in one direction or another.

He climbed the steps and drew up a chair for me, then dropped into one beside it.

"You carried it off very well today," he told me.

"No—I only sleepwalked. I didn't know what I was doing half the time."

"Then your performance deserves all the more credit. You're tired now. A night's sleep will help."

He was tired again too. I could hear it in his voice. Much more strain and responsibility had rested on him than on the rest of us, and I wished I knew how to thank him properly. But, for all his sympathetic words, something in him that seemed forbidding held me off.

There were a hundred questions I needed to ask, but this wasn't the time and I had no heart for them, any more than he was likely to have heart for the answers. Anyway, there was just one question everything boiled down to: *What am I to do?* I had asked it of him before, and it was still too futile to be repeated. I thought dully of Myra and her disturbing news.

"I've just learned that Brett Inness isn't Gretchen's real mother," I said.

Jarrett was silent for a moment, looking no more or less somber than before. "Who told you that?"

"Your secretary. Vasily apparently spilled this out to Myra at a time when he was upset because Brett and Gretchen were quarreling. She could hardly wait to come and tell me, though I don't think she was being malicious about it."

"I'll speak to Myra. That was pretty idiotic of Vasily."

"Have you always known?"

"Not until I'd been with Ross for a couple of years. It's hardly common knowledge."

"Why hasn't it come out?"

"That's a long story. I suppose you might as well know—though I'm not sure it serves any good purpose now. I understand that Gretchen's real mother was a young woman who worked here. A girl whom Ross took a fancy to while he was married to Brett. Neither of his wives had given him a child, and he wanted a son. So when he knew the girl was going to have a baby, he made secret arrangements. Brett had no choice. He sent her away, and then brought her back with the child when the time was right. Unfortunately for him, it was a daughter. Brett had to accept her, while the real mother was sent to some distant state with a sizable payoff if she would never return. She hasn't been heard from since. Allegra knew, but no one else until I was told."

"Has Gretchen always known?"

Jarrett shook his head. "I think she should have been told early, so that she could grow up with the facts. But she was fifteen when Brett lost her temper one day and told her the truth—rather scornfully. She couldn't even offer Gretchen the solace of having been deliberately chosen, as most adopted children are. And it was never enough that Ross was her real father. I suppose Gretchen had spent her childhood trying to win Brett's affection, never understanding why she was rejected. Oddly enough, after she knew, Gretchen and Brett became better friends, and they could plot together against Ross when it suited them."

When it came to rejection by a mother, I had more in common with Ross's daughter than I'd dreamed, I thought wearily. Even though I'd been the child of both my parents, Ysobel and Brett had felt alike about their daughters. Yet while this might have given us a basis for some understanding at least—by willing Poinciana to me, Ross had made Gretchen my mortal enemy. I turned away from so painful a subject.

"How is Allegra?" I asked.

"She's magnificent. It's good to see her taking a stand with Coxie and telling *her* what to do for a change. Just the same, she's frailer than she believes, and all this has been a strain for her."

"Tomorrow I'll find out whether she wants to move back into the house."

He brightened a little as he stood up. "I'd hoped you would do that. You'll be here to look out for her now. I suppose I should offer you my formal resignation in the next few days."

My alarm was complete and so shattering that it astonished me. He smiled as he put out a steadying hand.

"Hey—don't look like that! Your ship isn't sinking. Of course I want to stay. I *need* to stay. But I had to give you the chance to make a choice."

"There isn't any choice. I'm the one who has to think about leaving."

His hand tightened on my arm and he pulled me up from my chair almost roughly. "Not yet, Sharon. There's a lot you need to do before you go running away."

He could still make me angry. There was at least that much emotion left in me. I pulled away from his hand, no longer shaky.

"*I* will decide what *I* want to do," I said.

"That's the spirit! It's time you started telling a few of us off. Sleep well—tomorrow is a day of battle."

He grinned at me wickedly and went down the steps to the lawn. I was still feeling outraged, but my anger died as I watched him walk off toward his cottage. There was that new weariness in the set of his shoulders, in the slowness of movements that were usually brisk and assured.

These last days must have been terrible for him. I thought of the note that linked the wife he'd loved with the man he had served so long and loyally. How had he lived with this ambivalence toward Ross and kept his sanity? Jarrett was never a man to be pitied, yet there was a welling up in me of sorrow for him as I went back to my room. A sorrow I could do nothing about, because he, of all people, would accept sympathy from no one.

I didn't want to go to bed. Sleep was something far away, for all my weariness. I longed for some distraction to occupy my too active mind. As I sat there, I could not control the pictures that insisted on unrolling. Sharpest of all was my memory of Ross slumped across his desk, with all the vitality that had been so much a part of him gone forever. I could weep for him now. Weep for him, not as my husband, but as a man who had suffered and been struck down in a moment of shock and anger. In a sense, he had been destroyed by a few typed words on paper. All of this, however, was more than I could face right now.

In the end, I was left with just one thought in my mind—one phrase that played itself over and over. The words Jarrett had spoken before he left.

Tomorrow is a day of battle.

Since when must I become a warrior? Since when must I stand and fight? Yet I knew that tomorrow this would have to be done, and that sooner or later, I had better put on my armor.

Chapter 13

The battle began early in the morning, when Gretchen sent for me right after breakfast.

She waited in the Japanese room, and Vasily was with her. The moment I went through the door I knew by her look and manner that she considered herself the rightful mistress of Poinciana. A few mere facts of law would change nothing in the mind of Ross's daughter. Her purpose was clear and uncomplicated—to drive me out. Once all the workings of the law had been performed and the will probated, the house would revert to her if I decided to move away. I couldn't help but feel that this would be a greater justice than Ross had done in leaving it to me.

Except for Vasily. He was still the question mark that Jarrett had raised. Was I willing to have it all wind up in his hands? As Gretchen's husband, his influence would be very strong. While I had no wish to see him parted from his wife, as Ross had been so determined to have happen, there were still uncertainties that troubled me. His past was a little too checkered, to say the least. It might be easier for me to turn Poinciana over to Gretchen and leave at once, but I still had an obligation to Ross, and perhaps even to Gretchen herself, that I couldn't sidestep. Even though Gretchen wanted me gone, and would do what she could to make life at Poinciana uncomfortable for me, I must stay for now. Later, perhaps I could let her have it, and get away.

When I walked in, Vasily was standing at a tall window, where morning sun streamed in to light his fair hair. Gretchen sat at the desk that had been Allegra's, tapping irritably on its surface with a pencil.

"Good morning," I said, including them both.

Vasily sprang to fetch me a chair, placing it on the other side of the desk from his wife.

"You look more rested," he said. "You've slept well?"

That didn't bear talking about, and I gave my attention to Gretchen. She scowled at me with no greeting.

"What have you done with my father's manuscript?" she demanded, going straight into her attack.

Such a challenge was the last thing I expected. "I don't know what you're talking about."

"Of course you do. He always kept everything right here in this desk. The manuscript and the photographs I did for his book were always here, and they're not now. Neither are Dad's receipts and vouchers that he kept on every item he purchased for the collection. Only the record book that you started is here. So what have you done with the rest?"

Her small face, with its pointed chin, and its frame of dark hair, looked more pugnacious than ever this morning, and I didn't know how to deal with her attack. I hadn't thought about the netsuke since Ross's death.

"I haven't been in this room for days," I told her.

"I haven't even thought about the collection, or about Ross's manuscript."

"Of course you're lying," she said. "Why?"

Vasily made a small, placating sound, but she waved him aside.

"I'm not very good at lying," I said evenly. "Surely these things will turn up. Your father must have put them somewhere else himself. In one of his safes, perhaps?"

She ran both hands through the mop of short, straight hair. "Don't talk nonsense! I've already searched and they're not anywhere. They make a big package, along with the pages he'd done and my glossy prints. So they should be found easily. But why would you want to hide them?"

"I haven't hidden anything. If you want me to help you look, I will."

Perhaps something in my face, in my tone of voice, began to get through to her, and for the first time she looked faintly shaken in her conviction.

"Then why are these things gone? Who would take them?"

I could only shake my head. The whole thing seemed unimportant in the face of all else that was wrong at the moment.

"Why is it so urgent to find the manuscript right now?" I asked.

"It's urgent because I want to work on it. It's something I can do for my father. It's the only thing I can do for him. I could have done the cataloguing. I know all about his collection. I've worked with him, making those photographs, and he's told me about every item in this room. Now the book must be finished and published under his name, as he wished."

I could recognize and understand her intense need to be close to her father and preserve his work. In a sense, she could keep him alive by throwing herself into this project. In a situation where nothing could be done, she could find consolation in performing a task closely connected with her father. While I was still in London, I had helped to instigate the publishing of a new collection of Ysobel's songs—that would have pleased both her and Ian—and Ross had thrown himself into helping me. I realized now that we'd been doing exactly what Gretchen was trying to do now. And I would help her all I could, if only she would let me.

"This is a fine idea," I said. "Of course it should be carried out, and you're the one to do it. Perhaps we can look through his office and his bedroom and see if we can find where he put the package."

"I've looked," she said.

This was a dead end for the moment, and I let it go. I had come downstairs armed with something else that must now be dealt with.

"I've been wanting to talk to you," I went on. "There was one item that was held back from the police after Ross's death. It's something that might have so upset your father that it could have brought on his attack. Jarrett felt that it should not be given out because of all the ramifications."

I placed before her the note typed on Poinciana stationery and signed with one of the little faces she had adopted as her signature.

She read the few lines, and a flush came into her face. "You'd better explain," she said.

"I thought you might be able to explain. Jarrett found this in your father's possession when he reached his office that night in response to Ross's call and found him dead."

Vasily had come to stand behind Gretchen's chair, and he read the note over her shoulder. "What is this? What does it mean?"

"I think," I told them carefully, "it means that someone was threatening him. Perhaps with blackmail, or for vengeance. Perhaps to frighten him into taking some action, or not taking some action. Someone knew, or pretended to know, something that would have caused the loss of Jarrett's services if he was told."

Gretchen stared at the sheet of paper. "This was typed on my machine. I can recognize that crooked *w*. And someone has copied the silly way I sometimes sign my notes. But I didn't write this. I would never have threatened my father—no matter what I suspected."

"Not even if it could have stopped him from sending Vasily away?"

I half expected outrage at my words, but she answered me openly. "I might have tried. I meant to try. But not this way. Besides, it's foolish. Dad wouldn't have been afraid of anything like this. Jarrett already knew about Pam and my father. I think he was trying to decide what to do at the time Pam died in the car accident. Afterwards, it didn't matter enough any more, when there were so many big issues to keep him here." Gretchen looked at Vasily. "What do you think?"

He didn't touch the sheet of paper, but he leaned forward to read the words again. "Your mother?" he said to Gretchen.

"Maybe. I'll show it to her."

"I'd rather do that myself," I said, and picked the note up to slip it into the handbag I'd brought downstairs with me.

Gretchen made no effort to stop me. "Why would Brett try anything like that?" She was still speaking to Vasily. "It's too silly. Too weak."

"Perhaps not," he said. "Brett was here on the grounds that night. She was here in the house."

I caught him up on that. "When? At what time?" This was the question I should have asked Brett myself, when Jarrett and I came upon her that night.

Vasily shrugged delicately and returned to stand beside the window. Either he didn't know, or he didn't mean to say.

"There's no reason why my mother would do this," Gretchen said to me. "Dad paid her a lot of alimony. He even loaned her money to start her shop. Indirectly, that is. She didn't know for a while that it came from him. Anyway, he would never have given her a cent more for anything—let alone blackmail."

"On the day before your father died," I said, "I found some letters that had been left on my dressing table. In one of them—"

"Oh, so you read them? I thought you would."

"Was it you who put them there?"

"Of course. Vasily didn't want me to. He thought I was being too mean to you and—"

Her husband broke in. "I felt that you were really on our side, Sharon. I saw no reason to try to hurt you."

"But I *wanted* to hurt you!" Gretchen cried. "And that was a good way, wasn't it? All those drippy letters Dad wrote to Ysobel Hollis!" She turned back to me. "I wasn't sure you'd read them, but I hoped you'd see that he never loved *you.*"

"I didn't read them." Somehow I managed to speak quietly. "I only read a snatch here and there, to see what they were. But when I came to one that mentioned Brett's name, I did read that part. Ross wrote my mother that he held some sort of weapon over Brett's head. In case she became a threat to him. Apparently you didn't read the letters yourself."

"Of course not—except to see what they were. But Brett knew about them. He was writing to Ysobel even while they were married. She knew that Ysobel used to send them back to him, and that he kept them in his bedroom safe. So one time when he was away, she took them. She said they might be useful sometime. Anyway, I thought it a good idea to give them to you now."

"Then your mother would have known that Ross might call in that note he held any time he chose?"

"Of course she knew that. She found out quickly enough, but she never tried to do anything about it. What could she do, except hope that he wouldn't call it in before she was ready?"

I didn't speak aloud the thought in my mind—that Brett Inness might have come to see Ross in those early-morning hours in order to threaten him. Yet if, as Gretchen believed, this note hardly made a strong enough threat, then this theory was probably wrong. I let it go for now.

"There's something else I've wanted to consult you about," I said. "Do you think your grandmother would like to be moved back into her own rooms at Poinciana? Do you think we should ask her?"

Gretchen's face could take on the look of a small, impudent monkey when she grinned. "Of course she would. I've already thought about that and discussed it with Brett. It isn't up to you. She's *my* grandmother."

I had been properly snubbed, and I could feel a flush rise in my cheeks. Gretchen was right. It wasn't up to me to make arrangements of this sort, even though I was supposed to be the owner of Poinciana. Yet it was important to my own sense of justice that I make the effort first.

Vasily turned from the window. "My wife has only been *thinking* of doing this. I believe it would be a fine thing if you two could act together in this matter. Allegra knows that Poinciana has been left to you, Sharon, and not to my wife. There are certain courtesies that should be considered, and it would be more reassuring to her if you approached her together."

To my astonishment, Gretchen threw her husband a wildly angry look, burst into tears, and ran out of the room. He made no effort to follow her, but took her place across the desk from me.

"You must forgive my wife. Her father's will has hurt her deeply. She is feeling very bitter against you at the moment. I hope this will pass. You will not send her away from Poinciana?"

"Of course not," I said. "This is her home. Much more than it can ever be mine."

"Then perhaps you will not choose to go on living here, now that your husband is dead?"

Somehow, I thought, I was being maneuvered with

these soft, apparently kindly words, and I stiffened a little. "I'm not sure what I will do."

He smiled at me, and if it hadn't been for that faintly lifted eyebrow, I might have been inclined to trust him more than I wanted to. He was a surprisingly compelling man, but that scar reminded me of too many things.

"Last week," I said, "Ross told me that Gretchen knows about your former marriage."

"Of course." He remained unabashed. "Oh, perhaps I should have told her sooner than I did. But my wife has a temper, and I wanted to make her happy first. Then I knew she wouldn't care so much about the past. Now she understands that my previous marriage had already ended before I met her. When her father brought it up, it only made her angry with him, and anger is an ugly emotion. Don't you agree, Sharon?"

As I stared at him helplessly, he reached across the desk to touch my hand. "There has been too much anger and ugliness under this roof. I hope we may all live together amicably now. I suggest that you speak with Gretchen when she is calm again. Persuade her to let you accompany her when Allegra Logan is invited to return to this house. This would be a good thing for all of you."

I could almost believe in his effort toward peacemaking. Almost, but not quite. Because Vasily Karl's motives were never clear, and I was never exactly sure what he was after. He had a talent for being on everybody's side. Whether I would do as he asked, I didn't know, and I drew my hand from beneath his, resisting the charming way in which I was being manipulated.

Instead of answering, I asked another question. "What do you think about my husband's manuscript and Gretchen's photographs disappearing?"

He seemed to consider my words solemnly, closing his eyes as though he consulted some inner muse. When he opened them he wore a quizzical look.

"If I were you, I would check very carefully to see

whether any of the netsuke collection should prove to be missing. Now, if you will excuse me, I shall go and look for my wife. By this time she will be feeling regretful over her outburst. She loses her temper quickly, but fortunately, she also recovers just as quickly."

He stood up, gave me his quick little formal bow, and went out the door. I sat where I was, thinking about his words. That was very good advice—to check the netsuke collection to see if any items were missing. Except for one thing. Without the manuscript, the photographs, the invoices, nothing could be checked. Or at least only that portion of the collection that I had already catalogued could be tallied. Which, of course, could be the reason why these things had disappeared—the reason Vasily was pointing out to me. I found the thought disturbing, and I didn't want to accept it.

Nevertheless, I went to the shelves of tiny carvings and stood looking at them, trying to remember. But I hadn't gone far enough with my listing. I had examined with care only those I had listed for Ross.

Last time there had been a hullabaloo about two missing netsuke, but they had turned up in Allegra's possession. A thought that gave me no comfort now, because Allegra herself had probably not put them there. The netsuke thief was still operating, and Ross was no longer here to know what had been taken.

Idly, I picked up a carved brown ball, hardly bigger than a marble. A tiny rat was cunningly curled around itself in the wood. Every detail was perfect—ears, lacquered black eyes, sharp teeth and claws, a broad tail held amusingly in one paw. One hind foot was scratching an ear. When I turned the piece over, I could see the characters of the sculptor's name etched on the bottom beside the curving tail. Strange to think that this small item might be worth several thousand dollars. Such a sum would mean little to Gretchen, but it might represent a fortune to someone who needed money, and could see it multiply in such tiny, easily taken objects. Where would one dispose of such things?

Who would have the sophistication and knowledgeable background to find a market for them?

I wondered, too, how large an allowance Vasily was given. Had he amusements, indulgences that were expensive and of which Gretchen might not be fully aware? Or might want to discourage? How disarmingly innocent he would seem in suggesting to me what would become obvious soon anyway—that some of the netsuke could be missing.

But I didn't want to think this. I didn't want to believe that Vasily would steal from Poinciana. To some extent, he had won me.

I put the carving aside and picked up Allegra's favorite, the Sleeping Mermaid. Perhaps this could be given to her now, as Ross had given it long ago, and on second thought had taken it back. It might please her to own it, and this was a small thing I could do for her. But not yet. It didn't belong to me yet, and I mustn't tamper with the collection until it was really mine.

How still the house seemed with all the commotion of the last few days quieted. How empty of everything except its memories. Strange how strongly I could feel Ross's presence in this room. I could see him clearly at the desk where he had worked, almost hear his voice admonishing me. An odd little quiver went through me, and I recognized in distress that it was once more a feeling of relief. But how could one feel relief over a death? This was a totally unacceptable emotion.

"Mrs. Logan?" a voice reached me, and I turned to find Mrs. Broderick in the doorway, looking more worried than I had ever seen her.

"Has something happened?" I asked.

"I've been looking for Mrs. Karl. She would know what to do. No one has told me—we weren't prepared—

"I'm sorry," I said. "I don't understand. Perhaps I can help?"

A look which doubted that flicked across her face.

To Mrs. Broderick too, Gretchen was the real mistress of Poinciana.

"Mrs. Allegra is moving in upstairs," she continued reluctantly. "But her rooms aren't ready. I was not told this would be happening. When I tried to object—"

I broke in, smiling. "But that's wonderful! She's taken things into her own hands at last. Mrs. Karl and I were thinking of arranging for this, but she's a whole move ahead of us."

"Mrs. Allegra is not the same person she used to be," Mrs. Broderick said, thoroughly disapproving. "Mr. Logan would not have allowed this to happen."

"*I* will allow it," I said, keeping my tone pleasant. "Let's go upstairs and see what we can do to make her comfortable."

The emotions that crossed Mrs. Broderick's usually passive face made me smile again. I could read them so clearly: *That I had no right to give orders in this house. That Ross Logan's wishes were still to be obeyed. That if anyone made changes, it should be Gretchen Karl.*

"Come along, please," I said. "We'll need you to see to the new arrangements."

There was nothing else for her to do, and she followed me upstairs, stiffly forbidding and displeased, but not yet in open rebellion. I felt astonished that I had been able to give an order and have it obeyed. That she was still trying to tell me something, and that I wasn't listening, didn't come home to me until later.

Chapter 14

When we reached the upper hall, Mrs. Broderick tried to speak to me again. "Mrs. Logan, there is something you should know—"

Unfortunately, I still didn't listen. I had the bit between my teeth, and short of open rebellion, I knew now that she would do as I said. Which gave me a heady feeling. I was delighted that Allegra had taken action herself and returned to the home where she belonged.

Aware that I was paying no attention to her, Mrs. Broderick gave up and opened the suite's bedroom door, stepping aside, every inch of her exuding disapproval.

I burst into the bedroom, eager to show my pleasure—and stopped in surprise, barely across the sill. Brett Inness was unpacking a suitcase on the bed, and behind me Mrs. Broderick made a further clucking sound of disparagement. She would have told me, if I'd given her a chance.

Brett glanced around in mild surprise at my abrupt entrance. She looked as elegant as ever, in a light pull-over and pants of saffron silk. There were gold bangles on her bare, tanned arms, and a gold skewer thrust through the knot on top of her head.

"Hello," she said. "I decided that no more time should be wasted, and that I would do as Gretchen wishes. So I've brought Allegra back to her own home."

I could find no words of response. Near a window, Allegra sat in her own small rocker, still dressed in robe and slippers, looking bewildered and ill at ease. Her inner disturbance was evident in the trembling of her lips.

I went to her and took her hands in mine. "Are we rushing you too much? I meant to come down to your cottage this morning and ask if you would like to move into these rooms again."

"Of course she wants to move into them!" Brett said. "Don't you, darling? Look now—I'm putting your toilet things in the bathroom, where you can find them. Coxie is packing everything else for you at the cottage. I've sent Albert to bring up your suitcases. You needn't lift a finger."

Allegra's bewilderment hurt me. "Tell me," I said, ignoring Brett, "what do you really want to do?"

"I—I'm not sure," she managed. "Brett and Gretchen want me to do this, I know. But I'd gotten used to the cottage. I could get outside so easily down there. Now there are stairs."

"You must stay exactly where you wish to stay," I told her. "I think we've all been in too much of a hurry to have you do what we believed you'd want. It's time we asked you."

"I'm tired right now," she said. "Perhaps I could lie down on one of those beds for a little while?"

"Of course. Let me help you."

"I'll get her into bed," Brett said. "I'm used to this."

She turned down one of the spreads with its yellow sprinkling of buds, and came to help Allegra out of her robe. In a moment the old lady was snug beneath a light quilt, her eyes closing with weariness. Brett put a finger to her lips and nodded toward the adjoining parlor. I went in ahead of her, and she left the bedroom door ajar, dropping onto the long oyster-colored sofa before an empty fireplace. Mrs. Broderick followed us.

"You can go, Broderick," Brett said. "You can fuss about the rooms later."

"Yes, madam." Mrs. Broderick had long been accustomed to taking orders from Brett Inness, and she went out the door, her back still stiff, but with less open disapproval than she'd shown me.

"She's going to be hard to handle with Ross gone," Brett said cheerfully. "You'll never manage her. But I expect Gretchen will take her down a notch or two. Broderick's been spoiled because Ross has been here so little and she's become rather a tyrant in the house."

I said nothing. Both outrage and alarm were warring inside me. Outrage at the audacity of this woman, and alarm because I was beginning to doubt whether I could handle any of what was happening.

"I'm glad of this opportunity," Brett said. "We need to talk. I think you're probably right that we've rushed poor Allegra into a move she wasn't prepared for. The old like what they're accustomed to, and we should have thought of that. Of course she must come back to the house. But we haven't been altogether sensitive to her wishes."

I wanted to say, "*You* haven't been sensitive," but not speaking at all seemed the best defensive weapon I could use. I hadn't seen Brett since the funeral—to which she'd come with the air of belonging, even returning to the house with Gretchen afterwards. And she had been much more at home with family and friends than I could be, since I was the suspect stranger who had probably married Ross for his money.

"There's something I've wanted to ask you," she went on, undisturbed by my silence. "Have you decided yet whether you will move out of Poinciana? I'm sure this can't be the pleasantest place in the world for you now, and it would seem wise to leave."

In the face of such arrogance, I found my voice. "Since it's going to belong to me, I expect I will stay." That might not be true, but I had no intention of raising her hopes, or Gretchen's. Not until a number of things had been cleared up could I make a decision about Poinciana.

"Oh, dear!" I heard the mock distress in her voice. "Gretchen has been so sure that you won't want to stay."

"I don't want to. But I have a few obligations. To Ross, first of all. He wanted me here. I'm not sure of his reasons, but I expect I'll learn about them."

"The only reason is because he was angry with Gretchen and made impulsive changes in his will. Given time, he'd have come to his senses."

"You mean as soon as he got rid of Vasily?"

"Oh, Gretchen would have got around him on that. Ross really adored her, you know. However, there's something else I've wanted to consult you about. My daughter can be obstinate at times. Her current attitude is to pretend that you don't exist, no matter what Ross's will may say. She needs to accept reality more gracefully."

Brett paused to take a cigarette from her bag, lighting it with an initialed gold cylinder. Her every move was one of calm and graceful assurance. Or, as I had thought before—arrogance. She was far more suited to being mistress of Poinciana than either Gretchen or I, and I resented her with all my heart, knowing that Ross's wishes would be on my side in this at least. Nevertheless, I felt ineffectual in the face of such poise and self-confidence. I'd once been able to assume just such a manner of aplomb, but with me it had always been a screen, hiding the uncertainty that lurked underneath. With Brett, it was the real thing, grown from years of nurturing, and it intimidated me more than a little, much as I wanted to stand up to her.

When she had taken a puff or two, she went on, still unconcerned by my rigid silence. "Gretchen has invited me to live here again. My apartment in town has become rather much to keep up when I must give my time to my work. Also she rather depends on me in a number of ways. Vasily is charming and loving, but his advice isn't always wise. I hope you will have no objection. I can be of some help to my daughter."

I made a slight movement of indecision, but before I could speak, she went on quickly. For the first time I wondered if her self-confidence, too, might be partly bluff. Was everyone fooling everyone else?

"Gretchen, of course, had no business issuing such an invitation to me. You and I both know that, but I hope you'll forgive her." Brett's smile suggested that she and I were women of the world, and could solve our differences amicably. "I can only do this with your permission, naturally. My rooms would be in Gretchen's wing of the house, and she'll want, in any case, to open up one of the downstairs rooms for our dining. Your path and mine would hardly need to cross, and you would have all the solitary time you wish in which to decide what you'd really like to do with your life. The world is your oyster now." A slight acerbity crept into the last words, belying the cordiality.

I reminded myself that the world was no longer Brett Inness's oyster, and that she wouldn't be human if resentments against me didn't go deep. I remembered Ross's letter to Ysobel concerning the note he held for Brett, and which he'd hinted he might use against her. I thought, too, of how she must have come to hate him. Had she hated him enough to forge a letter from her daughter in order to shock him into taking some move that she wanted him to take? Such as returning her note?

She was waiting for my answer, batting away cigarette smoke with a gesture not entirely controlled. There were perhaps chinks in an armor I'd thought altogether attack-proof.

"I don't know if this would work out well," I said a bit stiffly. "I'd like to discuss it with Gretchen first. Of course, she may decide that *she* wants to live elsewhere."

"You'd better not count on that." The slightly acid smile appeared again. "Anyway, there's no need for hostility between us, is there? We're not likely to be chums, but we can behave in a civilized manner."

Implying that if I gave her a negative answer, I was hardly civilized? How badly did she need money? I wondered, and thought of the letter again, folded in my bag. I took it out and handed it to her.

She read the words with no show of emotion and gave it back. "You mean this was sent to Ross?"

"I don't know how it came to him, but it must have been one of the last things he read before he died. Gretchen says she didn't write it and never would have tried to hurt him that way."

"It does seem rather pointless, doesn't it? Something that happened more than two years ago. Whoever wrote it must have been naïve to think it could upset Ross at this late date. The fact of his affair with Pam Nichols would come as a surprise to no one. Not even Jarrett, I'm sure. And there are always those around whose job it is to protect the reputation of a man like Ross Logan."

She seemed entirely open and casual, unimpressed by the note, yet I sensed an inner stiffening. As though something that she kept from the surface disturbed her. Perhaps even frightened her. Why I received this sudden flash of insight, I didn't know, but something—for just an instant—told me that Brett Inness might indeed be far less calm and assured than she was pretending to be.

In the face of this sudden strong awareness, my own assurance began to revive. "Did you see Ross the night he died?" I asked.

Her hand with the cigarette moved nervously. "See him? Why should I see him? When I came to Poinciana

I always tried to avoid running into Ross. I'd hardly be likely to seek him out."

There was no way in which I could put pressure upon her to tell the truth—if she wasn't telling it—and this unpleasant interview had continued long enough. I went to the bedroom door and looked in. Allegra lay sleeping peacefully. Perhaps this bed would seem familiar to her when she awakened, and she would have a feeling of belonging again in Poinciana. If she decided to remain at the house, I would talk to Jarrett about having a stair seat installed that could take her up and down stairs easily.

Brett stood up as I returned to the room. "I must run. There's so much I need to do now. My shop has been neglected and I haven't worked at my designing board for days. Thank you, Sharon, for being so generous and understanding."

I had been neither, and I merely nodded. We left Allegra's suite together, to find Albert coming along the hall carrying a suitcase in each hand. Miss Cox trotted after him, her plump face tinged with pink in an effort to keep up. She didn't look in the least pleased with this move, which would probably interfere with her own authority, but she gave us each a careful smile, clearly uncertain as to where the source of real power lay.

I stopped to speak to her. "Mrs. Logan is asleep. She was very tired. When she wakes up, tell her we can solve the stair problem for her so she can get outside when she wishes."

The nurse nodded, directed a questioning look at Brett, and followed Albert down the hall. Brett hurried away from me, presumably to look for Gretchen. I would not be surprised if she moved into the house immediately, whether I granted permission or not. And without an ugly confrontation, there didn't seem to be much I could do about it.

I went on toward the branching corridor that led to my room, no longer certain of anything. That nothing was what it seemed to be was a recurring theme in this house, and I hated the confusion and uncertainty. I wanted only to believe and trust, yet such simple virtues seemed to have disappeared from my life.

Beside me, the wall appeared to move, and Keith Nichols popped out of the very woodwork. We stared at each other in surprise, as we had done that other time when I'd been with Ross and *trompe l'oeil* had deceived me.

"Hello," I said. "One of these days you must introduce me to some of Allegra's secret passages."

The apprehension in his eyes faded. "You mean you don't care if I come inside the house sometimes?"

"It's all right," I said, "if your father approves, and providing you don't touch anything you're not supposed to."

"Like the netsuke? I wouldn't do that. Not ever."

"Why did you think of the netsuke?"

"I don't know. I guess somebody said there were some more missing. Only Mrs. Allegra doesn't take them. I know she doesn't, because she's told me not to. They're awfully valuable, aren't they?"

"I believe they are. Is there someone you're looking for now?"

"Her. Mrs. Allegra. Albert said they'd moved her up to the house, and I wanted to visit her and see if she's all right."

His young face looked up at me with such open candor that I felt a certain relief. Keith, at least, could be taken exactly as he was—a small boy with an attachment for an old lady that was refreshing.

"She's asleep now," I said. "But perhaps you can come back later and talk to her. Only you can use the stairs nearest her room and not startle people by coming out of the wall."

"I was in there looking for something. Something Mrs. Allegra wants me to find. Only she doesn't remember exactly what it is, or where she put it. She thinks that she hid it somewhere in the house a long time ago. She said it was important. I was looking the other day too, when Mr. Logan brought you into the art gallery."

"You mean it was you who watched us through the door at the far end that day?"

"Sure. I know how to turn off the alarm. And I didn't let him catch me that time. But I didn't find anything there either."

I let the matter go. "Come back later," I repeated. "I know Mrs. Logan will like to see you. And will you do something for me when you come, Keith? Will you try to find out whether she really wants to stay here in this house, as Gretchen thinks she should?"

"She'll want to," Keith said with confidence. "After she moves things around in her head, she'll want to. She's always telling me about how wonderful the house is, and about those rooms she fixed for herself when she got pretty old."

I put a hand on his shoulder. "Thank you, Keith. You've just said something more sensible than anything the rest of us have come up with. I may want to use you as a counselor again sometime."

"Or a detective? There are a lot of mysteries around here, aren't there?"

"Indeed there are."

"Like how that alarm went off the night Mr. Logan had a heart attack?"

I answered carefully, suppressing any eagerness that might stop him. "Do you know anything about that?"

He looked pleased with himself. "That's not really a mystery, is it? Because Miss Inness turned it on. Didn't you know about that?"

I could only stare at him in astonishment. "Keith, why do you believe she turned it on?"

He wasn't ready to tell me that, however, and his gaze shifted to a point far down the hall. "Oh, I guess I just knew," he said, and ran off toward the stairs.

What was it I'd been thinking? That Keith, at least, was exactly the small boy he seemed? Ingenuous and believable? Only now it appeared that he had his secrets too. This would bear looking into, when I found a way to do it. Why would Brett, of all people, have turned on the alarm?

When I reached my room, the phone was ringing, and I picked it up, to hear Jarrett's voice.

"Are you all right?" he asked.

"I'm fine. But I have a lot of things to tell you."

"I thought you might. Would you care to come down to our cottage tonight and have dinner with Keith and me? We dine early, so six-thirty would be fine."

"I'd love to," I said, and when I put down the phone I felt better than I had all morning. Perhaps Jarrett Nichols was the one person in this house to whom I could talk openly. But what was I to do with my day that would be useful until it was time for dinner?

The answer came readily. I could look for Ross's missing manuscript and the photographs Gretchen had taken for his book. The obvious place to start was in his office, even though Gretchen claimed to have searched it thoroughly.

I went downstairs and found Myra working at her desk. Ross's door was closed, but Jarrett's office stood open and empty.

Myra caught the direction of my look. "Mr. Nichols has just gone out." Again she had discarded her casual slacks for a neat cotton dress—perhaps still being respectful to a proper atmosphere of mourning? Her smile was one of sympathy. "You look tired, Mrs. Logan."

I went directly to my purpose. "Mrs. Karl hasn't been able to find the manuscript my husband was working on, and I thought I might look through his office. It isn't locked, is it?"

"Nothing's locked except the safe." She left her desk and went to open the door for me. "Mrs. Karl was here earlier, but she wasn't able to find that manuscript herself."

"Then I probably won't find it either."

As she stepped aside, I went past her with a sense

of apprehension and stood looking around the big, handsome room. Nothing had changed about its impressive air of luxury, from black leather chairs and walnut desk to the Chinese carpet, bordered by polished parquetry. The last time I had stepped into Ross's office had been on that terrible night when I'd found him slumped across his desk, with Jarrett beside him. The memory was vivid in my mind, and I could almost hear the shrilling of that dreadful alarm.

Myra was still at my elbow. "I don't know if it's any help, Mrs. Logan, but on the same day that it happened, Mr. Logan brought his manuscript and those photos Mrs. Karl took, into his office and was working on them here. So perhaps he never put them back where he usually kept them."

"Did you tell Mrs. Karl that?"

"She didn't give me much chance," Myra said ruefully. "And probably it's no help anyway, since I don't know where he put them after that."

I hardly knew where to begin my search. The obvious starting place was Ross's desk, but I was sure it had been gone through carefully by this time, and not only by Gretchen. In any case, I was reluctant to touch Ross's desk at all. Memory was too vivid.

"Do you mind if I speak out of turn?" Myra asked.

"You don't usually wait for permission," I said, and she grinned.

"We're in the same boat, in a way, aren't we? Oh, I know you're the top lady of all this now, and I'm hardly a speck on the horizon. Just the same, we're both outsiders, aren't we? And I don't know what to do now, any more than you do."

As usual, she had penetrated through all the subterfuge. Perhaps it would be more useful to talk with Myra Ritter than to start what was sure to be a futile search.

"Why don't you sit down," she said, "and I'll fix us some coffee."

I sat in one of the big leather chairs and let her

minister to me, feeling oddly grateful. She remembered that I took my coffee black, and when she'd put a mug in my hands, she pulled another chair around and curled herself up in it, rather like a small cat.

"I suppose the main thing we have to remember," she said, "is not to let them railroad us into doing what we don't want to do."

"I don't feel that I'm being railroaded," I said. "I'm making my own choices, such as they are."

"That's what you think. But aren't you letting them make you stay at Poinciana, when all you want, really, is to get away?"

"How can you possibly think that?"

"Because it makes sense. I can put myself in your place. And if I were there, I'd get out so fast you wouldn't see me for smoke."

I sipped coffee and smiled at her. "That is what I want, and you're perfectly right. But it's not what I can do. There are responsibilities."

"For instance?" She was openly curious.

"My husband's will. He wanted me to stay here. He must have thought that it would be best for Poinciana in the long run."

"It's only a house."

"Nevertheless, it should be preserved. Perhaps turned into a museum, or a trust eventually. That is, if Mrs. Karl and her husband should decide not to live here. Or when Allegra Logan dies."

"So you'll hang on and be miserable here, when all that would probably come about anyway?"

I couldn't confide my uneasiness concerning Vasily Karl. I couldn't talk to her about the note that had been sent to Ross. I couldn't say, "Perhaps someone frightened my husband to death and I want to know who and why."

"I can understand," she said. "I know it must be hard to decide. I feel the same way. I mean, Mr. Nichols isn't going to stay here after everything's settled. His work is in New York and Washington. He only came here regularly because Mr. Logan insisted. But it's not very convenient to run everything from Florida. So I expect he'll take his little boy and leave before long."

The sinking feeling at the pit of my stomach was not wholly unexpected. I had felt this way when Jarrett spoke of resigning. The very thought of Poinciana without Jarrett Nichols here to depend upon gave me a shivery feeling, as though I'd suddenly stepped into a cold wind.

"Of course, I suppose you're his boss now," Myra went on, watching me shrewdly. "I suppose you could order him to stay, if you want."

"I couldn't do that."

She sighed. "I didn't think you would, but I had to find out. You see, what he does affects me. Oh, I think he'd take me along. I've worked for him pretty well. I like it here in Florida. I like my little apartment, and I don't want to leave. I suppose I can get another job here, but it won't be the same. I've enjoyed working for Mr. Nichols. Being at Poinciana has been like living in a play. So you see I have a dilemma too. Though it's not on the same level as yours."

I remembered her mentioning earlier that I might need a social secretary. But that time hadn't come as yet, and I wasn't prepared to make a decision now.

"Anyway," I said, "I expect everything will run along as usual for a while. At least until the will is probated."

I'd finished my coffee, and she got up to take my empty mug. "I suppose that's true. Then there will be the litigation while Mrs. Karl tries to get Poinciana back."

Such a thought appalled me. The last thing I wanted was to be embroiled in an unpleasant contesting of Ross's will.

"Surely that won't happen," I said.

"Maybe not. Especially if you wind up leaving. They'll try to get you out between them—Mrs. Karl and her mother. And I think if you're smart and like your freedom, you'll go."

I might want to go, but I didn't mean to be forced out by Gretchen and Brett Inness. Where did Vasily stand in all this? I wondered. What did he really want? But I knew I couldn't count on anything Vasily Karl said, even if I asked him straight out.

"I'm not sure what I'll do," I told Myra. "Except that now I had better see if I can find my husband's manuscript. Can you think of any place where she might not have searched?"

Myra considered. "Only the locked safe. She wasn't able to look into that because Mr. Nichols wasn't here to give her the combination. You could ask him about that."

It seemed the logical place, and perhaps if Jarrett had been through it, he hadn't recognized the manuscript package for what it was.

"You're probably right," I said. "There's not much point in searching where Mrs. Karl has already looked. I'll get Mr. Nichols to open the safe for me later."

I thanked her and went into the long corridor. At the far end, one of the maids scuttled out of sight, still restrained by the rules of invisibility Ross had laid down. Mrs. Broderick would probably see to it that they were adhered to, and would allow no slackening.

Were the things I was doing merely a marking of time because I hadn't come to grips with a real purpose for my life? Was I keeping busy with mere intrigue, while larger issues escaped me?

But even if this were true, I couldn't deal with anything larger now. Keeping busy at *something* was all I could manage. So a visit to the tower rooms next would be as good to do as anything else.

Not because I expected to find any answers there, but because those rooms might tell me something further about Gretchen, and perhaps about Allegra herself. I hadn't been up to the belvedere since my first uncomfortable encounter there with Gretchen and Vasily.

Once more I climbed the circular iron stairs, holding

on to the curving rail. The steps were wedge-shaped and difficult, and I wondered that Allegra had wanted to use these rooms for herself. However, she had been agile and athletic enough, even into her fifties and sixties. The clippings I'd seen had told me that.

The lower room that she had called her "nap" room was one I hadn't explored, and I stepped off the stairs and stood looking about its square expanse. Blinds were closed, the furniture still shrouded. Again, as in the room above, there were windows all around, though more wall space had been allowed here. There was no outside balcony at this level.

As my eyes became accustomed to the shuttered light, I saw that an elegant French armoire had been placed across one corner. I remembered the time when I'd stood in the ballroom downstairs and wondered if any of Allegra's gowns from her earlier days had been preserved. Perhaps this was one place to look.

Double doors pulled outward as I turned the handles, swinging wide to emit an odor of mothballs and faded sachet. The big armoire was hung solid with covered dresses. The plastic protection they wore belonged to a later day than the dresses themselves, and I could see them through the transparency. How beautiful they were—all ball gowns, apparently, and of every imaginable style. Nothing must ever have been given away that she had worn to a party. I lifted a hanger from the rack and held up a long, slim frock of midnight blue satin, trimmed with crystal bugle beads. It rustled softly, as if stirring from a long sleep. Its décolletage was low, front and back, and there was a tiny train that she must have picked up by its wrist cord when she was dancing. How Allegra must have glittered as she moved, holding every eye.

I heard my own sigh as I replaced the dress among its sisters. Strange that these things should remain in all their perfection, while the woman who had worn them aged and faded. Another time, I would come here to examine every gown in the armoire. Perhaps I would even ask Allegra about their stories. "A long time ago" was a time she would remember more easily than yesterday.

I closed the doors softly, so as not to disturb old ghosts, and climbed the stairs to the top of the tower.

There seemed little change in this upper room since the last time I had seen it. If Gretchen still used it for her studio, however, there was no evidence, though the two contrasting photos of Ross still hung on the wall near the desk. I felt a pang as I studied them again.

How sure—how almost sure—I'd been on that innocent day when I'd first seen them that Ross's true character was revealed in the dynamic picture in which he moved toward the camera with a confident smile, exuding the power and vibrant spirit I had known him to possess. Now, I could look at the second picture and remember all too well that the darker side of him had existed too, and perhaps been in ascendancy here at Poinciana. That far more dangerous side. Yet in the end the danger had ricocheted back to him.

A clang of metal from the stairs startled me. Someone had stepped onto the iron wedges and was coming up. An instinctive reluctance to be found here sent me to the balcony door. I pulled it open and stepped into the wind, closing it after me. I wasn't sure why I'd moved so swiftly and fearfully, except that I had once been pushed down a flight of stairs, and that nothing since then had caused me to feel safe and secure in this house. I wanted to know who climbed those stairs before I made my presence known.

The climber paused at the floor below, but only for a moment, and then came on to the upper room. I moved around the narrow wooden balcony that followed the square turns of the tower, and found a window where I could watch around the edge, with a minimum likelihood of being seen.

Vasily Karl's fair head emerged from the stair opening, and he stepped into the studio room and stood looking about. Looking for what? Had Gretchen sent him here on a search for her father's manuscript? But surely Ross would never have brought it to the belvedere.

As I watched Vasily standing there, studying the room, I still thought that some search must be in his mind. But his next move showed clearly that he knew what he was looking for, and where it was hidden. He went to a wicker chair and lifted out the chintz-covered cushion. Reaching beneath it for something, he found whatever it was and dropped it quickly into his jacket pocket. In a moment he would be gone again, down the stairs.

Vasily didn't frighten me. Though perhaps he should have. I ran around the balcony, not bothering to be quiet, so that he heard me coming and turned to stare at the door as I entered the tower room.

"Hello, Vasily," I said.

For once I had taken him by surprise. Accustomed as he must have been to difficult situations in which he had lived by his wits and clever deceptions, he was able to think of nothing to say or do in the face of my sudden appearance. Only after a long pause did he recover and smile at me brightly.

"Are you up here admiring the view, Sharon?"

"I'm not sure why I'm here," I said. "ESP, perhaps. Something pulled me to the tower. And I was right, wasn't I? I had reason to come here."

His shrug was as easy and comfortable as though he had not been taken by surprise a moment before. "Oh, well. I suppose it doesn't really matter now. I told Gretchen that her idea was foolish, and that you would have to know sooner or later."

He went to the desk and opened a bottom drawer. From it he drew a large red folder and placed it on top of the desk. I knew what it was without the slightest doubt.

"How did Ross's manuscript come to be here?" I asked.

Again the careless shrug. "Let's not go into that. Isn't it enough that it has been recovered?"

"Does Gretchen know it was here?"

"Of course. She put it in that drawer herself."

"In order to make a stir? In order to upset me?"

"Sit down for a moment," he said, suddenly grave as he motioned me into the chair where the cushion had been replaced. "It will be just as well not to confront my wife with this, Sharon. Sometimes her moods aren't altogether rational, and it's not wise to disturb her unnecessarily. This is a difficult time for her, as it must be for you. I've been wanting to assure you that I will do everything possible to persuade Gretchen to leave Poinciana. I would like to travel abroad with her. There are so many places in Europe that we could see together, and I hope to convince her that this would be a good thing to do right now. It would also help to heal her loss."

"You mean you'll try to persuade her to give up Poinciana?"

"Not exactly. She needn't live in the house to fight this will, if that becomes her desire. Neither does she need to outwait you here. I suspect that you may find that you don't want to live in this mausoleum of a place alone. Everyone will be leaving, you know. And will you enjoy being its custodian all alone? Especially during the summer. This isn't a house that can be air-conditioned, except for a few rooms."

"Allegra and Charles Logan sometimes spent their summers here without air conditioning."

"I don't want to argue with you. I shall try to persuade Gretchen that if we all leave, and that will include Brett and Allegra—whatever must be done about her—then some of the servants will give notice, and you will find that you have no wish to stay here, no matter what selfish thing Ross may have asked of you."

He seemed strangely eager to convince me, and he had grown less mockingly assured. There was almost an urgency of need in him to persuade me.

"It isn't just that you want me out so that Gretchen will inherit Poinciana, is it?" I asked.

His usually easy manner evaporated. I had never seen him so grave. "No, it is not. For your own sake, Sharon, you are better away."

"But why, Vasily? Tell me why?"

"There have already been attempts to injure and torment you. Isn't that enough reason? Do you believe in primitive force, Sharon?"

This was a surprising turn. "I'm not sure what you mean."

"I'm not being esoteric. I have come to believe that there are contrasting natures in all of us. One is the primitive side that we learn to suppress as children, and it must be kept suppressed, or it can become a primitive force for destruction. As happens in some people."

I glanced at Gretchen's photograph of Ross. "My father used to say it in a different way—that things are seldom what they seem."

"Exactly. Have you felt this force in yourself at times, Sharon?"

"I don't think so." There had been occasions when I was with Ross...but I had hardly turned primitive.

"I have felt this in myself," he went on, "and sometimes it has frightened me."

That was what I had begun to sense in Vasily—that he was frightened—and the very fact alarmed me.

"I'd like to leave this house right now," I told him. "But there are certain things I must know first, and I mean to stay and find them out."

"Don't stay," he pleaded. "Don't try to find out." He hesitated and then went on, still deeply in earnest. "There are times in a life when one may be caught in a net of one's own weaving. The strands are there to hold you, and there is no way to cut yourself free. So move now, Sharon. Get away before the deadly strands tighten."

As he was caught in his marriage to Gretchen? I

wondered. But all this about primitive forces and deadly strands grew a little too melodramatic. Vasily was skilled to perfection in building the sensational, and I must not be convinced by his efforts. I began to relax a little.

When he picked up the manuscript and turned toward the stairs, I held out my hand. "I'll take that folder, please."

He gave it to me, though I sensed his reluctance. There was a new eagerness in him to escape my company, and I could easily guess why. He had said all he wished to say, and he didn't want me to pick up on something he wanted to conceal. I picked up on it.

"What was it you retrieved from this chair?" I asked him.

His stiff smile seemed to warn me that I was going too far. "Let's say that is my own small secret. You must not push too far, Sharon. You are still young and somewhat heedless—as I used to be. Now I count safety as a virtue in itself, and I value it greatly. I recommend that you do the same. You have lost your powerful protector, and you must remember that."

I watched as he gave me a mocking salute and disappeared down the turning stairs. There had been absolutely nothing I could do or say in the face of his veiled warnings. If I'd demanded to see what he had taken from the chair and dropped into his pocket, he might either have laughed at me, or become angry. For the first time it occurred to me that I would not like to see Vasily Karl angry. Not that he had seemed in the least enraged. He had been more fearful than angry, and the knowledge that something was frightening him was rather terrifying in itself. He might deal in melodrama, but I couldn't dismiss what he said because of that.

The folder was in my hands, and I opened it and looked inside. The pages Ross had finished were there, as were the photographs and invoices. Had Gretchen really been the one to bring these things to the tower room? I couldn't be sure that Vasily had told me the truth about anything he had said. His reluctance to have me mention this meeting to his wife seemed to suggest that he had not told me the entire truth.

At least, with the manuscript in hand again, I knew what I must do before anything else happened. I must go downstairs immediately and check every item on the netsuke shelves against the records I held in my hands.

Chapter 15

I worked meticulously, systematically, and I was now familiar enough with many of the individual netsuke so that I could find them to check against the records. Two that were missing showed up quickly. Vasily had been right in his first wry suggestion that these records might have been hidden so that subsequent thefts would not be discovered. But surely Gretchen—oh, the very thought was ridiculous.

The missing items this time were a carp with a baby turtle in its mouth—in itself an amusing reversal of nature, since snapping turtles were more likely to bother the fish—and a Daruma, who was described as reading and chuckling over an erotic "pillow book" when he should have been doing his religious meditations. Both items were signed and were valuable in themselves. But only to the extent of a few thousand dollars.

Either or both would have been small enough to hide beneath the cushion of a chair, and later slipped into a jacket pocket if Vasily had wanted to carry them away.

Yet I could hardly accuse Vasily of the theft, or even be sure that the netsuke, like the manuscript, had been hidden in the tower room. It would seem a good place for such concealment, since Gretchen never allowed the maids to come up there to clean, and apparently she had seen little of those rooms herself in recent days.

But who was the thief? Perhaps this was just another trick of Gretchen's to give her an excuse to keep me off balance. Or it could be that Vasily was stealing for his own profit. Gretchen, being her father's daughter, might very well be keeping him on a short leash. The strands of that net he had mentioned?

A deep, unreasoned conviction was growing in me that some missing element existed in all this. If I could uncover the one connecting link, everything else would fall into place and be tied together—from Ross's death, to the alarm-setting, to the hiding of the manuscript. Even to the fact that two valuable netsuke were missing. Also, as Vasily had reminded me, there were those hands that had pushed me down a flight of stairs—an intent that might have killed me. To say nothing of the harmless, yet utterly disturbing trick with a rotting coconut. All were connected, and I must somehow learn in what way.

Earlier, I'd wondered if I had been simply busying myself with intrigue to avoid meeting larger issues head on. Now I was growing certain that everything was part of that larger issue that still escaped me, and with which I must eventually come face to face. When I knew the answer to this and this, then the dark human motives, the primitive force that Vasily had spoken of, would be revealed. Only then would I see clearly where danger lay, and I could only pray that my knowledge wouldn't come too late. That was the awful part—

not knowing the face of my enemy, or from what direction the next attack might come.

In the meantime, I had better keep busy if I wasn't to be shaken into flight. One problem now was how to protect the netsuke collection from further raids. But even if they were removed from their shelves and locked away, there was still the rest of Poinciana—an enormous collection of far more valuable items, many of them small enough to be easily pilfered. When the will was settled, perhaps I could return the netsuke collection to Japan as Ross had mentioned doing. But there was little I could do now about all these treasures except to try to be as watchful as possible.

A certain rebellion and resentment began to stir in me. This was a dreadful way to live! To be constantly in fear that valuable possessions would be stolen was to be owned by those possessions—and that was not for me. The house should be turned into a museum, and be supported and guarded as such, however much of Ross's wealth this might cost. Once I had thought nothing could be more marvelous than to live in such a place—my own private museum. I didn't think so any longer. There were treasures here and they should be seen, appreciated, not kept selfishly private as Ross had wanted to keep them. He had wanted me to stay here, to restore, to give myself to Poinciana. And that was something I had no intention of doing.

Nevertheless, until the house and its property were clearly in my hands, there was little I could do. It might even be that the pilfering lay within the family, and that would be very hard to deal with.

One thing I knew. For the moment, I'd had enough of Poinciana and all it contained. Except for the funeral, I hadn't been outside the gate for days. Perhaps I could even think more clearly if I got away for a while. Tonight at dinner I could pour everything out into Jarrett's sensible ears, but I didn't know where he was right now.

I went upstairs and changed into something suitable

for town. When I was ready in beige linen and brown pumps, with a touch of coral at neck and ears, I went downstairs and asked for the car and Albert.

I was told that Mrs. Karl had already taken the Rolls, with Albert to drive her, and had gone into town to view her exhibit of pictures in the library. Would I care to drive myself? There was, of course, a choice of cars.

There was no reason why I shouldn't drive myself. I accepted a white Ferrari that Vasily sometimes used. It would do as well as any, and perhaps it would be an advantage to catch Gretchen away from the house. I too would visit the exhibit at the library.

I had overlooked what it was like to be a Logan at this time. As I drove through the gate, photographers and reporters swarmed upon me, hurling questions, snapping their camera shutters. I had seen such assaults on television news programs, but this was the real thing. Away from the protection of the house, I had to roll up my windows, and try to drive without running anyone down.

For days I had scarcely looked at the newspapers, and I hadn't realized what I should have taken for granted—that the world was fascinated by Ross Logan, his death, his family, and that repercussions would take a long while to die down.

Until this moment, no one had been able to get near me. Now I was uncomfortably aware that cars were following me into town and that I would be surrounded again the moment I left the Ferrari. Better to join them than fight them! When I came to a place where I could stop on the narrow boulevard without blocking traffic, I pulled off and waited. A car squealed behind me, and a woman got out and came running up to the window of my car. She was young and eager, and I rolled it down and smiled at her.

"Would you like to act as my guide?" I asked. "I'm going into town to see Mrs. Karl's exhibit of photographs. If you mean to follow me anyway, you might as well go on ahead and show me where the library is."

She agreed cheerfully. "Sure. If you'll answer some questions for me at the other end."

"I'll try," I promised.

She grinned in the direction of two other cars that had slowed behind us, and got into her battered Chevy. When she drove around me, touching her horn, I followed, and the rest of the entourage fell in behind.

Oddly enough, away from Poinciana, I didn't mind so much. These people were doing their job, and after all I was one of the reading public who had followed with interest what happened to the world's celebrated. Except that I couldn't see myself existing in that category, even after my marriage to Ross Logan.

We drove into the center of Palm Beach to Four Arts Plaza, and parked. My guide whipped out of her car and came to slip into the front seat of mine.

Strangely, I felt more relaxed than I had in days, as, notebook and pencil in hand, she began her questions. I tried to keep my wits about me, and remember what everything would sound like in print.

For the most part, her questions were straightforward enough. What were my plans? Would I stay on in Poinciana, or leave and allow Mr. Logan's daughter to inherit? (So news of the will was common property?) How did I feel to be one of the world's wealthiest women? What would I do with my time?

I asked a question or two of my own. My inquisitioner's name was Meg, and she worked for the woman's page of a Florida paper.

It was my own feelings about what was happening to me that most interested her. In most cases I had to answer with an I-don't-know. I really hadn't thought about being wealthy. I hadn't had time to get used to it. I hadn't thought about a lot of things, apparently.

How did I feel about my husband's daughter? I told her cautiously that we hadn't had time to become well acquainted, but that I admired her work in photography, and was interested in seeing her exhibit at the library. No, of course there was no antagonism between us. Already I was discovering that one lied glibly to the press. Not until I asked to be let off from any further questions did she put the one that most upset me.

"How do you feel about the rumors that your husband's death was not due to a heart attack?"

After the first shock, I tried to answer carefully. "I haven't heard any such rumors. You have only to check with his doctor."

"Oh, we have. But there seem to be unanswered questions about just what brought on the heart attack."

I mananged to keep myself in hand. "I was *there,* and there is nothing more to know."

The girl beside me recognized that her interview was at an end.

"You'll enjoy the library," she said. "An interesting building. It's not a public library, you know. Local residents support it. Don't you love those bronze jaguars on either side of the steps?"

"I'll go in now," I said.

"Thanks a lot for letting me talk with you," she told me, and returned to her Chevy. I could hope that she would be reasonably kind in whatever she wrote.

There were more reporters waiting, having followed me here, but I hurried through and went up the wide steps between the two prowling animals. I had a quick glimpse of a white stone building—Quattrocento Italian in style—and then I was through the arches of the red-tiled portico.

The interior was cool after bright sunlight, and I stopped to look up at the stunning portrait that hung over the desk. It was a painting of a seated woman, her white hair partly hidden by black lace, her eyes of arresting intensity. A remarkable face.

The librarian behind the desk greeted me as I came in. "Good morning, Mrs. Logan. If you're looking for Mrs. Karl, she's already here."

I supposed that my picture must have appeared in

papers across the country, and I had to get used to being recognized.

"Thank you," I said. "I've come to see her photographs."

"They've been hung upstairs in the children's room, where we have more wall space," she said, and directed me.

I took the elevator up and found the big room with its bright book jackets, low tables and small chairs. It was empty when I walked in, except for Gretchen, who stood looking up at a matted photograph she had taken of her husband.

The photo seemed extremely posed, yet, knowing Vasily, I suspected that she had caught him quite off guard. He fell naturally into poses. In the black-and-white full-length, he leaned against the trunk of a coco palm on the grounds of Poinciana. A familiar glimpse of the belvedere identified the setting. His blond head rested against the trunk, his arms were folded, and one foot crossed over the other. The collar of his white shirt was open at the throat to reveal a gold coin he wore on a chain—a gift from Gretchen. He seemed completely relaxed and unaware of any camera nearby, his expression one I'd seen before—the look of a man who accepted life as it came, and was entertained by it. The face of a romantic, an adventurer. *The Thief of Baghdad*, I thought to myself. That was where Vasily belonged—in the *Arabian Nights*. But this was a dangerous look for a modern man to wear.

"You've caught him very well," I said softly to Gretchen.

She whirled to stare at me, quick anger rising in her eyes.

"Please," I said. "A truce. I only want to talk with you. We're really on the same side, but you never give us a chance to find this out."

From beneath the fall of short hair, her look was one of hostility. She said, "We can't talk here. But come along, and we'll find a place."

She led the way to a narrow room with a table and chairs placed near an end window. Books lined the shelves, and Gretchen waved a casual hand at them as we entered.

"This was the personal collection of the architectural books that belonged to Addison Mizner. He's the man who gave Palm Beach its Spanish-Mediterranean look." She sat down at the table. "Okay. What do you want to talk about?"

"I have the netsuke manuscript," I said, sitting opposite her.

Her look of surprise seemed real. "Where did you find it?"

"Oddly enough, it was in the upper room of the belvedere, in a drawer of your grandmother's desk. I thought you might have put it there."

"Of course I didn't!" Again her outrage seemed sincere, but before she could further vent her indignation, I went on.

"I took it down to the Japanese room and started checking. I haven't finished, but I've found two netsuke missing. I suppose that's why these records were hidden. So there would be a delay in our discovering a theft."

Her first angry flush had died away, leaving her pale. So much for Vasily's veracity in telling me that it was Gretchen who had hidden the manuscript.

"How did you happen to look in the belvedere?" she asked.

"You'd looked everywhere else," I said. "Though I didn't really go up there for the purpose of searching for the manuscript. I stopped to look at an armoire full of Allegra's gowns, and then I went upstairs and—and found the folder with Ross's papers and your photos." I would keep Vasily out of it for now.

Gretchen was silent, still pale. And frightened? Yet with a different fear from that I'd sensed in her husband. He had been afraid of something or someone. There had been an awareness, a direction about his fear that I had sensed distinctly. Perhaps a fear of his wife. Gretchen was afraid without knowing why. Or perhaps she was afraid *to* know why.

"How much do you trust your mother?" I asked bluntly. I wanted to ask how well she could trust Vasily, but I didn't dare.

For once, she took no offense. "I can trust her as long as her interest coincides with mine." An old bitterness sounded in the words.

"I'm not making accusations," I said, "but I can't help wondering. Just this morning Jarrett's son, Keith, told me that it was Brett who set off the alarm that night."

This time I hadn't surprised her. She reached across the small table and grasped me tightly by the wrist. "Don't think whatever it is you're thinking. Brett's okay."

So she knew. So it was true. "I'm not able to conclude much of anything," I told her. "That's the trouble. Perhaps none of it matters now anyway. These things aren't what is real—old grudges, suspicions. It's our lives *now* that matter. What I am going to do, and whether you're happy in your life. Are you, Gretchen?"

"Of course I'm happy! Except for what's happened to my father, more than I've ever been. Vasily wants us to go on a trip through Europe, until after things are settled. I think perhaps I will. There's so much he wants to show me over there, and we need to get away from Poinciana for a while. Until it can belong to us. As it will, Sharon. As it has to!"

"Of course it has to," I agreed. "That's what I'd like you to understand. I don't want any part of it. Your father was angry with you when he changed his will. But he would probably have changed it back if there'd been time. I only wish he had."

She was staring at me again, in disbelief. "But I thought—"

"You didn't think, Gretchen. You only made accusations and jumped to false conclusions. I can understand that you never wanted your father to marry me. I know my coming couldn't have been more unwelcome. But that's over now. I don't want Poinciana for myself. But I'd like to see it preserved and protected, as your grandmother and your father would wish. So I'll stay for now. Especially if you're going away. Later you can decide what you want to do, and how you mean to take over. Besides, with Allegra back in the house, someone has to stay around."

"Allegra? Back in the house? But how—"

"Your mother brought her there. Brett moved her upstairs with most of her things this morning, and she went to bed in her old room. But I'm not sure she's happy about the move. Brett said you wanted it, and so did she, and I think she acted out of good intent. Only it was too fast for your grandmother to realize what was happening. It must have been a shock to be suddenly uprooted like that."

"Brett!" Again Gretchen put bitterness into her voice. "She never even consulted me."

This was the moment for attack. There was something I could probably settle now. "I'd rather not have your mother stay in the house," I said. "She has told me she plans to move in."

I could sense the quick rising of resistance to me that was second nature to Gretchen, and I hurried on.

"I don't believe you want her there either. It's not necessary to spite me any more."

She made a sudden switch to a new attack of her own. "Did you ever really love my father, Sharon?"

Reasonable words were hard to find, and I answered with an indirection. "Do you remember those two photographs you took of him—the ones that I saw in the tower room? I was in love with the man in one of those pictures. I could never have loved the other one, but I didn't know he existed until I came to Poinciana. Which one was real? Perhaps I was only in love with a man I imagined. Perhaps Ross and I were both cheated. I wonder if women always marry imaginary heroes."

"I didn't! I know everything about Vasily. The bad things and the good, and I know how much I love him." She spoke the words defiantly, as though she slapped some sort of challenge down between us.

"Could he have taken the netsuke that are missing?" I asked.

"Of course he could have. It would be very like him. But I don't know whether he did or not. I'll find out. Is that all you wanted to talk about?"

"For now," I said. The feeling of depression and helplessness was returning. Perhaps I had wanted more from a meeting with Gretchen than was possible. Not information, not answers, but a lessening of the strain between us. And there I'd failed.

She went to shelves that lined one side of the room and took down a volume, riffling through its pages. "Maurice Fatio. He was the architect who designed this building, and he had a hand in Poinciana too. Though Grandmother Allegra went through a score of architects trying to incorporate her own ideas. That's why it's such a hodgepodge."

But it wasn't architects that concerned her now. "I still can't believe he's gone," she said as she returned the book to its place. "I still think of things I want to tell my father, share with him. Even argue with him about. At first I was just numb. But now feeling is beginning to come back, and I don't know how I can bear it."

"I know," I said. "I keep expecting him to come through a door at any moment. It's always that way for a while, I suppose. I still feel as though I ought to write my parents a letter, and I still wait for one from them. Perhaps it's a sense of unreality that helps us to get through until we can handle what has happened."

"Too many deaths," Gretchen said. "You've suffered too many deaths, haven't you, Sharon? Just the same—for me—there's a kind of relief as well. I don't have to fight him any longer. I don't have to worry about that terrible bargain he made with Vasily. Which doesn't mean that I don't miss him at every turn. It's strange how mixed up emotions can be." She broke off and stared at me. "Do you ever feel relief, Sharon?"

The tone of her voice had changed to one of challenge, and I knew she would never allow me what she felt herself. Whatever I said now, she would deride.

Without answering, I picked up my handbag and started for the door.

"Sharon?" she said more gently, and I turned to see that she looked almost contrite. "Listen—I know a little courtyard off Worth, where we can sit at a small table outdoors and have sandwiches and coffee. Will you come with me? I don't want to be alone right now."

Surprised as I was, I didn't hesitate. "I'd like that," I said.

We went downstairs together, and out the door between the guardian jaguars—to be greeted by the clicking of cameras. The throng had grown.

"Smile at them," Gretchen said between her teeth.

Albert came quickly from the Rolls to assist us, but Gretchen told him she would come with me and he could take the big car home. We were followed to the Ferrari, but Gretchen took it all in her stride and put on a good face. She got behind the wheel as her right, and I gave her the key.

"You might as well grin and bear it," she told me as we drove off. "Anybody with the Logan name is news all the time. But more so than ever now. You and I, especially. Just look at them cheerfully, or you'll find scowling pictures of yourself plastered across every newspaper you pick up."

"All I can manage is to look blank," I said. "I can't get used to any of this. It was never as bad with Ysobel."

"Then you'd better toughen up," she told me.

When we reached Worth Avenue she found a space between a Lincoln Continental and a pickup truck—the latter a sign of democracy moving in. We followed an arcade to a sunny courtyard, where umbrellas shaded small round tables.

Once an enterprising photographer popped in to snap a picture before he was banished by a waitress, but for the most part our lunch together was a green oasis in the dry and lonely desert in which I seemed to be lost. There was a relaxing of defenses at last, almost an approach to friendliness between us for a little while. I was to remember this hour we spent together—Ross's daughter and I. I was to remember it later in the face of all the dreadful things that were to come.

During the meal we talked at first about neither Ross nor Vasily. Gretchen spoke of her grandmother as she remembered her from the past. She told me some of the stories about her that had taken on the quality of legend. Once when Allegra was young and given to laughing at the proprieties, she had ridden a horse rudely among the tables of the Coconut Grove at the august Royal Poinciana Hotel.

"It really was a coconut grove and outdoors then," Gretchen said. "So it wasn't like riding under a roof. I wish I could have seen her. She used to tell me about the Royal Poinciana. Flagler built it way back in the 1890's, and he painted it lemon yellow, the way he did everything. It was the largest wooden building in the world, and the grandest of the grand hotels. But then people began to build what they called 'cottages' in Palm Beach. The Royal Poinciana was damaged in a hurricane, and finally torn down in 1936. All ancient history."

"At least Palm Beach still has the Breakers."

"Yes, and it's pretty grand. It burned down on three occasions, but every time it rose from the ashes, so that it has become a landmark, with those big white towers on the ocean. The Breakers was Flagler's baby too, in the beginning. One of these days I must take you to Whitehall. That was his home, you know. It's a beautiful museum now, with the rooms all intact."

How pleasant it was to be peaceful, to talk about ordinary things, to rest emotionally. I think Gretchen felt it too and that these moments were as welcome to her as they were to me.

The sense of peace lasted all the way back to Poinciana, and that was the end of it. Susan Broderick, home from her morning classes, waited for us as we came in.

"Mother told me to watch for you. There's a problem with Mrs. Allegra. She seems to be going berserk in the art gallery, and you'd better go there at once. Mr. Nichols is away and can't be reached. As usual, Coxie doesn't know what to do."

Gretchen and I looked at each other, and then started for the gallery at a run.

Chapter 16

Allegra was dressed once more in her running-away costume of brown slacks and pullover, her white hair braided out of the way and tied with a pert velvet ribbon. When we came in she was standing in the center of the long gallery, her arms set akimbo, hands on hips. Coxie and Steve, the guard, were both remonstrating with her.

"I want to know where those two pictures are!" Her voice managed to be indignant and still ladylike at the same time. This was not the Allegra who would ride a horse impudently through the Coconut Grove. Instead of flying in the face of authority, she was authority itself.

Gretchen ran down the room to fling her arms about her grandmother. "I'm so glad to have you home!" she cried. "Even if Brett shouldn't have done this when I wasn't there to help."

Allegra released herself gently from her granddaughter's embrace, eyeing me over Gretchen's shoulder. It was to me she spoke.

"You're my son's wife, so you're in charge now, and you must answer my question. There are two paintings missing that always hung on that wall."

I looked up at the wall she indicated, and saw no empty spaces.

"I'm sorry," I said. "I don't know the collection well as yet. Will you please explain?"

"There were two Lautrecs that always hung right there. I didn't like Ross's arrangement, but I got used to it, and I know every painting on these walls. Now he seems to have hung a couple of unimportant Hudson River schools there. Why? What has happened to the Lautrecs? They are valuable."

Gretchen flung up her hands. "Oh, Gran! There's no use asking Sharon. What does she know? Dad moved things around whenever the notion struck him. You've been away for a long time, and he might have done anything at all with those paintings. There are a lot put away in storage, you know."

I was staring at the wall. "Wait! I think I do remember one of those pictures. I noticed it especially because it wasn't the Moulin Rouge sort of thing that Lautrec made so popular. It was an oil of a carriage drawn by a single horse, with a driver on the high seat, wearing a top hat. A lovely picture."

"That's it!" Allegra tapped me smartly on the arm in approval. "That was one of them. So you must have seen it on this wall recently."

"I believe I did. It could even have been here on the day Ross died."

"I knew it, I knew it! There's been a theft. Two Lautrecs are missing!"

Gretchen gave me a look of reproach. "Gran, we don't know that. Dad moved the portrait of Ysobel Hollis that last day. He might have moved others as well."

Allegra looked at me brightly. "*You* don't think so, do you?"

I didn't think so, but Gretchen was shaking her head at me in warning.

"I can't be absolutely sure," I said.

Allegra seemed to wilt a little, suddenly a very old lady. "I'm tired. Take me upstairs," she said to Gretchen. "*If* I can climb those stairs."

She climbed them between Gretchen and me, with Coxie trailing after us, and on the way Gretchen whispered sharply in my ear. "Just let it alone," she warned me.

Mrs. Broderick had taken the opportunity to get two of her maids into Allegra's rooms, and they were being tidied and dusted. Gretchen shooed them out of the bedroom, kissed her grandmother lovingly, and turned her over to the nurse. "I'll come visit you later, Gran."

We went into the corridor together. "Do you think those paintings have been put somewhere else?" I asked.

"I think they've been stolen," she said. "Just as the netsuke have been stolen. But I don't want Gran worried about this. I'll see what I can do about it."

She went off looking grim and tense, and I wondered if Vasily was in for a bad time. If he'd taken these things, he deserved it. Perhaps it would be easier for everyone if she took him off to Europe for a while. Yet somehow I was glad to have them both in the house. I hated to think of these echoing halls with so many of the family gone. It would be especially lonely at night, when the servants all vanished to their own quarters. But I mustn't start frightening myself.

When I stepped into my room it seemed more alien than ever. I must move out of it soon. Perhaps to a smaller bedroom, with a sitting room. In some strange way, I could feel Brett's presence here, and I was always aware that she had planned and furnished its pale elegance for herself. Besides, I didn't want to stay here, with Ross's room and all its unhappy memories right next door. And there was still the portrait of Ysobel Hollis to be dealt with. It must be hung somewhere else—or put away.

But I didn't want to decide anything now. All I needed to do was mark time until I could see Jarrett this evening. Always, through this strange morning, the thought of him had been warm at the back of my mind. I would talk to him tonight, tell him everything of my day, and of fears that he would help me to dismiss.

Something inside me said, "Wait, wait! You've been wrong before. You mustn't trust so easily. You mustn't care so easily." But I wanted to trust. I wanted to care. I didn't want to live by that cynical rule of my father's—that things were seldom what they seemed. There had been an unexpected warming in me toward Jarrett and I *wanted* to turn to him.

Once more, the outdoors drew me, and I went down the gracefully curving stairs to the yard. I'd hardly stepped out of the house since Ross's death, except for the funeral and my trip to town just now. I needed to push walls away from me, to breathe clear, salty air blowing in from the Atlantic.

The afternoon was warm and sunny—a real taste of Florida. I would go down and walk on the beach, I thought. It was time I faced those sands again, and banished memories that hurt me. But as I turned in the direction of the water, I saw with delight the flame tree—the flamboyant—the poinciana! It had burst into full bloom with every spreading branch ablaze with glorious fire. I stopped to drink in its beauty. All over southern Florida, these trees would be flaming now. Allegra must have seen to the planting of this one, since she'd honored the name for her own Poinciana. For how many seasons had Ross watched this blooming? Yet now he would never see it again, and the realization brought sadness with it. I walked on slowly.

As usual, there were two or three men at work on the grounds, tending the mowing, the watering, the flower beds, ready to pounce on any weed that showed itself. I stopped beside a man who was inserting something through a funnel into the trunk of a coconut palm and asked what he was doing.

He shook his head gloomily. "All over Palm Beach the coco palms are dying of a disease. The town is having them all injected, but I'm not sure it's doing much good."

These palms were plentiful at Poinciana. From every upstairs window one looked out upon their shaggy heads and slim, leaning trunks. In the days when there had always been visitors at the house, I'd been told that these trees were kept free of coconut clusters, lest they fall upon the heads of innocent guests.

I found my way to the tiled tunnel through which Ross had taken me on our way to the beach. Overhead, traffic was zooming past, while I walked on echoing stone. When I came out upon the sand at the far end, I saw the bathhouse and swimming pool Allegra had built, but it was the ocean that drew me.

Today the wind was strong and whitecaps rolled in, curling a froth of lace onto the sand. The ocean's voice roared in the sound of the waves, and where the beach was wet and firm I followed the edge of the water as it reached my feet. Sea grape grew against the wall that protected the boulevard, rusty brown from salt winds, with spiky branches as thick as my arm, and big tough leaves. In the summer I would come down here and swim. *If* I were still here in the summer.

I'd been afraid of being haunted by the memory of that night of a Florida moon when I'd walked here with Ross. Strangely, however, that was beginning to seem another lifetime away, another man I had walked with. A man I had lost because of the stranger he had turned into. I couldn't mourn for the stranger. Gretchen was right. We must both admit to a sense of relief some of the time.

I walked on, looking up at the roofs of large houses that fronted on the water across the boulevard, and when I began to tire I turned back toward the tunnel again. But as I went down the steps to its sunken floor, I heard echoing voices. At once I drew myself close to the wall, where I wouldn't be silhouetted against the light, not wanting to meet anyone now.

As my eyes became accustomed to the dim mustiness of the tunnel, I made out the two people standing together at the far end. There was an air of secrecy, perhaps of conspiracy, about them, and I knew instinctively that they had come here separately to a private meeting. One was Vasily Karl, the other Brett Inness.

The clattering echoes of their own voices must have warned them, for they began to speak more quietly, and I couldn't make out the words. Crouching against the wall, I didn't hesitate to listen, to strain to pick up any phrase I could catch.

Once I heard Brett's words, "She knows..." and then her voice was lowered. The clamminess of unreasoned fear dampened my arms. Ever since I'd come to Poinciana, I had sensed secrets that were hidden beneath our everyday lives. I'd tried to speak of this to Ross, and he'd shrugged it aside. Perhaps that very shrugging off had been fatal for him. Perhaps what he had chosen to ignore so arrogantly had in the long run killed him. The troubling question returned to me.

Why had Brett turned on the alarm system?

A voice was raised again—Vasily's voice: "...stop this."

"Hush," Brett said. "You have no other choice."

I began to wonder how visible I might be if they really looked this way. But I was afraid to move, lest the slightest sound betray my presence. There was something terribly wrong at Poinciana. Something—evil. Yet I wasn't sure against whom it might be directed. There seemed only two choices—Gretchen and me. And I was the likely one. *She knows,* Brett had said. I could only think she meant me. But *what* did I know? And why should it matter when I'd already made it clear to everyone that I meant to leave Poinciana to Gretchen as soon as it was possible for me to get away?

Or was there a more far-reaching plot against me? If something happened to me, then *everything* would revert to Gretchen. That would mean investments, the controlling shares of Meridian Oil stock, property in other towns—I really had no idea of all that Ross had left me. I only knew that it had not been a gift of love, but one of revenge and punishment against his daughter.

The murmuring voices had stopped. There was movement now at the other end of the tunnel, and I saw Brett's elegant figure stand briefly against the sunlight of the arched opening. Then she disappeared up the steps to the yard. After a moment Vasily followed, moving to the left, approaching the house from another direction.

I returned to the sand, where children were playing with a beach ball. Out over the water a flock of brown pelicans caught my eye. They were spectacular birds, diving accurately into the water from a great height to capture fish in their huge yellow beaks.

When I'd watched long enough, I returned and dared to go cautiously through the tunnel. Even then, I didn't step immediately into the sunlight, but clung to the wall as I climbed the steps and looked carefully around the grounds.

Except for a gardener, no one was in sight, and I stepped onto the grass and started toward the right wing of the house. If anyone saw me approaching, it might be thought that I'd come from somewhere else than the tunnel.

"Good afternoon, Sharon," said a voice behind me.

I whirled in alarm, to see Vasily Karl leaning against the coquina rock wall that ran along the edge of the boulevard. Beyond him cars whipped past. I was totally unable to speak. He smiled at me easily, but I sensed watchfulness in his eyes, and suspicion.

"Don't look so astonished, Sharon," he said. "Did you think you were being clever by waiting a while before you came back through the tunnel? Of course I saw you all along, standing there, listening. Though I think Brett did not. When she left, I decided to sit here and wait for the rabbit to come out of the hole."

I made a desperate effort to collect myself. "Much good it did me," I told him. "I couldn't hear a word either of you was saying."

"I quite believe you," he said cheerfully. "When I saw you come into the tunnel, I took care to keep my voice down, and I persuaded Brett of the need for quiet. So now you have another mystery, don't you? This strange meeting between Gretchen's mother and her husband. Whatever can they be up to?"

"Would you like to tell me?" I asked.

"Good! I like a lady who can bluff when she is frightened. You are frightened, aren't you, Sharon? And with good reason. It would be very wise at this time to turn everyone out of Poinciana, including Allegra, and close it up for a while. Then take yourself far away from Palm Beach. Where you will be safe."

"Safe from what?"

"You wouldn't even begin to guess," he said. "Just take my word and leave."

"Is that what you're really advising?"

"Advising, yes. But I think you will refuse to go. You are just stubborn enough to refuse to give in to your fears. Isn't that so, Sharon?"

"I don't want to talk to you!"

I moved away from him across the grass. The lawn seemed to go on forever, but I didn't stop or look back until I was safely inside the house. Then I paused beside a window from which I could see the ocean and the entrance to the tunnel under the boulevard. Vasily was nowhere in sight.

My first thought was of Jarrett. He was the only one I could turn to and I hurried to his office. He still hadn't returned, but Myra took one look at my face and said, "Sit down, Mrs. Logan."

She went through her usual ministering of refreshments—her cure for everything—and for once was discreet enough to ask no questions. After a while I stopped shaking.

"Tomorrow," I said, "I'm going to move out of my room upstairs. It's too big for me now."

"And too lonely," she observed wisely. "*I* wouldn't want to rattle around in that empty wing all alone. Especially not if I had a feeling that there were those in the house who didn't mean me any good."

I stared at her. "Why do you say that?"

"It's obvious, isn't it? Mrs. Karl has hated your marriage from the beginning. She can't be happy about you now."

But it wasn't Gretchen I feared, though I couldn't tell Myra that.

"Anyway, moving would be fun, wouldn't it?" she went on. "I mean, to have all the rooms there are in this house to choose from? To be able to furnish your own apartment any way you wish?"

"I don't suppose I'll bother," I said. "I doubt I'll be here long enough."

She sighed, and I could see the wheels going around in her head. Obviously, she thought me foolish not to take every advantage I could of being Mrs. Ross Logan. I couldn't tell her that Mrs. Ross Logan was someone I didn't want to be.

"There's one thing I'd like to ask you," I went on. "Do you happen to know whether Mr. Logan removed any pictures from the gallery on the day before he died?"

She thought about that for a moment. "There was the portrait of your mother. He brought it to his office in the afternoon, and I wondered if he was going to hang it there."

That would have been like him, I thought. But he had a better idea.

"That's not the one I mean. Mrs. Logan thinks there are a couple of Toulouse-Lautrec paintings that are missing. And I believe I've seen one of them hanging in the gallery since I came."

She thought about that solemnly, and then hopped up from her chair and scooted toward Ross's office, flinging words back at me.

"I don't know for sure," she said. "I mean I don't know what pictures they were, but I believe he brought some things from the gallery here either that last day or the day before. Let's look."

I followed her and watched as she opened a deep cabinet, gesturing for me to look inside. I could see the edges of frames standing on their sides, and I drew one of them out. It was an oil on wood of coach and horse, the driver sitting up in front, with his whip and top hat. I pulled it out in delighted relief and reached in to pull out the second picture—the portrait of a lady in a garden. Another Lautrec.

"That's wonderful!" I cried. "Now I can put Mrs. Logan's mind at rest. But I wonder why my husband brought these here?"

Myra managed to look both wise and arch at the same time, while she said nothing.

"Stop playing games," I told her impatiently. "Even if you're only speculating, I'd like to know what you're thinking."

She bent to close the cabinet, and then looked at me with a half-smile that was both appealing and apologetic. "I really do like you, Mrs. Logan. You don't look down your nose at the help, and you've tried to be kind to my friend."

"Your friend?"

"The old lady. Mrs. Logan. I understand she's back in the house again. Just the same, I don't want to stick out my neck with things I'm not really sure of at all. And I don't want to hurt you."

"I can stand being hurt," I said. "And I expect you're perfectly sure about a lot of what goes on at Poinciana."

She was still hesitant. "But this is pretty crazy—really far out. Do you suppose rich men ever steal from themselves?"

I went to the big leather armchair opposite Ross's

desk, remembering that it was in this chair I'd sat that night when I'd run away from him and come here with Jarrett. The last night.

"Maybe you'd better explain," I said.

She was airy about her reply, still being cautious. "The rich don't always keep a lot of cash in their pockets. Isn't it true that sometimes they have to liquidate funds in order to pay big debts? So couldn't a rich man who owned a great many valuable possessions put some of them—well, in hock, so to speak, in order to raise money if he needed it?"

I had never thought of such a thing. If Ross had needed cash, I was sure that Jarrett could have raised it for him in a moment. Millions. We had never been short while we traveled, though now that I thought about it, most of the time we'd managed on lavish credit. One thing I knew. Not for a moment must I openly accept such an idea from Myra Ritter. I owed it to Ross not to give her fertile imagination anything to build on. Besides, even if it could possibly be true, it had all been brought to a halt now. It didn't matter. The paintings had been found.

I shook my head emphatically. "Mr. Logan would never have touched his netsuke collection, or his precious paintings. So I'm afraid that idea is out. Anyway, thank you for the coffee, Myra."

I left her and started up the stairs that led to the wing where Allegra had her rooms, but I couldn't put her words from my mind. Certainly Ross's anger over the first two missing netsuke had seemed real. And he had seemed convinced that his mother might have taken them. Yet I knew too that he would have been perfectly capable of putting up a smoke screen to serve his own ends. Perhaps there were funds he didn't want to touch. Or he might not have wanted to ask Jarrett when so many vast interests were involved. The rich *were* different, as Scott Fitzgerald said.

The netsuke, no, but about the paintings I was less sure. Ross hadn't collected those himself, even though he had enjoyed owning them. In any case, I was too close to all of this to judge what Ross might or might not have done. Myra, the outsider, might well have cut through to an unpleasant truth.

Jarrett would know. Increasingly, this was becoming my refrain. Tonight at dinner I would be able to talk to Jarrett. But now I could at least set Allegra's mind at rest about the Lautrecs, and if she was awake, I would tell her now. I must also let Gretchen know—and soon.

Allegra was no longer in bed when I reached her rooms. She had installed herself at the desk in her parlor and was making notes with a pencil. I hoped she wasn't back in the past planning another ball.

Coxie sat knitting in a chair by a window, and both of them looked up when I appeared at the door.

"Good," Allegra said. "I wanted to talk to you. I want you to tell Coxie to throw out all those pills and things she keeps pushing at me."

"The doctor—" Coxie began.

"Let me know the next time he comes," I said. "Mrs. Karl and I would like to speak with him."

"Then there's the matter of those missing paintings," she went on, making a check beside an item on her list.

"That's what I came to tell you about, Mrs. Logan," I said quickly. "Both the Lautrecs have been found. Ross had put them away in his office for some reason."

"In his office?" Her look sharpened. "I wonder what he was planning? Anyway, I'm glad you found them."

When I'd made sure there was nothing else she wanted at the moment, I left her and followed the corridor, looking for rooms I might move into. If I chose this wing, I would be close to Allegra and her nurse as well, and not off in lonely, isolated grandeur. I would also be at the opposite end of the house from Gretchen and Vasily, which would suit me very well.

I selected a room that opened toward the lake and would make a pleasant sitting room. Next door would serve as my bedroom, and the changes in furniture would be simple enough for my temporary purposes. I would have a phone connected, and move in here tomorrow. Mrs. Broderick could manage all this, I was sure.

I found the housekeeper supervising the cleaning of a suite in Gretchen's wing. She explained with barely concealed satisfaction that these rooms were to be for Miss Inness, who was moving into them later this afternoon.

So Gretchen had paid no attention to my request. Or else Brett had overruled her. This was not something I could settle with Mrs. Broderick. I explained about the change I wanted to make in my own living quarters.

"I'll wait until tomorrow to move," I said. "That should give you time to make a few changes. I'll show you the rooms I've chosen whenever you're free."

Mrs. Broderick inclined her head. "As you wish, Mrs. Logan," she said, and I knew that she guessed the reasons for my moving and was scornful of such weakness. Since Ross's death, she had become even more of a fortress of authority, as though the uncertainty of all our lives at the moment must not be allowed to touch the running of Poinciana.

I made a small effort to placate her. "We must have a talk before long. I know very well that you are the one who keeps the house running smoothly."

"Thank you, Mrs. Logan," she said, but I knew I was still the stranger, of whom she disapproved.

The rest of the afternoon I spent in the Japanese room checking through the remainder of the netsuke. No more seemed to be missing, and when I'd examined them, briefly, I was able to give my attention to the ivory carvings, the cloisonné and Satsuma that I'd wanted to learn about ever since I'd come to the house. My old excitement over such treasures had weakened, however, and I knew I was only waiting for the hour when I could go to Jarrett's cottage.

In the late afternoon, I showered and dressed carefully. The coming visit might not be altogether easy and enjoyable. There was too much that was unpleasant that I had to tell Jarrett—even to the question Myra Ritter had raised about Ross and the paintings. Thus my dressing was, in a sense, like putting on armor for the evening.

I wore my lime green silk from Hong Kong, and added no jewelry, except for the rings Ross had given me. In a sense, my rings were the symbol of my right to be in this house. I was still Mrs. Ross Logan, whether I liked it or not, and their presence on my hand prevented me from tossing everything over and running for my life. Which was what Vasily had suggested that I ought to do, and which was what I really wanted to do. Yet I must stay. For a while.

Somewhere in all those frantic years with Ysobel and Ian, a sense of duty to others had somehow been inculcated in me. Perhaps a stodgy, old-fashioned principle, but it was still there, operating in me, and I had to obey its edicts. Once Ian had told me that I was the one responsible member of the family, and I recalled that I'd laughed at his words.

An unexpected flash of memory swept through me. There had been a night in San Francisco...I had been waiting when Ysobel returned to her dressing room. Something had shaken her confidence during her performance, and she, who was determined to remain forever young, had felt suddenly old. Ian had been out front checking on the house, and we were alone.

"I'm losing it," she said bleakly. "Something's slipping away, and I can't stop its going. They weren't responding out there tonight. And if they don't respond, I'm not anything."

I couldn't bear to see her in such a mood, and I had given myself to reassuring her. Just before she went on again she came to put her arms about me, and her cheek against mine. I could still remember the scent of her stage makeup, and her special perfume.

"Thank you for being my friend," she said, and went

out to where the applause that greeted her sounded as enthusiastic as ever.

I had sat down before her dressing table and looked at myself in the mirror in astonishment. I touched the cheek hers had touched, and felt a comfort I'd never known before. Her *friend*, she had said. And if she had lived, perhaps that was what we might have been eventually—friends.

Now, looking into another mirror in another time, something seemed to melt the coldness inside me. In the past I had allowed harsh words, perhaps carelessly spoken, to freeze me, so that I could never see Ysobel as vulnerable and human too. I'd been absorbed in my own self-pity.

The poignancy of loss was intense at that moment, and yet there was a healing too, a beginning of true comfort for me. I went downstairs with a new courage lifting my steps.

The grounds were empty as I followed the shell path to Jarrett's cottage. Keith saw me coming and ran to open the screen door, with Brewster at his heels.

"Dad's in the kitchen," he told me, smiling and excited. "He's making lasagne, and he makes it better than anybody. Mrs. Simmons had to go home to see a sick daughter, so we're on our own tonight. I'm fixing the salad."

He ran off, with the dog after him, and while I hesitated, Jarrett called from the kitchen. "Sit down, Sharon, and I'll be with you in a moment."

I sat down and looked around. The cottage had been charmingly furnished with old, well-worn pieces that suited its character. A few throw rugs were scattered across polished floors, and the sofa wore cheerful chintz. Part of the wide room had been separated into a dining area, from which steps led up to an outside deck. A plain oak table was set with woven place mats and old silver.

Jarrett came out of the kitchen with a spatula in hand. "Hello, Sharon." His red hair was in his eyes, and from beneath it his look approved of me. "We're nearly ready. So come and bring things in."

I began to relax as I carried salad bowls and a basket of bread sticks to the table. From where Jarrett seated me I could look out toward the fiery poinciana tree and see beyond it the belvedere that rose above the roofs of the big house. I wished I need never go back under that roof again.

The lasagne was perfection, as Keith had promised, and for dessert there were sweet Florida melons. No long silences troubled us while we ate, though the talk was of the inconsequential. Brewster had had his own dinner, and he lay watching us with bright doggy interest. I could almost believe that life was normal, and that the threats of Poinciana had ceased to exist. Tonight I was seeing a Jarrett that I'd never glimpsed before. An easier, more contented, simpler man. Which only meant that I'd not even begun to understand his complexity.

When we'd eaten, I helped to put dishes in the washer, and it seemed pleasant to be doing those small domestic chores that had never been a part of my nomad's life.

When Keith had taken his bicycle and Brewster and gone off to visit a friend, Jarrett led me up inside stairs to the raised deck he had built along one side of the cottage. We stretched out in long teak chairs to watch the sun go down over the lake, and I hadn't felt so peaceful in months.

"Is this the way you always live?" I asked him.

"When I'm in Florida. Pam and I had a home in Maryland, but I've let that go. I'm not sure where we'll live when you close Poinciana—or do whatever you decide to do with it. Perhaps Gretchen and Vasily will stay, if you leave it to them. But my work is up North. If I'm to continue, that is."

Again the certainty of Jarrett's leaving was a fact, and I closed my eyes, not wanting to think about it. For this little while there had been no antagonism between us, and he had treated me with a solicitousness that seemed almost tender.

But the sense of peace, the deceptive atmosphere of normal living could not last.

"You'd better tell me," he said. "I could see the strain in your face when you came in. Has it been a bad day?"

Slowly, groping for words at first, I told him everything. About the missing netsuke and the uncomfortable meeting with Gretchen. About our lunching together, and my surprise glimpse of Vasily and Brett in the tunnel. About Vasily's words to me afterwards, and especially of his coming to the tower and retrieving Ross's manuscript. I spoke too of the missing Lautrecs, and of how they were discovered in Ross's office. Finally I told him what his son had said about Brett Inness turning on the alarm. This last didn't surprise him.

"Yes, I know. Keith told me the next day. He was up late that night and he's always loved to roam the grounds after dark. He was near the house, down at the art gallery, and when the alarm went off and he saw Brett come running out of the house, he was sure she'd turned it on. But what was happening scared him, and he came straight to the cottage and sneaked back to bed. Of course, he wasn't supposed to be out in the first place."

"What do you make of this?"

"Nothing—yet."

"But you didn't bring it up with the police?"

He smiled at me ruefully. "There's an old Logan rule dating back to Allegra's time. We protect the family. I'll talk to Brett when I have a chance."

Once more, I disliked the concealment that always seemed part of the very atmosphere of Poinciana.

"I don't believe she left that 'Gretchen' note for Ross, if that's what you're thinking," he said. "Brett would take stronger action than that."

I was considering this when Jarrett surprised me by reaching out to take my hand. The gesture seemed to happen quite simply, and the touch of his fingers quieted me, easing my turbulent thoughts so that a sense of contentment filled me. His touch asked for nothing and offered nothing. Only friendship. Yet something in me knew that if I wanted it, this might very well be a beginning. If only I could trust again as easily as I had done with Ross. Instead, I thought of women who built those imaginary heroes they fell in love with, and I was wary. After a moment I slipped my hand away. It was myself I distrusted, more than Jarrett.

I went on to tell him what Myra Ritter had said about the possibility of a rich man stealing from himself. Jarrett seemed neither surprised nor outraged, as I'd half hoped he might be.

"I don't know that this is what happened," he said. "But it's not impossible. Ross enjoyed the little games he sometimes played. Power games, meant to fool those around him and subject them to his will. There's no telling now what he might have been up to. I'm glad the Lautrecs have been found. Perhaps the netsuke will also turn up."

"Why did you work for him?" I asked. "Why did you go on working for him?"

"I suppose the trap closes. One gets caught. Getting out becomes hopelessly complicated. If I'd left, a number of projects that I believe are important would have been abandoned. Ross was never a philanthropist at heart. It was my job to make it seem that he was one. But I've already told you this."

"You must have hated him."

"Not always. Not entirely. There were times when I was sorry for him."

"Sorry for Ross Logan?"

"He wasn't a happy man. He was caught in the trap too. A trap set up in the beginning by Charles and Allegra, and baited with all the things they expected of him."

At that moment there was no compassion in me for Ross. "But how could you *not* hate him, when—?" I broke off because the thought of his wife could not be spoken.

"Sometimes I suppose I did," he agreed.

A voice spoke out of the darkness that had gathered around the deck. "And when you did, you could have killed him. Is that not so?"

The voice was Vasily's, and there was both mockery and challenge in the words.

Jarrett left his chair to move to the rail, and I sensed a barely controlled violence in him. "You have some reason for a remark like that?"

"Not I," Vasily said cheerfully. "Gretchen. It's her latest theory. Will you permit me to come up and join you? I thought it might be well for you to know what she is saying, and what she plans."

He didn't wait for Jarrett to answer, but came up the outside steps and leaned against the rail beside him. "Good evening, Sharon. Have you been thinking over the things we discussed this afternoon?"

"Sit down," Jarrett said. "You'd better tell us what's on your mind." He had already suppressed his first instinct to anger.

Instead of taking a chair, Vasily perched on the broad rail, swinging his legs. "My wife has, I believe at Brett's prompting, decided that you and Sharon caused the shock that resulted in her father's death. She has been claiming that all along, as you know. But now she means to give an interview to this effect. I've tried to dissuade her. Give me credit for that, at least. But when Gretchen goes on an emotional binge, I know of no way to stop her."

Jarrett swore softly under his breath. "Nor does anyone else. I'll try to talk to her, but that might be only a red flag. Thanks for coming to tell me. Incidentally, why did you?"

In the reflection of light from the windows behind me, I could see Vasily's face, see that for once he looked a little anxious.

"Let's call it self-preservation," he said. "I lack the

talent for destruction that Gretchen has. What she cannot win, she destroys. That she herself may be ruined in the process never seems to stop her."

I broke in. "But she can't have any possible basis for claiming such a thing. Oh, I know she's thrown out wild accusations, but I didn't think she took them seriously herself. I had lunch with her today, and she seemed almost friendly. Why should she do this now?"

Vasily moved his hands in an eloquent gesture that was thoroughly European. "She has been brooding. You were both there immediately after her father's death. Perhaps you were even there before he died?"

I knew that *I* had not been, but for the first time I wondered if Jarrett could have reached the office while Ross was still alive. By his own admission, he too was capable of subterfuge. I hated my own mistrust, and I had to answer Vasily.

"That's nonsense! Anyway, why would Gretchen do this? I've already told her she can have Poinciana. What more does she want?"

"Brett has convinced her that you will never give it up. Tomorrow she will act. She's planning to call a press conference in the early afternoon. I myself think this is unwise, and I would like to see her stopped. Among other things, she will claim that there have been thefts at Poinciana, and that one of you may be filching valuable items to sell outside. Items that ought to belong to her."

"She's absolutely mad!" I cried.

"She may very well be," Jarrett agreed. "I'd better go talk to her now, and see if I can coax her back to reason. I'm sorry to end the evening this way, Sharon. Would you like to come back to the house with me? Do you want to talk to Gretchen?"

"I'll go back," I said. "But I've had enough of talking to Gretchen for one day." What I didn't want was to be left alone with Vasily, who was making me increasingly uneasy.

"Remember," Vasily said, "you didn't see me. It wouldn't do for Gretchen to know that I came down here." He faded away into the darkness of the grounds, out of which he'd come.

All the lovely evening had been spoiled, and I felt hopeless again as I walked beside Jarrett toward the house.

He put an arm around me as we came near. "There's nothing to worry about. Gretchen can't back up her wild claims. People in the media will see through her, and I'll call a conference of my own if necessary. Though news of conflict at Poinciana won't do us any good."

"Why would Brett urge her into this?"

"Because she is a vindictive woman. Because she's still trying to punish Ross for all he did to her. She has some grounds for feeling the way she does, you know. But she has always managed to keep her influence with Gretchen. Love can be a very strange and mixed-up thing between mother and daughter, as well as can all the other kinds."

How well I knew that. "I doubt that Brett ever loved Gretchen."

"That's probably true. It's Gretchen, unfortunately, who grew up wanting Brett's affection and approval as she never wanted anything else, especially since she wasn't her natural child. She didn't have to work so hard with her father."

"In spite of everything, I feel sorry for Gretchen," I said. "She has so much going for her, and she doesn't use it."

When we reached a side door, Jarrett put his hand on my arm. "Take it easy, Sharon. Things will work out. Don't try to solve everything inside your head all at once. I'll phone you later, after I've talked to Gretchen. Will you be in your room?"

I said I would wait for his call, and went upstairs. Even when I was away from him, I could still feel the touch of his hand and see the kindness in his eyes.

The corridor that led to my room seemed emptier than ever as I hurried along, and I closed my door quickly, locking it. I wondered now why I had been willing to spend one more night in this room.

Chapter 17

When I was ready for bed, I sat propped against my pillows, reading one of the many books about early Palm Beach that I'd found in the library. Mainly, however, I was waiting for my phone to ring.

Nearly two hours passed and I'd dropped my book and fallen into a doze when the shrilling woke me.

Jarrett's voice sounded calm and reassuring. "I've done what I could. Fortunately, I caught Gretchen alone, without Brett, and in her way she's been fond of me since she was a little girl. So at least she listened. Part of the time she argued furiously, but I don't think she believes a word of her own accusations. She wants to make trouble for you. Brett has managed to instill that purpose in her, though I think something else is operating too. It's almost as though she may be covering something up with this outburst. Something that frightens her. I'm not sure what."

"But if it's me she wants to hurt, why is she accusing you too?"

"I'm tarred by the same brush, apparently. We were both in the office soon after Ross died. So she wants to claim that we were there before he died."

"Will she really call that news conference?"

"I'm not sure. She can change so fast. Are you all right, Sharon? If you're worried about staying at the house, Mrs. Simmons's room is empty and you can spend the night here at the cottage, if you'd be more comfortable."

For an instant, I wanted to accept his invitation joyfully. Instead, I held back. It would not be wise. There would be gossip and there were dangers at the cottage too. I mustn't move into that until I was sure. I had moved too soon with Ross, and I couldn't entirely trust myself. Besides, my own fears of this house were something I needed to overcome. I would be safe enough in this room for one more night. It had been Ross I had been afraid of here.

When I'd thanked Jarrett and hung up, I went to check the locks again, both in my own room and in Ross's. I hated to go in there and when I went through the door I didn't turn on the light. I didn't want Ysobel to watch me from her place on the wall. Moonlight showed me my way, and I made certain that the door to the hallway was locked.

Then I took a mild sleeping pill and went to bed.

Somewhere around midnight the music began in my dreams. The music and the singing. I could hear the words clearly: "... purple shadows and blue champagne ..."

I threw aside the covers and sat up in bed with cold sweat breaking out all over my body. My throat felt constricted by fear. In the remaining moonlight I could see that the door between my room and Ross's was open, and Ysobel's disembodied voice drifted through with a clarity that sent shivering fingers down my spine. The room beyond the doorway was as dark as my own, and shadowy—but the voice sang on and I didn't know what hand had set the tape running.

In my muddled, still half-conscious state, I thought first of Ross. If he could come back, this was just the sort of trick he would relish. I shook myself awake and slipped out of bed. That singing had to be stopped. If it went on, I might lose all self-control. I might cower here in terror forever if I didn't stop it. I might even start to scream.

Again I found my way, stumbling. I couldn't remember where the light switch was—probably by the door to the hall, so I eased around the edge of the bed, discovered a floor lamp, and turned it on. The room was empty. I fumbled my way to the record player and flipped the switch. Ysobel's voice slurred in the middle of a phrase, and I dropped onto the side of the bed and covered my face with my hands.

A cool breeze touched my shoulders, chilling me further, and I looked around to see that the door to the loggia was ajar. That door I must have forgotten to lock, and someone was out there in the darkness, watching me. I felt sure of it.

Shivering, I stood up, meaning to pull the spread from the bed and wrap it about me. But when I grasped a corner to turn it back, something rattled in the center of the spread. I paused to stare at the two tiny objects nestled there, clicking against each other. The Daruma and the carp with the turtle in its mouth—the two missing netsuke.

Moving automatically, I picked them up and placed them on a corner of the bed table. Then I went back to pull the spread free, and wrapped it about me. That felt a little better. When I'd picked up the netsuke again, I moved toward the open door to the loggia. I knew very well who was out there, and now I'd begun to tremble with rage as well as with the cold.

"You'd better come in," I said.

A small, square hand appeared to push the glass doors wider, and Gretchen slipped through the opening.

She was dressed in a long blue robe, with the collar turned up, and she was grinning her monkey grin that had little mirth in it.

"I've been watching you," she said. "I really frightened you, didn't I?"

My anger rose. "How could you possibly do a thing so cruel?" I demanded.

"It wasn't hard. I've grown up with two very good teachers—my father and Brett. I'm a prize, graduate pupil."

"Where did you get these?" I held out the netsuke.

"I have my ways," she said, and I knew she would never tell me.

My own urge to do violence surprised me. I wanted to slap her, shake her, punish her, but I knew that *my* control was the one thing I must not lose.

She was watching my face almost gleefully, as though she knew very well the emotions she aroused in me. "After all, I brought the netsuke back to you, didn't I? Why not give me credit for that?"

There was no possible answer. Not when she had deliberately turned on the recording of Ysobel's song, and waited outside in the dark to see what I would do. In spite of myself, my eyes were drawn to the portrait, and my mother's gaze seemed directed at me. In the shadowy room, where only one lamp burned, the generous warmth that she'd always given her audiences flowed out to me. If only she could have looked at me like that in life.

I turned again to Gretchen. "You'd better go now. You've done enough."

But she too was staring at the portrait. "Did you love her very much?" she asked softly.

The words surprised me. Even Gretchen's sudden changes of mood spoke of her unbalanced state. It was not for the first time that I wondered if everything that was unpleasant which had happened to me since I came to Poinciana had stemmed from just two sources—Ross and his daughter.

"I don't think this is the time for philosophical discussion," I said. "I'm going back to bed." I held up the netsuke. "I'll sleep with these under my pillow for the rest of the night."

She paid no attention, and her voice stopped me as I reached the door. "Just tell me the answer. Did you love your mother very much?"

"You've asked the wrong question," I said.

"I suppose I have." Her eyes didn't move from Ysobel's face. "I should have asked whether she loved you. Do you dare to tell me the answer to that, Sharon?"

I was very still as anger slipped away, leaving a strange pity behind it. I knew why she had asked me such a question. She had asked it because for all her life she had longed to be loved by Brett, just as I had longed to be loved by Ysobel Hollis. In this one thing we were sisters, Ross's daughter and I.

"I loved her a great deal," I said gently. "At least I did when I was small. And I wanted more than anything else to have her love me."

"I know," Gretchen said. "I understand that very-well."

As had happened between us at odd moments in the past, enmity fell away, and we were kin. I reached out from under the spread I'd wrapped around me and took her hand.

"Come in here," I said, and led her into the room that was still mine, away from Ysobel's watchful eyes and Ross's invisible presence. I pushed her down upon the chaise longue and pulled the throw over her. Then I stretched out on my bed, propping myself on one elbow.

"Have you ever tried to find your real mother?" I asked.

Her eyes were closed, and I saw a tear coursing down her cheek. "No! I've never wanted to. Not when she sold me to my father. I don't really care who she is. I've never gotten over wanting Brett to love me as if I were really her daughter. Fathers are important. But it's mothers we're closest to in the beginning. Or want to be closest to. Until we find someone outside to love us. I have that now in Vasily. And Brett and I are friends, in a way. I still want to please her, make her like me. Though I can see her more clearly now."

"Is that why you're planning a press conference tomorrow? Because she wants you to?"

She opened her eyes wide and stared at me. "How did you know that?"

I repeated her own words, faintly mocking. "I have my ways."

"Vasily," she said. "Of course."

I didn't give him away. "No—it was Jarrett. He phoned me tonight after he'd talked to you."

"Oh?" I heard the note of relief in her voice. "I suppose I thought it was Vasily because he can never be trusted any farther than I can see him. Yet I know he loves me. I *do* know that!"

I said nothing, hoping this wasn't a whistling in the dark for her.

"I wish I could tell you something," she went on, "but I can't trust you either."

Again I was silent. Later, I would wish I had urged her to confide in me, but I missed the chance with my silence.

"Just the same," she mused, "I'm lucky to have Vasily. I'm luckier than you are, Sharon. Because my father never really cared about you, did he? He only cared about Ysobel Hollis."

The cruel intent was back, and I lay silent on the bed, already regretting the impulse that had caused me to bring her into this room.

"There!" she said. "You see—I've done it again! Vasily says I use my tongue like a sword. But it's only because I speak my mind. I don't pussyfoot. I don't really mean—"

"You didn't mean to open the door to my room and set that recorder playing? You didn't wait deliberately for me to come?"

She sat up, somehow looking young and defenseless—which she certainly was not.

"Nobody's ever stopped me from doing the first thing that came into my head. Except maybe Grandmother Allegra. Everybody else let me go my own way. I guess my father was disciplined a lot by his parents when he was a boy, so he wouldn't do that to me. And Brett never cared, unless I bothered *her*. At least you've learned something about self-control, haven't you, Sharon? You've behaved admirably."

"I don't know if that's what you'd call it. In the end I suppose we all have ourselves to blame, whatever we do."

"I know. Take responsibility for our own acts! That's what Gran is always preaching. But she never does it herself. None of us looks at ourselves as we really are, do we? Never mind. I'll go now." She walked to the door and stood for a moment, hesitating. "I can't tell you I'm sorry, because I'm not. I enjoyed what I was doing. I really did. And that's pretty sick, isn't it?"

I said nothing and she scowled at me.

"My father should never have left you Poinciana," she said, and went out the door, pulling it shut after her.

I got up to lock it again. Then I went into Ross's room, where the lamp still burned, and this time I locked both doors. But I didn't turn off the light. I didn't want to think of darkness pulsing in that empty room. Back in my own bed, I thrust the two netsuke under my pillow and lay on my back with my eyes closed, all emotion draining from me, all sleep hopelessly far away. Limbo.

I must have slept eventually—heavily, deeply—for it was mid-morning when I opened my eyes to hear rain at all my windows. In the next room the lamp still burned, and memory returned sickly. The two netsuke were still beneath my pillow when I reached for them, but I closed my eyes, listening to the rain, remembering mornings when I'd been eager to rise and start my day because so much that was lovely and exciting awaited me. For a little while Ross had given me that. And I could almost believe that he had enjoyed giving it. If we could have stayed away from Poinciana...

Better to make plans, I thought. Today I would change my rooms. I would visit Allegra. I would make lists of things that must be done. The thought brought a smile. List-making was something I'd learned in self-defense when I traveled with Ysobel. My mother had been cheerfully heedless, depending on others to see that she arrived where she was supposed to be at the right time, that she didn't overspend her allowance, that she dressed herself in the right assortment of clothes. She must always be on stage, and others must help to get her there. After which she performed beautifully on her own.

A flash of memory slanted through my thoughts, to bring back another moment I'd had with Ysobel on that tour that ended in San Francisco. Before we'd flown to Ireland for that last performance. She had come into the wings after taking numerous bows, and the applause was still ringing with all the love her audiences held for her. She pushed through those who waited in the wings, and came to where I stood alone, watching her. I could remember the way she put a finger to her forehead, rubbing as though a headache were starting, and she'd looked at me in a puzzled way.

"I'm only real when I'm out there," she said. "What's going to happen when they don't want me any more?"

In that instant I'd felt older than Ysobel, and I'd put a comforting arm about her. "They'll always want you," I said.

At once she had laughed and pushed me away and was herself again. But I had glimpsed again her vulnerability, and love for her had welled up in me, stronger than old resentments.

Had Gretchen given me something last night, in spite of malicious intent? She'd said, "None of us looks at ourselves as we really are." It was time now to look, whether I liked it or not. Look and stop blaming.

Not something easy to do.

When I'd showered and dressed in slacks and a light pullover, I stood at the loggia door and watched rain slant across the tiles and stream down the drains. The palm trees looked wet, their trunks glistening dark, and the lake was a murky froth. Good! I was tired of everlasting sunshine. Rain suited my mood.

Susan brought my breakfast tray, since it was once more a Saturday and she was on duty. I was grateful for her unobtrusive presence as she set the tray down, drew up a chair for me, poured coffee—and waited.

"What's happening around the house?" I asked.

"I don't know really. Everything is spooky quiet, except that Mr. Nichols is working in his office, and has Miss Ritter in for the day so he can dictate. And my mother's turning out the rooms you want to move into, though I'm afraid she doesn't approve."

"This room belonged to Brett Inness."

"Yes, and Mother was devoted to her. She's upset because you don't want to stay in a room she thinks is absolute perfection."

I glanced about at pale elegance. "It's not for me. I like things cozier."

"Anyway, you shouldn't stay here."

"I agree. But why do you say that?"

"It's just a feeling. As though everyone in this house is plotting against everyone else. It's creepy."

"Including me?"

"Maybe you're not plotting enough," she said, and went quietly away.

I ate my breakfast in a thoughtful mood, wondering about the hint of warning in her words. Fine! I would plot. I would make lists, I would take action. I sat at my desk and wrote. It was easy enough to make lists. I was an expert.

When I was done I read through what I had written—all the earnest duties that I could begin to perform about the house—and found it utterly boring. I didn't want to live my life by the clock any more, or by making lists. And I didn't want to *plot*. There were things to be done, and I would do them. I tore up the list.

First, a visit to Allegra. I must tell her about my move into her wing.

I found her propped up in bed with her eyes closed, and Brett in a chair beside her, reading aloud about a certain Mrs. Pollifax, who was apparently an adventurous lady after Allegra's own heart.

The reading stopped as I appeared in the doorway, and Allegra opened her eyes. "Today I want to go up to my rooms in the tower," she said to no one in particular.

Brett closed the book. "Darling, those stairs would be hard for you. I've always hated them myself."

"Nonsense! Everyone used to complain about them. Because they are steep and make people dizzy. They are very easy stairs, really. You just put one foot after another very carefully and pull yourself up by the iron rail. I never had any trouble."

"But, darling, you're not as strong as you were then," Brett reminded her.

I had said nothing, and no one greeted me. Now Allegra gave me a rather wicked look, and lowered one eyelid in a wink that made the years fall away. I had a feeling that she would need to be watched very carefully today or she might indeed try to climb those stairs to the belvedere.

"There's something you wanted?" Brett asked, making it clear that I intruded, and that she had no intention of recognizing me as mistress of Poinciana.

I went closer to the bed, speaking to Allegra. "I wanted you to know that I'm moving into this wing today, Mrs. Logan. I don't want to stay off there by myself. Besides, if I'm closer to you, you can tell me more about the house."

Her nod was lively, pleased. "Come visit me any time."

I didn't wait to see how Brett took this exchange, but returned to the corridor, skirted a bed that had been moved out of what was to be my sitting room, and found my way downstairs to the office wing.

Myra apparently didn't mind working overtime on Saturday, and she was at her desk typing briskly. She looked up and shook her head. "If you're looking for Mr. Nichols, you can't go in right now, Mrs. Logan. He has an appointment with a man who has just arrived from New York."

I'd wanted to see Jarrett to tell him about Gretchen's visit the night before, but that could wait. Moving idly, I went toward Ross's door, and Myra stopped me again.

"Better not," she said. "Mrs. Karl is in there and I think she's having a bang-up fight with her husband. We'll probably have to get a new coffee set. She was throwing the crockery around." Clearly Myra was enjoying the whole scene.

Voices could be heard from beyond the heavy door, but no words came through. It was an awkward moment to have Brett follow me downstairs and walk in just as Ross's door flew open and Gretchen came storming out. She saw us both, and stopped for a moment, wildly angry.

"Vasily is threatening to divorce me!" she cried. "Him! I'll show him! I'm going to change my will as soon as I can!"

Brett put out a hand to stop her daughter, but Gretchen brushed blindly past. We followed her to the door and looked out. Halfway down the hall, she pulled open the door that led to the tower stairs, and I heard her clattering up the circular treads on her way to the upper rooms. Vasily came out of Ross's office, looking oddly helpless and white-faced.

"Those damned netsuke!" he said. "I gave them back to her, but she wasn't satisfied. She's gone a little crazy."

"You did have the two missing ones, then?" I asked,

surprised that he would admit it. "You had them that time in the tower?"

"Yes, yes—what does it matter? I returned them to her, didn't I? So why must she ask so many questions? Why did she have to go searching among her father's papers?"

"Searching for what?"

He was recovering himself and growing calmer. "My wife has decided to check up on me—as her father was doing. Instead of taking my word, she has decided to find out everything he thought he had uncovered about me."

I became aware of Myra, listening eagerly as usual.

"Let's not talk here," I said. "Come across the hall."

He was too excited to pay attention. "I've taken enough from her! I told her to divorce me and have done with it! I tried to make everything clear to her when we married—but it wasn't enough. So I will move out now!"

If Vasily walked out on Gretchen, she would lose everything she most valued—no matter what she was saying now in anger. Even if Vasily had taken the netsuke, it didn't matter in the face of his wife's unstable condition. I dreaded to think what might happen to her if he left her at this time.

"Just wait a while," I said. "You know she'll cool off when she stops to think."

He seemed to see me for the first time, and a faint smile returned to erase the anger. "You are a good person, Sharon, and you are also very naïve," he said, and went toward the door. He didn't speak to Brett, but she blocked his way.

"Sharon's right," Brett told him. "Give Gretchen time to come out of it. Maybe I can talk to her. She's gone up to the belvedere now. That's always been her refuge, just the way it used to be Allegra's. When she comes down, she'll feel better. So don't go running out on her, Vasily. After all, you've got a lot to lose if you do."

I watched them both intently, and I saw the strange look of understanding that passed between them. It was a look that made me think of their meeting in the beach tunnel, when I'd surprised them.

Vasily was already shaking his head. "It's too late. This time it's too late. I've had more than I can take—and perhaps she has too. So let her do her worst."

Brett started to speak, but he brushed past us both and disappeared down the hall. She looked after him soberly and I wondered what dark thoughts she was thinking. As always, she seemed an enigma. But I had no wish to stay and discuss what had happened with her, so I left the office and found my way outside to where a sheltered courtyard offered protection from the rain.

Wrought-iron chairs were grouped around a table, and I pulled one out, and sat down beneath the overhang. This little court was another of the curious indentations that Allegra had built into the house. Because of them, all the upstairs rooms had windows that opened upon the outdoors. Near where I sat, a strange twisted tree that Ross had called a gumbo-limbo shook its wet leaves as a breeze stirred them. I lifted my head, breathing the fresh scent of the rain.

The scene in the office had shaken me badly. Gretchen seemed intent upon destroying her own happiness. Or had Ross been right from the beginning, and had all possibility for happiness ended on the day when she'd married Vasily Karl? Strangely, there were times when I almost liked him. I didn't trust him, and I thought it might be characteristic if he had taken the netsuke. Yet there was something oddly likable about him—even while he was following his own devious bent. In a way, I could understand how he had captivated Gretchen. I could also imagine him doing quite dastardly things in a most charming and disarming way. As though to say, "You see—I know it is wrong, but obviously I cannot help myself."

I remembered his saying that I should close Poinciana up while the will was being settled, and go away. Probably that would not negate my ownership. Certainly Ross hadn't meant that I couldn't take a trip or a vacation, or stir out of the house. As long as I was in residence legally, I could go away and come back. If there really was a divorce—though I couldn't see Gretchen letting it go that far, unless she had driven Vasily away for good this time—then it would be safe to let Gretchen inherit Poinciana. But if they made up again, Vasily might receive all of it should anything happen to Gretchen. Ross hadn't wanted that, and I didn't believe it was wise myself. Not unless the time came when I could be more sure of him. If he had taken the netsuke to sell, this hardly improved my opinion of him.

Besides, this wouldn't have been the first time. Again I wondered about the Lautrec paintings. Had it really been Ross who had removed them?

No, even though I might like Vasily at times, I didn't trust him for a moment.

Beyond the dry nook where I sat, rain sounded on the tiles of the courtyard, and I listened to its soothing rhythm. Always, I felt more peaceful when I was outside the house. How long I sat there, I don't know, but suddenly the morning was pierced by a thin, high scream. A chilling sound of terror, followed almost at once by a shattering crash. I came to my feet, tense and listening. The morning was still except for the rain.

I ran out upon wet grass, to where I could look back at the house. The scream had come from the direction of the tower, and I stood for a moment staring up at the circling windows of the belvedere, and at the balcony that ran around the top. Nothing moved, and all the windows I could see were closed.

Running again, I rounded the end of a wing, and came out on the other side of the tower. Now I could see the glass door that gave onto the gallery. It stood open, and a portion of the rail had broken through, with a piece hanging down. My throat closed with fear as I rushed across the grass.

Gretchen lay face down upon the paving stones at the base of the tower—lay in the one place where the tower stood away from the house, with no tiled roofs below. There had been nothing to break her fall.

She lay still, chillingly still, with rain beating around and over her, her arms outflung. Before I could reach her, others came running. One or two men first, and then a frightened maid. Jarrett was next, rushing out a nearby door, and it was Jarrett who knelt beside her.

In that dreadful suspended moment, while we stood around them, waiting, I was intensely aware of unimportant details. One of the girls, already soaked by the rain, was crying in choked sobs. The loose bit of balcony rail flapped in the wind, and the poinciana tree shed its bright petals as rain beat them into the earth. One of Gretchen's hands was curled about some small object that she must have clutched at the moment of her fall.

Jarrett looked up and spoke to one of the men. "Call for an ambulance. Hurry!"

He saw me among the others and shook his head, his face grim. "There's only a feather of pulse. Get me something to cover her with." A servant went back to the house.

As he touched her sad, broken body, something tiny rolled from her hand, and I bent to catch it. I felt a compulsion to stop for an instant to look up at the tower. It seemed to me that something moved up there. Not at the balcony level, but in the room below. It was no more than a flash, an impression at a window. Then I rushed inside and began to call for Vasily or Brett—or for someone to go and find them. From the direction of the boulevard came the screaming of an ambulance siren.

I opened my wet hand and stared at the tiny object

that I had caught from Gretchen's fingers as she opened them. It was a netsuke—the small carving of the Sleeping Mermaid that was Allegra's favorite of all the collection.

Chapter 18

When the others drove to the hospital, following the ambulance, Jarrett asked me not to come.

"There's nothing you can do," he said. "Stay at Poinciana and hold things together. Be with Allegra if she needs you."

I told no one about the little mermaid. Its presence frightened me. When I was alone I took it out and examined it carefully. It was just as I remembered—a mermaid sweetly asleep in pale pink coral, her tail curled neatly around her body—but it told me nothing. Or everything? Had Allegra indeed gone to her tower rooms? And if she had—? I put the puzzle away from me. Allegra had loved her granddaughter dearly. As she had once loved her son?

For the rest of that gloomy day, while I awaited word from the hospital, I did what I could. Though my clothes were still damp, I put off changing them, and talked to Mrs. Broderick. Badly shaken as she was, she called the staff together and informed them of what had happened.

Since Jarrett no longer needed her, Myra went home in an upset state, muttering that the house was accursed.

Then, when I'd put it off long enough, I climbed the stairs to talk to Allegra, uncertain as to whether I should explain at once what had happened, or if it might be better to wait for certainty later. Mostly, I tried to keep myself from thinking, from believing, from facing what had happened. More than anything else, I was afraid to question the presence of the mermaid in Gretchen's hand.

The door to Allegra's bedroom was open and I went in, to find that her bed was tousled and Allegra gone. Coxie sat placidly knitting in the next room. Nothing of what had happened had touched that remote wing, where sounds from the rest of the house were inaudible and the tower far away.

"Mrs. Logan is asleep," Coxie said as I looked in at her.

"She's not asleep. She's not there at all," I told her.

The nurse took the news calmly. "Well, don't worry. She likes to wander around the house when the spirit moves her. Do you want me to search for her?"

"I'll do it myself," I told her, and hurried off.

I knew where I would look first, reluctant as I was to go there. I remembered what Allegra had said about climbing to the tower. With all my heart, I hoped she had not been there when Gretchen fell, but I had to make sure those rooms were empty, and that nothing had happened to Allegra.

Along the corridor that led to the belvedere, I met Susan and saw that she was crying. "My mother's just phoned the hospital and talked to Mr. Nichols. He says there's very little hope."

I patted her shoulder and went on toward the tower stairs.

After the first sick shock of Gretchen's terrible fall, I had seemed to exist in a suspended state, where nothing about me had reality. There were duties that must be performed, and I would do them. My mind seemed to tick off what was necessary. It wasn't possible to face the fact that Gretchen might at this very moment be breathing out her young life. Numbness was a blessing. I could act without thinking or feeling.

As I climbed the iron treads I remembered Allegra's words—that the stairs were easy enough to mount. One set one's feet carefully on the wedged steps and clung to the rail. I went round and round to the top and stood looking about me. The little studio room seemed undisturbed. The two pictures of Ross hung in their usual place on the wall, and I was glad he couldn't know what had happened to his daughter.

Rain slanted through the open glass door and I went to look outside. The loose piece of railing still flapped in the wind, and there was an opening wide enough for anyone to fall through. Reality hit me like a blow to the pit of my stomach. Gretchen had stood exactly here. Had the rail broken when she leaned on it—or had she thrown herself against it, meaning to break through?

Yet she had screamed as she fell.

How awful, how terrible, to experience those seconds of falling—to be alive, with the ground rising—and then not to be. I felt so ill that I had to go inside and sit down for a little while. I must return to that safe state of being numb and not thinking. I mustn't let my imagination go. Yet the fearful record was ready to play itself over and over in my mind. I prayed a little—but without hope. Even though I had only glimpsed her face, I knew.

How different deaths could be. My mother's and father's—too horrible to be borne. Ross's had been shocking and sudden. But none of them had been terrible in the same way as this. Ross had lived a long, full life, and death could never destroy what he'd had and what he'd been. My parents had lived happily and successfully for many years. But Gretchen's life was still beginning. And she had been unhappy for so much of it. All those pages of years might never be written for her now, and I couldn't bear to think about that. Or of the fact that I hadn't tried hard enough to befriend her. This was familiar too—the blame one took upon oneself when someone close died.

Nevertheless, I held back my tears, afraid to let them come. If I cried now, I would be crying for too much recent loss, for too much pain, and I might not be able to stop. I must still find Allegra.

Returning to the stairs, I circled them to the room below and looked into it. One glance was enough to shock me. I walked into the small square area where Allegra had liked to rest, and looked about. The armoire where her ball gowns were kept was open, and dress after dress had been taken out and spread across shrouded chairs and over the couch, where Allegra had once napped. The room was a froth of satin and lace and rainbow colors strewn everywhere. No damage had been done to any of them, as far as I could see. It was as though they had been laid out for display. Perhaps in order to make a choice?

Now, with dread, I knew the answer to the faint movement I'd seen at a window of the tower. Allegra herself had been here, looking at her old gowns, perhaps savoring memories connected with each one, living her old life again. She must have brought the mermaid here, to give her once more a glimpse of her home, the sea, as she used to say. Gretchen must have found her grandmother here and taken the mermaid from her. After that—what? I wasn't sure I wanted to know. I was afraid to know.

I was certain of only one thing. I must find Allegra at once, and these gowns suggested where I might look.

I ran outside through the rain to the closed door of those stairs I had first explored, and which led down from the loggia to the ballroom. This was a place I hadn't cared to visit again, but now I ran down curving tiled steps in the gloom, and opened the door at the bottom. Brilliance dazzled me.

All the chandeliers were lit, and she was there—beautiful, resplendent in chiffon the color of primroses, her white hair pinned carelessly on top of her head, her arms raised as she danced with an imaginary partner. The dance, obviously, was an old-fashioned waltz, and she moved to an echo of music I couldn't hear, swaying gracefully as she turned—forever young and untouched by the years that stretched behind her, as they might never do now for her granddaughter.

Though she must have seen my approach, she gave no sign of recognition, her eyes raised dreamily to a partner only she could see, her beautiful, lined face filled with love. Of course. She was dancing again with her Charlie.

I knew myself for the intruder I was. What was I to do—rush up and say, "No, no, you mustn't wear yourself out like this"? Was I to cry out that calamity had once more fallen on Poinciana, and this was no time for dancing? Or ask if she had seen Gretchen in the tower? Of course I did none of these. I went to sit on one of the small gilt chairs that edged the room. I sat very still and watched and thought of nothing but the present moment.

So beautifully did she dance that I could almost see her partner, almost hear the lilting three-quarter pulse of the music. In my imagination I could people the room with couples moving beneath great chandeliers that set gold leaf shining across the coffered ceiling. All this she had created out of her own will and imagination, and I would not stop Allegra Logan from dancing.

She stopped herself eventually, and came smiling to sit beside me. "Isn't it a lovely party?" she said.

"It's the most beautiful party I've ever seen," I told her, "and you're the most beautiful hostess."

She smiled at me benignly. "Thank you, my dear. I'm sorry, but I'm not sure of your name. There are so many..."

My heart did a turn as I realized that this wasn't make-believe for her. She had slipped entirely back into another world, and lost all touch with the present one.

"I'm Sharon Logan," I said. "I'm Ross's new wife."

Once more that puzzled her. "But Ross's new wife is named Brett." Her hands fluttered lightly, uncertainly, and I took them in mine.

"It's time to come home," I said gently. "This is another day. Ross and Brett have been divorced for years. And of course you—you do remember Gretchen?"

"Gretchen? I don't know anyone named Gretchen. Really, this is becoming a foolish conversation. Will you please find Charles for me? Our guests are beginning to leave, and we must be together to bid them good night."

I almost envied her. She had slipped into the past more completely than I had ever seen her do—a past in which there was far less pain than the present. There seemed no way in which I could call her back. I held her hands more tightly, frightened for her because she was living in a happier time, and the return to today would be all the more terrible. Yet I couldn't leave her in the place to which she had gone, lest she never return.

"Allegra, please come back," I said again. "Of course you remember Gretchen, your granddaughter. You must have seen her this afternoon in the tower rooms."

"No, no, stop it! I don't like to play games like this." She drew her hands from mine and looked eagerly about the room. "I can't think where Charlie can have gone. He was here only a moment ago."

How could I tell her? How could I tell her that Charlie was long dead, and Ross more recently, and that now Gretchen might very well be dying?

"Let me help you upstairs," I said.

She was growing bewildered, and her mind was still far away. She allowed me to raise her to her feet, and we walked out and stood for a moment in the center of that vast parquet floor. I looked from arch to arch of the doorways, wondering how to get her quickly back to the main part of the house.

"I want to take you up to your rooms," I said gently. "Miss Cox will be waiting for you."

That only drew a blank. "Miss Cox?"

"You do remember the rooms, don't you? Your beautiful silver-gray rooms that you enjoyed so much?"

"My gray rooms? Yes, I think so." Her bewilderment was growing, but she made an effort to recover her air of authority. "Of course—my gray rooms! I'd like to show them to you. Come along—this is the simplest way out."

She led me down the great ballroom, not toward one of the doors, but to a panel in the wall. She touched it lightly and it swiveled in. Without faltering, she reached for a switch that lighted a narrow interior passageway which ran back toward equally narrow steps. She was laughing a little now.

"Charlie used to worry about me. He said I would get lost in my own house and never be found if I kept using my secret routes. Come along, dear. Don't drag your feet."

I wondered who she thought I was by this time, but I went with her, feeling claustrophobic. The panel had closed behind us at a touch of her hand, and the passageway smelled of musty dampness and mice. There were probably all sorts of insects too, this being Florida. Allegra picked up her chiffon skirts, not letting them brush against the walls or floor, and moved lightly ahead of me. Not walking like an old lady now, but like the young, strong woman she had once been. So much for what our minds could do for us! Believing herself young, she walked with the lightness of youth, and climbed the stairs without faltering. I followed her, hating the tight walls that seemed to press in upon us, the airlessness, and the horrid sense that if anything happened we really could be lost in here, as Charlie had said—and never be found.

At the top, the passage came to an end and Allegra reached out to push another panel. Again the wall swiveled and I saw that this was where Keith had popped out at Ross and me that time. She waited courteously for me to step through, and then touched another switch that turned off lights that were strung all the way from the ballroom. The panel pushed shut behind her, and there was only a *trompe l'oeil* doorway painted on the wall.

Only then did she falter and grow uncertain. Youth crumbled away in an instant, and she seemed to age before my eyes. Yet the change brought only bewilderment with it, and no recognition of the passing years, or of my identity.

"We'll go to your rooms now," I said gently. "You'll want to rest. You must be tired from dancing."

She tossed her head and careless hairpins went flying. "Of course I'm not tired! I never got tired the way the others did—not even when I danced the whole night through." She broke off and looked at me piteously. "No—you're right. I am tired. Why is that?"

I put an arm about her and drew her along the corridor. After a few steps she resisted me, and clutched at her breast in a sudden frightening gesture, so that I wondered if her valiant heart had at last betrayed her.

But she wasn't clutching at her heart. She slipped a hand into her low-cut bodice and drew out something small and oblong, like a flat box.

"I forgot about this," she said. "I don't know what to do with it."

She held the box out to me, and I saw that it was a cassette tape. Uncertainly, I took it from her. "What is it? What do you want me to do with it?"

"I finally found the tape!" she cried, suddenly excited, and I heard the triumph in her voice. "I've been trying to remember what I did with it. I used to come to the house from the cottage to search for it sometimes, and today I found it—right there in a corner of the armoire, under my ball gowns."

With surprising ease she had slipped from past to present, and was with me in reality again. The small flat case seemed to have a life of its own in my hands, and I knew that I was afraid of whatever it contained.

"Help me," she said, and clung to my arm as she had not before. "I want to sit down. My—my knees feel very strange."

We went along the corridor to her own gray and crimson parlor. Even with the dark rain at the windows and the ocean stormy beyond, the Turkish rug glowed with its muted colors.

At the sight of Allegra in her primrose chiffon, Coxie dropped her knitting and jumped to her feet.

"Oh, dear! Oh, dear!" she cried. "What have you gotten into now? Where have you been?"

"Never mind," I told her sharply. "Mrs. Logan wants to sit here and rest a little."

"I'll put her to bed at once! Come along now, dearie. Coxie will help you."

"No!" I said, and led Allegra to an armchair, lowered her into it. Then I faced the nurse. "Just go away for a while."

Clearly, I'd outraged her, and she drew herself up to her bulky height. "I don't take orders from anyone but—"

"You're forgetting," I said. "You take orders from me. So go downstairs and talk to someone. Find Mrs. Broderick. Something has happened that you should know about. But don't come back here for at least an hour."

For a moment she looked shocked and a little frightened. Then she ducked her head and almost ran from the room. Allegra sat very straight, with her bright dress fluffed around her, looking incongruous now, her unrestrained locks coming down about her face.

"Good for you!" she cried. "I'm glad you told her off—whoever you are. I don't know when that woman came into my life—I can't remember. But she's a dreadful nuisance."

When she leaned back and closed her eyes, I was afraid she would slip away too deeply into the past again. Pulling a hassock close to her chair, I sat down and touched her hand.

"This tape, Mrs. Logan—tell me what it is." Strange, I could call her Allegra when she was in the past, but not in the present.

"I don't know," she said without opening her eyes. "I've never listened to it. I've never wanted to know what it contains."

"But where did you get it? Why did you hide it?"

Her time sequences might be confused, with lapses of memory bewildering her, but a thread of sense ran through her words.

"Pam Nichols gave it to me only the other day. She said I mustn't show it to anyone unless something happened to her. But of course nothing will happen to her—will it?"

I could almost lose myself in Allegra's mixed time periods. "I—I don't know," I said. "What else did she tell you when she gave it to you? Try to remember, please."

Her effort was clear in her face. "She told me that—that someone was trying to kill her. She told me that she had put all her suspicions down on tape, so that if anything happened, the guilty person would be accused."

"And then what? Try to remember."

She turned her head from side to side in anguish. "I don't know. I was sick for a long while afterwards. I'd put the tape away, and when I was well again I couldn't remember where it was. I tried to get that little boy, Keith, to help me find it, because he knows all the hiding places in the house. But he never could. Of course, he didn't think of looking among my dresses up in the tower."

"You still don't know what's on it?"

"No. Pam asked me not to play it unless—unless—I don't remember. And then when I was well again, I couldn't find it."

"Have you told anyone else about its existence?"

"Yes—I think so." The fogs were slipping away a little now. "I told Gretchen. And I think I talked to Brett about it. And perhaps to others. Ross was married to her when Pam was in that accident, you know. She did die, didn't she? But no one ever found the tape—until I did myself—today!"

"Do you want to hear what it says?" I asked.

There was a long silence while she considered painfully. "No, I don't think so. He's my son. I don't want to know. Because if I know I might have to do something about it." Her look was suddenly wise, perhaps a little crafty. "That's too often the way, isn't it? We have a choice and we do nothing. And then suddenly it's too late. Afterwards, we don't dare admit what we haven't done."

"What do you want me to do with the tape now?" I asked.

This time she didn't hesitate. "I think you must play it. I think you must know whatever there is to know. You're Ross's wife, aren't you? I remember now. You need to know how dangerous he can be. You need to know, for your own protection. But you mustn't tell *me.* I'm too old to bear any more. Ross was always an impossible boy. We hoped for so much for him. We gave him so much."

Everything except understanding, I thought with sudden clarity, seeing for the first time a lonely small boy lost in the grandeurs of Poinciana, fearful that he could never live up to all this, yet driven for all his life into trying—in no matter how unscrupulous a way—because he couldn't believe in himself. This would be something that Allegra could never understand. Her generation had not been given to much self-awareness. That was difficult enough for a far more psychologically oriented age to come by. We could only make beginnings out of ignorance.

She spoke to me again. "The tape is yours now. Your responsibility."

I wasn't sure this was a responsibility I wanted to accept, but the small, frail woman in the chair sat up straighter than ever and fixed me sternly with eyes that were quite clear. She was Allegra Logan, and hers was the authority that ruled this house.

"You have no choice. I had a choice. For a long while I had a choice, but I did nothing. Then when I knew that Ross meant to put me away in some terrible place, so that no one would listen to anything I said, I decided. I told Brett and Gretchen they must find the tape and stop Ross from what he meant to do. I'm sure they searched and searched, but neither of them found it. So now *you* have no choice. Take it away and listen to what it says. Listen to it right now!"

I sat on the edge of the hassock, with the cassette in my hands, and knew I would have to obey. But first there was something else I must ask, something that I'd postponed out of my own fears. I must face it now.

"Will you tell me, Mrs. Logan—when you were in the tower room today, did you see Gretchen there? Did you talk to her?" I took the little mermaid from my raincoat pocket and held it out to her. "What do you know about this?"

Before my eyes, she seemed to crumple in upon herself, shaking her head from side to side. "No, no! I didn't see anything! Where is Gretchen? I want Gretchen to come to me right away!"

Either she had seen nothing, or she had blocked out whatever had happened in the tower. Blocked it out then and there, so that she could journey into the past and dance in her ballroom again. I knew I could urge her no further now.

"Let me help you out of that dress," I said. "I'll find a robe for you, and—"

Once more she stiffened, recovering. "Go right now!"

she ordered. "Before anything happens to stop you. I'm perfectly comfortable here, and after a while Coxie will come and see to me. She irritates me, and sometimes I fight her. But I'm used to her, and she does look after me."

"All right," I said. I kissed her cheek, and she reached out to pat my arm vaguely, again not quite sure who I was.

There were several tape recorders around the house, and one was in the library. So that was where I would go.

On my way downstairs, I met Coxie hurrying up, and knew by her face that she had been told about Gretchen. She hadn't waited out her hour.

"This will kill Mrs. Logan!" she cried. "She can't take any more, poor old thing."

"She's not a poor old thing," I said, "and she's probably tough enough to outlive us both. But don't *you* try to tell her."

The nurse fled from me up the stairs, intent on succoring her charge. I knew by now, however, that Allegra had her own means of escaping from whatever might disturb and injure her, and I could almost envy her that facility.

For me, the library was filled with memories, and Ysobel's recording was still in the machine. I took it out and replaced it with the first side of the unlabeled tape that Allegra had given me. Outside, the storm was growing stronger, slashing against window panes, bending the palm trees, banging a shutter somewhere in the house. The air seemed close inside, yet I felt cold and a little ill. Allegra's voice still commanded me. *Play it now.* I reached out and pressed the lever.

The voice was clear and sweet and filled with sorrow. I listened with all my being.

"Someday, Jarrett, you will hear these words I'm recording. And so will others. Because all the family must know. I watch you now, and I suffer for both of us. I know that you know, and I can see how hopelessly you are trapped. As I am trapped. You're angry with him—with Ross—and you're sorry for me because you know how foolish I've been. I think the time will come when you'll leave Ross because this is more than any man can bear. But it mustn't come to that. You will surely find a way to stop him.

"I know how much depends on you. There are all those people out there who will be damaged if you leave Ross. Because *he* doesn't care. None of what you're doing means anything to him. I've heard the callous way he talks. I know how indifferent he is. Yet he needs you to keep him in power, and he depends on you, much as he hates this very thing. You're the man he would like to be—perhaps that's his tragedy—and he can never forgive you for being what he isn't. So you are bound together, despising each other—and trapped. The thing I am most afraid of is violence. From either one of you."

"How did it happen? I mean between me and Ross. You have a right to know, and yet I'm not sure that I can tell you. It happened—that's all. Perhaps it was his revenge against you. But that's not what this tape is about. It's not what I'm trying to tell you now. I've loved him and hated him, and I have never stopped loving and admiring you—but in a different, healthier way. Let it go. As you'll have to let me go. But you must not let Ross get away with everything.

"He's grown tired of me, as he grows tired of anything that comes within his grasp. He always thinks he has to reach further. And perhaps Allegra is to blame for that. I know that part of my appeal for him lay in spiting you, but he has become like a drug for me, and I don't know how to go on living without him. So—foolishly—I've tried to threaten him. When he said he wouldn't meet me again, I told him I would go to you—inform you of everything. He laughed at me—but with that look in his eyes that told me he wasn't laughing inside.

"I think—I *know*—that he means to be rid of me,

top me from talking. Somehow he will make it look ike an accident, but I want you to know that it won't e one. Perhaps I could prevent this. Perhaps I could ind a way to make him really afraid. But I shan't try. don't want to go on living like this. I don't want *you* o go on living in this terrible way. So—I will let it appen, whatever it is. And I will not go to you as I hreatened. My greatest sorrow is that I must leave Keith. But you will be a better father to him than I ave been a mother. And someday you'll find another voman to mother him. Just make him understand al-vays how much I loved him.

"Yesterday I saw Ross in the garage when Albert nd the others were gone. He was working on my car. went away and said nothing. Very soon I will drive ut again—and then who knows? It will be best for all f us if it happens. For me and for you. And Ross will t last be exposed for what he is, because when you ear this tape you will have to act against him. It would e foolish to say I'm sorry. That would only be weak nd useless. But I wish you had never gone to work for Ross Logan.

"Try not to hate me. You are the finest man I've ever nown. I will put this tape in Allegra's hands to give o you if anything happens to me.

"This is Pam—signing off."

The tape recorder clicked to a stop, and I sat for a long while in the dim library. All about me on the shelves were a storing of words. Millions of words, ready to come to life whenever anyone opened a book. But only Pam Nichols's words echoed terribly through my mind with all their ramifications—their power to affect the lives of those who lived after her.

The evil I had sensed in this house had stemmed from Ross. Rather than see the man he depended upon turn against him, he had destroyed Jarrett's wife. First, he had satisfied his own need for power by seducing her, to spite the man he envied, but he could not risk

Jarrett's permanent loss, so he had rid himself of the danger she had threatened. Brett had been wise to get away. Perhaps I would have escaped eventually myself. Allegra knew her son. What she had never seen was the hand she had taken in forming him. Not that she could be blamed either. This wasn't a game of find-the-blame. Everyone was guilty—including those of us alive now. Allegra must have guessed. Ross had destroyed her too. Even though she had never played the tape herself, she had known, and when Pam died, she had become ill with the knowing, never again to be her old self.

What was I to do? What was the right thing, the wise thing, to do? Jarrett had every right to hear this tape. Yet how dreadful it would be for him to listen to Pam's voice, and learn all these things now, when he had at last begun to heal a little, and when Ross was gone and no longer could be held answerable. Jarrett had the right to hear it and Pam had the right to be heard. But I would wait a little while. I mustn't rush foolishly into damaging him further.

"May I come in?" a voice asked from the doorway.

I looked around in something of a daze, to see Brett Inness, bright in a frock printed with flame-colored blossoms. Poinciana blossoms? At once the present swept back.

"Gretchen?" I said with the painful question in my voice.

She walked into the room, turning on a lamp as she came down its length. She looked no less elegant than usual, and the gold bangles on her arms glittered in the light. When she reached my chair, she stood quite still, staring at me, her face devoid of emotion.

"Gretchen is gone," she said. "From the first there was no hope. The fall smashed her too badly. She was never conscious again, and she didn't suffer."

Even though I'd feared and expected this, my breath caught, and I leaned back, closing my eyes. Brett pulled over another chair and sat beside me.

"I went up to see Allegra just now. She will care most about this, you know. Her one grandchild—her only hope for immortality."

Words which might have carried sympathy were only scornful, and I shrank away from her. At once she sensed my rejection.

"You can't expect me to mourn as a mother would," she said. "I think you know the truth—that I never had a child of my own. I took Gretchen because she was forced upon me. The child of one of Ross's infidelities. How could *I* love her?"

I ached for Gretchen. "She needed your love."

"Need? Don't we all need? But I didn't have it to give. Though perhaps I made it up to her a little in recent years, when we became reasonably good friends."

They'd become friends because Brett wanted the power, the influence that close association with Gretchen could give her. Perhaps even the means of revenging herself upon Ross.

"Have you told Allegra?" I asked.

"No. She's slipping in and out of her fog. Coxie didn't know what to do, so I suggested that she say nothing for now. Though Allegra can sense things sometimes that the rest of us don't even know are happening. So she's uneasy now. She told me she'd found Pam's tape that she's been searching for all this time, and that she gave it to you to play. I thought you might come directly here." She glanced at the recorder beside me. "You've listened to it?"

I left my chair and removed the tape from the machine, slipped it into the case, and started from the room. "Yes, I've listened to it."

She came after me, caught me by the arm. "Wait! There are things we need to talk about, you and I. Sit down for a minute. Don't worry—I won't ask you to let me listen to it. I've been pretty sure all along what that tape contained. Ross managed Pam's death, didn't he? He fixed that car?"

Near the door were two massive Spanish chairs, and

I sat down on a cracked leather seat. I had better listen to anything she had to say, whether I liked her or not.

She took the opposite chair. "I'm sure you're all mixed up with feelings of loyalty toward your dear departed husband. Or had you already come to hate him as much as I did?"

I held to my silence. I would listen, but I wouldn't talk. I would tell her nothing.

"He deserved what came to him," she said, and I heard the anger in her voice. "I'm glad I was able to have a hand in his punishment."

In spite of myself, she had surprised me into words. "What are you talking about?"

"You might as well know. There's nothing that can be done to me now, and I'm sure you won't open things up with the police again. Or the press. I was there that night. I was with Ross when he died. Oh, don't look so shocked. Gretchen was the only one in this house who had mourned him at all, and even her feelings were mixed—because of Vasily. At least you can take some satisfaction in knowing that poor, silly Pam has been avenged. And so have the rest of us."

"You'd better explain."

"All right, I will. As long as Gretchen was alive, I meant to keep this to myself. Now it doesn't matter. I knew he was working late and alone that night. So I went to see him. He was planning to call in that note of mine he held—out of sheer spite. So I decided to fabricate a little. Every now and then Allegra has talked about the tape she'd misplaced. From bits and pieces I knew Pam had given it to her, and I couldn't guess why. So I told Ross that the tape existed and that it would incriminate him in Pam's death. I told him I would use it if he acted against me—and that perhaps I might use it anyway."

"And he had a heart attack?"

"Exactly. It all went better than I'd hoped. So you see it wasn't that silly note signed with one of Gretchen's little faces that set him off. That must have been one of Vasily's futile efforts. That young man can be pretty juvenile at times. It was what I told Ross about the tape and how I meant to use it that did it. Perhaps he'd have tried to attack me physically right then, he was so angry. But instead he turned purple and fell over on his desk. I knew he was dead and there was nothing to be done. Of course, I didn't want to rush out screaming and admit to my own presence in his office, but neither did I want him to lie there unattended. I have some sensibilities. And of course I didn't know then that he'd already phoned Jarrett."

Her words had left me stunned. "So you set off the alarm to waken the house and cause someone to come and find him?"

"That's right. I turned it on at the far end of the gallery, where the guard couldn't see me. And before he could get there, I went down to Allegra's cottage and stayed there for the rest of the night. Keith saw me coming out of the house right after the alarm went off, and he may have guessed that I'd turned it on, but he didn't give me away."

So much was being explained. Yet I knew that it was as she said and none of this would be told against her now. Of what use would it be?

"It must have been cozy at the cottage, with Vasily hiding out there too," I said.

She smiled vaguely.

"Why have you told me this now?" I asked.

"Because you have Pam's tape. Because Ross has already been punished for what he did, and there's nothing further you can do by letting anyone else hear it."

"I haven't decided about that. Why are you interested in seeing it kept quiet?"

"If it should become public, there would be a huge scandal. And when one scandal comes out, others follow. The ripple effects could be devastating."

"To whom?"

"To the entire Logan empire, of course. I suggest

that you destroy this tape as quickly as you can. Otherwise, we may all be damaged."

"Jarrett has a right to hear it. And Pam has a right to be heard. Jarrett wouldn't use it in any way that might hurt Keith."

"Ah? I see. I had an idea the wind was blowing that way. You and Jarrett—well! Lovely possibilities for both of you there."

I'd endured enough, and this time when I stood up, I walked out the door. Nevertheless, she came with me, so I asked one more question.

"How is Vasily taking his wife's death?"

For the first time, Brett seemed puzzled. "I'm not sure. He rushed away from the hospital looking wild-eyed, and left all the complications in Jarrett's lap."

"Complications?"

"The police, of course. There'll still be all the questioning to go through again, before they decide it was suicide. I suggest that you say nothing to anyone about Allegra being in the tower today. Oh, of course she admitted it to me just now. But an insane grandmother who was present when her granddaughter fell to her death would give the media a field day. To say nothing of poor Allegra being driven further out of her head with questioning. Best to say nothing at all, Sharon my dear—just in case it wasn't suicide, after all."

She went her way then, bangles jingling, wafting behind her a trace of Givenchy perfume. I had always believed that every human being had some redeeming traits. Now I wondered in Brett's case. But I really knew nothing about her, knew nothing of what had formed her into the way she was. In any case, I could hardly feel generous toward her.

Chapter 19

Brett had been right in her forecasting. With Gretchen's death, all the police inquiries opened up again, and we were once more in a state of siege from the outside world, which was clamoring to know what had really happened at Poinciana. Even the small, unimportant interview I'd given the day I saw Gretchen at the library was blown out of all sensible proportion, with implications that had little to do with reality.

The official conclusion was one I didn't believe in, even though my own testimony seemed to support it. Unfortunately, there were too many witnesses to the last quarrel between Gretchen and her husband, and this couldn't be evaded. Brett and Myra and I had all heard Vasily angrily threatening divorce, and everyone knew how impulsive and emotional Gretchen could be. No one could claim that she had been in a calm and rational state when she rushed off to her grandmother's tower and climbed those stairs for the last time.

At least nothing ever came out to hint that Allegra Logan had been in the tower that day. Allegra herself still didn't seem to know exactly what had happened while she was taking out her gowns and Gretchen must have rushed past her on the stairs. It was Mrs. Broderick who saw to putting the gowns away before the police came.

I had told Jarrett of finding the mermaid netsuke, and we'd agreed that nothing could be gained by discussing this with anyone. Whatever had happened, Allegra must not be brought into this.

It was Jarrett, finally, who told Allegra of Gretchen's death. I was with him when he sat beside her in the silver-gray parlor and held her hands gently. Perhaps some of his own strength flowed into her frail person, for she took it better than he might have expected. In fact, she took it so calmly that I wondered if she already knew that Gretchen was dead. What *had* she seen in the tower? Perhaps we would never know, and perhaps it was better that way.

This time, Allegra did not come to the funeral. We all thought it would be too great a strain, and she herself escaped the day in her own happy manner, slipping back to a time when her husband and her son were with her at Poinciana, and there was not yet a Gretchen to think about.

When the funeral was over, she seemed to know, and came back to us quite sensibly, and to our surprise was even able to talk a little about what had happened.

"Gretchen would never have committed suicide," she insisted. "She was much too self-centered a girl. I can imagine her being violent against someone else, but never toward herself. She was like her father in that. Self-preservation came first. The harm she sometimes did herself could be serious and damaging, but that was because she never thought one minute ahead. To kill herself, however—no!"

I leaned toward Allegra and spoke to her quietly. "Mrs. Logan, was anyone else in the tower that day? Did anyone go up there to join Gretchen?"

She drew away from me at once, and I was to learn that any pressure of questions about that time in the tower was sure to send her into one of her "fogs." As quickly as though she closed a door, she shut out reality and escaped from any probing. When this happened, there was no calling her back until she chose to come of her own free will. Gretchen's death was something terrible for her to live with consciously for very long, and when she went into her retreat she might talk about her granddaughter happily, as though she were alive.

Strangely enough, in the days that had followed the funeral, Allegra never once asked what I had done with Pam's tape, and I didn't remind her of it. The tape seemed to matter less, when so much else that was agonizing in the present crushed in upon us.

When we left Allegra that day she had spoken of suicide being impossible for Gretchen, Jarrett and I went down the hall and sat in my cozy living room. I had unpacked a few things of my own that I'd brought with me to Poinciana and never used until now. It was good to have my own books and a few pictures and ornaments that I'd collected around me. For the first time, I could feel reasonably at home—even though I knew the feeling wasn't permanent. I couldn't stay here forever now.

"I like this room," Jarrett said, settling himself into an armchair that had belonged to my father, and which Ian had insisted on carting with him wherever he went.

"Do you think Allegra is right?" I asked. "Could it have been an accident?"

"She didn't say that, did she? She only insisted that it wasn't suicide. The railing was firm enough, as the police found out. Only if Gretchen had flung herself against it deliberately could she have broken through."

We didn't speak further of the third possibility that

was in both our minds. After all, the evil at Poinciana had died with Ross, and no one would have tried to kill Gretchen. Surely no one would have?

Jarrett left his chair and came to sit beside me on the sofa. "You're not taking care of yourself, Sharon. You've been losing weight and you're growing frown lines between your eyes."

I liked his concern. I wanted it. Gradually in these weeks, as I watched him taking on most of an impossible burden, I began to know myself a little. And to know him. Everything between us was too fresh and recent for expression, and we were both learning caution. Or perhaps I was. He already knew. Nevertheless he showed me in small ways that he was watching over me when he could, and I tried to let him know that I was grateful.

Because of our closeness at that moment, I could at last do what I had been postponing, and which I knew must be done. I had no right to keep Pam's tape from him because of the pain I would feel over his pain. I went to the drawer where I'd put it and took out the cassette. Just beneath it was a folded sheet of Poinciana notepaper, and I took that out as well, not thinking much about it, because I was intent upon the explanation I must give Jarrett of how I'd come by the tape.

He listened without emotion except for a tightening of the muscles around his mouth. When I put the case into his hand, he closed his fingers about it reluctantly and I knew that he sensed what lay ahead.

"Perhaps you'll destroy it without listening to it," I said. "I only wish I could have thrown it away myself. I've given up trying to decide what's wise, or right or wrong. This was meant for you and you must have it."

He sat very still with the cassette in his hands, and I longed to say something that would comfort him. Only I could find nothing comforting to say in this bleak moment.

For the first time I really looked at the sheet of

notepaper I still held, and then I sat down abruptly in the nearest chair, completely horrified.

This note was very much like the one that had purported to be from Gretchen—the note that had been on Ross's desk when he died, signed with one of Gretchen's signature faces. This time the face was grinning and the words were different:

> Be careful, Sharon. Don't be as foolish
> as I was. Stay away from high places.

Words from Gretchen—when Gretchen was dead?

My hand shook as I gave it to Jarrett. "Now we know the first note was never written by Gretchen."

Jarrett scowled, reading it, and shook his head wearily. "Perhaps this is the time to move you out of Poinciana."

"How can I go? There's too much that I'm responsible for."

"I know," he said. "At least when you're in here, lock your door."

He slipped the cassette into a pocket and stood up. I wanted to touch him, feel his physical presence, but I knew this was not the time. First he must listen to Pam's tape and fight his own demons, find his own peace. There were depths of emotion in Jarrett that frightened me a little when I glimpsed them. I remembered what Gretchen had said one time—that he held too much in. A release might come in words, if only we could talk, but at that moment we were poles apart, and Ross and Pam stood between us.

In the coming days he seemed unchanged. He was always grave, and now he became more seriously busy and more remote than ever. If there was a deepening of the lines in his face, I could very well guess the cause, but there was no opening for me to say anything. Not once did he mention the tape, or admit that he had listened to Pam's words. I bled a little, knowing his pain and unable to offer him comfort.

I wanted to tear up the note I'd found and burn the pieces, but I kept it in the drawer where I'd discovered it. Now and then I took it out and read it again, willing the words to tell me something that would betray the writer. But the grinning little face mocked me, hiding its identity, and I knew that evil was still alive at Poinciana.

Then one day, quite unexpectedly, Jarrett took me away from the house. We gave reporters the slip by running off in a boat across Lake Worth to a place where a friend had a car waiting for us. On the mainland side, we drove south, and I was aware of Florida blooming lushly all around us. There were even more blossoms and flowering vines and shrubs than before in a riot of tropical growth. Jacaranda, breathtakingly blue, azaleas of all shades, bougainvillea more colorful than ever.

In Boynton Beach we had lunch at Bernard's, a building of white stucco and red tiles that was a Mizner creation. In the dining room I sat in a wicker chair that spread behind me like a great open fan, and looked out through surrounding glass upon a jungle garden, gone wild with undergrowth and twisted banyan trees.

I felt almost happy to be away from the house and alone with Jarrett, and because he had wanted to bring me here. Yet at the same time I was uneasy. I could never be sure of what lay behind anything Jarrett did. For the moment he seemed almost relaxed and I began to relax a little too, postponing the time of reckoning that might lie ahead.

The wild tangle beyond our table had once been the famous Rainbow Tropical Gardens, he told me, where rare palms and plants had been gathered for visitors to enjoy. Gretchen had said once that she would bring me here "sometime."

Sometime! There was never enough time. It could be too late so quickly. I looked into what had once been an orderly garden and shivered at its dark, mysterious depths.

Jarrett reached across the table, and I put my hand in his. For the living there was still time. Time to take hold, to keep the days from being wasted. His warm clasp told me what I wanted to know. Perhaps Jarrett too was aware of hours speeding away with our lives.

We went outside then and followed a curving white wall roofed in red tiles. At a place where an arched wooden gate with great iron hinges opened into the wild garden, we went through. The days were growing hotter now, but here in this tangle of uncontrolled underbrush and plant life, a shadowy coolness welcomed us. We were in a quiet and secret place, and we sat together upon a fallen log.

"We've needed to talk," he said. "But Poinciana constrains me, and I haven't known how to begin. I don't really know now. I wanted to get you away from the house and have a little time with you first. Something pleasant to remember. Sharon, I've listened to Pam's tape."

I put out my hand. "You needn't talk unless you want to. I can understand."

He went on. "In these last days I've been thinking a great deal about truth—whatever that is. Sometimes it seems a hopeless abstract, impossible to grasp and hold on to. Maybe meaning something different to everyone who looks at it. Perhaps even dangerous to touch. Yet somehow one has to try. The lie can be even more damaging."

He paused as if waiting for some response from me. I had little to offer that was comforting, but I tried.

"My father used to tell me again and again that nothing is as it seems," I said. "I don't think he believed in truth as something in itself. It was always the lies of others that he thought about and feared, and he tried to make me distrustful. But I've never wanted to live that way. I want something I can believe in, even if I have to get hurt by believing."

"You're finding your own way, and it's a good way, Sharon. My trouble is that I've lost myself in a jungle as wild as this little counterpart where we're sitting. I know now that it wasn't good enough to believe in a kind of truth, if I couldn't live it. Oh, I had a dozen noble excuses. I've given you some of them. The good of the many! That always sounds laudable. But it can mean the beginning of the lies. If I hadn't gone down that road of deceiving myself as well as everyone else, Pam might be alive today. The good of the many might have been taken care of if I'd stood up to Ross and told him off. And I might have saved Pam. My own confusion doesn't excuse me."

Again there was that waiting pause, and I spoke into it, smiling faintly in memory. "Once when I went to school for a little while in Chicago, I had a teacher—an older man who was a devotee of H. L. Mencken. He had a favorite quotation that I liked so much that I memorized it. And I can still quote.

"'I believe that it is better to tell the truth than a lie. I believe it is better to be free than a slave. And I believe it is better to know than be ignorant.'"

I was relieved to see Jarrett smile too. "Yes, I know that one, and I've always liked it. Truth can be a pretty hazardous commodity, but it doesn't breed the same kind of dangers that the lies breed. It *is* better to know. I'm glad you didn't follow your kinder instincts and hold that tape back from me, Sharon."

"I wanted to," I said.

He put an arm about me, and for a little while no more words were needed between us. They could wait until Jarrett had come through his own dark passageway.

We returned to our borrowed car and I felt closer to him on the drive back to the boat than ever before. The return trip across the lake was companionable, and I think his anguish had lessened a little because of talking it out. We crossed the lawn together, and then Jarrett turned in the direction of his office, while I went into the inner court where I'd sat in the rain that terrible day.

The table and two chairs were occupied. Allegra and Myra sat in the shade, finishing plates of cheesecake. Allegra smiled at me vaguely, and I knew this wasn't one of her better days.

"There's enough for you, Mrs. Logan," Myra said. "I made it myself last night. But now I see Mr. Nichols is back, so I'd better scoot before he misses me."

She jumped up and gave me a quick little nod, beckoning me to the nearest doorway.

"She's way out of it, poor lady," Myra said when we were alone. "Miss Inness was just here trying to find out if Mrs. Logan saw anything in the tower that day. Imagine tormenting her like that! That woman ought to stay away from her."

Myra waved her arms indignantly and rushed off in her abrupt way. I returned to the courtyard and sat down at the table. Allegra looked at me with a modicum of the rational in her eyes, and I wondered if she sometimes dissembled, to serve her own purposes.

"Brett just came to say goodbye," she told me. "Of course, with Gretchen gone, she feels she must move out of Poinciana. I said I didn't think you'd mind if she stayed, but she didn't agree with me."

"I'm afraid she's right," I admitted. "It will be more comfortable with her gone. And now there's really no need for her to stay. Did she try to ask you anything else when she was here?"

Allegra looked unhappy, confused. "All that about the tower, you mean? I don't know what she was getting at. I told her about taking out my beautiful gowns and dressing up. That's all I can remember. Except that I danced in the ballroom, and you found me there."

Her bright eyes were candid, guileless. I couldn't believe she was dissembling. A door had closed firmly somewhere in her mind, and if there was more she had no wish to remember it. The very fact was a relief. If ever she remembered something more, she might be in very real danger.

"I'd better tell Brett goodbye," I said. "Will you be all right if I leave you here?"

"Of course. I'll finish this delicious cheesecake. Coxie will come for me after a while, since she knows where I am."

I went upstairs to the wing that Gretchen and Vasily had occupied, and into which Brett had moved. It was not that I ever wanted to see her again, but that there were some untied threads left dangling that I still wanted to pick up.

The door to her room stood open, and I looked in to find her packing.

"Hello," she said. "Come in, do. I was about to go look you up. I've decided to return to the apartment over my shop in town. Everyone's leaving the house, I gather. You're going to have a big place to rattle around in alone. Do you mind if I come to see Allegra occasionally, while she's still here?"

"Of course not. But what do you mean—everyone's leaving?"

"Vasily too. Hadn't you heard?" She paused in packing her toilet case and regarded me thoughtfully. "Perhaps there are a few more things you ought to know. I don't suppose anyone else will tell you—if anyone even knows. You remember that bang-up argument Vasily and Gretchen were having that last day?"

I nodded.

"I know what it was about. In fact, I knew the cause earlier. I met Vasily one day down by the beach. He wanted to talk to me without being seen. He wanted to urge my silence. I told him what he had to do—that he had no other choice. But he wouldn't listen. Or perhaps he didn't know how to handle this himself. I tried to tell him that I thought Gretchen knew and that he'd better talk to her, reassure her, if he could. Before it was too late. I told him that again the night Ross died, and Vasily and I found ourselves camping out in Allegra's cottage, not trusting each other. I expect you've noticed his state of mind lately. He was scared then, and I think he still is."

I had noticed that he seemed to be under some strain, but I had set his distraught condition down to his grief over Gretchen's death. Though he had seemed more devastated than I might have expected him to be.

"What was it that he should have told her?"

Brett gave up her efforts at packing and dropped into a chair. "His big problem is that his ex-wife has turned up over in West Palm Beach, and he's been seeing her there. I suspect there's still some sort of attachment between them. Gretchen guessed that he was seeing another woman, only he never told her who it was. She might have understood better if he had. Instead he admitted it to me."

I remembered that time when Gretchen had come to Ross's room. There had been a moment when I thought she was about to tell me something, and then had held back. Was this the unhappy secret she'd been carrying? I could feel all the more angry with Vasily now.

"Why should Vasily tell you?" I asked.

"I think he couldn't handle it himself, and I suppose in a way I was in a neutral camp. He's turned to me on other occasions when he felt the world was closing in."

This was quite possible, I thought. Brett was intelligent and worldly wise, and she had few scruples that would make Vasily uneasy.

"Is this matter of the ex-wife one of the things Ross tracked down?" I asked.

"He knew about the wife, of course. She called herself Elberta Sheldon when she was an actress in London. But I don't know if she was here when Ross was alive. Anyway, Gretchen started to go through her father's files to find out about this."

"Will Vasily go back to his first wife now?"

"Maybe you'd better ask him," she said, and got up to close her last suitcase with an air of finality. "I'll be leaving now, just as soon as Albert comes for my bags. You don't mind if he drives me into town? Then he can help me at the other end. I'll send for my car later."

We didn't shake hands. There was a strange moment when we looked at each other across the room. A moment in which there was a certain wary appraisal, each of the other. Then I acted on an impulse and took from my handbag the little mermaid netsuke that Gretchen had been holding when she fell from the tower.

"You remember this?" I said.

She recognized it at once. "Yes, of course. Allegra's favorite. The one she was always picking up because she said it was hers."

"Gretchen had it in her hand when she fell from the tower," I said.

Color seemed to drain from Brett's face and she sat down suddenly on the edge of the bed. "Then Gretchen *did* see Allegra that day in the belvedere! Allegra must have stolen the mermaid again, and then Gretchen took it from her. So Allegra knew very well that Gretchen was there and that she'd climbed to the upper room."

"Does it matter now?" I asked.

Brett answered me almost absently, and with indirection. "I remember Allegra the way she used to be when I first came to this house. She was the only one who was really kind to me. She knew all about Ross and she knew what he would do to me. She was more like a mother to me than my own mother ever was. In the end, she was the only one I could care about in this terrible place. And she was fond of me too. So of course it matters!" Brett gave me a suddenly baleful look. "I wouldn't want to see any further unhappiness come to Allegra."

"No one but Jarrett knows about the mermaid," I said. "And he thought it best not to mention it."

She nodded in a way that dismissed me, and I went off, leaving her to finish with her suitcases.

From the hallway I could hear sounds coming from Gretchen's rooms, where Vasily too was preparing to leave. I went to the door of the parlor and looked in. He had set open bags around the room and was carrying out clothes from the bedroom to stuff into them. Through the open door I could see the bed piled with the suits and coats that Gretchen must have bought for him. Standing there silently, waiting to be noticed, I could see how wild and agitated he looked. Not at all the easy, confident man I had first seen in this house.

"You're leaving?" I asked after a moment.

He started and looked around at me, then made an effort to recover himself. "Ah—Sharon. I would have come to tell you, of course. It is necessary to get away from this house with all its terrible memories. I can't stay here another night."

"Where are you going?" I asked.

"France, perhaps. Paris. Perhaps the Greek isles." He almost smiled. "Strange to think that I can now go wherever I wish, do as I please. Now that it's too late."

"You'll be taking your former wife with you?"

That really startled him. "Who told you that?"

"I've just been talking to Brett," I said.

He seemed to relax a little, as though this somehow reassured him. "Brett, of course. But that lady doesn't know as much as she thinks she does. I tried to persuade her of that the time when we met in the tunnel and you discovered us so inopportunely."

"But your ex-wife *is* in West Palm Beach?"

"If you must know—yes. I am hoping to get out of the country before she knows I am gone. She hasn't been making my life easy. So I hope you will not send out any spies. Though, now that Gretchen is gone, there isn't much she can do."

I went on conversationally, wondering if I was on the track of something. "Gretchen admitted to me once that you'd probably married her for her money. Not hard to guess. Was that true?"

He didn't seem to mind my frankness. "In a way, yes. But there was more to it than that. Gretchen was a—a very special person. She—needed what I had to give her. With her there was something—something—oh, God!" He flung himself into a chair and buried his face in his hands. "If only she could have believed in herself a little more! If only she had not tried to punish and torment me for what I could never help!"

"I think," I said, "that you mustn't leave Poinciana right away, Vasily. In fact, if you try to leave, I will ask Jarrett to have you stopped. You must stay here a little while longer."

There was something like terror in the look he gave me. "No, no, Sharon! Don't ask this of me."

"We need your help," I went on. "If you should leave now we might never know who was in the tower with Gretchen before she died. I don't think it was an accident, Vasily. I believe that Gretchen was pushed through that railing to fall to her death. Just as I was pushed on the stairs that time by the same person."

Vasily had grown up in a culture that was not afraid of tears and emotion, and now he was weeping helplessly.

For a moment longer I stood staring at him. At any moment he would look up and see what was in my face. I had said too much, and I couldn't stay here a moment longer. Everything was beginning to fall into place now.

"Just don't leave the house yet, Vasily," I said softly, and went away from him, hurrying toward the stairs, hurrying to Jarrett's office.

Myra was at her desk typing, making up for lost time. She looked up in surprise as I rushed past her and through the open door to confront Jarrett.

"I know what happened to Gretchen!" I cried. "She was threatening to change her will because Vasily had been seeing his former wife in West Palm Beach. He wouldn't have divorced her, but she might've divorced him. So he must've followed Gretchen up to the tower. He must have fought with her there. Maybe he never meant to have it happen, but it was Vasily who threw her against the railing so that she fell through to her death."

"Whoa!" Jarrett said. "Wait—calm down a bit, Sharon."

I wouldn't be stopped. "There's no time to be calm! He's getting ready to leave right now. He's planning to leave the country! He's going to get away if we don't stop him."

"This is all supposition, Sharon. Even if you're right, we can't rush in and act on a conclusion you're jumping to."

That stopped me for only an instant. "Never mind that! Allegra knows. She knows very well who went up to the tower with Gretchen, and she's trying to shut the whole thing away so she won't have to face it. We must get her to talk. Now!"

Jarrett shook his head at me sadly. "You're going off half cocked. If you tackle Allegra in that state, you'll probably shock her into hiding forever. Wait until you cool down, Sharon."

All my life I had been trained to be calm and cool and let nothing disturb me. Now all the bars were down, and I was out and free. Cool judicial thinking would let Vasily get away. If Jarrett wouldn't help me, I would have to do this myself.

Again I ran past an astonished Myra and down those endless corridors, up the stairs, and into Allegra's suite. Coxie was putting her to bed when I flew through the door.

"I want to talk to her," I told the nurse. "Just leave us alone for a little while."

Reluctantly, Coxie left and I turned to the bed. Allegra watched me with sudden alarm in her eyes, and I brought my voice down, forcing myself to speak quietly.

"You must help us now," I said. "For Gretchen's sake, you must help us."

I could almost see the curtains come down as she

retreated, escaping once more from what she dared not face.

I reached for one frail hand. "Please, Allegra. Don't go away from me now. I know what happened in the tower. I know Vasily went up there and fought with his wife. You saw it all, didn't you? You know what happened. You mustn't run away from it any longer, no matter how much Gretchen's death hurts you. Help us, Allegra!"

She stared at me with a total lack of comprehension. Jarrett was right. In my need for haste, I had frightened her into retreat. Though I knew it was hopeless, I stayed a little while longer, trying to talk to her, struggling to break through those protective barriers she had raised. But it was no use, and I knew it. In the end I gave up and returned to the hall.

I was on my way to my room when Vasily appeared around a far corner and came walking toward me. I didn't like the strange look in his eyes.

"You've been talking to Allegra?" he said. "So what has she told you?"

I shook my head, trying to hide my sudden fear. "Nothing. She doesn't remember anything."

He still looked frightened, and in a man as unstable as Vasily, that was dangerous. Yet he spoke to me quietly enough.

"Sharon, you don't understand. There is nothing you can do now. I want to go away quietly, while there is still time. You must permit me that."

He took another step toward me, his eyes very bright, and I backed away, flat against the corridor wall. At that moment, from somewhere downstairs, I could hear Myra calling me. I knew Jarrett had sent her after me, and blessed him for it. Vasily turned, momentarily distracted, and I felt the panel move behind me. I stepped backward as it swiveled, and I let it close upon darkness. With a frantic hand I fumbled for the switch that would light my way of escape to the ballroom.

Lights came on down the long passageway, and I

moved toward the stairs, trying to make no sound behind this secret wall, uncertain of whether Vasily knew that the passage existed. I'd reached the top of the hidden stairway when I heard the panel in the corridor behind me open again, and when I turned to look, I knew I had lost. Vasily stepped in and swung the door closed behind him.

I gave up trying to be quiet, and shouted for Myra, praying that she would know about this way to the ballroom and that she would hear me. The rickety railing broke under my hand as I stumbled down the stairs. I recovered my footing and ran for the turn in the passageway, while walls seemed to press in upon me.

But clearly, Vasily knew the passage well, and he was coming after me. I heard nothing from Myra. Perhaps she had gone for help. Or more likely, she hadn't heard my cry at all. It took only seconds for Vasily to reach me, and I felt his wiry strength as he swung me around. "No, no, Sharon! You must not run from me. I would never hurt you."

I knew better than to believe him. I knew everything now.

"It was you all along!" I cried. "You thought I was a danger because you were afraid I would recognize you, give you away. That I'd spoil your plans to get your hands on Gretchen's money, and then go back to your first wife. You wanted to frighten me away from Poinciana, didn't you?"

"No, no! No one meant to push you on the stairs. You were there at the wrong moment. It became necessary."

It was all becoming horribly clear. "You were behind that child's trick with the coconut! And the two notes! The one left for Ross and the one I found in my room! It was you, Vasily! Gretchen suspected, didn't she? And tried to protect you."

"No, no—I never thought—"

"You've been cruel—utterly cruel! How did you kill Gretchen?"

He caught me by the shoulders, shaking me hard. "Stop it, Sharon!"

I squirmed desperately in his grasp and managed to break his hold. Blindly, I ran toward the ballroom and the way out. But the door was so far away—so far! And he was coming after me again with a wild strength moving him.

Then at the far end the concealed door opened and a shadow filled the slit. Rescue was coming, after all! I cried out, and ran toward the opening. It closed again, and in the wall lighting I could see Myra coming toward me.

"Help me!" I called to her. "Help me to get out!"

"I don't think so," she said. "It's all right, Vasily. We've got her cornered now. I think you'd better tell her everything."

Behind me, Vasily made a strange choking sound. I stood where I was, stunned with disbelief. What had Myra to do with anything?

"Oh, so you don't want to tell her?" she ran on, sounding almost pleased. "Then perhaps I had better do it for you."

I could see her clearly down the passageway, and there was a change in her that was astonishing. Her very look, her manner was different. She was a woman far more arresting than the Myra I knew.

She spoke with a self-assurance I'd never seen in her before. "I'm his wife, Sharon. I'm his *real* wife. Oh, we were officially divorced, of course, because we worked out this fine plan between us. Gretchen used to come into Vasily's gallery in London as a customer, and he had only to play up to her, win her—marry her! Then when enough of the money was in his hands, he would get a divorce and he and I would be together again with everything we'd never had before."

"Don't, Myra," Vasily said.

I'd had it right, and I'd had it all wrong.

She ran on again, paying no attention. "I rather liked you, Sharon. We had good visits together, didn't we?

It was too bad about that time on the stairs. But I was afraid of what you might do to our plan. You were beginning to remember who Vasily was. So I tried to warn you to go away. I didn't mean to hurt you, and I made it up to you afterwards, didn't I? Though I was laughing inside over the way you trusted me. Nothing more would have happened to you, if you hadn't turned into a real threat with all your poking and snooping. I used to watch you, Sharon—so many times when you never knew I was about. Why didn't you understand when I left that coconut for you, and that note? Of course I left the one for Ross, hoping it would make him change his mind about Vasily. And it gave me the idea for the one to you. Why didn't you get out while you could?"

The whole chilling picture of someone completely amoral was coming clear. This was the most dangerous kind of evil—never to recognize the truth about oneself. Vasily had understood and suffered over his own villainy. But Myra had played without conscience the role of a friendly, well-meaning woman—all the while appallingly bent upon her own venal purposes. I had seen only the character an actress had developed, mannerisms, attitudes, and all. Perhaps the best role Elberta Sheldon had ever played.

"Let her go," Vasily said. "You know I never intended any of this."

"Yes—you were always the weak one. You'd have let Gretchen get away with changing her will, divorcing you, fixing it so that in the end we'd have nothing. You found the netsuke under the cushion in the tower, where I hid them, and you made me return them both times. And the Lautrec paintings, when I could have sold them through people I know. Though at least you tried to protect me by hiding those manuscript pages, so what was missing couldn't be checked. I was pleased about that."

There was anger and grief in Vasily's voice. "You've lost, Myra! You must give up now."

"Because you thought you'd fallen in love with your temporary wife? Don't be foolish! I knew you would always come back to me. You had to come back, didn't you?"

"No! I told you it was over when you played that idiotic prank and got yourself a job as Jarrett's secretary. I told you you couldn't work in this house!"

"But I did, didn't I? I fooled them all! What fun I had playing that character. Though in a way, she *is* part of me. And you kept coming to see me over in town."

"To persuade you to leave. To keep you from any more scheming acts. I wasn't playing your game anymore."

"It's not a game you could stop playing, Vasily. Yet only today you've tried to run away—without letting me know. How very foolish of you! Now you've brought us to this. We can't let Sharon go. You see that, don't you? Look what I have here."

She was holding something up, and Vasily cried out with a despair that shook me even more.

"It's Sharon's own husband's gun," Myra pointed out. "That nice little automatic he kept in his desk. How appropriate if Sharon commits suicide with it because she is grieving so for her beloved husband—and mother and father. It's all been too much for her. You can see that. But it must be done very convincingly, Vasily."

He moved then. I felt myself thrust against the wall as he plunged toward the woman who had been his wife. They were struggling together down near the ballroom entrance when the gun went off. Its cracking echoes seemed to reverberate forever in that narrow passageway. And then there was only a terrible silence.

Until the sobbing began.

Following the shot by moments came a distant shouting and the clatter of running feet. Everything resounded through the thin walls of Allegra's secret passage, until the door opened once more at the ballroom end, and this time it was Jarrett who came through.

"Sharon?" he called. "Sharon, are you there?"

I moved toward him with a greater relief than I'd ever felt in my life. Slipping past Vasily and Myra, not sure which one of them sobbed, I flung myself into Jarrett's arms. For a moment he held me, making sure I was unharmed. But others were crowding the narrow doorway now, and he set me aside, moving past me toward the place where Vasily crouched, holding Myra in his arms. Now I knew that it was he who wept, and I could see that Myra was bleeding.

Chapter 20

The immediate excitement is over. I can sit beside Jarrett on his deck above the lake and talk with him almost calmly. Myra has been taken to a hospital, where she will recover from the flesh wound inflicted when Vasily struggled with her for Ross's gun. The police have been questioning them, and the whole miserable story is out.

There can be no escaping the horror ahead that will keep everything painfully public for a long while. Myra will be tried for Gretchen's murder, but Jarrett believes that Vasily, for all his original intent, has done nothing legally criminal, and he certainly saved my life. All along he had been trying to stop his former wife from carrying out the plan she had launched them into. They were two adventurers, and perhaps that was her greatest appeal for him. Yet I think Gretchen was not wholly cheated by Vasily in their marriage.

Brett had managed to leave the house before everything exploded. She and Gretchen had been coming close to the truth, but neither had suspected that Vasily's former wife, Myra Ritter Karl, alias the actress Elberta Sheldon, had installed herself so impudently right under their noses at Poinciana.

When Jarrett had left for the hospital, along with the police, I had gone upstairs to see Allegra. She had heard the shot and it had brought her out of bed in trembling fright. I helped Coxie to quiet her, and then we sat together in her little gray and red parlor, while I told her everything. And at last she talked to me.

The sound waves of that shot shattering their way through Poinciana seemed to have broken through her defenses. That she had seen her granddaughter fall from the tower had nearly destroyed her sanity. Perhaps would have, if she hadn't been able to retreat into her own refuge. She had known Gretchen was in the tower, because her granddaughter had stopped to see what she was doing, had discovered that she had the Sleeping Mermaid again, and had taken it for safekeeping.

Yet Allegra had never known who was in the tower with Gretchen that day. She had been engrossed in examining her lovely gowns, lost in her memories, her fantasies, and she hadn't seen Myra climb the stairs. However, she had been standing near a window, holding a dress up to the light, when Gretchen had fallen past the glass. She had heard her scream, heard the crash of her fall—and the shock and horror had been too much for her to bear. She had fled into the past, dressing herself in a favorite gown and going by way of her secret passage to dance in the ballroom—where I had found her.

After that, she had drifted in and out, between past and present. Whenever the present came too close and threatened her with terror and collapse, she ran from it, saving herself. But she could have told us nothing useful anyway.

A few tumultuous days have passed, and now for this little while we can sit on the deck outside Jarrett's cottage, watching the brilliance of a Florida sunset. The poinciana tree is green now with plumy leafage, and I feel a deep sorrow because Gretchen will never see it again. Or Ross.

Jarrett and I are making our plans quietly, because we know now that there is never enough time. We will be married as soon as possible. When we can leave Poinciana, we will take Keith and Allegra with us to some suburb of New York or Washington, where we can find a smaller house, and live the sort of lives that will better suit us all.

Though I know we will return. Allegra must have her say about what will be done with Poinciana. She too wants it to be shared with those who come to visit in the future. Perhaps as Flagler's beautiful Whitehall is being shared.

But for now—for this little while—I am content to sit beside Jarrett, my hand warm in his, while Keith and Brewster play on the lawn nearby, rolling coconuts. I am content to experience these last peaceful moments at Poinciana.

We can never forget what has happened here, but there are good new memories to be made, and so much lies ahead for all of us.

About the Author

Phyllis A. Whitney was born of American parents in Yokohama, Japan. Today she lives in Virginia. She has always worked with books—as a librarian, bookseller, reviewer, teacher of writing and, of course, bestselling author. She is one of America's most successful writers of romance and suspense. All her books have been bestsellers and major book club selections.

About the Author

Phyllis A. Whitney was born of American parents in Yokohama, Japan. Today she lives in Virginia. She has always worked with books—as a librarian, bookseller, reviewer, teacher of writing and, of course, bestselling author. She is one of America's most successful writers of romance and suspense. All her books have been bestsellers and major book club selections.